A city-loving book addict, peony obsessive **Katrina Cudmore** lives in Cork, Ireland, with her husband, four active children and a very daft dog. A psychology graduate, with an MSc in Human Resources, Katrina spent many years working in multinational companies and can't believe she is now lucky enough to have a job that involves daydreaming about love and handsome men! You can visit Katrina at katrinacudmore.com

Christine Rimmer came to her profession the long way around. She tried everything from acting to teaching to telephone sales. Now she's finally found work that suits her perfectly. She insists she never had a problem keeping a job—she was merely gaining "life experience" for her future as a novelist. Christine lives with her family in Oregon. Visit her at christinerimmer.com

Also by Katrina Cudmore

Tempted by the Greek Tycoon
Christmas with the Duke
Resisting the Italian Single Dad
Second Chance with the Best Man

Royals of Monrosa

Best Friend to Princess Bride

Also by Christine Rimmer

Almost a Bravo
Same Time, Next Christmas
Switched at Birth
A Husband She Couldn't Forget
The Right Reason to Marry
Their Secret Summer Family
James Bravo's Shotgun Bride
Ms Bravo and the Boss
A Bravo for Christmas
In Search of the Long-Lost Maverick

CHRISTMAS ENCOUNTER WITH A PRINCE

KATRINA CUDMORE

HOME FOR THE BABY'S SAKE

CHRISTINE RIMMER

MILLS & BOON

First Published in Great Britain 2020
by Mills & Boon, an imprint of HarperCollinsPublishers,
1 London Bridge Street, London, SE1 9GF

ISBN: 978-0-263-27900-9

1020

This book is produced from independently certified FSC™ paper to ensure responsible forest management.

For more information visit: www.harpercollins.co.uk/green

Printed and bound in Spain
by CPI, Barcelona

CHRISTMAS ENCOUNTER WITH A PRINCE

KATRINA CUDMORE

To Helen, for all the childhood memories.

CHAPTER ONE

ALICE O'CONNOR SHOT out of her chair as another thud sounded downstairs. Could it be burglars? Had some opportunist, on seeing the entire staff leave for their Christmas holidays earlier, decided now was the time to break into the London residence of the Monrosian Royal family?

She had to call the police. But where was her phone? Damn. She had deliberately left it downstairs to avoid wasting yet more valuable writing time internet browsing.

She glanced around the library for some form of weapon. But the only objects to hand were books. Thousands of them. She grabbed a sturdy hardback with sharp corners and crept towards the door.

She paused in the hallway, ears pinned back, but the faint sound of traffic out in Fitzalen Square was all that was to be heard. She counted to ten, but no further noise came from downstairs. She lowered the book, doing a mental eye-roll.

The house was old and bound to creak and heave like an old ship. She swung around to return to the library. And froze. Her eyes widened. Downstairs a voice spoke. A male voice. Wait! That voice was familiar…

deep and smooth with a sexy Mediterranean accent that sent a flow of heat through her body…a voice that had irritated and fascinated her with equal measure at her cousin Kara's wedding six months earlier.

She darted down the corridor and leant over the banister of the grand staircase.

It couldn't be. Oh, please, not him. Of all people, especially not him.

'Relax, Edwin, I promise to be in Monrosa for Christmas.' Silence followed and then he spoke even more impatiently. 'Yes, as soon as I take care of some business here in London.'

She leant further over the banister.

He was staying in London? Here?

'There's no need for security.' Silence followed that statement and then an exasperated breath. 'Don't blame them; I left the Bahamas without informing them. And I insist that you allow me some space—I don't need my protection team. I have to go, I have an urgent meeting.'

Beneath her, he appeared in the hallway, a hand raking through his dark, wavy hair, before he disappeared out of sight again.

She jerked back. The book leapt out of her hands. She went to grab it. Her fingertips glanced across the dark green woven cover but then it dropped fast and hard down through the stairwell. She stared after it and jumped when it smacked against the black and white tiles of the hallway two floors below.

She gasped and felt herself go the colour of a vine-ripened tomato.

A long silence followed and then slow footsteps. His feet came into view. It was the middle of winter. It was cold and wet. Then why on earth was he wearing flip-flops? He stepped forward, those broad shoulders lifting in question at the book sprawled on the floor. Pages had come loose.

Please don't make it a rare edition. My credit card will go up in flames if I try to load any more debt onto it.

His head lifted, and for a moment she was tempted to run back to the library and pretend that she had taken no part in events. But having backbone was everything to her. So, arranging her features into a blank expression, she waited for the humiliation to come.

As he studied her his puzzled expression only intensified and then shifted into incredulity. And then he laughed.

Indignation fired through her.

She dashed down the stairs towards him—Prince Luis of Monrosa, who was waiting at the bottom step for her with a grin and a raised eyebrow. She tried to slow down on the final turn of the stairs, suddenly feeling rather shy and ridiculous. But her momentum was too great and she hurtled towards him, expecting his glee at meeting once again the stranger who had ambushed and kissed him before fleeing into the night.

Alice O'Connor flew down the stairs towards him like a hacked-off doe, her long legs and arms performing an uncoordinated dance. Luis leapt forward, to save her from going head over tail, but at the last moment she sidestepped him.

'Your Highness, I didn't know… Kara told me that the house would be free for the entirety of the Christmas period. I have my PhD thesis to complete and need absolute solitude.'

So that explained why Kara's curious cousin was in the house.

Her black T-shirt had fallen off one shoulder, exposing a twisted black with red edging bra strap. He stared at it, a strange but strong compulsion to twist it back into place transfixing him. His hand moved out but just then she took the book that had dropped from the skies like a heat-seeking missile from him and added, 'You startled me.' She opened the book and leafed through the pages, her dark eyebrows knotting when she lifted the torn pages. 'Oh, no, I've damaged it.'

'What about me? I was almost impaled by it,' he pointed out.

That only earned him a brief shrug. Her hand stroked the cover of the book, her long fingers caressing the spine. He touched his neck to where her fingers had stroked his skin the night she had kissed him. 'You certainly know how to make an impression.'

Those grey eyes of hers lifted and she studied him with the same considered seriousness she had regarded him with at Edwin and Kara's wedding. He had only spoken to her, as they had waited for the newlyweds' departure for their honeymoon on the marina, because he had been concerned that she was about to fall into the sea, given how much she was swaying on her feet. At first he had thought she had drunk too much. But without him having said a word to this effect, other than to warn her of the water's edge, she had indignantly informed him that she had never touched alcohol in her entire life. Then, after serving him a rather impressive withering look, she had bent down, untied the strap of her sandal, stepped out of it, and yanked it out of where it had become stuck between the wooden planking of the jetty and had turned her back on him.

Her long brown hair had been tied up, faint freckles visible along her bare shoulders. He had shrugged and stepped away but then had turned back, intrigued by the fire in her eyes. She had reluctantly chatted with him after Edwin and Kara had left but had refused his invitation to dance with him back in the ballroom. He had forgotten about her and danced with other guests. But later that night when he had been walking through the gardens in search of his brother, Ivo, Alice had appeared before him. For a few seconds she had hesitated but then in the barest of whispers she had asked if she could kiss him. He wasn't given to kissing women he barely knew, it wasn't his style, but her quiet seriousness, her lack of pretence and flirtatiousness, had him nod yes, his amusement swiftly being replaced by intrigue and desire thanks to the mind-blowing, perfectly pitched kiss she had delivered. Tender, warm and full of promises.

But the moment his hand had brushed against her bare arm, the moment his mouth had opened to her parted lips, she had yanked back and walked away. When he had called out for her to stop she had given a firm shake of her head. By the time he had caught up with her, she was already in one of the cars taking guests to their nearby accommodation.

Now she lifted her chin, cleared her throat and offered, 'I believe I owe you an explanation.' She hesitated for a moment, her hands rubbing against the blue denim of her jeans. 'I've always wondered what it would be like to kiss a man with a beard. It was inappropriate of me and I hope I didn't offend you. It was a silly dare I had with one of my cousins. A silly dare and a silly mistake.'

A silly mistake.

Really?

He rubbed his hand against his jawline and said in a deliberately heavily accented and husky timbre, 'Am I safe now that my beard is gone…or do you want to see what it's like to kiss a guy with a day's worth of stubble?'

She blinked at that. Went to answer, but, her eyes narrowing, realising he was teasing her, she asked instead, 'You're on your way to Monrosa? Are you leaving tomorrow?'

Her voice was full of hope.

He gave her a lazy grin. 'I haven't decided yet.' His gaze ran from her startled eyes, down over her high cheekbones and wide mouth, down over her lean body that only gave a hint of curves, down to her bare long and narrow feet, her toenails unpainted, a satisfying and pleasurable thought forming in his mind. 'I guess it depends on whether there's something better to keep me here in London.' Maybe Alice O'Connor was just the distraction he needed in his life right now.

'But surely you want to spend Christmas with your family. Kara told me that Edwin is looking forward to you all spending Christmas together this year. That it will be the first time in years.' Pausing, she frowned and asked, 'Why are you wearing shorts and flip-flops?'

Without answering her, he took the stairs down to the basement kitchen. Opening the fridge, he pulled out a beer. Alice appeared behind him. Popping the bottle open, he took a long, deep slug, his eyes never wavering from Alice's disapproving scowl. Dropping the bottle to the worktop, he looked at his watch. 'Twelve hours ago I was in the Bahamas. I decided I wanted a change of scene.'

'Couldn't you have at least changed your clothes?'

'I didn't have time.'

Her eyes widened and she edged away to stand on the other side of the kitchen island. 'Were you running away from something…or someone?'

He gave a chuckle. 'Just myself.'

'What do you mean?'

Well, Alice, I've just achieved my life's ambition—to win the Global Power Boat Championship Series. Right now I should be back in the Bahamas, celebrating with my team. But I tried that for a few hours and I couldn't stand it. I couldn't stand the thought of it all being over. I couldn't handle the prospect of saying goodbye to my team. Knowing that now I had to keep my promise to return to Monrosa and take up my royal duties.

Can you believe that I even considered messing up my last race and losing the championship so that I wouldn't have to honour that promise? That I was prepared to give up my life's ambition in order to avoid returning to Monrosa. To avoid a life of boredom and protocol and being under the constant scrutiny of my father. The man who couldn't even be bothered to call me and acknowledge my win. Like a fool I had waited for hours for him to call.

But why had I expected him to do so, knowing just how much he disapproved of my career? Why had I expected him to be proud of me, when I was nothing but a source of disappointment?

He took another slug of beer. 'It was a joke. You do get jokes, don't you?'

She eyed his now almost empty beer bottle disapprovingly and answered, 'Yes, Your Highness, but only when the joke is explained to me…really, really slowly.' Then, walking over to the basement French windows, she pointed out to the rain-soaked rear patio. 'Why on earth would you want to come back here anyway? It's wet and miserable. Surely a Mediterranean palace or the Bahamas is preferable to this?'

She considered him, her hands reaching around to rest in her back pockets. She was cranky and unpredictable… but right now he needed something that would distract him, and Alice O'Connor would do nicely.

He finished his beer, set it down on the worktop and said, 'London does have its attractions.' Moving towards her, he added in a low voice, his eyes holding hers, 'Especially at Christmas time, when everything is so beautiful. I like beautiful things. And you can call me Luis… I think we've already moved beyond the formal, don't you?'

Alice could understand why so many women fell for Luis. When it came to a checklist of desirable must-haves, he had them all. A prince. *Tick.* Tall, dark and handsome. *Tick.* A charismatic sports star who was at the top of his game and lauded for his commitment and bravery. *Tick.* A man with the unerring but addictive ability to make you feel as if you were the most important person in the world by holding your gaze with those soft hazel eyes and smiling gently at you. *Tick.*

But beneath the veneer of all those deceptively attractive qualities she was certain that he was just like her dad—self-regarding, self-centred and driven at all costs. And with those traits came manipulation and pain for those surrounding them. Which made the fact that she had kissed him all the more confusing and galling. At times since Kara's wedding she had been able to convince herself that the kiss was all about her gaining control of that strange chemistry he had stirred up in her, but at other times she had had to admit to herself that it had been nothing more than ill-advised lust. And she hated herself for it. She hated losing control. She hated deviating even an inch from the life she had planned out for herself. And Luis had sent her careering off that path, okay only for a few crazy minutes, but it had seriously unsettled her. And it wasn't going to happen again.

She held out her hand. 'How about we start again… Luis?'

He took her hand and, giving her one of those heart-melting smiles of his, he said, 'It is the season of goodwill after all.'

His grip was strong, his skin warm. A buzz ran up her arm and down her entire body. Flustered, she snatched her hand away. 'Can I take it that you are yet another fan of Christmas? Don't you get bored of it? It's the same ding-dong every year, the same songs that are so sappy they make my skin crawl. Not to mention the same crazy buying of gifts that nobody wants. A law should be introduced whereby only under-tens are allowed to celebrate Christmas. Everyone else should have to just grow up and go to work. Think about just how unproductive it all is.'

He gave a chuckle and shifted closer to her. 'My, aren't you a modern-day Miss Scrooge?' Something dark and mischievous glinted in his eyes. 'Maybe you need to be shown just how magical Christmas can be.'

His voice was low, sexy. Beneath his black sailing fleece his pink polo shirt was open at the neck, revealing a fine dusting of dark hair and tanned skin. Something warm stirred in her veins.

'I'm going to a party after I shower and change; why

don't you come with me…' he paused, his lips curled up into an even more seductive smile '…to the party, I mean?'

What would it be like to watch him undress? Watch him step into the shower? Follow him into the warmth of the water? Get to know his body?

She jerked away from him. What on earth was the matter with her? She had a schedule to keep. A word-count to maintain. She had ten days to get her PhD thesis under control. Ten days of hiding away from the world, ten days of thankfully being able to avoid the silly season that was otherwise known as Christmas. Ten days before she would have to return to work and the erratic temperament of her boss at the coffee shop. And two weeks until her next meeting with her university supervisor, who, given the tone of their last catch-up, was seriously starting to question Alice's ability to complete her thesis. And no PhD would mean she could kiss goodbye to any hope of securing a full-time lecturing position. She shouldn't be wasting time having schoolgirl fantasies about her cousin's brother-in-law. A real-life Prince Charming who was born to break women's hearts. 'Sorry, but I'm busy. I have to focus on my thesis.'

His head tilted. 'That's a shame…it's Christmas, after all. You should be enjoying yourself.' The teasing disappearing from his eyes, he added, 'I'll feel bad leaving you here all on your own. Are you sure you won't come?'

For a moment she actually thought he was being sincere. The tone of his voice, the gentleness in his expression almost fooled her. She had to give it to him, he was a seriously good actor. But she trusted Prince Luis just about as far as she could throw him—and, given that he must be close to six feet four, and therefore had a seven-inch advantage over her, she wouldn't be able to throw him far. He was trying to charm her. Why was beyond her, as they had nothing in common and it wasn't as if there was a shortage of woman keen to date him if media reports were anything to go by. But she didn't have the time or interest in working that particular puzzle out. Not with a PhD to complete.

And the idea of attending a Christmas party frankly left her feeling cold. All that forced and pretend gaiety. When in truth for many Christmas was about bickering and arguing, the unleashing of simmering tension and anger. She grabbed Luis's empty beer bottle and rinsed it at the sink, before wiping it dry. Dropping it into the recycling, she answered, 'I have a schedule I have to keep.'

Opening the fridge door, he considered its contents. 'It's Christmas. Everyone should forget about schedules and work at Christmas.'

'Not me. I don't do Christmas.'

He shut the door with a frown. 'So I gathered.' Spotting the tin of chocolates on the counter beside the fridge, he prised the lid open. Alice winced. He rifled through it, his frown deepening. 'Who eats all of the chocolates and leaves the wrappers behind?'

Earlier, after she had deleted all her day's pathetic word-count, she had tossed herself into the tin of Christmas chocolates her mother had sneakily hidden in her luggage. There was no way a professional sportsman would understand how a grown adult could devour an entire tin of chocolates in one afternoon thanks to bored frustration, so she wasn't even going to bother trying. So instead she backed towards the kitchen door and said, 'If I don't see you tomorrow before you leave for Monrosa…well, it's been nice seeing you again. Enjoy your time with your family. Give my love to Kara.'

Unwrapping a chocolate in a purple foil wrapper that he must have found at the bottom of the tin, he gave a resigned shrug and said, 'If you change your mind then you can join me at the Stewart Club. I'll leave your name at the door.'

About to head up the stairs, she paused. His party was at the Stewart Club? Where it was said that Lady Radford had frequented. She'd love to have the opportunity to see the interior of one of London's oldest and most exclusive private clubs. She eyed Luis. But to do so would mean accepting his invite. She moved back into the kitchen. Watched as he popped the dark chocolate into his mouth, his eyes lighting up with delight as he savoured the praline inside.

She should turn around. Go back up to the library. But instead she heard herself say, 'My thesis is on the writer Lady Maud Radford. She used to dine frequently in the Stewart Club—in fact, it's said that it was there she found the opportunity to influence those in government at the time with her political and social-reform ideas. So in the name of research I would like to join you tonight. But only for a short while. And strictly on a work basis.'

He laughed at that. 'Do you ever chill out, Alice?'

She gave him a death stare. 'I'll change and be working in the library when you've finished your beauty regime.' Climbing the stairs to his laughter, she groaned. Hating just how prickly she became at Christmas. Hating how prickly she was when life took an unexpected turn.

CHAPTER TWO

'So, your thesis, tell me...' Luis had no sooner returned to his seat beside her when he was interrupted once more. Standing up, he gave her an apologetic smile before kissing both women in the group on the cheek and back-slapping the three men, laughter and chatter dancing between them.

Sitting back into her chair, Alice decided a Christmas party at the Stewart Club would make for a great social anthropology study. Somehow, without any formal organisation, those attending understood where they stood in the social hierarchy. Those on the lower social rungs were the ones who were expected to travel the thronged room, greeting those higher up the ladder, who stayed put in the vicinity of their table. And, of course, Prince Luis of Monrosa was the prize person to talk to tonight. Within minutes of their arrival at the club, Luis had been drawn into an unending cycle of greeting acquaintances and friends. Not once had he failed to recall a name, and his keen attention on everyone he spoke to only seemed to up the excitement and general air of goodwill and celebration in the room.

How easily people fell for the affirmation of attention. What was it in us humans that needed the acknowledgement of others? Even when it was to our detriment? After her parents' divorce, even when she had known for years the ugly side to her father, she had craved his attention. Believed that this time things might be different. How many times had he not turned up to meet her? Or turned up steaming drunk? How many times had she forgiven him when he told her he was sorry and that he would never let her down again? He had been so charming and funny and warm. A born entertainer. In his good moments he'd made life seem magical. But then he would drink and become bitter and belligerent and blame her for not understanding him.

Now she smiled as a waiter placed a pot of tea and teacup on the table. With Luis otherwise occupied she had earlier explored the club, taking in the historic rooms upstairs, the gallery and library, taken photos of the grand dining room with its heavy chandeliers and dark wood panelling, imagining Lady Radford dining there.

When she had finished her tour of the club she had dithered in the hallway before eventually deciding to join the party, the guilt of not meeting her writing milestones losing out to the temptation of spending more time in the place where Lady Radford had socialised in the vain hope it might just provide her with the inspiration she desperately needed to get over her writing slump.

Around her champagne and laughter flowed. Out on the dancefloor guests danced to the DJ's Christmas playlist. When she had returned to the main party, which was taking place in the reading room of the club, Luis had gestured for her to join him and he had introduced her to the people he was talking to with great enthusiasm. Several times he had sat beside her and begun a conversation but time and time again he had been interrupted. Watching him now, gesturing wildly, those around him wide-eyed at whatever story he was telling them, she marvelled at the fact that earlier, on their way to the party, he had admitted to being jet lagged. But nobody would guess that now. For a moment she wondered what it must be like to be so carefree, so open to others, but then she remembered that the outer persona so often masked the truth of the inner person.

Dressed in black tie like all of the other male guests, Luis had assured her that her choice of a knee-length black dress was perfect for the party…which was a good thing, as that and a leather skirt were the only half-decent items she had brought with her to London. Unfortunately, however, all the other female guests were dressed in festive golds and silvers and reds and she had been stopped several times in her tour of the club and given a drinks order. She didn't belong here amongst all the glitz and glamour and bonhomie.

His story over, Luis turned to a woman standing to his right. Bowing his head, he whispered something into her ear. The woman nodded and then, curving into him, flung her arms around his neck. They embraced well beyond what was socially polite.

She placed her teacup down on the saucer. It was time she left.

Standing, she grabbed her bag.

'I'm not being a good host, am I?'

She shrugged, looking away from Luis's apologetic smile. Hating how easily he could make her heart leap with just a smile. 'I didn't expect you to play host. I only came to see the inside of the club. And now it's time for me to go home.'

His hand touched against her arm. 'Stay and dance with me. I do want to hear about your thesis.'

With a grin he removed his tuxedo jacket and threw it on his chair. She wanted to say no. This was not how she had planned out her trip to London. And something way too giddy was stirring in her blood at the gorgeous shape of his torso beneath his shirt—incredibly broad shoulders tapering down to a narrow waist. For a person with embarrassingly limited experience when it came to men, the effect Prince Luis of Monrosa was having on her was baffling beyond all measure. She *should* leave. *But* she was staying in his family's home. Wouldn't it be impolite for her to refuse to dance with him?

She nodded and he held out his hand to her. Inhaling deeply, she took it and allowed him to lead her out onto the dance floor, trying to resist the urge to grab her hand back out of his grasp, the heat, the strength, the callused skin of his hand disturbing reminders of the raw maleness that lay just below his outward display of the equable Royal Prince.

On the dance floor she groaned when Luis began to dance. Damn it, but he could move. Whereas she, as her friend Toni liked to joke, danced like a giraffe on acid. Luis's hips swayed, his arms moved in time with the beat, his eyes fixed on hers, inviting her to join him. She gave her hips a tiny sway. He nodded encouragingly. She moved her hips in a wider circle, trying to smile and pretend it all came naturally. She lifted her arms and shuffled her feet, bumping into Luis in the process. He placed a steadying hand on her waist, his eyes dancing with amusement. Was he aware that her breast was squashed against his arm?

'I'm starting to think that this is going to be a particularly good Christmas.'

She arched her neck away from the warmth of his breath, her pulse whooshing in her ears at the huskiness of his voice. His hands shifted ever so slightly, his thumbs fixing on the points of her hips. His scent was like a mixture of freshly washed cotton and earthiness…with a pinch of goodness.

She stared at the crisp whiteness of his dress shirt, thrown by just how wrong it was that someone so dangerous could smell so…pure and right. He weakened her. Something about him stirred a chemistry inside her that she seemed incapable of controlling. Now, for the first time in her life, she understood why people took reckless decisions that went against everything they strove for.

She shifted her gaze upwards, knowing it was time to stay goodnight, when a commotion to the side of the room had her shift her attention in that direction instead.

A group of middle-aged men were making their way into the room, calling out to a friend who was standing at the bar. She gasped. Pulled herself away from Luis. At the centre of the group, his arms thrown around his companions on either side, was her father. She knew by the gleam in his eye, the high colour in his cheeks, that he was drunk.

This could not be happening. She needed to run…but her feet felt as though they were glued to the floor. The DJ played a new track, killing the men's overbearing voices. She was vaguely aware of Luis asking her if she was okay.

And then her father looked in her direction.

She twisted away, crouching over. A service entrance was in front of her. She stumbled towards it, panic pounding in her ears.

Dio! Didn't she realise he was only flirting with her? Luis watched Alice run from the room, pushing past startled partygoers, heard their surprised laughter at her desperation to leave. For a moment he considered just letting her go. Alice O'Connor unsettled him. She was impossible to read. Up to a minute ago she had seemed to be enjoying the night…in her own quiet way. But now she was bolting away—just as she had done at the wedding. But he couldn't let her go without at least seeing her to the safety of a taxi.

Chasing after her, he raced through an empty service corridor and then the club's kitchen, and outside the kitchen's double swing doors he saw Alice in the distance at the main entrance door.

He called out her name, but she disappeared outside.

It was raining hard. Raindrops bounced off the footpath. He cursed as a passing black cab sprayed him. Shoes soaked, he stared after Alice, who was sprinting down the street. Couldn't she at least have collected her coat before rushing away?

'Alice!'

Passing traffic and the heavy rain meant she probably couldn't hear him. He broke into a run, a car horn blaring when he crossed a side street without looking. Ahead Alice was slowing as she waved frantically for a cab to stop, but they all rushed by, already occupied.

He was fast gaining on her when she turned a corner into a pedestrian side street. He followed her, the rain pinning his dress shirt to his skin. He cursed and stopped. The street was empty. Where had she disappeared to?

'Alice!' His call echoed down the narrow shopping street, the blue and white overhead Christmas lights swaying in the breeze.

He shouted her name again. 'Alice!' This time more angrily, panic taking hold. What if something happened to her? How well did she know London? He broke into a jog. There were several arcades and narrow lanes leading off the street. She could have gone down any of them.

He bellowed her name again, frustration adding to his panic.

And then he saw her. Pushed into the furthest reaches of a darkened doorway, shivering, her eyes that of a hunted animal.

He came to a stop. Waited for her to come out. But instead she cowered even more into the darkest recesses of the store. She was terrified. Of him? Had he triggered something in her?

'Please don't shout.'

He flinched at the desperation in her voice.

He took a step backwards, holding his hands up.

I won't do you any harm.

'I was worried—that's why I was shouting.'

For long seconds she considered him. He waited for her to speak, to explain what was going on. But it seemed as though she was incapable of speech.

'You need to be indoors.' He held out a hand, wanting to lead her out of that dark and cold place she was hiding in, but she didn't react. He took the smallest of steps forward, lowered his voice. 'I'll take you wherever you want to go—a friend's house or a hotel if you don't want to return home with me.' He let out a long exhale. 'I'm sorry, Alice; I've upset you. Let me make this right.'

She shook her head. 'It wasn't you.'

Then what? He wanted to ask a hundred questions but knew he had to wait until she was ready to talk.

She stepped out of the doorway, wrapping her arms tight against her waist. 'Can you find me a cab?' Her hair was soaked through, its heavy weight emphasising the height of her cheekbones, the almond shape of her eyes. Her long, narrow frame seemed so fragile he longed to pull her into a hug, to make things right for her. Which, of course, was the last thing he should do right now. She nodded in the direction of the club, and added, 'You must return to the party…' Her eyes flicking over him and lingering for a moment on his rain-saturated shirt, she grimaced. 'I'm so sorry, I didn't mean for you to follow me out. I've ruined the night for you.'

He shook his head and gestured that they should walk back in the direction they had come from. He waited until they were out in the main street, where there were people walking by, wanting her to have the security of having other people nearby before he said, 'I don't understand what has just happened, but I do want to help.'

Her eyes flickered towards him, studied him for a few seconds and then moved away. A shudder ran through her body. 'I saw someone… I thought he was chasing me.' Those grey eyes of hers that were so wary and cautious met his again, an apologetic smile trembling on her lips. 'I didn't realise it was you…and now you're soaked through.'

He wanted to know who she had seen. Who had terrified her so much? He wanted to go back to the club and thump whoever had caused this fear in her. But instead he waited until a black cab appeared down the street and, stepping out into the road, he forced it to stop. The driver wound down his window and started to hurl a barrage of abuse in his direction. Luis interrupted him by pulling out his wallet and withdrawing a large number of notes. Calmly he explained that it was an emergency, and on the offer of a substantial sum of money both the driver and two male occupants happily agreed to Alice and him taking the cab, the two men heading in the direction of a nearby pub.

He instructed the cab driver to drive around the block while he phoned ahead to the club. As they pulled up to the door, Jana, the general manager at the Stewart, ran down the steps with both of their overcoats.

He helped Alice into her black wool coat and, despite her resistance, insisted that she use his as a blanket.

They travelled back to Mayfair, passing by the Natural History Museum and Hyde Park, both decked in festive lights, in silence. He clenched his fists to stop himself from reaching for Alice, who despite the coats was still shivering fiercely. He wanted to make all of this better for her.

Outside a department store, people were standing on the pavements looking at the Christmas scenes in the window fronts. He had hoped for a night where he could forget about the life, the friends and team he was leaving behind and the unwanted future that stood in front of him. But instead he had half frightened his house guest to death. Yet another example of him getting things wrong.

'I'm ashamed to be your father.'

His father's words to him as a fourteen-year-old boy. Words only uttered once, but conveyed ever since in every look and criticism of his life choices. In his father's eyes he brought shame on the family and Luis did nothing to combat his father's opinion, wanting to antagonise him, wanting to hurt him as much as his father's behaviour in the aftermath of his mother's death had scarred him. They had once been close, had shared a passion for sport. Intuitively they had understood one another, mirroring each other's personality. They were both outspoken, impetuous, extrovert. But after his mother's death his father had withdrawn into himself, had become ever more defensive and irritable. Their once close relationship had crumbled and Luis had learnt the fickleness of love. He had learnt to never fully engage with or trust another person. He had learnt that you never truly know what others were truly thinking and wanting and feeling, beyond the smoke and mirrors that collapsed in a moment of crisis. He had learnt that a life lightly led, a transitory life, was far more preferable to one where you overly relied on others. He was never going to overly rely on another person again and he certainly wasn't going to allow a relationship to destroy him as had happened to his father following his mother's death.

Sure, he had a reputation for dating countless women, but that reputation was media-driven and one he didn't go out of his way to dispel, given how much it maddened his father. He enjoyed socialising. Had a large circle of friends. He adored the buzz, the distraction of other people; it suited his personality…and the need to forget the hole inside himself.

A hole that Alice O'Connor's reserved and watchful

presence made a whole lot bigger as though she were holding a magnifying glass up to it.

He offered her a smile. And his heart tugged when she attempted a smile in return, heat flaming in her cheeks. She looked away towards the lights of Green Park and the groups of people heading to the nightlife in Piccadilly, but not before he saw tears glisten in her eyes.

The cab swung down a side street, the passing street lights flickering over the soft, full shape of her lips, the long, straight line of her nose, the sweep of her eyelashes, the darkness of her brows, that perfectly framed her once again closed and reserved expression.

He reached out his hand, resting it next to where her hand lay on his coat. She startled when his finger touched hers, an inch of skin on skin.

Her gaze swept back to meet his; it was wary, as though she was trying to gauge whether she could trust him. He tried to shrug off the disappointment that came when her hand shifted away.

Alice walked to her bedroom door. Stopped. Spun around. Paced the soft, dove-grey carpet, circling the blush-pink two-seater sofa at the centre of the room. She owed Luis a proper apology and explanation. But should she wait until the morning, when she'd be less emotional?

The past hour had been nothing short of a nightmare. Luis must think that she was completely unstable. The first time they met she had ensnared him in a kiss and tonight she had bolted out of the party with no explanation.

How was she going to explain her behaviour to him, without having to unearth memories and feelings she wanted to keep buried? It wouldn't be so hard if he had just been disbelieving and impatient with her like her ex, Rory, had used to be when her dad would call her phone number. It was over a decade ago but Rory's irritation with her fears, how he'd used to ask her if she was sure that her dad was as bad as she claimed he was, had made her question her own sanity and her memories and reading of her own life. No wonder their relationship hadn't lasted more than a year. And since then her romance history had consisted of a litany of disastrous first dates, that she had half-heartedly gone on in the first place, giving into her best friend Toni's insistence that she couldn't remain single for ever. Her dates had included guys she had thought were lovely and kind at first, who made her feel hopeful but then would let slip towards the end of the night that they were already in a relationship. Others had thought it was okay to lie about most things—their age, their job and their interests—in order to secure a date. The guy who had given Toni the best laugh was the one who had turned up to the restaurant carrying a bag of 'leather items' he thought they might use later that night. Alice had walked straight out, swearing never to look at a dating app again.

She approached the bedroom door again, placed her hand on the doorknob and took a deep breath. She was his guest. The least she could do was apologise again for dragging him away from the party early. She closed her eyes, remembering the image of him standing on the pavement, the irritation in his eyes, in the tight scowl on his mouth, softening to concern. The street light had flashed on the beads of water dripping down the sharp edges of his face, his soaked shirt stuck to his torso like a second skin. For a moment she had wanted to weep with relief that he was there for her. But thankfully she had pulled herself up on that particularly delusional hope—her judgement on men had been disastrous in the past and she could see zero reason why that would have changed now. Especially with a thrill-seeking, restless prince with a reputation for playing the field.

She found him in the basement kitchen. He had showered too and was now dressed in grey cotton lounge pants and a navy long-sleeved top. Leaning against the kitchen counter, he was eating trifle from a crystal serving bowl, not pausing when she appeared.

'Would you like some?' he asked, nodding to the bowl.

'I don't like custard.'

'All year or just in protest at Christmas?'

Despite her nerves, or perhaps because of them, she laughed. He raised an eyebrow. No wonder. Her laugh was bordering on hysterical.

Using her sopping dress as an excuse to escape, she took refuge in the adjacent laundry room and tried to gather herself as she placed it in the washing machine.

Back in the kitchen once again, she found Luis now tucking into a fist-sized piece of Christmas pudding covered in a small mountain of cream.

Shaking her head when he offered her some, she cleared her throat. 'I'm sorry about earlier... I really thought it was someone else following me.' A drop of water from her hair oozed down onto her pyjama top. She shivered in memory of how cold she had felt as she had hidden in the shop doorway.

He nodded to the counter behind her. 'I made you a pot of tea. There's milk in the fridge if you take it—I'm assuming you don't take sugar.'

Tea was exactly what she wanted. But why was he

making the assumption that she didn't want sugar? 'Why would you think that?'

Amusement shone in his eyes. 'Because I reckon you like to do everything by the book, including having a clean diet…' his eyes trailed over to the chocolate tin on the counter '…although perhaps at times, despite yourself, you are human like us all and give in to temptation.'

She tried to pretend she had no idea what he was talking about and poured some tea. God, was she that obvious? Well, they said sugar was good for shock. Opening the kitchen cupboard where she knew the sugar was kept, she took down the silver canister and put a teaspoon into her cup.

Approaching the fridge, which Luis was standing in front of as though guarding its contents, she said, 'I need the milk.'

Opening the fridge, he took out a milk carton and was about to pour it into her cup when he stopped and said gently, 'Why don't you put it down on the counter?'

Damn. She hadn't realised that her hands were trembling so badly. It was as if the cold from earlier had seeped into her bones. And as he poured the milk into her cup she realised just how tired she was. Not just because of what'd happened tonight, but she was tired to her bones trying to work full-time in the café, sometimes working double shifts to pay her rent and trying to complete her PhD. And she realised just how nice it was to have someone to do something as simple as make her a cup of tea. Living alone gave her the independence she craved…but a solo life had little softness. There was no one to cheer you up on a bad day, to help pick up the pieces when things went wrong.

With a smile that undid her with its soft kindness, Luis pushed the teacup in her direction.

Shifting back to the other side of the kitchen island, she sipped the tea, trying to keep her expression neutral when the overly sweet liquid made her want to grimace.

She took another sip, preferring the sickly taste to explaining why she had fled from him earlier. But Luis deserved some honesty. 'I…' She paused, a heat spreading from her stomach out onto her skin. 'I saw my father tonight, at the club. We don't speak.'

'You're scared of him?'

She inhaled at his question. 'Scared, no…' She wanted to turn away, say goodnight. Forget about her father.

'Do you want me to call the police?'

'No. No, nothing like that. I just got a shock. I didn't expect to see him. My aunt had told me that he had moved to France a few years ago to be a rugby coach at a club there. I didn't want to speak to him—it never turns out well when we do. I needed to get away, and when you followed me out of the club I thought you were him.'

'I'm sorry that I scared you.'

She smiled at that. 'You're not the one who should be apologising. I ruined your night.'

'There'll be plenty more of them—don't worry.'

Was there a hint of boredom in his voice? But she shook off that thought. Why would there be? Luis was a party animal.

'Has he hurt you, Alice?'

The gentleness of his voice grabbed her by the heart. Crazy tears filled her eyes. The stress of her PhD was getting to her. She swallowed hard. 'No…not really.' And then she made the mistake of looking up to see Luis move across the kitchen to stand opposite her. Not too close, but near enough for her to see the lines of tension at the sides of his mouth.

'He's an alcoholic, not that he'd admit to that. He used to be a professional rugby player. He had to retire early due to injury and found a friend in alcohol. He never hurt me...'

She stopped, her heart pounding. Remembering the arguments, the thuds and the silence downstairs that would follow. How her mother would try to cover up her bruises the following day.

'But he did hurt others...your mum?'

She nodded at that. Her heart pulling apart to remember how her mum had used to try to pretend it never happened. Her shame of it transferring to Alice. It was something not to be spoken about. How could the town's famous son, Freddie O'Connor, possibly be a domestic abuser? He was the genius rugby player who charmed everyone in his wake. Even his wife and daughter found it hard to comprehend the dichotomy in his personality.

'We don't have to talk about it if you don't want to, Alice.'

She nodded, grateful that he wasn't going to push her, and touched her hair, glad to have an excuse to get away. 'I need to dry my hair.' She went to move away but stopped. 'Thank you for being so...so kind tonight.'

He made an amused sound. 'You sound surprised.'

'I guess.'

'Maybe we have misjudged one another.'

Taken aback, she studied him for a moment, the seriousness in his expression making her wonder who the true Prince Luis of Monrosa was. Had she totally misread him? Perhaps.

'Sleep well…and be kind to yourself; none of this was of your making.'

She nodded to his quietly spoken words, and climbed the stairs, her heart pounding in her chest at how utterly dangerous and beguiling he was.

CHAPTER THREE

ONE HUNDRED PER cent focus. That was what she needed to give this thesis. Plain and simple. Just get the words down and forget about that voice in her head that was telling her to give up, that she was an imposter and that there was no way she was going to finish it.

For God's sake, Alice, are you going to crumble now, when finishing it is within your grasp? Where has your fire, your determination disappeared to? Where's your passion for this career that has consumed you for the past decade? Remember how you used to say you'd prove the father who had told you that you were wasting your time on a subject with zero employment possibilities wrong when you made something of yourself?

She scrolled through the pages and pages of her already written words on her laptop screen, barely remembering writing them—it was as though they belonged to someone else.

She breathed against the panic in her chest. She was scared. Scared of not finishing this. Scared of what her future would look like. What if she didn't get a lecturing position? How many years would she have wasted chasing that dream? And what if she did get a position and it wasn't what she wanted after all?

Her passion for history was gone.

As evidenced by today. Here she was, sitting in a near empty reading room in the British Library, with its perfect lighting, silence and soothing architecture for inspiration. But instead of producing a blockbusting word count she was just faffing about. She knew what sections of the thesis she needed to address. There were gaps in her exploration and analysis of Lady Radford's writing and advocacy on the right to a free education for all. In her head she knew the points she wanted to make, but articulating them, actually typing the words, was proving impossible.

She closed her eyes. Breathed deeply.

Don't panic. You have this under control. You are strong.

She shrank inside herself, a series of images floating in the darkness behind her lids. Christmas Eve in her childhood home. The year her dad had been away all summer. The laughter. The unspoken disbelief that this year things might be different. They had gone Christmas shopping together and afterwards had eaten in their local Chinese restaurant. But on their way out he had bumped into some fans, complete strangers to him, who had persuaded him to join them for a drink in a local bar. Her mother had pleaded with him. Had cried when she had driven herself and Alice home. Alice had woken in the early hours of Christmas morning to the sound of her mother's scream for him to get out and then the sound of her body slamming against a wall.

She ground her teeth, anger flaring inside her. He had ruined her childhood. He was *not* going to ruin her future.

She needed to delve deeper into Lady Radford's influence on government policy.

But instead an uncomfortable thought and accompanying heat flamed her skin. Luis had come to her rescue last night—a fact she was grateful for, but she hated that he had seen her so weak. It was a side of herself she kept hidden from everyone. Even herself. Why was she so vulnerable these days? Was it tiredness? The uncertainty over her future?

'Finally! There you are. I've been searching for you.'

Alice leapt in her chair and screamed. Opening her eyes, she blinked hard.

What on earth was Luis doing here and why did he look so pleased with himself?

From somewhere across the room, someone made a disapproving tutting sound.

Pulling out the chair next to her, Luis sat, his grin growing wider. He tutted too. And, those hazel eyes of his sparkling with amusement, he leant into her and whispered, 'Are you a screamer, Alice?'

She tried not to redden.

Act blasé. If he knew the truth, would he laugh?

'What are you doing here?'

He rocked back in his chair. 'Now, that sounds like you're unhappy to see me. Do you know just how difficult it was to persuade Security to allow me in here?' He raised both arms into the air, stretching long and luxuriously, gave a yawn. 'I found your note saying you were going to work here for the day, so I decided I'd come and take you to lunch.'

'Aren't you supposed to be travelling back to Monrosa right now?' She didn't mean to sound so peeved, but the sight of Luis stretching like a giant and powerful cat, sending unfair pheromones into the air, made her feel irritable.

Eyes on her blank computer screen, he shrugged. 'There's no rush.'

She angled the laptop out of his line of sight. 'I'm busy.'

He smiled at that, raised a disbelieving eyebrow. 'It sure seemed like a flurry of activity when I arrived.'

'What do you want, Luis?'

Placing an elbow on the desk and resting his head in his hand, he studied her for a few moments, his expression now earnest. 'To make sure you're okay before I leave.'

'I told you this morning that I'm fine.' Earlier, as she had been heading up to the library, Luis had come out of his bedroom, all sleepy eyes and tousled hair, and in a husky voice had asked why on earth she was up so early.

For a fraction of a moment she had wondered what it would be like to follow him back into the darkness of his bedroom, feel his arms wrap around her, have his mouth on hers once again.

And their eyes had met and something raw and elemental had spun between them.

Heart thumping, she had turned away from him, terrified of just how vulnerable she felt around him. And when she had heard him leave the house later in the morning, irritated by just how skittish and distracted she had been all morning at the thought of him sleeping downstairs, she had flung her laptop and notes into her bag and fled for the sanctuary of the British Library.

'I know a great Peruvian restaurant close by—I'm sure the break will do you good.'

She didn't deserve a lunch break. Not with such a

dismal word output today. She was about to say no, but the concern in Luis's gaze had her reluctantly stand and nod her acceptance. Her behaviour last night had obviously alarmed him greatly; she needed to prove to him that he could leave London with a clear conscience and that she would be okay on her own. With Luis gone, then just maybe the words would come.

Beyond the Christmas lights surrounding the restaurant window, head bowed, her phone to her ear, Alice paced the Marylebone footpath. They had just ordered their food when her phone had rung, and with a concerned expression she had excused herself and stepped outside.

Okay, so he knew by taking Alice to lunch that he was procrastinating. Putting off travelling back to Monrosa. But being in Monrosa agitated him. How the hell would he cope with living there full-time? Palace life stifled him. It made him feel like a shadow of his true self. Royal expectation and formality choked him. It was as though he had to suppress every truth about himself. But he had promised his father…and, despite what his father thought, he did not go back on promises. Maybe it was because of his father's low opinion of him, but integrity and honour were vital to his self-regard and esteem.

Outside, Alice placed her phone in the back pocket of her jeans. But didn't come back inside. Instead she seemed to stare blankly at all of the last-minute shoppers rushing by. Was something the matter? Perhaps it was something to do with her father.

What kind of animal created such fear in his own daughter? This morning she had been up at some ungodly hour, looking tired and tense, and had barely spoken to him before she had bolted up to the library, insisting she had work to do. Later on, when he had returned from his run, he had found a note from her informing him she had decided to work in the British Library and wishing him a happy Christmas.

And he had got to wondering what her Christmas would be like.

How was he supposed to walk away from her, knowing she would be all alone for Christmas, especially after witnessing her distress last night?

Coming back inside, she handed her black padded jacket to the waiter and, putting her phone on the table, dropped down to her seat opposite him with a sigh.

Wearing a black and white T-shirt with the logo *TOMBOY* emblazoned on it, she gave him an apologetic smile. 'Sorry. That was my mum. I didn't want to miss her call. I knew that she was driving to my aunt's house today and she's a nervous driver, so I wanted to make sure she got there okay.' She let out another sigh. 'Although now I wish I hadn't: she wants me to go back to Ireland for Christmas.' On the table her phone pinged. She glanced at it before dropping it into her handbag at the side of the table. She rolled her eyes. 'I'm now going to get a barrage of calls and texts from her. My mum thinks I'm nine, not twenty-nine.'

'Why does she want you to go home?'

She hesitated for a moment before admitting, 'I made the stupid mistake of telling her that I saw my father last night.'

What was she not telling him? Why was her mother so concerned? His own concern had him ask sharply, 'Is your father a danger to you?'

She blinked, rightly taken aback by his tone. He raised his hands in apology. 'Sorry,' he placed his hands on the table between them, 'I can't get out of my mind just how terrified you were last night. It's not right.'

She studied his hands for a moment and then briefly she touched her fingertips against his. 'Thanks for being concerned.' Her eyes held his; there was a flash of uncertainty, deep vulnerability, in her expression, but then, sitting back in her seat, her expression once again closed to scrutiny, she gave a shrug. 'My father isn't a danger to me. My mum was never happy about me spending Christmas alone in the first place. It's the first time we haven't spent Christmas week together—I've tried to get out of it other years but she's very good at persuading me into spending it with her family. God, it's a nightmare—too many people, too many presents to be bought and exchanged, too much food and too much singing.'

'It sounds like fun to me.'

She laughed at that. 'I'm guessing any party is fun to you.' Then, her expression growing quizzical, she said, 'Your life, it seems so busy. You seem to be in a different country every week, hanging out with a different crowd. That constant travel, racing and socialising would exhaust me. Do you ever just long for an easier life?'

He raised an eyebrow. How and why did she know what his life looked like?

He watched their waiter place their food on the table—*tajarin* pasta with wild mushrooms for Alice and roasted venison loin for him—before he asked, 'Are you keeping tabs on me?'

Her mouth dropped open. 'Good God, no. My mum is an avid reader of celebrity magazines, and ever since Kara married into your family she thinks it's her duty to keep up with all of your lives. I could equally tell you about Ivo's win in Henley and your father's trip to Canada this autumn. But you leave both of them standing when it comes to coverage in the media—do you ever take time out? Does being so hectic make you happy?'

He laughed at her question but it came out half-heartedly. Under her calm grey-eyed gaze he started to feel undone. No one had ever asked him that question before—if he was happy. And she seemed genuinely intrigued by his lifestyle. Not in a judgemental way, but more as though it was something she really wanted to understand about him. But how could he explain the restlessness inside of him to her? The need for change and novelty and the energy of others? The need to feel alive? How being alone brought demons he didn't want to know about to the fore? He focused on cutting into his venison, anything to break the unnerving way she was studying him, and nodded towards her plate, encouraging her to eat too. 'Your mum will be reading less about me from now on—I'm moving back to Monrosa to take up my royal duties.'

'What about your powerboat career?'

He cleared his throat, the thought of what he was leaving acting like a punch to his heart. 'I promised my father that as soon as I won the Global Series I would return to Monrosa.'

Laying her fork back into her pasta bowl, she said, 'You don't sound very enthusiastic.'

He shrugged. 'It's what I need to do.'

Lifting her fork again, she rolled the pasta on the prongs. 'At least you'll be able to spend time with your family now.'

'As long as my father doesn't try to force me to marry.'

Alice dropped her fork. Damn it, he had forgotten

that she knew nothing about how his father had forced Edwin to marry Kara.

'Why on earth would he do that?' she asked.

'Because it's tradition and what's expected of all royals. We're expected to settle down, produce heirs and live happily ever after.'

Alice's head tilted as she studied him. 'And you don't want any of those things?'

He never had this type of conversation. His friendships and past relationships were based on having a good time. Not this type of soul-searching. And despite his better judgement he heard himself admit, 'I don't want to spend my life second-guessing the feelings of someone else for me.'

'I don't understand what you mean by that.'

The need to get up and walk away itched inside of him. He pulled at his shirt collar, his eyes shifting away from hers. *Dio!* It was hot in here. He was about to make a joke of it, but looking her in the eye again, her calm intelligence, had him confess, 'You think that my lifestyle is exhausting…well, I find relationships exhausting. Despite media accounts, I am not a serial dater. I've had a handful of serious relationships but they have never worked out. I get restless in relationships. I don't like the constant worry of what someone else is thinking and feeling. I've now decided it's easier to be alone. And despite my father's wishes, I never intend on marrying.'

She gave a faint smile at that. 'Whatever makes you happy, Luis—that's what's important. We all don't have to follow the same path in life. Even if others can't or refuse to understand and accept that decision.'

Taken aback by the sad resignation in her voice, thinking of her spending the next week alone, he said,

'Maybe your mum is right and you should return to Ireland.'

'Have you not been listening to me? I have my thesis to finish. And right now that's not happening anytime fast.'

'How long have you been working on it?'

She rolled her eyes. 'Three very long years.'

'Maybe you need a break from it for the next few days. Is there anyone in London you could spend time with, just relaxing?'

'No—my best friend, Toni, is the only person I know who lives in London and she's in Australia at the moment. You may have heard of her boyfriend, Dan Ferguson?'

'No.'

Taking her phone from her bag, she said, 'Last year his TV series on Italian history was a major hit.' She showed him the screen of her phone. On it, a tall blond-haired man wearing dark-framed glasses was surrounded by a large group of beaming women, his expression one of utter bafflement. 'He's especially a huge hit with female fans. Apparently they all love his geeky look. Toni thinks it's hilarious. Her awkward and shy boyfriend a sex symbol.'

He studied the photo. Suddenly not too keen on Dan Ferguson. 'Do you think he's a sex symbol?'

She laughed at that, her eyes dancing with merriment. 'Dan? No! God, no!' Then, pausing, she looked at him with bewilderment.

He cleared his throat. 'Is there anyone waiting for you back in Dublin, a boyfriend?'

She pushed her pasta bowl away. She had barely touched it but suddenly she had lost her appetite. Would Luis stop staring at her so intently? Did he somehow know, detect something in her? She tried not to redden. It was no one's business what her relationship history was like and the decisions she had taken, but she could never shake off the dread for being judged for it. Even by a guy who had admitted to not being particularly good at relationships himself. 'No.'

For the longest while Luis studied her across the table. She felt herself grow even more scarlet. He would laugh. She knew he would. Of course, one of the world's most eligible bachelors, a sophisticated prince, a champion sportsman, a man who had dated some of the most beautiful women in the world, would be amused to know that she was still a virgin.

'Let's go for a walk.'

She glanced down at his half-eaten plate of food. 'What about your lunch?'

Not answering her, he motioned to the maître d', who, after a quick conversation with Luis in Spanish, reappeared with their bill. Luis refused to allow her to pay for the lunch or even pay for her share.

Outside, they walked back in the direction of the British Library. From every shop doorway came the sound of cheerful Christmas songs.

At the entrance to Regent's Park he said he knew a shortcut to the library. The park was quiet but for some runners and families all bundled up in rain gear for yet more forecasted heavy rain later in the day.

'I'm guessing we have messy relationship histories in common?'

She shrugged at his question. 'I wouldn't say so.' She should change the conversation but for some reason the need to tell Luis the truth burned inside her. Why, she couldn't understand. But there had been something in their kiss, something in his care last night, and in all of those awkward moments when their eyes locked and neither of them seemed capable of looking away, that had her add, 'You have histories, I don't.'

Under a towering bare-branched oak, he pulled her to a stop. 'What do you mean…you must have *some* relationship history?'

Did he have to sound so surprised? She tried not to wince and decided to try to laugh it all off. 'I don't think I can count my one and only very brief relationship, as it was so long ago. I was nineteen and it only lasted a year and even at that we lived in different cities, as he was away at university. But, trust me, it confirmed my belief that I'm better out of relationships. He said that I made him unhappy. And I guess I did—he wanted more from the relationship than I could ever give. And with the benefit of hindsight I can see that he wasn't good for me—he wasn't the most patient of people.'

Over his white shirt he was wearing a heavy woollen coat, the seam of the collar done in dark bronze thread. She stared at the collar and the tanned skin of his neck. Evening shadow was already there. No wonder he had grown a beard. The effort of keeping clean-shaven must be a tiresome daily battle. But she preferred him clean-shaven. Preferred seeing the sharp, clean edge of his jawline. This was new to her. Not once before had she been drawn to a man like this.

'And you haven't been in a relationship since?'

Heat flamed in her belly at the soft tone of his voice.

She swallowed hard. Fell into the beauty of his eyes. Deep, deep green with flecks of brown. 'No.'

He tilted his head, shifted his body to stand even closer to her. 'Why?'

They were alone on the tree-lined path, the day darkening around them. When other people asked her that question she always told them that she was too busy with her studies, that she was perfectly content on her own. But with Luis she wanted to tell him the truth, especially after last night. 'After my dad, I never want to be dependent on someone else.'

His hand touched her jaw. 'I guess we do have that in common—an aversion to relationships.'

His head tilted closer. Her head spun. His nose came close to touching hers. His hand on her jawline was warm and gentle. Seconds passed. His eyes held hers.

Kiss me! Kiss me before I pass out. I know I should walk away. I have work to do and you have a flight to catch. But would one more kiss matter? We wouldn't see each other again for a very long time.

What was he waiting for? She wasn't experienced when it came to men but surely the way his pupils were enlarged meant he was feeling the same pull of desire? Was she going to have to kiss him…again?

She shifted onto her toes. Their noses touched.

His gaze darkened. Her heart pounded in her ears.

Before you go, kiss me one more time. I want to soar, to feel alive.

His mouth brushed against hers. She felt faint with the need for more.

She almost cried out when he pulled back way too soon.

He raked a hand through his hair, his mouth tense. 'I'm staying in London with you for Christmas.'

CHAPTER FOUR

ALICE LET OUT an impatient breath. The house on Fitzalen Square was ablaze with lights, so she took it that Luis was still at home. She had hoped that he would have already left for the dinner party he had invited her to earlier by text message. She had messaged back saying she couldn't go with him. In return he had sent her a video clip from an old black and white movie, of a guy standing outside a department store, impeccably dressed and carrying a bunch of flowers, looking comically hangdog and forlorn as he realised that his date wasn't turning up. Despite her pledge after his shock announcement that he was staying in London for Christmas that she was going to do her best to ignore his presence and the knots he was tying her up into, she had laughed long and hard at the video, earning herself stern looks from her fellow readers in the library.

Why couldn't he have gone home to Monrosa? It would have made her life a whole lot easier. She needed peace and solitude. She wasn't able to figure him out. Why was he really staying in London? He claimed it was to keep her company, but why would someone forgo their Christmas to spend it with a stranger? What was he up to?

Turning, she studied the small park behind her at the centre of Fitzalen Square, which had been transformed for the festive period into Christmas Central. Beneath a huge Christmas tree a temporary stage was playing host to a gospel group who were entertaining a large audience. To the rear of the central fountain, a Christmas market was busy with shoppers now that the earlier heavy rain had given way to a crisp, clear night sky.

She shuddered as the choir broke into a popular Christmas song. Her dad had used to sing it in the car. She glanced back at the house. And then at her phone. It was close to eight. Luis must be leaving for his dinner party soon.

Bracing herself, she entered the park, deciding to take refuge in the Christmas market. She would find a stall selling coffee and buy a triple espresso. She had a long night of writing ahead of herself.

Head down, she ignored the stalls, but from the corner of her eye she spotted handcrafted baubles and a stall selling pine wreaths with enormous red bows. She came to a stop, intrigued, when a little boy exclaimed in delight at a stall laden down with a ceramic Christmas village snow scene that featured the most exquisite crafted churches and houses and miniature people and animals straight out of an Alpine village. Bending down, she gazed into the window of a wooden cabin, smiling at the scene inside of a family hanging Christmas stockings, the youngest child hanging both hers and that of the family dog, who was seated at her side. When the stall owner asked her if she wanted some help, she shook her head and backed away.

The food stalls were all placed to the rear of the market. She groaned to see a long line at the stand selling hot beverages. She eyed a couple walking away from the stall, both of them laughing in delight at the huge dollop of cream and chocolate shavings on top of their hot chocolates. Her stomach growled. And she turned away when the couple stopped and kissed, laughter and happiness shining in their eyes.

A few stalls down there was a doughnut stand. She hesitated for a moment but then marched up to it. Stood in line. Ordered one doughnut but then changed her mind and ordered three. Well, it was a three-for-the-price-of-two offer after all.

She found a bench, not as far away from everyone else as she would have liked, but it was the best she could do and, sitting down, she bit into the doughnut. She closed her eyes as the sugar melted in her mouth. She took a second bite, opened her eyes, but almost choked when she tried to swallow. Luis was walking in her direction, eyeing her half-eaten doughnut hungrily. Could she find any peace in this world?

With a grin he sat beside her.

She passed the box of doughnuts over and he picked one out.

She wanted to ask him why he wasn't dressed for a dinner party but thought better of it. Instead she nodded towards the box. 'I reckoned I need some sugar before I get back to my writing. I'm going to have to work until past midnight at least.'

He raised an eyebrow, studying her way too closely for her liking. Why did he look at her that way and yet when she virtually offered herself on a plate earlier he had backed away from really kissing her? She was useless at all of this. She didn't understand flirting…was she reading all of his signals wrong? The best policy for the next few days was avoidance—at least that way she wouldn't make a fool of herself. Again.

She jumped up. Put her half-eaten doughnut back into the box and tossed the box into her already heaving handbag, squishing it next to her laptop and notes. 'Talking of work, I'd better go and do some. Enjoy your evening out.'

Luis nodded, but instead of staying where he was as she had hoped he would he stood and began to walk with her, back towards the pedestrian gate opposite the house. 'I'm not going out. I said that I was staying in London to support you. And I meant that. I'll stay in and cook you dinner while you work.'

'There's no need...' She paused in her protest, realising it was futile, given that the recipient had decided to wander off to a stall where two surly-looking teenagers were glaring out at the world. All of the other shoppers were wisely giving their stall a wide berth.

Luis smiled at the teenagers, who were selling dark blue football jerseys.

In unison they folded their arms, their glares intensifying even more when he lifted up a rain-soaked jersey. She guessed that at one point the jersey would have had the same logo as that printed on a display football at the side of the stall—*Our Place FC*—but some of the adhesive letters had lifted off the jersey and now it just read *Our lace*.

The boy wearing a bobble hat nodded at the jersey, his scowl deepening. 'We didn't know it was going to rain. No one warned us.' He stared at Luis as though it were Luis's fault that the heavens had decided to open that afternoon, and added, 'We've tried getting in contact with the supplier for a refund but there's no telephone number on the website and he's not answering our emails. My mum says we've been had.'

Luis nodded. 'Bad luck.'

The other boy, who was wearing a bottle-green parka jacket, gave an angry laugh. 'You can jog on now, mate. There's nothing for you to buy here. We're only here because my mum won't let us go home. She said she didn't waste all that time convincing someone to allow us to have a stall for us to leave on our first day.'

Luis picked up the football, bounced it on the ground and did some impressive solos. Alice rolled her eyes. Was there anything this man couldn't do?

'So where's *"Our Place"* located?' Luis asked as he flicked the ball towards the boy with the hat.

The boy caught it, his scowl for a moment replaced with an awestruck expression at Luis's skills. 'There's an empty field behind our flats… we're trying to get a team together from the neighbourhood. There's no local team. And the kids are bored.' Remembering the rain-soaked jerseys, the boy picked up one, his expression one of disgust, before flinging it back down on the table. 'We need to raise money for goalposts. We had hoped to sell these jerseys.'

Luis nodded. Considered the two boys for a moment and then gestured to the entire table. 'I'll buy everything.'

The two boys looked at him as though he had lost his mind. The guy in the parka said, 'All of the jerseys are destroyed.'

Luis shrugged and then smiled in her direction. 'I'll take two, one for myself and my friend Alice. Who knows, we might come along and watch you play some time?' Pausing to take business cards from his wallet, he passed one to each boy, along with a healthy number of banknotes, 'I trust this will adequately cover my bill? Take the rest of the jerseys home and see if they can be rescued. If they can, hand them out to local children and encourage them to join the club.'

They walked away from the speechless boys.

He called me his friend.

She eyed him warily, more confused than ever as to what to make of him.

Are we friends? I suppose I should be pleased that that's how he sees things...that's way safer than there being more to this. Two friends sharing a house over Christmas. Nothing complicated or worth spending time fretting over. Friends who just might meet up again in the future if they happen to cross paths.

As they neared the gate out of the park, the boy wearing the green parka raced after them. Fist pumping Luis, his eyes aglow, the boy then gave Luis an awkward hug before running away, giving a whoop.

Luis laughed, his eyes shining with pleasure. This she did not expect from him—other people had given the boys a wide berth, but not Luis. What was it in him that had seen their story, their disappointment masked by belligerence? He had an innate intuition and kindness that was so at odds with his public wild and carefree image.

Inside the house, she followed him down to the basement. 'That was an incredibly nice thing to do.'

Shrugging, he went into the utility room and deftly loaded the wet jerseys into the washing machine, popping in some detergent and putting the machine onto a wash cycle. Turning, he raised an eyebrow. 'I'm not sure if the jerseys will survive a wash, but it's worth a go.'

She eyed the washing machine and then him. 'You wash your own clothes?'

He laughed at that. 'Why shouldn't I?'

She followed him back up to the sitting room, where he used a remote control to switch on the lights of the Christmas tree that was sitting in the bay window. 'You could have just bought a few jerseys from the boys—why buy everything?'

Moving to twist around a decoration of a girl on skis that was facing backwards, he answered, 'They reminded me of myself when I was a teenager.'

She stood in front of him. The white lights of the tree flashed against his dark skin like snowflakes. 'Really? I thought you were born smiling.'

'I went through a long and protracted teenage rebellion. It was only when I found powerboating that I changed. It gave me a sense of purpose. Something to aim towards.'

She caught the emotion in his voice—was it regret? 'And now that you're leaving that career—it must be difficult?'

He stepped back from the tree. Unbuttoned his grey wool coat. Unwound his dark grey and cream scarf from around his neck. 'Resuming my royal duties is what I have to do.'

She raised an eyebrow at his unenthusiastic tone.

He yanked off his coat, ran a hand against his neck. Rocked on his heels for a moment, eyeing her all the while. 'Come to dinner with me. I have been hearing great things about the new restaurant in Hotel Russo. I need to get out.'

She went to say no but he interrupted her as though guessing what she was about to say. 'It's two days before

Christmas. We should be celebrating. Not stuck inside.' He moved away, his restlessness clear. 'Come on, Alice. It's only dinner. You can work tomorrow. I'm a terrible chef—you really don't want to have to eat whatever I manage to cook for you tonight.'

She wavered for a moment. Swayed by his eagerness but even more so by his kindness towards the boys. He waited for her answer with a forced patience. And she remembered his soft gentleness with her last night. How could she turn him down? But she had to at least make an attempt to call a halt to how he was throwing her completely off schedule. 'Why not go to the dinner party you were invited to?'

He stopped and considered that for a moment. And then with a hint of bewilderment, as though something was just dawning on him, he answered, 'I guess I'd much rather spend time with you.'

She blushed, smiled, felt rather faint at the softness of his voice, at the way he was concentrating on her with one hundred per cent focus. It would be so easy to fall for every word he said. She needed to tread carefully. No, scratch that: she needed to take this man and any notions he fostered in her down with a sledgehammer. She folded her arms and tilted her chin to deliver one of her best unimpressed stares. 'That's not true—what are you up to, Luis?'

He laughed. Long and deep. His eyes sparkling with amusement. His laughter wrapped around her, and despite herself she smiled, taking far too much pleasure in being able to create that happiness in him. He eventually controlled himself enough to say, 'I like chatting with you. Your crankiness is refreshing.'

With that he tilted his head, those eyes of his watching her, softly appealing to her to accept his invite.

She rolled her eyes. Let out an irritated breath. 'How can a girl possibly say no to such flattery?' She turned for the door. 'I'm warning you though, once tonight is over, I'm one hundred per cent focused on my thesis.' She stopped at the doorway, adding, 'After tonight I don't want to be disturbed…or reminded that it's Christmas. Is that a deal?'

He sauntered over to her. She waited for him to say yes. But instead, his voice disturbingly intense, a dangerous heat in his eyes, he said, 'I'll try…but do you really want me to stay away?'

She knew she should give him a sharp retort, but her throat was suddenly dry. All she could muster up was a weak smile, her pulse pounding in her ears, the memory of their kiss in the palace garden, the heat of his mouth, the beauty, the rightness of his touch, his scent, leaving her with no option but to walk away from him now without an answer, her skin flaming with the knowledge that he watched her every single shaky step as she climbed the stairs.

Following Alice as the maître d' led them to their table in the dimly lit restaurant, Luis tried not to stare at the curve of Alice's bottom encased in soft black leather. She had removed her coat to reveal a cream open-neck silk blouse tucked inside a black leather mini-skirt. He wanted so much more with her. He wanted to kiss her again and experience that heart-jolting, addictive hunger her mouth, her taste, the feel of her skin against his had stirred in him. He wanted to move beyond that tough exterior she presented to the world and know her better.

But to do so would be selfish. How would getting entangled with him help her in any way? *And* she was practically family, so that was another reason he needed to draw a line in the nature of their relationship—he'd allow himself some light flirting, he was only human, after all, but ultimately the next few days were about Alice not having to spend Christmas alone.

He took his seat opposite her at their table, which was placed next to the floor-to-ceiling glass window that spanned the entire length of the restaurant located on the top floor of the hotel. The candle on their table flickered in the window's reflection and he smiled when Alice placed her hands against the glass and peered out. 'I can just about see the Thames—the view from here must be spectacular during the day.' She let out a disappointed sigh. 'It's a shame it's so hard to see anything at night.'

Their waiter, who had come alongside the table, cleared his throat. Alice leapt away from the window.

'We dim the interior lights to allow a better view, but we do have a number of outdoor areas that diners can avail themselves of for their desserts and coffees.' Pausing to glance in his direction, the waiter added, 'Usually they are booked in advance, but I can organise for an area to be reserved for you, Your Highness.'

Across from him Alice squirmed in her seat. He raised an eyebrow in question as to what she thought of the idea of having dessert outside and she nodded with a sheepish smile.

The waiter presented them with their menus and after disappearing for a few minutes returned with water and amuse-bouches and took their orders. They agreed to forgo a starter and head straight for the main course, both of them choosing the restaurant's signature dish of halibut and oysters.

Sitting back in his chair, he nodded towards Alice's reflection in the window. 'Personally, I like the view—I get to see you twice.'

She scowled. He laughed, knowing he enjoyed teasing her way too much but that it was proving to be way too entertaining to stop.

'You mean you enjoy being able to see your own reflection.' She tilted her head, impending revenge glittering in her eyes. 'So, what's it like to be considered one of the most eligible men in the world? That accolade must go to your head.'

'I stopped reading anything about myself a long time ago. Trust me, disassociation from your public image is the best thing anyone in the public eye can do. The person portrayed in the media is not me.' He paused as the waiter brought the glass of Merlot he had ordered and a sparkling water for Alice to the table. When the waiter had left he raised his glass in a toast. 'If you stick around long enough you might actually believe that.'

She considered him for a moment. Her hair was tied up, her long, slender neck seeming even more vulnerable without the weight of her hair. A plain silver chain hung around it, resting in the hollow of her throat. 'So how would you describe yourself?'

'A professional sportsman,' he paused, catching himself, 'or should I say an ex-pro?'

'Are you definitely leaving powerboating?'

He took a drink of his wine; the tannins were smooth, but something caught at the back of his throat. 'I haven't publicly announced it yet…' He trailed off.

'It must be a hard decision, given how successful you were—will you miss it?'

With all my heart.

'Not the losses or the frustration of mechanical problems and bad weather and wrong tactics.'

She studied him with that unnerving quiet perceptiveness of hers that totally unsettled him. She was waiting for him to say something more…she knew he was holding back the truth. He took a drink. Looked to see if there was any sign of their waiter. When would their food arrive? And still she said nothing. The silence was too much. He admitted in a rush, his voice carrying how much he begrudged and felt exposed at doing so, 'I'll miss the sense of purpose, the camaraderie… The team are like a family to me.'

Placing an elbow on the table, a hand cupping her cheek, she said, 'That's a huge amount of things to have to give up.'

He arched his neck, his legs beneath the table restlessly moving with the urge to get up and go, the understanding in her voice, the understanding of what he was leaving behind, too much to handle.

'Tell me about the team. Tell me about what it was like to chase the world championship.'

Surprised by her question, he hesitated for a moment. But then he realised he did want to talk about Justin, Ryan, Anna and the rest of the team and the lows and highs they had endured over their eight-year campaign to become the top team in the world. He told her about them throughout their meal and as their waiter cleared away their dinner plates he realised that, though it was crushing to know that that time in his life was over, having a chance to reminisce about it, to share the highs and lows of all those years with someone, made it just that little bit easier.

'What will your responsibilities be when you return to Monrosa?'

He grimaced at her question. *Dio!* He dreaded the arguments that would come in the New Year as the exact nature of his role was thrashed out. His father no doubt would be as scathing and dismissive of his abilities and commitment to Monrosa as he always was.

Across the table, she waited for his answer with a calm understanding. She knew only too well the dysfunction of families. Was that why he found it so easy… okay, none of this was easy…but was her own past the reason why he was talking about things he had never spoken to another person about before?

'With my father abdicating and Edwin taking over as monarch, my role has not been fully decided. My father when he was monarch had been making noises about me joining the treasury—my degree was in Finance and Economics…well, it was until I left university early to take up powerboating. I reckon he thinks I can do least damage there, hidden out of public view and under the careful watch of his close ally, the Chancellor.'

'But now that Edwin has taken over, if powerboating is so important to you, why can't you—?'

He interrupted her, knowing where this conversation was going, 'I'm not going back on my promise that I would return to Monrosa. Edwin has ambitious plans for it and is looking for my support. Which I unquestionably will give him, even if it means joining the treasury to appease my father—I'm sure it will be more fun than it sounds.'

'That's very honourable…' Pausing, she bit her

lip, cleared her throat. 'I admire you for keeping your word…so many people promise things and never follow up on them. But can there be a compromise? Can you have a role where you can use all your experience in sport? And, though I'll admit to not being the best judge of character, to me you have the most incredible people skills. People gravitate towards you. You should be in a role that inspires others, not be stuck behind a desk. Look at how well you dealt with the boys this evening in the park. You're a leader, a role model, a mentor; use those skills.'

He took a drink of water, trying to process everything she had said. Her passion, her conviction, her assessment of him, throwing him.

Was that who he was?

But no—he was the dissident of the family, the one who caused the trouble, the one who constantly locked horns with their father. A brother who put socialising and winning above the needs of his siblings. Wanting any excuse not to have to acknowledge all that was wrong in his family. He had walked away from them—not wanting to have to deal with his father's bitterness, Edwin's pointless attempts to keep their father appeased and Ivo's complete withdrawal from them all.

Leaning further into the table, she placed both arms on the white linen cloth. 'Kara rang me earlier; she's disappointed you won't be in Monrosa for Christmas.'

'Trust me, I know. Edwin has made that perfectly clear.'

For long moments she eyed him and then, pushing back into her chair, she folded her arms and said quietly, 'You're not staying in London just for my sake, are you? It's an excuse not to go home, isn't it?'

For a split second he was going to argue that she was wrong. Hating to be called out, suddenly feeling like a cad. He closed his eyes for a moment and then, opening them, admitted, 'Wanting to help you was my primary reasoning...but I will admit that it was a convenient excuse not to spend Christmas in Monrosa too.'

'At least you admitted it...' She bit her lip and stared towards their reflections, a deep heat colouring her cheeks. 'My father used to play mind games with me...' yet another deep inhale was followed by a shrug, and then she looked at him. 'Promise me you won't do the same. Promise me you'll always be honest with me.'

The simplicity of her words but the emotion behind them, the depth to them, the endless possible implications of them, left him momentarily bowled over. His heart was racing for reasons he couldn't comprehend and on a shaky exhale he reached his hand across the table. 'I promise.'

Ever so slowly she laid her hand in his.

They smiled at one another. An unsure but intimate smile. That felt as through every certainty he believed in was being pulled right from underneath him.

CHAPTER FIVE

ALREADY PRETTY SHAKEN by the unexpected powerful intimacy of her conversation with Luis, Alice stared in disbelief when their waiter led them to their outdoor space that was positioned in the seclusion of a small upper terrace on the restaurant roof.

What had she got herself into?

The waiter had promised them views and yes, there they were—the Thames and all the stunning iconic buildings that lay along her meandering path through London—but what he had failed to mention was that instead of sitting at a table they were going to have dessert whilst lying on a double daybed. And he had also failed to mention that they would be all alone up here.

'We can go back downstairs if you prefer,' Luis said.

Was her dismay that obvious?

For crying out loud, Alice, it's a daybed. You're both fully clothed and wearing heavy overcoats. Relax and enjoy yourself... How many times in your life will you get to lie next to a real-life prince in one of the most beautiful cities in the world? At least now, for once, you'll have a story that will beat Toni's exploits as the partner of a reluctant celebrity.

Grabbing the cream and green striped woollen blanket at the bottom of the bed, she stepped out of her high heels and tried to lie down as gracefully as that manoeuvre would allow, trying to ignore his amusement.

The rear of the bed was propped up, so after offering him a share of the blanket, which he refused, as she had hoped he would do, she tucked her legs beneath her, anchoring the blanket under her bare feet.

Settling in, she closed her eyes, the distant traffic, the heat from the overhead outdoor heaters all surprisingly soothing. She tried to focus on her breathing…and not on Luis lying next to her, the way the mattress sagged at his movement, his arm brushing against hers. She shifted away. Breathed deeply into her lungs.

Silence followed. She opened her eyes and let them wander in his direction. He was looking at her. She smiled. Feeling unaccountably shy.

He smiled back.

'Are you sure you were a sullen teenager? I can't imagine you being one, given your perpetual sunny nature,' she said.

He raised an eyebrow. Unbuttoning his coat and then his navy suit jacket, he yanked his white shirt out of the waistband of his trousers and, lifting it up, revealed a small tattoo beside his ribs.

She edged closer to see it, unconsciously touching a fingertip against the beauty of the tree tattooed on his golden skin—the powerful trunk giving way to soaring green branches.

Seconds passed. Her finger lingered on the warmth of his skin. She knew she should pull away but something kept it there. She tried to ignore the tight awareness in the air between them. 'I don't think something this beautiful can be classed as rebellion.'

He laughed. Caught hold of her finger, mischief glittering in his eyes. 'It can if you're a fifteen-year-old royal. Show me your tattoo.'

'I don't have one.'

'What a surprise. I take it you were a model teenager.'

She laughed at the fact that he had rightly guessed her clean-cut teenage years. But then, sobering, she admitted, a lump in her throat, 'My mum had enough to contend with without me going off the rails.'

He grimaced, lowering their hands to the mattress but not letting go of her finger. 'I'm sorry.'

She shrugged, wanting the hole that had opened up inside herself in remembering how haunted, how fragile her mum had been during her teenage years to disappear. 'It's okay.' Taking her hand away from his, she pretend-frowned, wanting to keep this conversation light. 'Why a tree? Most teenagers go for something dark, like a skull. A flourishing tree doesn't exactly represent teenage rebellion.'

Luis tucked his shirt back in and fastened his jacket button. 'It's on my mother's family crest.'

She grimaced. 'Now it's my turn to say sorry.'

He went to speak. Stopped. And then gently said, 'Sometimes I struggle to picture her, to remember her voice.'

'It wasn't fair that you lost her at such a young age… I still remember hearing about her death on the radio, I was in the car with my mum. The newsreader listed your ages, Luis was the same age as me—we were both only ten.' Pausing, she rested her hand on his arm before admitting, 'I remember crying, thinking about you all losing your mum and how terrible that must be.'

For a moment his hand rested again on hers. And she

stopped breathing at the hint of a grateful smile that lifted ever so slightly on his mouth. But at the sound of approaching footsteps he moved away.

Their waiter placed their desserts on the tables on either side of the bed.

She grinned at her chocolate mousse tower that had a disc of chocolate on top. Lifting the disc, she bit into it. 'I adore chocolate.'

He laughed. 'So I gathered, given the state of that tin of chocolates last night.'

Lifting her plate, she cut into the mousse tower. 'If you'd had the day I had yesterday, you'd have eaten them too.'

'I hope you're not talking about my arrival?' he asked with a grin, lifting out a spoon of his crème brûlée.

'Well… I have to admit, your arrival was unexpected… Kara had promised me that the house would be empty.'

'It's surprising that we never met before Kara's wedding—she's mentioned you a lot over the years.'

'I'd intended on visiting her but work always came in the way. And then things got awkward when I moved in with her dad.' Seeing his quizzical look, she explained, 'After I left school, I stayed working locally—I wasn't sure what I wanted to do, and I didn't want to leave my mum. We had only moved to the town a few years previously and she didn't know that many people. She struggled with panic attacks after she left my dad. One of the jobs I had was as a tour guide in the town's Norman castle. I fell in love with history, thanks to that experience, and when my mum was well enough I went to university. I was twenty-two. I couldn't afford any accommodation in Dublin so I moved in with Kara's dad.

But it wasn't just because I was penniless—all of the family were worried about him.' Placing her dessert back on her side table, her heart suddenly sore with emotion, she admitted, 'Kara's brother, Michael, you know…'

'Yes. I know he died…' he paused, his expression one of utter kindness and understanding, 'and that he took his own life.'

'It was such a shock. He and Kara used to spend their summer holidays with us at my Aunt Nina's house. We had been close—we grew apart as teenagers, but I have such lovely memories of Michael sitting on Cloghroe beach, reading his book or telling us over dinner some obscure fact. It was only in later years that I realised he used to make some of them up—he had once convinced us that Sir Walter Raleigh had stopped in Cloghroe Bay and was seen by locals burying something on the beach. All of us cousins spent the entire summer digging up the beach, which of course suited him perfectly, as we were too busy to pester him to play with us. He must have thought we were daft to believe him—but to us he was our cool older cousin who could do no wrong.'

Luis gave her a sympathetic smile. 'Kara doesn't talk about him a lot—I think she finds it too hard—but I know she misses him terribly.'

'After his death and then Kara's parents' divorce, my mum and her sisters were worried about her dad—they asked me to move in to keep an eye on him. Thankfully we got on really well. But I could see how low he was; if I hadn't already been turned off marriage, seeing how destroyed he was by the divorce would definitely have convinced me that nothing is worth that heartache. I thought Kara felt the same way about marriage—the few times we talked about relationships over the past few years she had hinted as much. But now she's happily married to Edwin.' Pausing, she waited for him to say something, to join in with her amazement over Edwin's and Kara's surprise marriage, but when he didn't she added, 'Did they send you their Christmas card? I usually just put any I get into a drawer, not wanting to be reminded that it's that time of year again. But even I felt compelled to display their card on my mantelpiece—it's so good to see Kara happy. How it happened I'll never understand—what do you think changed between them?'

Dio! What was he supposed to say? Just a little while ago she had asked him to always be honest with her. But would he be betraying Edwin and Kara by telling her of their wedding secret? Could he trust Alice not to tell anyone else? She was waiting for his answer, her expectant expression turning puzzled and then suspicious. Why was he even hesitating?

Because Edwin's and Kara's trust and closeness, how they are both blossoming as people within their marriage, the power of their togetherness, mocks everything you like to believe about love.

'Their marriage…at first it was not as it seemed.'

'What do you mean?'

'My father changed the law of succession—for Edwin to succeed to the throne he had to marry.'

Alice's mouth dropped open. 'You are kidding me.' Then, her brows slamming together, she demanded, 'Are you saying Edwin convinced Kara into a sham marriage?'

'Don't get mad with me. I was totally against the idea at the time. I thought they were both crazy.'

She shook her head. 'What? And now you agree with it? Knowing everything Kara has been through?'

He shrugged. 'They're in love—or so they claim. They have both admitted to being in love with one another for years, but after Michael died everything became complicated.'

Alice made a disbelieving snort. 'I can't believe Edwin persuaded her…honestly, what was Kara thinking of?'

Last month Edwin and Kara had travelled to watch him take part in his penultimate race in Corsica. It had been sickening…and kind of enviable just how in love they had been with each other—constantly touching, sharing looks and intimate smiles when they thought nobody was looking. 'But if they're happy now—isn't that what's important?'

'I guess,' she answered with a disgruntled expression.

'You're not jealous, are you?'

'No! Obviously. Why would I be jealous of something I don't want?' Slamming her arms together, she stared at him suspiciously. 'Why, are you changing your mind about not wanting to marry?'

He gave a shiver. 'No.' But then his gaze caught hold of hers and something unaccountable broke apart inside of him. And without any thought or sense he heard himself say, 'To have someone close, it must be…' Coming to an abrupt halt at her appalled expression, he scrambled to change the subject away from himself. 'So if marriage isn't on the cards for you, what are your dreams for the future?'

For long seconds she considered him but then with a sigh she answered, 'Up to a few months ago I was certain as to what I wanted—to finish my PhD and get a full-time lecturing position—but I'm not sure any more. I just can't find the motivation to finish my thesis—and that must say something. Sometimes I wonder if I was wrong to start a history degree in the first place.'

'It sounds to me as though you need a break away from writing.'

Shifting back to rest against the daybed, she answered, 'Maybe you're right.' For a while she looked up towards the night sky and then back to him. 'What about you—what are your dreams?'

'I've just achieved it—to win the global series.'

'You must have others.'

'Not particularly.'

Alice considered him with a puzzled expression. 'I had you pegged as someone who always had something else to achieve, some other grand plan. Uber-positive about everything in your life.'

He shrugged, trying not to give away how much he hated how she was pinpointing all that was wrong in his life right now. He was rudderless. Without an identity. A purpose in life. 'Positivity is my defence shield.'

'Does it work?'

He laughed. 'Most of the time, but with you it seems to fade.'

She laughed and then, sobering, she said, 'Okay, I'm going to admit that I don't know what you mean by that, and whether you're pointing out a flaw in my personality.'

She had asked for his honesty. He pulled in a breath, doubt and uncertainty tightening his chest at the wisdom of this conversation. 'I manage to hide what's really inside of myself from others...but not with you.'

Alice grimaced. 'I'm sorry—I don't mean to ask so many questions…it just seems right with you.'

He nodded. He understood what she meant—neither of them was looking for what was happening between them, neither of them wanted this depth of understanding and attraction.

He edged a little closer to her. His arm against hers, inches separating their heads, which were resting against the pillows. The silver in her eyes glittered. Her cheekbones reddened. Her full lips parted ever so slightly. *Dio!* But she was beautiful. 'Just make sure that you don't hurt me.'

'Me hurt you?' she asked in a low whisper.

He moved even closer. 'Well, you did kiss me.' He paused, remembering his initial doubts that soon transformed into a wave of physical pleasure and chemistry. He contemplated her lips, their wide, full shape. The night of Edwin's wedding she had left traces of her lipstick on his mouth. 'And then you ran away. I was left wondering what I had done wrong.'

She let out a tiny sigh of disbelief. 'Trust me, you didn't do anything wrong.'

He touched his hand against her jawline. Desire zapped through his body, the urge to kiss her and a whole lot more tingled in every nerve ending. 'Prove it—kiss me and this time don't run away.'

She smiled but quickly realised he was being deadly serious. She hesitated for a moment but then moved towards him, until inches separated them. He could feel her breath on his cheek, the light scent of her perfume. His own anticipation and desire were reflected in the silver pools of her eyes. Her lips found him, tentative and soft. And then everything went crazy. Her mouth opened. He heard her sigh. Her hand was on his neck. Pulling him closer. Lost to the power of the kiss, he went with her when she pulled him down the bed, so that they were both lying flat. She unbuttoned his coat and then his jacket, her hand hot over the cotton of his shirt. A charge went through him to feel her thumb move against his ribcage in small, rhythmic movements as though she wanted to caress his soul. His hand wound around the soft, silky length of her hair, loving the warmth of her mouth, the smoothness of her skin. His body buzzed with a hot craving that came from the most elemental part of him.

She moaned when he shifted his weight onto her. Felt her body buckle beneath him. He deepened their kiss, her hand shifting around to run the length of his spine.

He wanted to sleep with her. He wanted to know her body, whip her coat and clothes away. He wanted to taste her skin, cup her breasts in his hands, watch her fall to pieces. Would she scream? What would her favourite position be? He pictured her on top, her hair cascading down around her breasts, her hips moving in a slow dance, his back arching to meet her.

But, this was madness. She didn't need this complication in her life. He dragged himself away from her addictive mouth and rolled onto his side.

She looked at him with a dazed expression, her mouth bruised, heat glowing in her cheeks. But then she bolted up to sitting. 'I… Sorry…that went on longer than I intended,' she gave him a guilty smile, her eyes fleetingly meeting his before she looked away, 'but I can definitely confirm that there's nothing wrong with your kisses.'

She leapt off the bed. 'Well…it's been…lovely. But I guess it's time that we called it a night.' With that, she gestured vaguely in the direction of the stairwell that would take them back to the restaurant and bolted away.

CHAPTER SIX

SHELTERED IN THE safety of the department store entrance, Alice surveyed the mass of humanity sidestepping one another along the length of Oxford Street. The pandemonium of last-minute Christmas Eve shopping. A chaos that was far removed from her usual Christmas shopping, which was always done online, a week before the big day. She refused to be pressured into buying gifts any time earlier than then, hating the frenzied flurry of consumerism the marketing companies loved to create. In a few simple clicks she always bought a spa day for her mum in a local hotel and a book hamper from her local bookshop for each of her extended families. A few simple clicks and her Christmas obligations were over and done with.

She checked her phone. It was close to lunchtime. How was it possible that she had spent three hours shopping? It was as though she had stepped into a time machine when she entered the doors of the famous department store earlier that day. Who knew there were so many things to buy…? And yet it had proved near impossible to find anything appropriate.

Adjusting the shopping bags in her hands, she frowned and wondered what Luis would make of the presents she had eventually bought. He was probably used to receiving scarily expensive presents—would he find hers laughable? Should she just return them? She glanced back into the store. The queues at the tills were even longer than when she had waited in line to pay. There was no way she was going back in there. Bracing herself to step out into the stream of shoppers rushing by, she caught the eye of an older man waiting by the doorway. He looked as unimpressed with this shopping malarkey as she was. She did an eye roll to her fellow sufferer and said, 'It'll be all over by tomorrow thankfully…bar the arguing, of course.'

The man frowned and in fairness to him attempted to laugh along with her, but then he backed towards the door and fled inside, obviously preferring the madness that lay within to having to converse with a crazy lady outside.

What should she do now? Well, the obvious answer was to get herself back to Fitzalen Square and her thesis. But that meant having to see Luis. And after last night she just knew that she would blush and be all awkward and she didn't want to give him that satisfaction.

She really hadn't meant for their kiss to get so hot and heavy. If he hadn't rolled away…but he had. And now she was mortified. She had been up at six this morning. Determined to work. But after two hours of fidgeting, and rewriting the same paragraph over and over again, she had thrown in the towel and decided to escape the house before Luis climbed out of bed to postpone her embarrassment a little longer. But before she headed out into the misty morning she had gone to her bedroom to fetch a jumper and spotted all her Christmas presents her mum had insisted she bring with her to London. And it had dawned on her that Luis would probably have no presents to open tomorrow. All because he had decided to stay in London and keep her company. For a few moments she had toyed with the idea of sharing her presents with him, but, given what her mum and aunties had gifted her in previous years, she reckoned that Luis wasn't in need of an assortment of girly shower gels and body creams.

Now, bracing herself, she stepped onto the footpath and was quickly swept along by the human train of shoppers. But when, for the fifth time in as many minutes, she ran into the back of someone who decided now was a good time to check their phone, she diverted off onto a side street. It would take her longer to get home—but, as much as it pained her to admit it, she was happy to find any old excuse to avoid the dual taunts in her life right now—her thesis and Luis.

The side street was lined with restaurants and cafés. In spite of the rain-laden skies, shoppers had bravely opted to sit outside. And, instead of fretting about the weather, the groups of families, friends and couples all seemed buoyed up by the season, their laughter deep and excitement shining in their eyes.

Ahead of her, a little girl dressed in a knee-length red wool coat with white fur trim broke away from her mother and raced along the footpath to a man who swept her up into his arms, kissing her forehead and then embracing the woman, all three of them forming a tight hug that cocooned them into a huddle of love and giggles.

She crossed the road. Walked by a Belgian-chocolate shop, the gold interior of the store shining out into the greyness of the day like a beacon. She came to a stop, spun around and went inside, and bought herself a family-size milk chocolate and hazelnut bar.

She found a street bench. Dropped herself and her bags onto it heavily. Yanked the wrapper from the bar. Ate a square. And then another. It was hard to swallow. But she was ravenous. She squeezed her eyes shut. She was *not* going to cry out here in public.

What was the matter with her?

I'm just overwhelmed by my thesis. I'm in a strange city. And I'm missing my mum. That's all.

No, Alice. You're lonely.

She bit down on another square of chocolate, trying to tune out the voice in her head.

Let's face it. You're lonely. And spending time with Luis is driving that fact home. It's all very well living in your lovely bubble in Dublin, where work and studying distract you from every emotion inside you, but Luis is shining an unwelcome light on everything you want to pretend isn't wrong in your life. You didn't leave the house this morning because you were embarrassed by last night—you left because you were so desperate to see him again this morning. And that terrified you.

Tossing the chocolate bar into her handbag, she grabbed the shopping bags, her heart pounding. She tried to stand, but her legs wouldn't cooperate.

She really liked Luis. She *really, really* liked him.

And not just in a *you make me weak* type of way. That, she could handle. Not that she'd admit it to anyone, but she was given to crushes. She'd had a long-running one on a guy who came into the café every morning. After two long years he had asked her out. But they hadn't got beyond their first date. How hadn't she ever noticed his habit of sucking between his two front teeth in all those years that he had stood at the opposite side of the counter and waited for his Americano?

She didn't just fancy Luis. She actually liked him. Admired him. Thought he was pretty cool, in fact.

What on earth was she going to do with all of this? Get the first flight back to Dublin before she did something stupid? Okay, so she wasn't exactly experienced on the bed front, but she was definitely getting vibes off him that his thoughts towards her weren't one hundred per cent pure.

She smiled at that. Giggled. An elderly woman walking by diverted away from her.

She wanted to call out, *I'm not crazy, honestly!* But decided not to scare the poor lady any further. And anyway, she wasn't certain if she could actually claim to be the picture of sanity. Not when, despite her previous reservations about Luis's character, she was actually picturing them sharing a bed.

Okay, so it was only a fantasy. She would never act upon it. But the fact that she was even dreaming about it was worrying.

She needed to calm down. Remember that Luis would be leaving for Monrosa in two days. She was going to get a grip. Starting now. She stood. Straightened that backbone that had got her through many ups and downs in her life so far. She was going home, where she would greet him with a chilled-out air. And, most important of all, she was going to get back to finishing her PhD.

His feet pounding the footpath, Luis muttered a curse. Rain he could handle but this hail shower was beyond ridiculous. Thoughts of the blue skies he had left behind in the Bahamas mocked him as he rounded a corner, the wind firing the hailstones into him at full force.

If he had stayed in the Bahamas he would now be at Justin's beach house, taking part in his annual beach volleyball tournament or playing chase in the sea with Justin's kids, Flo and Jordi. Not out here, battling the weather and battling his own head.

She was getting to him. And not just because she kissed like an angel…with a few dirty thoughts in mind. Her strength, her vulnerability, her coolness, her sense of humour…they were all burying themselves deep inside him. Despite the hammering hailstones that were pinging off his skin, he chuckled to himself. How had she described his kiss last night? Oh, yeah—'of an adequate standard'.

Ahead in Fitzalen Square the Christmas tree swayed in the near gale. He jogged past some other equally foolhardy people also out in this weather, one of them, hidden beneath an umbrella, valiantly fighting the hail and wind to keep that umbrella upright. A few steps on and said umbrella went sailing by him, thumping against the footpath. He chased after it, passing his own front door in the process. On and on it bumped along the footpath, refusing to allow him to grab hold of it. Eventually its escape was halted by the black wrought-iron railings at the end of the square.

He turned to return it to its owner. And grinned when that owner came running towards him, melting hailstones streaming down her face, shopping bags thumping against her legs. She stood under the shelter of the umbrella and said breathlessly, 'I bet you're sorry you're not in Monrosa now.'

Alice attempted to wipe her brow where water was

dripping into her eyes but the bags she was carrying hit the umbrella and toppled it backwards, exposing her to the full force of the hailstones again. She gave a gasp and startled forwards, her body colliding with his. He placed a hand around her waist to steady her, drew the umbrella back up over them, and, though he knew it was wrong of him, smiled down into those grey eyes and said softly, 'I guess we're both in need of a long, hot shower.'

Her eyes widened. The hail pounded down on the umbrella. And as the light faded around them, thanks to the worsening weather, it felt as though they were the only ones on this earth.

It would be so easy to get this wrong.

He stepped back, took her bags from her. Gestured back towards the house. Gave her a smile. 'I stayed in London to make sure you're okay and here I am letting you get soaked to the bone. Come on inside; you need to get warm.'

A little while later, both of them having showered and changed, he carried two hot drinks up to the sitting room on the second floor. He expected to find Alice sitting on the sofa watching the Christmas movie he had earlier put on for them to watch, but instead she was kneeling before the Christmas tree, placing parcels under it. He knew he should let her know that he was there but there was something heart-warming about the way she rattled some of the presents as though trying to guess what was inside, the way her hands would then smooth over the paper, the way she would place the present against her chest as though invoking a well-meaning spell over it before gently placing it on the floor.

His chest tightened, realising that there would have been a time when she had liked Christmas.

He cleared his throat.

She jumped, almost toppling over the tree in the process. Standing, she studied him. She had changed into dark denim jeans and a plum-coloured wide-necked top that had fallen off one of her shoulders to reveal a cream vest-top beneath. Her hair was still wet and she had sleeked it back off her face, making her eyes, her cheekbones, her mouth seem even more pronounced than usual.

She was beautiful.

Not in a conventional way.

You could easily not spot her in a crowd. Which would be a tragedy. It was only when she spoke, when she challenged you, when you saw first-hand the essence of her spirit that you realised just how gorgeous she was.

He lowered the tray of drinks onto the coffee table beside the sofa.

He looked down at the large pile of presents under the tree and then back to her.

She shrugged. Looked uncertain for a moment, but then answered his unspoken question. 'My mum packed a whole load of presents for me, so I decided to buy you some too.'

Before he had an opportunity to respond she whipped around and, lifting a small handmade card close to the top of the tree, continued, 'You do know that soldier is spelt with a D and not a G.' She gave him a wicked grin. 'I thought I should point that out in case you ever have a need to write to the Monrosian Army.'

He held out his hand and she handed him the card. He laughed when he read his poorly formed and spelt message to Papá Noel. 'I remember writing this card! I must have been five or six and I wanted a ZX Marine commander toy soldier. My mother used to insist on us writing a card every year which was then hung from the tree for Papá Noel to read on Christmas Eve. Before my father inherited the throne from my grandfather we used to spend Christmas in different countries. My mother loved to travel. And she loved Christmas even more. She used to say that she wanted to experience Christmas in as many countries as possible.' He stopped and studied the card again, a solid lump in his throat to see his name sprawled messily across the bottom. Christmas had used to be such a magical time in his family.

'I'm sorry… Oh, I feel terrible now, moaning about Christmas, when it must mean so much to you.'

Taken aback by the upset in her voice, he touched her arm. 'It's okay…and totally understandable why you feel the way you do about Christmas.'

She shook her head. 'No, it's not okay—you shouldn't have to listen to me cribbing about it. I could have ruined your Christmas by being all Miss Negativity.'

'I don't expect you to change how you feel about Christmas just for me…' pausing to study the parcels beneath the tree—there were at least eight bearing the logo of a landmark London department store with a similar amount of variously wrapped parcels—he asked, 'Are we expecting some guests tomorrow?' Why did that thought bother him so much? Usually he loved having as many people as possible surrounding him. But tomorrow…he wanted it just to be him and Alice.

'No, they're all for us.' Reaching down, she plucked up one of the colourfully wrapped presents. 'My mum insisted I bring all of my presents with me. So I decided

I'd buy you an equal amount. Now we have the same number to open tomorrow. It only seemed fair that way.' She gave him an uncertain smile. 'I wasn't sure if you would have any other presents to open.'

His family were lousy present-givers. In fact, they had stopped giving each other presents over a decade ago. The same year that Edwin and he had had a fierce argument with their father over Christmas dinner about a proposed mass-tourism development on the coastline. That had been the last time they had spent Christmas together.

Picking up one of the presents, he touched his finger against the red velvet bow, knocked sideways by her thoughtfulness.

He knew she didn't like Christmas. But she had gone out and bought presents for him. He couldn't remember the last time someone had done something so meaningful for him. 'Thank you.'

She blinked at his whisper. Something soft and vulnerable entered her expression.

Long seconds passed. Seconds where an initial tenderness between them drifted into an electric longing so visceral you could almost touch it. He eased her into a hug. Her body slotted against his, her arms winding around his waist. He kissed the top of her head, inhaling her light floral scent, the longing inside of him melding with a rawness, a care, a need to protect her that surged like a powerful force within him.

When they broke away, they held each other's gaze, the connection between them wild and turbulent. Alice was the first to move away. 'I should get back to my writing…' Turning as a fresh hailstorm pinged against the windows, she sighed. 'This weather is so miserable it's hard to believe that it's Christmas. Christmas is supposed to be about cold, dry days with a smattering of frost or even snow if we're lucky. Not an entire monsoon season in one week. The forecast is even worse for tomorrow. We won't even be able to get out for a walk.'

Alice was right. Christmas should have been about snow. And it should also have been about leaving the world behind. Every worry, every obligation should have been forgotten on Christmas Day. He smiled, knowing what it was he wanted to do. He was going to make this Christmas magical for her. 'My family have a ski chalet in Switzerland—let's go there.'

She made a disbelieving snort and laughed before realising that he hadn't been joking. 'I can't; I have my writing...'

'You need a break.'

He pulled out his phone from his pocket. Searched for the palace's travel office while Alice recited a long list of reasons why she couldn't go. And, when he spoke to the on-duty travel officer in Spanish, she eyed him warily as though she was trying to decipher every single word of their conversation. Details arranged, he hung up. 'The palace's jet is free. It can collect us from City Airport in three hours' time and fly us to Sion.' Checking his watch, he added, 'By nine tonight we can be in Verbier. And tomorrow we can spend the day skiing. The decision is yours whether we go or not.'

Her mouth opened. She went to speak. Stopped. 'I shouldn't...and I can't ski.'

'I can teach you. In fact, I can teach you to snowboard, which I prefer.'

'You go... I'll stay here.'

'You're not spending Christmas alone.'

'Why not? I'll be perfectly happy.'

He folded his arms. 'Will you, though?'

She reddened, gave an irked shake of her head. 'You are impossible, do you know that?' Then, throwing her arms up in the air, she shook her head, sighed and said, 'I'll go and pack.' She was almost to the door when she came to a stop and added, 'Tell the travel office to book a ticket back to London for me on the twenty-sixth. You can travel directly to Monrosa by yourself.'

Her eyes tightly shut, Alice hummed to herself. She was not afraid. The helicopter pilot knew what he was doing. Landing at night in icy conditions was a piece of cake to him. Wasn't it?

The helicopter banked. Her stomach flipped over. A tiny murmur escaped her lips. She opened her eyes to find Luis, who was seated next to her, grinning. She slapped his arm. 'It's not funny.'

He attempted a contrite smile. But then, abandoning his pretence that her horror at flying by helicopter from the airport to Verbier in the dark, through mountainous terrain, wasn't amusing, he decided instead to distract her by pointing out the town and its picturesque landmarks beneath them.

When the helicopter eventually landed on a helipad to the side of the chalet, located on a hill overlooking Verbier, she greeted terra firma with shaky legs and a heavy sigh of relief to be still alive.

A path from the landing pad to the chalet had been cleared of snow. She and Luis immediately followed it to the welcoming warmth of the chalet, while awaiting staff took care of their luggage.

Inside, Luis led her from the entranceway through

various reception rooms, giving her a guided tour of the huge chalet, which even had an indoor swimming pool and cinema room.

When they finally made it to her bedroom, her luggage had already been unpacked.

Soon after, all of the chalet staff said their goodbyes, Luis reassuring them that there was no need for them to change their existing Christmas plans and that he and she would be perfectly capable of taking care of themselves for the next two days. As the lights from the staff cars made their way down the mountain she gestured around her, to the vast reception room that was softly lit with table lamps, to the huge log fire burning in the grate, filling the room with pine-scented warmth, the reflection of the flames dancing on the endless windows overlooking Verbier, and the longest and most luxurious sofa she had ever seen, and said, 'When you said a chalet, I was expecting a tiny log cabin.'

Luis grinned. 'We do own a small cabin further up in the mountains. We use it whilst skiing for refreshment breaks. We can decamp there if you'd prefer for us to be somewhere a little more intimate.'

For crazy seconds her heart folded over at the playful sparkle in his eye. But then she gave an exaggerated eye roll to compensate for her foolishness. None of this was serious to Luis. Now she could see that. He was looking for a distraction, an adventure, a new buzz. The man was an adrenaline freak. And she would be incredibly naive to believe that his attention was anything other than yet another entertaining diversion for him.

Walking over to the window, the bright lights of an outdoor Christmas tree in a far-off neighbouring property caught her attention. Spinning around, she scanned the room curiously. 'Something has been niggling away at me since we arrived and now I know what it is.' Pausing to gesture around the room, she added, 'There are no Christmas decorations.'

Leaning against the long wooden beam that served as the mantelpiece, Luis shrugged. 'I told the staff to take them down.'

For long seconds the crackling of the fire was the only sound in the room. She tried to respond but could find no words. Tears prickled against the backs of her eyes. She never cried. She so wished he wouldn't keep ambushing her emotions by being so considerate.

She breathed in and forced out a pretty shaky laugh. 'If we're going to spend Christmas in an Alpine chalet, in one of the most picturesque winter scenes in the entire world, we are going to have to do it justice. Where are the decorations stored?'

Walking towards her, he regarded her with such a depth of concern that those damn tears threatened again. 'We can pretend tomorrow is just a normal day.'

She folded her arms. 'Work with me here, Luis. I've given up two days of writing for this. I'm going to try to embrace Christmas—okay, I'll admit I'll never be a huge fan of its madness, but for you I'll try.'

'For me?'

Her heart closed over at the quiet delight in his voice. 'Yes, for you.'

'Why?'

Because you're the kindest, most generous person I have ever met. Because I'm tired of being sensible. I want to forget that I should be questioning everything that you do and I want to try to believe that there are good guys out there. I'm tired of fighting myself. I'm tired of pretending that I'm perfectly content in my life. I want some fun. For once in my life I just want to go with the flow and not be terrified by what-ifs.

'Because I spent three hours this morning buying gifts and I want to be able to leave them under a Christmas tree tonight.' Walking to the door that led out to the double-height hallway that held a masterpiece of design—the most incredible cantilevered wooden staircase she had ever seen—she asked, 'Now, are you going to show me where the decorations are or do I have to find them myself?'

An hour later Alice teetered on a stepladder, stretched just a little bit more, and with a grin managed to place the star on top of the enormous fir Christmas tree Luis had dragged in from outside.

It was a struggle to climb back down the ladder, thanks to Luis's hand being perilously close to her bottom as he guided her down.

When she reached the floor they both stood back and studied the exquisite white baubles and flashing icicle lights, then turned to each other at the exact same time and high-fived one another, laughing at their mutual delight at a job well done.

But then Luis frowned at the tree. 'It's tradition in Monrosa that, when people finish decorating the tree, they kiss. It's supposed to bring good luck.'

Alice laughed. 'No, it's not.'

His eyes twinkled. 'We could make it a tradition between us.'

How nice that would be. How nice it would be to spend future Christmases with him. To know that he understood why she struggled with past Christmas memo-

ries, to know that maybe she could heal those memories with his support.

She drew in a sharp breath. And came back to reality. 'I'll be in Ireland next year and, if Kara and Edwin have their way, you'll be in Monrosa singing Christmas carols with them. There won't be any future Christmases between us.' Pausing, she met his eye. 'Will there?'

He went to answer her question but stopped. Uncertainty clouded his expression. She turned away and adjusted one of the strings of lights.

When Luis came and stood beside her she glanced at him. Mischief was once again sparking in his eyes. He bent his head and whispered as though they were in a crowded room and didn't want anyone else to hear, 'All the more reason for us to enjoy this Christmas. Now can I kiss you or are you going to insist on debating the issue?'

She knew she should walk away, but when he was this close, when her head spun from his warm, intimate scent, from the sheer size of his body that made her feel tiny in comparison, when his gaze made her heart thump in her chest, a delicious warmth creep through her veins, she didn't want to know about logic or doing the sensible thing. 'Keep it brief.'

He laughed and hit a button on his watch. 'Is ten seconds brief enough for you?'

'That's too—' The rest of her words disappeared as his mouth found hers. It was a soft kiss, explorative and gentle. Her world shrank to the glorious heat of his mouth.

His alarm sounded.

She moved closer to him.

His arms wound around her as the alarm was silenced. His hand touched against her back where her jumper and jeans had parted. She sighed as his thumb pressed against her spine.

His alarm sounded again.

But, instead of breaking away, he silenced it again and deepened their kiss. Her chest was pressed against his, her body growing second by second more and more aware of every hard muscle of his powerful body. His kiss, his warmth, his assured movements didn't frighten her, didn't cause alarm as her previous dates had done.

On the third sounding of his alarm he pulled away from the kiss, leaving her a reeling mess of hormones and emotions.

Was she really trusting a man? After so many years of rightly protecting herself?

In the aftermath of his violence her dad had used to cry and plead for her mum's forgiveness, hugging and soothing her as though she were the most fragile thing on earth, placing tender kisses on her forehead. It had made Alice's skin crawl…yet she had also wanted to believe him.

Luis's hand cupped her cheek. 'You're so beautiful.'

She searched his eyes, looking for even a glimmer of deceit. But all she could find was honest certainty and integrity shining from his eyes. And she lost another piece of her heart to him.

CHAPTER SEVEN

'IT'S MY MUM!' Stumbling into the kitchen, yanking down a turquoise pyjama top covered in polar bears over matching shorts, Alice waved her mobile phone in the air. 'I slept in. Why didn't you wake me? I promised my mum I'd call her at nine on the dot. She's probably freaking out now, imagining all sorts of bad things happening to me.' Frantically looking about her, she mumbled, 'Not in here…the sitting room, in front of the tree.' She bolted towards the door, disappeared, but a few seconds later she was back. 'My mum thinks that I'm still in London—don't do anything to let her know otherwise.' She moved away again but darted back once more. 'And she doesn't know that I'm with you.'

Finishing off preparing their breakfast, Luis grinned. Alice's coltish legs were long and shapely. What would it be like to trail kisses along their length, to have them entwined with his? He groaned and plucked a blueberry off the top of the granola he had prepared for them, crunching down on it.

He poured himself a coffee. Not knowing where any of this was going. He knew he had to be honourable and protect her. But a hunger, a need to know her better, in every sense of that word, was tearing apart every good intention he had. To start with, he needed to stop kissing her. *Dio!* But it was addictive. The chemistry, the passion, the rightness between them was unbelievable. When he touched her he felt truly alert to the beauty and glory of life.

He strolled out to the sitting room. Alice, seated on the floor in front of the Christmas tree, was screen-chatting on her phone, which was propped up on a coffee table. She eyed him warily for a moment as he sat on the sofa opposite her, frowning when he grinned. He was going to enjoy this.

'What's the weather like?' asked a female voice.

She glanced out of the window, her eyes growing wide as she took in the heavy snow falling. He really should have checked the weather forecast before he promised her a day's skiing.

'Oh, the usual… So how are you all doing? I hope you're enjoying yourselves.'

A chorus of voices called out, 'Yes,' and then a male voice added, 'No.'

A vexed female voice immediately responded, 'Maurice, you heard what Dr Lynch said with your very own ears. Anyway, Alice doesn't want to be hearing about your new diet. Come on, Alice, give us a tour of the house.'

Alice blanched. 'Aunt Nina, there's not a lot to see.'

'Are you joking? It's the London residence of the Monrosian royal family. Of course there's things to see.'

She gave Luis a brief look, reddening. 'No.'

'Ah, Alice, you're no fun.'

Alice sighed. But then, sweeping her presents before her, she gave a wide smile, no doubt glad to find a way to move this conversation on. Lifting one up, she pulled away the wrapping paper. 'An exfoliate—thanks, Rose.'

A satisfied voice answered, 'The girl in the shop said we should all be using it, on our thighs especially, for cellulite.'

For a moment Alice looked down at her thighs in alarm.

Luis smothered a laugh. Alice glared at him.

One by one, Alice opened her presents, her enthusiasm and warmth towards those on the other side of the screen giving no hint of her dislike of Christmas. Did she keep it secret from them?

When it came to the last present, Alice read the gift tag and said, 'Oh, Sarah, I didn't realise that you had bought me a present.'

An excited teenage voice answered back, 'I saw it when I was out shopping. I thought you'd like it.'

Opening the present, Alice frowned. And then she reddened. Turning the present towards the camera, she attempted nonchalance. 'A calendar of Edwin's brother, Prince Luis. I didn't know you were fan, Sarah?'

'I saw you in the garden—'

Leaping for the phone, Alice interrupted her. 'Thanks again, Sarah. It was lovely speaking to you all, but I'd better go. I have to get back to work.'

A voice answered, 'Of course, Ally. But hold on for a moment, I'll go somewhere where we can chat properly.'

Alice smiled fondly at the person talking, everything about her softening with affection. 'You're busy, Mum. We can talk tomorrow.'

A door closed at the other end of the line. 'That's better. This house is crazier than usual. How are you? I miss you.'

'I miss you too.'

'Are you eating okay? Are you sure you're not lonely? It seems wrong that you're all alone, especially at Christmas when you love it so much. It's not the same here without you.'

'I'm fine, Mum, honestly.' Pausing, she glanced at Luis. 'And I'm not lonely.'

'Good. I like your pyjamas.'

Alice ran a hand down over her top, shaking her head. 'I'm thirty next year, Mum. I think it's time you stopped buying me Christmas pyjamas.'

'It's too cold at this time of year to be wearing nothing in bed.'

Blushing furiously, she swung away from Luis's line of sight. 'Mum! Honestly.'

Her mother laughed and then asked, 'Will you come home at least for New Year's Eve?'

'Mum, you know that I can't. I need peace and quiet to get my writing done. You know how noisy my upstairs neighbours are.'

Her mum sighed. 'I know. I love you, Ally.'

Turning back in Luis's direction, Alice smiled into her phone. 'And I love you too. I'll be home soon. Take care and enjoy the rest of the day.'

Something hard and obstinate stuck in his throat as Alice hung up, both women giggling as they made noisy kisses to one another. He missed that simple, uncompromising love. He missed his mother.

Coming to sit opposite him, she sighed.

'Your mum doesn't know how you really feel about Christmas?' he asked.

She curled her legs underneath herself. 'There's no point in her knowing.'

'But you seem so close…'

She shrugged. 'We are, but she went through enough with my dad without having to bear the burden of how it impacted on me. For a while I was angry with her. After she left my dad I just shut down. I was angry with her for taking so long to leave him, but I was also unfairly angry with her for not staying.' Sinking further into the corner of the sofa, she added, 'I hated my dad, but I loved him too. I couldn't understand how I could feel that way. When he played professional rugby, I'd beg him not to go to work. Most months he ended up with some type of injury. Concussion, pulled muscles. When he did finally retire, he didn't do so out of choice. He hated not playing, being part of the team. That was when his drinking worsened. He'd promise that he'd stop drinking, say he was sorry. I used to believe him. My mum rarely spoke to me about what was going on; I guess she was trying to protect me. I tried to speak to her about it, but she'd tell me not to worry. So in that vacuum of silence, not sure of what was the right thing to say, I'd tell her that Dad promised that things would get better. Why did I believe him? And what if I hadn't said those things to my mum? Maybe she would have left him much sooner than she did?'

He moved over and sat beside her. 'Your father, and only he, was responsible for what happened. No one else.'

She shrugged. 'I guess you're right.'

'And will you start actually believing that? That you weren't in any way to blame for what happened?'

She didn't answer him.

'You were *not* to blame.'

She nodded, her eyes full of emotion. 'You have an

incredible instinct for understanding people; you do realise that, don't you?'

He lifted up the calendar from the floor. 'Like the instinct that tells me that you're going to throw this into the bin at the earliest opportunity?'

She groaned, covering her face with her hands. 'I had forgotten about that. Sarah must have seen us together in the garden.'

'Isn't she the cousin you had the bet with?'

'Bet? No… Why…? Oh, *the bet to kiss you*. No! Sarah is only fourteen—I wouldn't be encouraging a teenager to gamble.' Taking the calendar from him, she flicked through it, laughing when he expressed his disbelief that there was a market for such a thing. 'I'm sure it'll be snapped up when I donate it to my local charity shop.'

He shook his head. 'Well, at least it'll be going to a good cause.'

She studied him. 'Are you involved in many charities as part of your royal duties?'

'I'm a patron of the national acquired brain injury charity and an ambassador for Kara's Young Adults Together, but my professional career meant that I haven't been able to dedicate myself as much as I would have liked to either of them.'

'I bet you're great in those roles though…with your energy and how engaging you are with people. And now that you're leaving powerboating you'll have more time to devote to them.'

How could he explain to her what a fraud he felt whenever advocating for any charity, when trying to influence change? As his father had liked to point out, he had achieved nothing in life other than to learn how to drive a boat really fast. 'I'm not sure I'm the best of role models. Especially as the British press has decided to label me The Reckless Prince.'

'Okay, so you're known for pushing boundaries, taking risks. But young people would relate to that. Your intuition and natural instinct to help are too valuable for you not to put them to good use.'

'I'm the last person on this earth who should be advising anyone on how to live their life, given my past. Expelled from school, a drop-out from university, and for the first few years of my career I came bottom in the rankings, thanks to too many rash decisions out on the course.'

'People, especially teenagers, aren't looking for perfection. Just someone who's honest and knows what it's like to struggle at times.'

Taken aback by the passion in her voice, in her belief in him, not ready to deal with just how disorientated he felt by it, he opted to tease her instead of carrying on this conversation. 'Are you saying that I'm not perfect?'

Leaning forward, her eyes silver pools of laughter but also affection, she studied him for a few moments and answered, 'I'm starting to realise that perfect is boring.'

Luis held her gaze, not blinking, leaning closer into her. And there it was again, that magic that kept springing between them, a magic of connection and desire, a recognition, she didn't fully understand. He gave her a lopsided grin.

For a heart-soaring moment she thought he was about to kiss her but instead he took hold of the calendar Sarah had gifted her and studied the photos. 'Given that you don't rate perfection so highly, perhaps I should stage some photos of me looking a little more dishevelled—it might encourage you to keep my calendar next year.'

For June, the calendar-makers had chosen a picture of him emerging from the sea, all golden-skinned and defined muscle. The room suddenly feeling way too hot, she took hold of the calendar and placed it behind her. 'It's your turn to open your presents.'

He raised an eyebrow, his eyes shining with amusement. Shaking his head, he stood and gathered up all of his presents. 'I'm hungry. I'll open them over breakfast.'

She stood too and gestured towards her pyjamas. 'I'll go and get changed first.'

His eyes twinkled. 'Don't. They're cute. And it's nice to see you wearing something colourful for a change.'

'You sound like my mother. She's always telling me that I should wear more colourful clothes, these pyjamas being a case in point. She insists on buying me a set every year. If I hadn't worn them for our call, I'd never have heard the end of it.'

'What's with your obsession with dark-coloured clothes anyway?'

She shrugged. It was just habit.

Because they make me feel safe. I don't want to stand out, be a target for anyone.

She blinked at that realisation. 'It saves time in the morning, and anyway I hate shopping. Sticking mostly to black and navy cuts out any time-wasting.'

Not looking convinced by her reasoning, he contemplated her pyjama top. 'Turquoise suits you…red would look great on you too.'

She rolled her eyes. 'What, are you a fashion consultant now? And I thought you said you were hungry.'

'So I did.' He said it in such a low rumble, mischief

glittering in his eyes, that she bolted for the door and in the kitchen went straight for the safety of sitting at the dining table, glad to be able to hide her legs from how Luis kept staring at them. God, she hoped she didn't have cellulite. A tummy given to bloating was enough to contend with.

The dining table was set into an alcove made entirely of glass, and cantilevered over the mountain. Heavy snow continued to fall on the sloping glass roof of the alcove, the village below invisible in the snowstorm. 'It's like being inside a snow globe,' she said.

'Except this has underfloor heating,' Luis said with a chuckle, bringing freshly brewed tea and coffee to the table.

While she tucked into the rich, flaky layers of a croissant, Luis ate a bowl of granola and yoghurt, and described the hair-raising off-piste ski runs he had done in isolated spots, having been dropped in by helicopter, shrugging off her disbelief that he had continued to take such risks even after once being caught up in an avalanche.

When they had both finished eating, he lifted up the largest of his presents, testing its weight in the palm of his hand. Thrown by how keenly he was studying the present, the expectation in his expression, she cringed and said, 'They're only small tokens…nothing special…don't expect too much.'

Unwrapping the first present, he studied it. 'A bonsai tree. Why a bonsai tree?'

She laughed. 'It's a reminder that great things of beauty take time and attention and patience. I hope you'll look at it and remember that it's good to slow down and that life doesn't have to be lived at a hundred miles an hour.'

He eyed her suspiciously. 'Why do I get the feeling there's going to be a theme here?'

Next came the aromatherapy pressure-point kit, which he received with a wry smile, and then the dark green polo shirt she had bought him, loving both the softness of the fabric and how it was a perfect match for the flecks of green in his eyes.

Opening the handcrafted dark praline chocolates, he asked in surprise, 'My favourite flavour—how did you know?'

'Just a lucky guess.'

And the fact that you ate that lone chocolate at the bottom of my sweet tin with such relish the other night.

Next came the limited-edition landscape print of the Thames at night. Her final present to him was a book. He held the hardback, studying the portrait painting on the cover before asking, 'You're not going to throw this one at me, are you?'

Alice laughed. 'Unless you provoke me.' Pausing, she wondered at the sense in giving it to him. Would he be interested? She swallowed. Suddenly wanting him to care, to want to know more about her. 'It's a biography on Lady Maud Radford—my PhD subject.'

'Why did you choose Lady Radford?'

'In the late nineteenth century she owned a huge estate close to where my mum now lives. When she was alive she divided her time between the estate and her house in London. She was very influential in Anglo-Irish politics but what she achieved hasn't been recognised because of her more famous son, the poet Henry Radford. She was incredibly progressive in her advocacy for women's rights and the rights of all children to a free education. Her views influenced education reforms and I think her contribution to that deserves to be acknowledged.'

Opening the book, he studied the photographs of Lady Radford and her family in the centre pages and then, reaching to touch the delicate branches of the bonsai tree, he said, 'I can see why it took you three hours to select all of these gifts; thank you for choosing them so carefully.'

Taken aback by the emotion in his voice, she responded, 'I'm sure these are nothing in comparison to the gifts that you usually receive.'

He shook his head. 'I receive gifts in an official capacity, but I always donate those to charity, or they are placed in the royal archive—and as for more personal gifts...well, as a family we haven't exchanged gifts in years.'

She pushed her plate aside, wanting to reach out to him, to ease the troubled lines now pinching at the corners of his eyes. 'I'll have to make sure to send you a present every Christmas.'

Her heart turned over to see him smile. But then he gave her an apologetic look. 'I thought, given your feelings on Christmas, that you wouldn't want a gift.'

She waved away his disquiet. 'Oh, I didn't want anything.' She gestured to the snow outside. 'To experience a proper white Christmas is more than enough.'

Liar! Okay, you hadn't actually thought about it up to now, but now that he has brought it up you do want something. Nothing big. Just a token to know he thought about it. Something to remember these days.

'I'll have to make it up to you next year.'

She gave him an uncertain shrug, her heart sinking, knowing there would be no reason for him to give her a gift next year. How would she feel about Christmas next year? Would she relive time and time again the whirlwind, the unexpected turns of this Christmas? How would she feel knowing that these few intoxicating days would never happen again?

For a crazy moment, as silence feel between them and he held her gaze, she thought they were sharing the same identical thoughts. But then he stood and, walking away, said, 'Come with me.' He led her back to the sitting room, where he opened a drawer in a console table. From it he took out a parcel wrapped in gold paper and handed it to her.

Her heart singing with pleasure and anticipation, she opened the present. Seeing what was inside, she laughed. 'Wow, my very own *Our Place*—or should I say *Our lace?*—soccer jersey.'

His eyes danced with merriment. 'We can become their first official fans.' Then he pointed towards the branches of the Christmas tree. 'Do you spot anything different to what we hung last night?'

Puzzled, she glanced over the branches of the tree, until she saw a small white bag with the world-famous gold insignia of Jarrad Jewellers of Bond Street sitting close to one of the flashing icicle lights.

She pointed at it, not sure where this was going.

Lifting the bag from the tree, he handed it to her.

'It's for me?'

'Well, I don't think it will suit me,' he answered.

Inside the bag there was a white velvet box. Opening it, she gasped before lifting out the falling cluster of white-gold flowers inset with diamonds on a white-gold chain.

'This can't be for me.'

Taking it from her, he placed it around her neck. She shivered as his hands touched her skin. 'My prize fund for winning the World Series was substantial. It's nice to be able to share it with someone.'

She closed her eyes. How could she refuse to accept his gift, given those words, given the emotional punch they delivered right into the centre of her heart? Meeting his gaze, she felt realisation barrel through her—he might have a hectic social life and a wide network of friends but perhaps he too understood what it was to feel alone.

She touched her lips against his cheek. 'Thank you.' And then stepped away, terrified by just how emotional she was feeling. She tucked the necklace beneath her pyjama top, confused by what it signified. Did he give such generous gifts to everyone in his life?

Returning to the kitchen, they both began to clear away the dishes. Wanting to lighten the mood between them, she said, 'Yesterday when I was shopping a store assistant asked me if she could help me. I must have looked *really* lost for her to have taken the time out from the chaos around her. Anyway, she asked who I was buying for and I was so frazzled I blurted out that it was for a prince. Without even blinking, she immediately directed me towards the pet section; she thought I was referring to my dog!'

Moving his gifts to a side table, he laughed. 'Are you saying I might have received some dog biscuits as a present?'

Searching for the glass cupboard, in order to stack

away some unused juice glasses, she said, 'Well, I was pretty desperate…and they had the most adorable dog beds in the shape of Santa's sleigh. But there was no way you'd have fitted into them.'

She grinned at Luis's laughter and, moving to the sink to rinse their plates and cups, she admitted, 'I wanted a dog so badly when I was a child, but my dad wouldn't let me. He said they were more trouble than they were worth.'

Coming alongside her, he shook his head in disbelief. 'Not worth the loyalty and affection and endless games of chase? Really?'

She snorted, something freeing in her, at his outrage. She had never thought she'd see the day when she would be able to laugh over anything concerning her dad.

Rinsing done, she watched as Luis settled himself against the counter opposite her. 'We had four dogs. Our mother allowed us to adopt one each on our tenth birthday provided we proved responsible enough by taking care of the family dog, Snuggles.'

This time she gave a hoot of laughter. 'Snuggles! What a great name.'

He regarded her with such warmth and affection that her heart felt as light and free as the snowflakes floating past the window. 'Yeah, it's a cool name, but not for him unfortunately—he was a grumpy schnauzer who refused to be cuddled.'

She laughed but in truth she was seriously distracted, thanks to how good he looked propped like that against the worktop. Blue shirt over blue jeans and tan boots. Height and power. Narrow waist, long and muscular legs. Hair a few centimetres longer than at the wedding. She preferred this length. Clean-shaven—this she also preferred, liking the warmth, the buzz of his skin against hers. He tilted his head in question. He was waiting for her to say something.

What had they been talking about? Dogs. Of course!

Now she just needed to find something to say. 'So… yes…what…what was the name of the dog you adopted?'

Moving away to grab his phone from the dining table, he came and stood beside her. 'He was a cross-breed from the local dog shelter.' Opening up his photo gallery, he scrolled through endless photos.

She caught brief glimpses of beautiful buildings and beaches and powerboats and gorgeous women. Okay, so these women were often in mixed groups, with nothing to suggest that they were more than just friends to Luis. But they were there. They were all part of his life, a life she knew nothing about. Luis had a whole life and friends and relationships she knew nothing about. That thought was odd…and disconcerting.

Finally pausing at a picture, he showed it to her. Her heart melted. 'Oh, gosh! He's so adorable.' The grinning dog looked like a mixture between a Wheaten and a Scottish terrier.

'Yes, he was…his name was Rocky,' he said, his voice full of emotion. 'I hated boarding school, not just because of the stupid need to conform and to obey rules that only made sense a hundred years ago but… I was homesick, for Rocky especially. After I was expelled my father was intent on sending me to a school in America but thankfully my aunt, Princess Maria, and her husband, Johan, persuaded him to allow me to stay with them. And, best of all, Rocky and I were reunited—my aunt smuggled him out of the palace without my father knowing. He was furious when he found out and accused my aunt of spoiling me—he thought I shouldn't be allowed to have Rocky as a form of punishment.'

'Were you happy living with your aunt and uncle?' she asked, hoping that he had been—what must it have been like to lose his mother and then be sent away to another country?

'Yes...in some ways. I had Rocky, and my aunt and uncle indulged me in whatever sport I was obsessed with at any particular time—I rode, sailed, played soccer and cricket, took up abseiling and kite surfing, and then I discovered a passion for motocross. I know they had concerns for my safety and the appropriateness of my involvement with some of the sports, but they always came to watch me compete.' He shifted away from the worktop and, grabbing hold of some paper towel and a spray bottle, he began to wipe the kitchen table with quick, wide, arching movements. 'My father refused to speak to me for over a year. He said I'd brought shame on the family by being expelled from his alma mater.'

'Why were you expelled?'

Head bowed in concentration as he continued to clean the length of the table that could seat at least ten, he answered, 'As I already said, I never settled in. The school was constantly calling my father over my behaviour. What finally got me expelled was when I let some pigs from the neighbouring farm loose in the school.'

Trying not to laugh, she asked, 'And what was the purpose of that little stunt?'

Tossing the paper towel into the bin, he answered, 'I was bored, and I had a science exam an hour later I was going to fail.'

'You wanted to be expelled?'

He folded his arms. 'Yes.' For a few seconds he considered her, shuffled on his feet, looking increasingly uncomfortable. He looked away from her. 'I wanted to get home to Rocky.'

'Did you tell your dad how—?'

He interrupted her, 'We don't have that type of relationship. After my mother died, he didn't want to know about our lives or what we wanted.'

'Losing your mum must have been hard for him too.'

Something dark flashed across his expression. He refused to look at her. His jaw working, he let out an angry breath. She shrank backwards.

He swung his head back in her direction. His eyes widened. 'Alice… I'm sorry.' He unfolded his arms. 'I'm angry with my father, not you.' And then on a sigh he said, 'And you're right. Her death did destroy him…and us as a family.'

Butterflies of panic still soaring in her stomach, she breathed against them. Any sign of annoyance panicked her. Impatient customers made her clumsy. Older men especially. She knew she had to stop equating other people to her father. She had thought that she had made inroads in doing so in recent years. But just now with Luis, it was as though she was looking for any sign that he would hurt her. Which was unfair, she knew that, but deep down she was increasingly panicking at how much he was getting inside her head…and heart.

'Did you tell your brothers about how much you disliked school?'

'No. Edwin was always trying to appease my father and Ivo was never to be seen. He spent most of his time painting model soldiers in his room and then he became obsessed with rowing. He and I are alike in our passion for sport…and in our desire to get away from Monrosa.'

He turned away and plucked a piece of paper from the noticeboard. 'The chef has left details on preparing tonight's dinner. I had better read it and try to decipher his instructions.'

She had never spoken to anyone before about her childhood, hating those memories. She glanced at the white velvet jewellery box, at the snow now falling in slow, dancing swirls, at her gifts to Luis, realising that sometimes, sharing what was deep inside, you could be the most valuable gift of all. 'I had no one to speak to when I was a child. I know how frightening that can be.'

He studied her before moving towards her, his eyes so gentle, so compassionate, swallowing up her heart. 'I wish you had had a Rocky in your life back then.'

She swallowed. Laughed in surprise, hot tears pressing against the backs of her eyes. 'I wish I'd had a Rocky too.'

His hand rested on her arm, his touch one of comfort. 'I reckon it's time we started having some fun. What do you think?'

She nodded. 'Agreed.' Looking out at the falling snow, she asked, 'Will we get to go skiing?'

'Unfortunately I don't think so.' Walking over to the window, he looked out. 'We'll need to think of something else we can do.' He turned around, a wicked gleam in his eye.

She braced herself.

'Do you have a swimsuit with you?' he asked.

'I'm on a skiing holiday—what do you think?'

'In that case I'll find you one.'

Following Luis as he rushed down the stairs to the basement with a little too much enthusiasm for her liking, she asked, 'Are we going swimming?'

Holding open the entrance door to the spa and pool area, he grinned. 'Something even better.'

She came to a stop. 'What?'

'It's a surprise.'

'I don't like surprises.'

'How about, just for today, you take a chance on relinquishing some of the control you insist on single-handedly gripping onto and let someone else make a few decisions on your behalf?'

She refused to budge even when he gestured for her to step into the spa area. 'What if they're decisions I don't like?'

He fake-considered this. 'Well, I agree that you mightn't like it immediately…' he paused and considered her with a dangerous and sexy glint in his eye '…but trust me: the pain and discomfort will be worth it.'

She swallowed. 'Okay, so now I'm worried.'

He lowered his head, looked directly into her eyes. 'I'll never hurt you. You do know that, don't you?'

Her heart kicked. Would she be terribly naïve to believe him? 'I'll hold you to that promise, you know.' Not waiting for a response, she stepped into the spa.

Luis followed her and opened a door to the side of the pool, the lights inside flickering on automatically to reveal shelves piled high with snow-white towels, dressing gowns and slippers. Brand-new swimming costumes still bearing their designer labels hung from a rail.

'Take your pick,' he said, walking to a row of wardrobes. He opened a door and took out a pair of pale blue swimming trunks and then grabbed hold of a towel and dressing gown.

'I'll meet you by the pool.'

Eyeing the swimsuits, she considered the only black

item on the rail but replaced it, realising just how tiny it was. It certainly wasn't designed for someone capable of eating an entire tin of chocolates in one afternoon. She stared at the other swimsuits. Why couldn't there at least be one practical item amongst them? They were all cut way too suggestively. She eventually plucked the least revealing costume in her size from the rail and, armed with a dressing gown and towel, she went to the changing rooms.

The swimming-pool changing areas she had ever frequented had featured the triple delights of musty odours, damp floors and temperamental showers. Here, the changing area consisted of six individual changing rooms, all the size of a small apartment, complete with a tropical shower, every beauty and hair product you could wish for, a TV and sofa and way too many mirrors. Stripping, she pulled on her swimming costume and after a quick grimace at her reflection she put on her dressing gown, yanking the belt tight.

Once she was out at the pool, her heart did several kicks when she spotted Luis waiting for her dressed in only his blue trunks. She sighed. His body was even hotter than she had thought it would be. His abs were like a tightly sprung mattress.

She gestured to the pool. 'You go ahead. I'll follow you in a few minutes,' she said, and darted to sit on a lounger, needing to gather herself.

But he had other ideas. 'We're not going swimming.'

She stared in confusion at the flip-flops he held out to her before reluctantly taking them. Pulling on his dressing gown and stepping into his own pair of flip-flops, he opened the door that led out to a covered terrace and the heavy blanket of snow beyond.

'We're going out…in that?' she asked, her voice as shrill as a bag of cats.

'We sure are.'

'We'll freeze.'

He gave her a stern look. 'Are you already refusing to give up control?'

Stepping into her flip-flops, she shook her head. 'I've always said you're dangerous, and you're doing nothing to dispel that impression.'

He chuckled. 'You haven't seen anything yet.'

Outside she squealed in shock at the wall of cold that slammed into her. Out on the sloping gardens the snow had drifted into high banks. He took her hand. 'Number one rule: don't stand still.'

He led her off the terrace and along a covered path that ran alongside the chalet. At the end of the path he opened the door to his right.

Stepping in, she breathed in the warm pine-scented air, shivering in relief. 'A sauna!'

He nodded, removed his flip-flops and dressing gown and went and sat high up on a bench, settling himself into the corner, a happy grin on his face.

He watched her. Daring her to give up control of the situation.

She'd show him.

Pulling off her gown, she went and sat in the opposite corner. 'Well, this is nice.'

He laughed but didn't say anything.

He closed his eyes. She did too. But then she peeled one open. Was he as chilled-out as he seemed? There was a faint silver star just below his right knee, a fresh bruise on his collarbone. Did he work out in the gym? Was that what gave him that impossibly flat stomach and biceps that could crush you? Her heart did a quickstep as she took in the long length of his eyelashes. He would have been too beautiful but for the unbalance in the shape of his lips—his bottom lip was slightly fuller. And she found it ever so cute…and sexy. She could spend a whole morning nibbling it. She shut her eyes, imaging waking up next to him…preferably naked and to his caresses. She shuffled in her seat, a tingling sensation in her limbs as she imagined his mouth and hands exploring her body. Heat spread along her limbs. What would it be like to have him between her legs? An ache unfurled low in her belly. She had never held a man… How would it feel? Would she know what to do?

'Ready for some fun?'

She leapt at Luis's quietly spoken question.

'A cold shower perhaps,' she suggested.

He stood with a chuckle. 'Something much better.' At the door of the sauna he said, 'We'll cool off outside.'

She stared out at the heavy drift of snow beyond the path and despite the searing heat of the sauna she shivered. 'You have to be joking me.'

'Nope.' He held out his hand.

She refused to budge. He folded his arms, settling against the doorframe.

For more than a minute they held a silent standoff, eyeing each other stubbornly.

With an exasperated exhale she stood up. He clearly wasn't going to back down and the open door was letting all of the heat out.

Passing Luis, she gave him the evil eye and took a few tentative steps outside. She gasped loudly and was so befuddled by the cold that she didn't fight him when he took hold of her hand and broke into a jog, pulling her with him.

Out in the open, beyond the covered walkway, the falling snow made her blink hard. They were heading directly for a huge snowdrift. She didn't want to do this. It was way too cold. She tried to pull Luis to a stop, but their momentum was too great. She screamed and fell into the icy blanket face first. She rolled onto her back. Screamed again. Screamed even more. Wanting to kill Luis. But then she heard herself laugh. Something freeing in her. It was Christmas morning and she was rolling in the Alpine snow with the most incredible man she had ever met. If this could happen to her, what endless possibilities were out there for her?

She gasped when fresh snow landed on her. Luis was pelting her with it! She gripped some herself and flung it at him. Laughing. Buzzing with happiness. He grabbed hold of her and they tumbled in the snow, their laughter rolling down the mountainside. He came to a stop lying on top of her, his twinkling eyes holding hers captive. Eyes that soon darkened, and, placing a kiss on her cheek and then on her mouth, he whispered, 'Happy Christmas.'

Her heart lurched. She wanted so much more with him.

Standing, Luis helped her up and lifted her into his arms. He carried her back to the sauna, grinning as she demanded that he let her down.

Inside the sauna he gently lowered her down and as he shut the door she laughed, shaking her entire body. 'That was so good.' Adrenaline was pounding through her. She high fived him. And then rubbed some snow from his collarbone.

They were now supposed to move back into their respective corners. But instead they just smiled goofily at one another. And then his eyes wandered lazily down over her body, lingering on her red swimsuit. Her skin, already on fire from the snow, took on a different heat.

'I told you that red would suit you.'

Her heart shuddered and stalled, the approval in his voice and eyes mesmerising.

His hand touched lightly against the cut-out seam above her hip. He twisted his finger into the fabric and pulled her forward, inch by slow inch. She didn't resist. Instead she smiled. Wanting this oh, so badly.

His mouth came to her ear. 'You're incredibly special.'

Her knees weakened.

His mouth moved down to nuzzle against her neck.

Her knees gave up and buckled, her body collapsing against his. His mouth found hers. They both groaned into the kiss. His hands moved to her back. Stroking, caressing her bare skin. His mouth took control of hers. Hot, probing, sensual. Leading the kiss. Pushing her to places she had never been before.

Dizzying desire flooded her, a solid ache beginning to throb in her core. His hands moved to run over her body, as though he wanted to know intimately every inch of her. Her hips, her bottom, her belly. Her body was moulded to his. The ache in her widened. Without conscious thought her body began to move against his, searching, hunting for a place that would ease the burning hunger inside of her.

They staggered backwards, Luis landing on the bench behind him. She stayed with him, her legs wrapping about his waist. As if this was the most normal thing in the world. Desire, hot and liquid, flowed through her.

She deepened the kiss, wanting more. His hand touched her side, running along her ribs, grazing over the side of her breast. She shuddered.

His hands moved under her swimsuit, one thumb touching against her nipple, the other running along the sensitive skin of her bottom. She jerked into him, deepened the kiss. She cried out as his hardness pressed against her. Cried out again when his tongue flicked over the light fabric, doing little to hide the bud of her nipple.

Her head spun as he whispered words to her, words adoring her body.

She was hurtling towards an edge no man had ever brought her to.

Her body felt ripe, wanton. Emotion and passion spun together, casting a spell on her. She felt powerful and desirable. Did he realise what he was giving her? The gift to enjoy her own body.

He knew exactly what he was doing, his mouth on her breast, his fingers pressing against her. He flicked the material of her swimsuit aside, his fingers finding the most sensitive points of her body. She gasped, spinning away from the conscious world to one solely filled with pleasure and need.

His mouth sucked harder. His fingers moved faster. He knew exactly the chaos he was wreaking on her.

She gasped again. Screamed. And fell into a long pulse of pleasure, her head thrown back. Wave after wave of ecstasy convulsed through her. She clung to him, her head thrown back, the hard press of his body driving her pleasure on and on.

When it had finally passed she collapsed against him.

He stroked her hair. Kissed her along her cheek. And whispered with a heartbreaking tenderness, 'I want to be with you.'

She nodded. But embarrassment had her bury her head even more into his shoulder. She wasn't supposed to have done that. She had totally lost control. What was she going to do? And all of a sudden she wanted to cry, feeling raw and exposed and vulnerable. How was she going to tell him?

She pulled back. Met his eye.

He grinned, pleased with himself. The desire in his eyes stole her breath away.

She breathed in deeply, searching for a way to tell him. 'I told you that I've never had a proper boyfriend.'

'Yes…so?'

He had no idea. She swallowed hard. 'I haven't had a proper relationship in every sense.'

He nodded but was still clearly puzzled, and then she saw realisation hit his eyes. 'Do you mean that you've never slept with anyone?'

She cringed at the incredulity in his voice. Standing, her limbs weak, she stepped back and whispered, 'Even what just happened there…' she felt herself go even redder '…it hasn't happened with a man before. I thought you should know before we do anything.'

Speechless, Luis stared at her, trying to gain control of his thoughts. And then he stood, fighting back the urge to pace. *Dio!* Sleeping with her was out of the question now. He needed air. He needed to clear his head. He needed to think straight before he said anything stupid. But instead he pulled her into a hug, his heart way too big for his chest, guessing as to why she had never slept with a man before.

Her body was rigid. He cursed. She must have seen just how thrown he was. He grappled for words, the physical desire he felt for her fighting against the need to protect her.

He sensed her about to pull away. He placed his hand on her hair, stroking it, wanting somehow to communicate with her that he understood even if he couldn't find the right way to express that right now. He mumbled out some words. 'I don't… I can't…'

She pushed against his chest, breaking away. Grabbing hold of her dressing gown, she pulled it on, refusing to look at him.

What was he supposed to say, to do?

She bolted out of the sauna. Cursing, he grabbed hold of his own dressing gown and chased after her. He followed her through the pool room and up the stairs to the ground floor. In the entrance hallway she turned to him, her expression devoid of all emotion. 'I need to get dressed. I'll see you later.'

'I can't be the first.'

She winced at that, but then with a shrug spun away.

Dio! He was getting this so wrong. He pulled in a long breath, trying to quell his panic. Her bare feet landed on the first wooden step of the oak staircase. And then the second. And the third. He was a quick thinker, had never been lost for words before. What was wrong with him?

She was nearing the top of the stairs. He couldn't let her go without explaining himself to her, without trying to say why hc could never sleep with her. 'I have never wanted to be with someone as much as I want to be with you.'

At the top of the stairs she spun around and studied him. Her expression was sceptical. 'You must find it hard to understand why someone my age has never slept with anyone before now. Odd even.' She paused, her mouth tightening. 'Your reaction is understandable.'

He climbed the stairs, hating how as he drew nearer she backed away into the corner of the double-storey height balcony window that gave an endless view of the neighbouring mountainside.

He flexed his fists. For the first time in as long as he could remember he was going to be truly honest with another person, and his heart was pounding at the prospect of doing so. 'I have never taken sleeping with someone lightly. I am not into one-night stands or casual hook-ups.' He paused, not quite believing he was actually admitting all of this. 'I know it might sound old-fashioned but for me making love to someone is about intimacy and respect and care for the other person.'

She shook her head as though trying to understand what she had just heard. 'So…what are you saying…that you don't feel those things for me?'

'No! No…what I'm trying to say and doing so badly is that you're leaving tomorrow…sleeping with you would be so wrong. I wanted to spend Christmas supporting you, not complicating your life even more or possibly hurting you.'

She tossed her head back. 'Who says I'll get hurt? And maybe you're not into casual flings…but what if I am? You're the one who keeps telling me to lighten up. Well, maybe for once I just want to do something reckless.'

He raised an eyebrow. His lips twitched.

She stared at him, clearly unimpressed that he might

find humour in her newly found rebellion. And then she swung around and looked out of the window, but not before he saw her mouth twitch too. Then on a sigh she said, 'It's stopped snowing. Let's head out. You can give me a snowboarding lesson like you promised.'

He could understand her need to escape from this conversation that was awkward and frankly way too close to the bone in revealing the connection that was between them, but there was more he needed to say before they escaped for the slopes. He went and stood beside her. Her eyes shifted for a brief moment towards him before she resumed staring out onto the silent white landscape outside. 'You're a beautiful, smart and brilliant woman. If you weren't Kara's cousin, if my life weren't such a mess at the moment…if I didn't care for you as much as I do…if making love wasn't so damn complicated, then I would be dragging you into my bedroom and into my bed right now and I wouldn't be releasing you until well into the New Year. But instead I want to be your friend… I want to be able to ring you in the future. I want to be able to face you at family events without any awkwardness. And most of all, I don't want to hurt you.'

'Who said you would hurt me?'

There was a fire in her eyes that reminded him of the first night they had met. Memories of her kiss, chasing after her through the palace gardens, the disappointment of seeing her drive away and the feeling that something important had escaped his grasp, had him say softly, 'Maybe I'm trying not to be hurt myself.'

Snuggled into the corner of the sofa, Alice tried to focus on her book but her gaze kept shifting over to study

Luis. For their dinner earlier he had changed into grey trousers and a white shirt, leaving the top two buttons undone. Head bowed, he was reading the book she had gifted him but how much he was taking in she wasn't sure, given that he was constantly checking his phone.

Was he waiting for someone to call or message him? A woman perhaps? She closed her eyes, dread forming in the pit of her stomach. She had spent most of the summer before she had started secondary school alone and isolated, having been dumped from her friendship group because they were going to a different school to her. One evening she had heard beeping and located its source to an unfamiliar phone she had found in her dad's jacket pocket. Confused, she had brought it into the kitchen, asking him if he had bought a new phone and why there were so many messages from one of her mum's close friends.

Her mum had cried. Her dad had yelled. And Alice had soaked up the way her dad had twisted the blame onto her, telling her that it was she who was responsible for her mum's devastation.

The lies people told. The games they played. And the self-destruct buttons they so easily pressed. And here she was, a perfect case in point. Instead of coming to her senses and counting her blessings that she hadn't slept with Luis earlier she was actually even more attracted to him than ever. Not only was she constantly reliving in her head the feel of his mouth on her breast, the magic of his fingers, the waves of bliss that had whipped through her body, but hearing him talk so sensitively about lovemaking, hearing the passion and sincerity in his voice, the way his gaze darkened when he had said that he had never desired anyone more than her, had her completely spellbound. And this afternoon, as she had watched him so effortlessly freestyle snowboard, the way he so patiently lifted her up time and time again after her disastrous attempts to stand upright, never mind actually snowboard, he had got even further under her skin.

She shifted in her seat and pressed a hand on her burning cheeks. And groaned as her glute muscles screamed in protest.

'Are you ok?' Luis asked.

She nodded but grimaced as she attempted to manoeuvre herself into a comfortable position and admitted, 'I don't think I'll be able to walk tomorrow. They might have to carry me onto the plane.'

He smiled but didn't say anything. Wood crackled in the fireplace. Tomorrow they would be saying goodbye. It was for the best. She had to get back to work, and Luis to Monrosa.

His phone pinged. She jumped at the sudden noise. He grabbed hold of the phone and smiled as he hit play on the video message he had been sent, a chorus of voices wishing him a happy Christmas from the Bahamas. But then with a sigh he put the phone back down on the velvet armrest of his chair.

'It wasn't the message you've been waiting for all evening?'

He frowned at her question but then shrugged.

It was none of her business but suddenly she really, *really* wanted to know whose message or call he was waiting for. She opened her mouth, looking for a subtle way of phrasing her question but quickly abandoned that search, the memory of her dad's phone burning in her soul.

'She must be pretty special to warrant how distracted you have been all evening.'

Closing his book and placing it on the coffee table, he sat back in his chair and studied her.

She blinked at the open way he considered her, as though he was trying to find the solution to a particularly difficult puzzle. 'If there were another woman in my life I wouldn't have kissed you the way I did this morning. I'm not that type of man.' He said it with such a softly spoken seriousness that for a moment she almost believed him, but then all her doubts and mistrust, driven by how raw and vulnerable she felt after their intimacy earlier, made her ask, 'Well, who are you waiting for, then?'

'You don't believe anything I say, do you?'

The disappointment in his voice made her wince but something deep inside her wanted to push him. She wanted to know that everything he had said to her earlier that day about why he wouldn't sleep with her was a lie. She was just a convenient distraction.

He wasn't really attracted to her. Did he think she was going to fall for all that baloney he had spun her? 'I know first-hand the signs of a man having an affair.'

'How can I be having an affair when we're not in a relationship?' he asked.

She wanted the ground to open up and swallow her swiftly. Why on earth had she so clumsily accused him of being involved with someone else? 'You know what I mean. I'd hate to think that there's a woman out there being hurt right now and that I have something to do with it. My dad had an affair and it nearly destroyed my mum.'

She waited for him to respond, a fire in her wanting to get things out in the open. With a start she realised she wanted a fight. She never wanted to fight. She hated confrontation. But here she was, deliberately antagonising him, wanting to push him further and further. Wanting to see the real man. Would he flip like her dad? Would she get to see the real man—the anger, the denials, the manipulation?

She jumped out of her seat. 'See, this is why I hate Christmas. Everything goes wrong.'

Standing up, he stabbed some numbers into his phone, his mouth a tight grimace, and handed the phone to her. 'Feel free to check through all of my messages. Maybe then you'll believe me.'

She took the phone and stared at it, the fire inside her dying, to be replaced by shame. Handing the phone back to him, she could barely meet his stare. 'I'm sorry…that was uncalled for.'

He said nothing.

Embarrassment made her throat close over. She walked over to the fireplace, studied the photos there of a young Luis and his family on skiing trips, looking so incredibly happy, Luis always standing at his dad's side, more often than not pulling a goofy pose.

She closed her eyes. And said with her back still to him, 'I'm scared of being hurt.' Turning, she studied him. 'It's easier to assume the worst in people rather than to be let down.'

'That's an unfair way to approach life…not just for the other people involved but also for yourself. You're pushing away good people because of the few and you're robbing yourself of a full life.'

She wanted to look away, she wanted to walk away from the truth in his words, but, pulling in a breath, she said, 'But it will keep me safe.'

There it was again, that sad, disappointed look of his that cut her to the quick.

'People need to be believed in.'

She shrugged. 'I'm not sure it's something that I can ever do—truly believe in everything that another person says.'

He walked over to her. 'Do you believe in what you say yourself, Alice? Maybe you should start there?'

She laughed. Not understanding his point. But then she stopped and stepped away from him. Her past insistence that she was content in her life, that she wasn't lonely, ringing hollow. She picked up a photo from the mantelpiece. 'Your mum was incredibly beautiful, and you look so like your dad when he was a younger man.'

He stared at the photo. 'I hadn't seen it before but there is a resemblance… It was my father I was waiting to hear from. I told Edwin earlier that I was delaying my return to Monrosa until the thirtieth. Apparently, my father is furious that I've cancelled my return yet again.' Flipping a switch on the wall, throwing the entire room into darkness with the exception of the light from the fire and the Christmas tree, he went to the terrace doors and, opening one, stepped outside. 'Come and see the stars.'

She stood at the doorway and shuddered. 'It's bitterly cold.'

He gave no response but instead, grabbing hold of a shovel hidden in an outside alcove, dug a path in the snow out to the terrace's balustrade. Path cleared, he turned and answered, 'Magic only happens when we take risks.'

She rolled her eyes but took a few steps out onto the terrace. She shivered fiercely but then laughed, the shock of the cold, the endless stars overhead, invigorating and magical.

She wrapped her arms around herself, dancing on the

balls of her feet to stay warm. 'Why have you delayed returning to Monrosa?'

His concentration fixed on stargazing, he answered, 'Because I'm hoping to persuade you to stay here with me for a few more days and then travel to the New Year's Eve ball in Monrosa with me.'

'What? Are you kidding me?' Her voice echoed down the valley. Was he serious? She gave him a disbelieving look. He shrugged. Shrugged! After landing that bombshell on her.

'I'm going back to London tomorrow.'

'Aren't you enjoying it here?'

Thrown, she paused. 'Yes… No… That's not the point.'

'Another few days and you'll master snowboarding.'

'Oh, please, we both know that is never going to happen—I'm way too uncoordinated.'

'If you allow yourself another few days of forgetting about your thesis, I'll guarantee that in the New Year you'll have the energy to tackle it again.' His eyes dancing, his voice dropping to a husky timbre, he added, 'And I'm more than happy to keep you distracted until then… in whatever way you'd like.'

She paused from crazily hopping from one foot to the other. Her eyes widened, her cheeks grew hot. He smiled, remembering this morning, remembering her falling apart in his arms. Sleeping together might be out of the question but that didn't mean that they couldn't find fun in other ways.

She frowned. 'Hold on. Are you claiming to be staying here entirely for my benefit?' Not waiting for him to respond, she added, 'I'm calling you out on that. My guess is that you don't want to go back to Monrosa and I'm an excuse for you not doing so.'

She was wrong. Well, sort of. He did think staying here would benefit her. The tiredness beneath her eyes was vanishing. The tension, the preoccupation, the distractedness he had seen in her in London were all fading away too. 'Perhaps it's the right decision for both of us right now.'

She let out an impatient breath that came out like a frosted cloud from her mouth. 'Will you stop twisting things and tell me straight why you want to stay here for another few days?'

That was a good question, given the conversation they'd just had—her mistrust, her prickly, guarded suspicion should have had him happily waving goodbye to her tomorrow. But he got why she was so wary of trusting him. Yes, it frustrated him, even hurt him, but there was so much more to Alice than the cynical wariness she had developed no doubt thanks to her father's behaviour. He enjoyed her company, her intelligence, her rawness, the way she challenged him. The chemistry they shared felt like a life force separate from them as individuals. None of it made sense. But he wasn't ready for it to end…just yet.

'Okay, so maybe I'm not ready to go back to Monrosa. There's no rush—it's not as if I won't be spending the rest of my life on that island.'

Stamping her feet, she said, 'You make it sound like a prison sentence.' Then with a deep shudder she added, 'It's way too cold out here.'

He followed her back inside and as he closed the door Alice asked, 'What is it about Monrosa that makes you so reluctant to go back there? I know there's the tension with your dad, but it has to be the most beautiful place I have ever visited. Endless sunshine, a rich and fascinating history, incredible beaches and food, and the warmest of people.'

He placed a log on the fire. 'Which is not something that can be said of my father.' He went and sat in the chair he had earlier been seated on. Instead of curling back into her space in the corner of the sofa, Alice sat on the footstool in front of him. She was wearing her black leather mini-skirt again, this time with a soft cream polo-neck jumper and black high heels. She pulled the sleeves of the jumper down over her hands and inched the footstool closer to the fire. He should switch the lights back on, but he liked how the flames of the fire flickered warm light across her face, dancing over the swell of her lips and the prominence of her cheekbones. She smiled at him, a hesitant smile but her eyes held his, an understanding, a recognition, making his heart stumble over in his chest.

'I spoke to your father at Kara's wedding. I liked him. He's blunt. But I prefer that to insincerity and lies.'

'You *liked* him? All my other friends are terrified of him. They try to be polite about it, but I see them slinking out of his way.'

'You know how sometimes you meet someone in life, and you click for some reason, and, as strange as it might sound, I felt that with your dad.' She shrugged. 'Maybe it's because we both use defensiveness to protect ourselves.'

'I would class my father's approach as attack rather than defence.'

'I know things must have been hard… I've been through it with my own dad. Ultimately I had to decide whether to keep working at our relationship or to break all ties. I know that's probably not an option available to you because of your roles and responsibilities, but maybe you need to redefine your expectations of what your father can give you. It may not be what you want and need, but at least you won't be constantly disappointed and hurt. That's what I found the hardest with my dad, the rollercoaster of hoping and expecting something from him, only to be let down.'

'Why should I have to adjust—why should I have to deal with his constant criticism?'

She shrugged. 'If you try to understand why he's so critical it might help you deal with his behaviour. After all, he must be hurting somehow to act this way.'

He sat back in his chair, knowing she was right. But trying to understand his father could mean having to let go of years of anger and frustration on his part. And perhaps even forgiving his father for the isolation and humiliation he had wrought on him. A forgiveness he wasn't sure he was capable of.

'There's more to your reluctance to return to the island than your dad though, isn't there?'

He shook his head. 'No.'

Shifting in her seat, her gaze holding his, she softly said, 'Last year I went back to the town where I grew up. I hadn't been there since my parents separated. I actually felt physically sick. I hadn't expected it, but seeing the town triggered huge panic in me. I couldn't wait to get out of there.'

Luis understood. He didn't experience panic, but he was always cranky and defensive while in Monrosa.

'What one word would you use about how you feel about Monrosa?'

He stared at her, undone by the gentleness in her voice, undone by the wave of grief he didn't even know he held on to. 'Sadness.'

'Because of your mum?'

He closed his eyes, suddenly wanting a drink. Or any other distraction that would serve to get him out of this conversation. He never, ever spoke to anyone about any of this. 'Every time I see the Monrosian coastline as we fly in, for a moment I think my mother will be there. That I will get to hug her again.' He swallowed, a barrel of emotion, of loss and regrets, sitting on his chest. 'I think that I'll be able to tell her one more time how much I love her.' He tried to stop there but it was as though the emotional break he usually had so firmly in place was out of action in the face of Alice's steady gaze. 'For those few moments I don't feel quite so alone.'

She tilted her head, smiled so kindly at him that he was forced to blink hard as tears stung the backs of his eyes. 'I had always thought you were the least alone person on this earth,' she said.

He threw his head back, running a hand through his hair. 'I spend my days trying not to be.'

'Do you like yourself, Luis?'

He shook his head. 'That's way too deep for me.'

She edged ever closer, her knees touching his, a playful smile on her lips. 'Now, don't go telling this to anyone, but I like you. In fact, I think you're pretty incredible. Yes, you need to stop and draw a breath every now and again. And find happiness within yourself. But I know that you're going to go on from here and be a force of good in this world. You have a unique opportunity and position of influence, a unique personality full of energy and optimism. The world needs good guys like you more than ever before.'

His heart turned inside out at her words. She really believed in him. He grinned, trying to regain control of his emotions. 'You're not expecting a lot from me, are you?'

'Nothing that you aren't capable of. Look at the courage and determination it took for you to win the World Series. I reckon you're capable of doing anything you put your mind to.'

'It's easy when you are in a job you love, with a clear goal in sight and surrounded by a brilliant team.'

She shrugged. 'Surround yourself with a new team. I get that transitioning from one life to another is hard, but take time out to understand what it is you actually want to achieve in life.'

What did he want in life? In his twenties he had thrown himself into anything that gave him an adrenaline rush and got him away from Monrosa. And anything that antagonised his father. He grimaced, knowing he had to accept some of the responsibility for his dysfunctional relationship with his father. 'Do you have what you want in life worked out?'

'Kind of. I know I want to create a love for history in students. I have some ideas on writing accessible historical fiction for teenagers focused on real-life events. So often, the way history is taught, teenagers can't relate to it. We can learn so much by the mistakes past generations have made. It frustrates me to see us make the same mistakes time and time again, more often than not allowing fear and ignorance, a narrow world view, to guide our decisions.'

He smiled at the passion in her voice. 'So why are you struggling with your PhD?'

She sighed. 'Good question. I guess that for so long my life has been predictable. I like that order. It makes me feel safe. When I finish my PhD I don't know what my life will look like, what changes I'll have to make.'

'So, I'm heading towards a life filled with structure and protocol and you're heading into uncertainty—the complete opposites of one another and what neither of us want.'

She tilted her head. 'We could swap. I think I'd love following royal protocol.' She laughed. 'It would suit me perfectly to be surrounded by centuries of history, and there isn't a rebellious bone in my body.'

He ran a hand along his neck. 'Don't say that within earshot of my father at the New Year's Eve ball or he'll try setting you up with me or Ivo—he's keen for us to marry too.'

'Of course I wouldn't! I wasn't implying...' She paused, her forehead puckering. 'Wait, I haven't said that I will go with you to the ball anyway. And there's no way I'm ever marrying, so you're safe on that front. I still can't believe Kara agreed to it in the first place.'

Picking up his phone, he opened up the photo gallery and showed the photograph Edwin had sent to him that morning, of him and Kara happily surrounded by the group of local children who as per tradition visited the palace on Christmas Eve to receive Christmas gifts. 'And look at how happy they are now.'

She studied the photo in silence. 'They really are in love, aren't they?'

He nodded. 'It looks that way...maybe starting as friends is a good place to begin a relationship.'

She gave him an uncertain look. And no wonder. He wasn't even sure himself why he had said that. He needed to lighten the mood. Rapidly. 'Come to the ball with me. It's always a spectacular event but this year it will be even more incredible because Kara is organising it and the proceeds will be going to her charity. She has doubled the numbers attending, and there will not only be the ball, but also an amusement fair, an aerial acrobatics team, a casino… She wants to make it into a huge fundraising event with guests coming from all over the world. Who knows, even you might enjoy it?'

She gave him an evil stare. 'Are you implying that I can be a grumpy pants?'

He laughed. 'Now, why would I ever have reason to think that?'

She studied him closely, as though trying to work him out. 'Tell me the real reason you want me to go to the ball with you—you know that it will raise eyebrows with your family and the media. Why risk endless and incorrect speculation?'

Because I want to dance with you. I want to hear your laughter when I drag you onto an amusement ride. I want your calmness. I want to be with you.

What was happening to him? Why was he feeling all these things?

He went to make a quip, intending to say that she could be his decoy around his father, but instead he answered, 'Because it's time that I started creating new memories in Monrosa.'

CHAPTER EIGHT

ALICE RAN OUT of the bathroom and scrambled through her suitcase. Underwear. Make-up bag. She scrambled even more. Where was her roll-up bag of make-up and hairbrushes? Oh, somebody please tell her she hadn't left them sitting on the bathroom counter of her bedroom in Verbier.

She checked her phone. She had forty minutes to get ready. Forty minutes! Her hair alone took nearly that long to dry…so not for the first time she cursed its thick length. She was going to look an absolute mess. At the New Year's Eve ball that the whole of Europe was talking about…according to her mum anyway. But it must be a big deal, given the amount of media parked outside the main gates.

She winced, remembering her mother's shock when she had rung and told her that she was going to the ball, but thankfully she seemed to believe her explanation that Kara wanted some support.

She felt so far out of her depth it wasn't funny. And Luis's father's reproachful look when they had rushed into the palace only fifteen minutes ago hadn't helped.

Giving up on her search for the make-up bag, she ran back into the dressing room to check that she hadn't imagined things when she had briefly looked in there before her rushed shower. The five exquisite ballgowns were still there, hanging on the rail—waiting for her to decide which one to wear tonight. Despite her protests that it was unnecessary, Luis had insisted on ordering a selection of gowns for her to choose from. She lifted a sleek beaded turquoise dress from the rail and placed it against her. It was beautiful…and tiny. Would she even fit into it? Had Luis given the designer the wrong measurements? Or maybe it was she who had got the measurements wrong in the first place. Which was no wonder, given her distraction thanks to Luis standing behind her, his hands on her hips and his lips on her neck, whispering a long list of things he wanted to find out about her body as she had struggled to write down her measurements. They had spent the last five days snowboarding…and making out. On the slopes, in the pool, in the sauna, on the sofa. Just about everywhere, to be frank. It had been exhilarating. Passionate. All-consuming. Unstoppable. She simply couldn't get enough of him. She craved his touch, the pressure of his body against hers.

Every morning when they met for breakfast he pulled her into a bear hug, and as his arms wrapped around her and she inhaled the citrus smell from his recently showered skin she'd place her head against his chest and hear the thump of his heart and a sense of peace would wash over her. And then he would kiss her. And that peace would be replaced with heat. A heat that would only grow throughout the day until in the darkness of the night, as he stood outside her bedroom door, which he insisted on walking her to every single night, they would make out like teenagers. Hot, lusty kisses. Intimate touches. He gave her the teenage passion she had been too scared to experience when she'd actually been a teenager.

'What is the matter with you?'

She could still hear the disdain in Rory's voice the one time they had come close to making love. The implication that she was damaged. She had panicked at the last moment and had leapt away from him, pulling her jeans and top back on as Rory stared at her with impatient and angry disbelief. Her dad's abuse had been too raw and recent. She had been too bruised to let anyone get close to her.

The passage of time and Luis's kindness, not to mention the chemistry between them, were all lowering the defences she had put around herself, and every night when she reluctantly shut her bedroom door to him she had battled with the urge to swing the door open again and beg him to sleep with her. Mostly pride holding her back. But also, just about enough sense to realise that in essence what was happening between them was nothing other than a short holiday fling.

Reckoning the turquoise dress wouldn't fit her, she checked each of the other dresses. The silver dress was equally tiny, the white sheath with a gold belt not her colour. Which left a full-skirted red dress and a jade-green fishtail dress. The red dress looked the most likely to fit her.

Back in the bedroom she pulled the towel from around her head, her wet hair falling around her shoulders. She jumped at a knock on the door. Gingerly opening it, she gave a cry of relief. 'Kara!'

Kara swept into the room, carrying the long train of her gold sequinned dress. Kara went to hug her, but

Alice ducked out of the way. 'No! I'll ruin your hair and make-up.' Stepping back, she shook her head. 'You look like a million dollars.'

Kara grinned. 'My hair and make-up team are miracle-workers.' Then, pulling Alice into a hug, despite her protests, she added, 'It's so good to see you. I was really worried your flight wouldn't be able to take off because of the snowstorm.'

Extracting herself from the hug, Alice pointed to her hair. 'I need to get this dry. And do my make-up… I'd like to say that I'm not panicking but I am.'

'My team should still be in the palace—I'll call them.'

Alice sighed in relief. 'That would be amazing, thank you.'

'Deal—but you have to tell me first, though, what's going on between you and Luis.'

'There's nothing going on between us.' Seeing Kara's disbelieving expression, Alice went and opened one of the shoeboxes sitting on the ottoman at the bottom of her bed. 'He got it into his head that I needed minding over Christmas. We get on. But that's all. We're complete opposites. Now seriously, can you go and call your team? I'm never going to be ready at this rate.'

'I'd never have put the two of you together, but the more Edwin and I discussed it, the more I realised that you are really suited. You balance each other out perfectly and you're actually not that different.'

Lifting a red sandal from the box, which must have been sent to match the red gown, she waved it at Kara. 'I have my make-up to do, I have to squeeze myself into a dress and hope that these sandals fit me… I don't have time to be chatting about a hypothetical relationship with Luis that's never going to happen. And for the record, he's an extroverted risk-taking prince and I'm a history student who struggles in a room with more than ten people.'

'Yes, but you are both incredibly intelligent, kind and compassionate.' Pausing, Kara considered her for a moment. 'Luis called Edwin yesterday to schedule a meeting tomorrow between him, Edwin and their father to discuss what his role will be when he returns to Monrosa. It's the first time that he's been willing to discuss his return. Edwin needs his support, so it's a huge relief for us—and I can't help but think that you've played a role in him taking this step. So isn't it any wonder that I reckon that there's a whole lot more going on between you two than either of you are letting on?'

Alice grabbed her phone and checked the time. 'I have half an hour to get ready. Can you please go and find your team?' Seeing that Kara wasn't about to budge, she added as way of a bribe, 'If you do, I promise that I'll take part in your mud-run fundraiser next year.'

'As long as you promise to persuade Luis to also take part,' Kara replied with a cheeky smile before disappearing out of the door.

Tugging off her towel, Alice pulled on a white lace thong and the dressing gown she had found in the bathroom. The red sandals consisted of endless rows of tiny straps, so, sitting on the ottoman, she undid the top five straps of each sandal before stepping into them, and cursed at how tricky it was to tie them back up.

Wrangling with the straps, she called, 'Come in,' when there was another knock on the door. 'That was quick…' She stopped, her heart missing a beat. Standing at the doorway, freshly showered and dressed in black tie, Luis let his gaze drop down to her sandals.

'Need some help?'

Before she was able to decline his offer he was already kneeling before her, his hand reaching for an ankle. He tied the straps in silence. A heated charge filled the room. She had sworn to herself this very morning that once they were in Monrosa everything would change—that she would stop being so aware of him, stop falling to pieces whenever they were in the same room.

His hands ran up the length of her calves, his eyes meeting hers. 'Great sandals.'

Such simple words but said with such heat and meaning, and they were followed up with him kissing her briefly but passionately on the mouth. And when he pulled back the intimacy in his eyes sent flutters of exhilaration and panic through her.

She was getting way too addicted to him. She knew it. She really, really was trying to fight it. But she might as well have been trying to hold back the tide.

'I'm supposed to be getting ready.'

'I think you look pretty great as you are.'

Yeah, right. Wet hair. No make-up. A fluffy dressing gown that made her look like a polar bear. But… Luis looked as though he truly meant it.

He reached into his inner pocket. 'I have a surprise for you.'

She groaned. 'Not another one.' Last night he had taken her to a local outdoor ice rink that was rather embarrassingly holding a date night. Not only had she had to endure the humiliation of having to cling to Luis for the night, but their slow movements around the ice had been accompanied by the most romantic playlist known to mankind.

From his pocket he pulled out a yellow and green ointment tube and held it out to her.

Puzzled, she picked it up.

'For all of your bruises—it's produced on the island and is famed for its healing properties.'

'Is this an apology for showing off on the ice last night and tripping me up in the process?'

He took the tube from her with a wry smile. Undoing the cap, he smeared some of the cream onto his finger and rubbed it onto the bruise on her knee. And then he parted her dressing gown, exposing more of her thighs. She knew she should protest, grab the ointment from him, but instead she watched with hypnotic fascination as he gently worked the ointment into every visible bruise, most of them a result of her poor attempts to learn to snowboard. Her heart dipped and soared, tongues of fire licked her insides and her poor brain tried its best to be heard amongst all that chaos, warning her that things were really getting out of control.

His thumb flicked over the lace panel of her thong. The tongues of fire burnt even more brightly. His head dropped down, his tongue trailing against her inner thigh. She threw her head back, all thought closing down as she became consumed with the sensation of his tongue, flicking against the fabric of her underwear. She grappled for some coherent thoughts. 'I need…to get ready…this isn't fair.'

He gently bit into the inner skin of her thigh. She yelped, not in pain but because it felt so good.

With a self-satisfied smile he popped the top back on the ointment and reached inside his pocket again. This time he pulled out another white velvet box from Jarrad Jewellers.

She eyed it warily.

'I'd like you to wear them tonight.' When she didn't take the box he added softly, 'It's a thank-you for coming to Monrosa with me…it's made the journey home easier.'

Her heart tightened. She blinked against a stinging sensation at the backs of her eyes. 'I'm glad.'

Opening the box, she inhaled sharply at the exquisite beauty of what lay within. 'Earrings to match the necklace you gave me on Christmas Day.'

'Jarrad's couriered it here today.'

Taking the box from her, he came and sat beside her and, taking one of the earrings out, pulled back the clasp and gently placed it on her earlobe.

'You noticed that I don't have my ears pierced.' Why was that fact so important, so bittersweet?

He placed the other earring on her other lobe, the soft wool of his dress jacket rubbing against her cheek. And then, holding her head so tenderly that she barely felt the pressure of his hands, he placed a kiss on each earlobe. 'I have to go and receive our guests with the rest of my family. I've asked a friend, Henri, to escort you to the ball. He will be waiting for you in the Blue Room downstairs.'

She nodded, and after one final kiss goodbye he left. She needed to get up, make sure she could walk in the sandals. But instead she collapsed back onto the bed behind the ottoman, exhausted by sexual frustration and by the knowledge that tomorrow she had to say goodbye to this Christmas tale. A tale, like all other Christmas tales, that was full of marvels and miracles but had no place in the real world.

Luis entered the ballroom and scanned the room for a red dress. He circled the room, waving to friends and associates but moving on, not stopping to chat, his eyes darting across the crowded dance floor. He came to a stop. A man was holding a woman in a red dress way too closely. He cursed as the man's hands ran over the pale skin of her bare back. He moved towards them but then the crowd parted, and he realised it wasn't Alice after all.

He left the ballroom, thrown by his jealousy and how desperately he wanted to track Alice down. He wanted to be with her. They hadn't spoken all evening. They had been seated at different tables during dinner and he had spent the entire meal juggling entertaining a sports-obsessed multinational CEO while trying to ignore the frostiness of his father, who had been seated next to him, and keeping an eye on Alice, seated to the side of the room.

By the end of the meal he had managed to convince the CEO that he should consider using the conference and sporting facilities on Monrosa for corporate events…and had developed an irritating crick in his neck from checking on Alice.

She had sat at her table, her reserve, the quiet way she occupied a space, so endearing, so positively Alice that he had wanted to stroll over to her and tell her just how amazing she truly was. Watching her from afar, he had wanted to turn to his father and tell him about the incredible person he had spent the last few days with. He had wanted to tell him about her determination to learn to snowboard, how at times tears of frustration had misted her eyes, but she had refused to give up. He had wanted to tell him of his pride in watching her complete a run. He had wanted to tell him about how they had talked about his future, how she had helped him move closer to identifying a new purpose in life, her intelligent questions, her constant positivity and belief in him enabling him to begin the process of deciding on what he wanted to achieve. He had wanted to tell his father how they had spent hours talking over their meals, something he had never been capable of before, always too restless, too uncomfortable in his own skin.

Now, out in the corridor, moving away from the sound of the orchestra in the ballroom, he took out his phone and began to dial Alice's number, but outside the library he came to a stop. Her back to him, Alice was pulling a book from a high-up shelf. Her hair was tied up into a loose bun. The strapless dress was cut low at the back, exposing the delicate workings of her shoulder blades and the neat, fragile bumps of her spine. The skirt of the gown, embellished with crystals, glittered in the low lights of the library.

He stepped inside. 'I'm glad you're continuing to take my advice to wear red,' he growled, remembering her cry earlier, how her legs had trembled uncontrollably as he had kissed and caressed her thighs. He pushed away the thought that what they were doing, the constant kisses and touches, the endless caressing and teasing, were almost more intimate than actually sleeping together.

She whipped around, blushing. 'I look like a Christmas decoration.'

Somebody chuckled behind him. With a start he spun around to find his father sitting on a sofa. Alice went and sat on the sofa opposite him. Both Alice and his father looked to him, waiting for him to say something.

He backed towards the door. 'I just came to see if you're okay and apologise for not spending time with you—Kara asked me to go and speak to the staff from her new offices in Sri Lanka and Auckland. They are rolling out a peer programme in both countries and it was encouraging to hear about the impact it is already having.' He came to a stop, feeling crazily emotional remembering some of the stories he had heard from the staff of teenagers alone and isolated, struggling with mental-health issues. He cleared his throat, hating to feel so vulnerable in front of his father. He looked at Alice. 'I need to go and speak to the guests in the ballroom; do join me when you are free.'

Alice patted the space beside her. 'Why don't you come and chat with us for five minutes first?'

His father sat back in his seat and studied him. It would be so much easier to go back to the ballroom. Be distracted by light-hearted chat and banter. Have a few drinks.

Alice's gaze met his and with the slightest of nods she silently said, *This is the right thing to do.*

He went and sat beside her. Alice smiled in his father's direction. 'Your father, His Highness, very kindly has been giving me an outline of your family history.' She threw him a teasing look. 'You're descended from warrior kings—no wonder you need to have challenges in your life.'

His father made a disapproving sound. Alice turned her attention back to him. 'You must be proud of Luis winning the World Series.'

His father mumbled something that was indecipherable.

'Did you ever go and watch one of his races?'

Luis stared at Alice. Where was she going with this?

'I was never invited.'

He stared at his father. 'I never thought you'd want to come.'

His father gave an indignant snort. 'Of course I would have liked to see you race—if I had been asked.'

He couldn't believe this. 'Why didn't you come anyway?'

His father's nostrils flared. 'You didn't want me there.'

'I never said that.'

His father gave a bitter laugh. 'You never said anything to me, full stop.'

Luis sat forward in his seat, anger and disbelief firing inside of him. 'That's because you stole all of the airtime criticising me.'

His father's mouth hardened. And then with a jolt of shock he realised that there were tears in his father's eyes. His father looked at Alice and then at him, as if deciding whether to respond. Eventually he said, 'Did you have to pick such a dangerous sport? And not just that—after your mother died, why did you insist on riding her horse? Even though I had banned you from doing so?'

He closed his eyes. 'It wasn't Cassini's fault; something caused him to bolt. Mum adored him. She'd have wanted us to care for him. She certainly wouldn't have wanted you to sell him.'

'I had no option but to sell him when you kept defying my orders.'

About to fire back a furious retort, he felt Alice's hand touch his thigh and he swallowed his words.

'Can you understand how difficult it was for me to see you riding him?'

He winced at the pain in his father's voice and quietly admitted, 'I hadn't realised… I wasn't thinking about you.'

He waited for his father to deliver some barbed comment, point out just how selfish and irresponsible he was, but instead his father asked quietly, 'Are you returning to powerboating—is that why you want to speak to Edwin and me tomorrow?'

Should he say yes, that he was going back to the life and career he loved? Beside him Alice shifted, the red material of her skirt landing to cover one of his knees. The past few days with her, the intimacy, the calmness of his days, how much he had wanted to find her just now—all of a sudden he was no longer certain the life he thought he loved so much was all that he really thought it was.

'I'm not sure… I want to discuss it with you and Edwin tomorrow.'

His father stood. 'Edwin needs your help—the role of monarch is becoming ever more demanding in the changing global environment.' He moved towards the door but before he left he added, 'And Edwin is right—it's time that we became a family again.' With a nod in Alice's direction he said, 'It's been nice to see you again, Alice; please come back and see us some time soon.'

They sat in silence, Luis's father's footsteps out in the corridor fading away.

'He likes you.'

She considered him. 'Why do you say that?'

'He doesn't usually speak to people outside his inner circle.'

Alice considered that for a moment. 'I think he was just looking for an excuse to get away from the ballroom—the music is pretty loud.'

'How did you both end up speaking in the first place?'

She laughed at his puzzlement. 'I just went over and started chatting to him; he looked bored.' She stopped and gasped. 'Did I just commit some social faux pas in approaching him?'

Luis grinned. 'Perhaps…but the fact that he remembered your name means you're forgiven in his eyes.'

Confused, she asked, 'What's the significance of him remembering my name?'

'He deliberately calls people by the wrong name when he's unhappy with them.' Leaning his head against the back of the sofa, he added on a sigh, 'I had no idea that he wanted me to invite him to my races…' He looked in her direction. 'Am I right in thinking he was saying that he was worried about my safety?'

She nodded.

Sitting upright, he took her hand in his. 'I'm sorry you had to sit through that conversation, and that I've spent so little time with you tonight.'

Threading her fingers through his, she answered truthfully, 'I hope things work out for you, Luis—that the differences in your family can be healed and that you find a career that will fulfil and challenge you.'

'I'm glad you're here.'

Her heart melted at the tenderness in his voice. 'I'm glad I'm here too.' But then, trying to gather herself, remembering that tomorrow she would have to go back to reality, she forced herself to smile and added, 'It's not often that I'll get to wear a designer dress and hang out with A-list celebrities. I can't wait to see Toni's expression when I tell her.'

Standing, he helped her up and with the sexiest of grins asked, 'Have you ever danced with a prince at a ball?'

She smiled. 'No, I can't say that I have.'

He led her to the ballroom, where elaborate cascades of white flowers hung from the ceiling, filling the room with a delicate floral scent. The lights were down low, and the orchestra was playing a slow number. They moved onto the dance floor, Luis saying hello to everyone they passed, and as they danced he continued to acknowledge those around them. But between them there was a private dance going on. Every touch, every look held a significance. His fingers ran down her spine. Hers touched the cords of his neck. His mouth beside her ear, he whispered, 'As much as I love that dress, I have to admit I can't help but fantasise about you wearing those sandals and nothing else.'

She blushed at the sensuous tone in his voice. But then frustration and bewilderment that these were their last hours together had her step away and say, 'Follow me.'

She led him out onto the terrace, heading in the direction of the bright lights of the Ferris wheel. But that was not her destination. Instead, she led him off the path and into a copse of trees, walking until they could go no further.

She backed him up against a tree trunk. And admitted, 'There never was a dare.'

He raised an eyebrow, waiting for her to further explain her confession.

'That first time I kissed you, here in the palace… nobody dared me. But I had to do it, I had to kiss you. I had never met someone I so badly wanted to kiss in my entire life. And it had nothing to do with your beard.' Desire was stripping away her every inhibition. She didn't care about the past or the future. For the next few hours she wanted to be truly alive. She wanted to forget every reason why this was a bad idea and live within this man's skin. She wanted to know every part of him.

He considered her words. Nodded sombrely. 'Thank you for sharing that with me.'

'I want to kiss you again.'

'No.'

She blinked. No! What did he mean? They had been making out for the past week.

His arm reaching around her waist, he whipped her around so that it was her back to the tree. The bark was smooth and warm. Monrosa was a long way away from the crisp coldness of Verbier and the dampness of London.

He placed a hand on the trunk, hit her with a dark look. 'This time, I'm the one doing the kissing. But be warned…it will be nothing like your kiss. This kiss…is going to be demanding and hard,' he paused, his mouth reaching for her ear, 'and perhaps even a little brutal.'

Her heart thumped against her chest. She was scared, but in a totally sensual way.

His eyes flashed. 'So, do you want me to kiss you?'

She nodded, her heart beating even faster.

His finger resting at the base of her throat for a moment, he traced a slow path down over her necklace and into the valley of her breasts.

Her back arched.

His mouth touched her neck. She inhaled the earthy tones of his aftershave, her head spinning as his mouth moved up her throat in a slow, tortuous path.

When his mouth reached hers, he drew back and whispered, 'You're extraordinary,' and then his lips were on hers. Soft. Light.

She moaned. 'You said it would be brutal.'

'Patience,' he whispered back.

His mouth parted hers. She gasped at the wonder of the heat of his mouth. One hand was on her waist, the other running over the outline of her breast, sending pulses of pleasure the length of her body.

His tongue touched hers, but it was all too teasing, too light.

She panted out, 'More. Harder.'

He pulled back. 'Are you sure?'

She nodded. His expression hardened with dark passion. His mouth found hers again. Demanding and in control, deep and seeking, sending a feverish heat through her. His hands wrapped around her wrists, drawing her arms above her head, and he pinned them to the trunk with one hand. Her body arched into the rigid planes of his. Her head spun. His mouth continued to wreak havoc on hers.

She arched even more when his free hand tugged down the front of her dress. She gasped as her nipples felt the warm air of the night. Her legs buckled when his mouth left hers and, dipping down, his lips slowly circled over her breast in ever-decreasing circles of tender kisses until his tongue grazed over her nipple. She cried out, her body buckling, needing the pressure of his weight, needing him. His mouth sucked on her nipple. She writhed, wanting to free her arms, wanting to touch him. He applied more pressure with his mouth. She gasped. His free hand touched her other nipple. She was already about to come apart.

'I want you... I need you tonight, Luis,' she whispered.

For a moment she thought he hadn't heard her, but,

lifting his head, he drew her dress back up over her breasts and he gently released her arms. He let out a sigh, touched his hand to her cheek, the passion in his eyes softening. He looked at her with such tenderness that she wanted to scream.

'I would like that more than anything in this world, but it would be wrong—'

She interrupted him, undone by his gentleness, 'Why? Why would it be wrong?' She stopped and let out a bitter laugh. 'Or am I getting what happens between us every single time we're in each other's company wrong?'

He considered her for a moment before asking, 'Why now?'

Desire and emotion had her speak without thinking. 'Because I know we have no future but that doesn't mean we can't have now. Because I'm about to explode with frustration and I'm so turned on by you that I actually want to cry.' She pushed away from the tree, her heart beating, beating, beating against her chest, and added, 'Because you make me feel safe.'

She moved to the edge of the copse but before she walked out into the open she turned and glanced at Luis. Her heart sank. He was watching her with concern, all evidence of passion and desire erased from his expression.

CHAPTER NINE

LUIS CURSED AS Lars Hendrick, an old university friend, potted the black. Placing the billiard cue back in the rack, he doled out his bet to a grinning Lars. Following the midnight fireworks the ball had ended over an hour ago and, as per tradition, all the diehard partygoers had decamped to the games rooms to continue the party with more dancing and drinking. He looked around at those out on the temporary dance floor and the loud groups chatting animatedly. He should go and join them. But instead he hung back.

Alice had said goodnight to him the moment the ball had ended. After their kiss in the woods he had caught up with her and persuaded her to ride the Ferris wheel with him, and then they had danced together again. And the whole performance had turned him inside out.

He wanted to lie naked next to her. Worship her body. But what if he hurt her?

He thought back to her gentle presence when he had spoken to his father earlier. His heart tightened. He had never thought to invite his father to his races. He had assumed he wouldn't want to attend. But what if the real truth of not inviting him was more to do with how frightened he was that his father would throw the invite in his face? Ever since his mother had died and his father had grown angry and detached, he had been waiting and fearing his rejection. And a self-perpetuating cycle of behaviour had evolved between them where he would make a preventive strike to either force his father's hand to push him away, or he would close down, not allowing his father any opportunity to hurt him.

The voices and music around him faded into the background as his mind became a whirl of uncomfortable thoughts. He went to the bar and fixed himself a whiskey. He didn't want to hurt Alice by sleeping with her. But what if there was more to it than that? What if he was scared of laying his soul on the line by sleeping with her, only to have her walk away?

He closed his eyes. Rocked by his own thoughts. He opened them again, knowing that the sensible thing to do was to go out onto the dance floor and lose himself in the music and the meaningless chatter. Once again, he should run away from everything inside of him.

But instead he pushed his untouched drink away and went and climbed the stairs to the guest wing.

He stood outside her door, wondering if he should wait until morning. He was terrified. Terrified of getting this all wrong. He undid his bow tie, opened the collar of his shirt. His rational self knew that he shouldn't be here. But his heart knew the truth. No doubt others would tell him that he was crazy, that there was no way he could feel this way so quickly. That he was only confusing his feelings for Alice with lust. He ran a hand through his hair. Dragged in a long, slow breath. And knocked on her door.

Minutes passed before she eventually answered. He took in the *Our lace* jersey she had changed into, her scrubbed face and the toothbrush in her hand.

She backed away, allowing him to enter. She touched the jersey. 'I was about to go to bed…'

He wanted to take her in his arms, kiss away the beads of water lingering on her hairline from washing her face. And no matter just how adorable she looked in the soccer jersey, he wanted to lift it over her head and see for the very first time her naked body. And, despite the desperate build-up in his body, he knew he would control it enough to make love to her slowly and tenderly, needing to show her how much he worshipped her.

But there were things he needed to say first. He gestured for her to sit on the bed and he pulled a low antique bedroom chair in front of her and sat too.

She sat looking at him, her eyes wide, the colour in her cheeks draining.

This clearly wasn't what she was expecting.

A whoosh of affection for her stole his words away. He touched his hand against her bare knee. He cursed once again at the large bruise on her thigh. He placed his hand over it, wanting to heal it.

He needed to talk, tell her. For a person whose school reports always contained the feedback, *Luis needs to stop talking and concentrate more,* and who spent his days constantly chatting, only now did he realise how little he actually said. In the past week he had spoken more honestly than he had done in his lifetime. But now, facing her, gaze to gaze, the hard shell of his true feelings cracked open—to actually share them with her felt like stepping into an abyss.

She pulled back from him, her expression growing wary. He opened his mouth, wondering what on earth he was doing. 'I want us to make love…'

She frowned. 'Well, it sure doesn't—'

He interrupted her, 'I know I'm messing this up, but there's something you need to know first.'

She sighed. 'There's another woman, isn't there?' She said it in a teasing tone, the accusation of the past no longer there, but clearly wanting to defuse the tension between them as much as he wanted to.

'You well know that there isn't.' He was finding it impossible to breathe. 'Before we make love, I want you to know that I'm in love with you and want us to be together, to be in a relationship.'

Alice laughed. She could hear herself. She knew she should stop but something had gone wrong in her brain. A defence mechanism of some sort had gone into overdrive.

Luis was staring at her, perplexed.

No, don't look confused. Don't look hurt. Don't look as though you actually meant those words. You can't love me. You simply can't. This is all too much. Too fast. Why are you telling me that you love me? What's really behind those words? My dad would yank my mum's hair until she screamed, punch her, threaten her, but then when the fury subsided he would hold her and plead his love. I don't want to hear that you love me because I might believe you and give you my heart, only for you to destroy it. This isn't what was supposed to happen. Laugh with me. Tell me you were only kidding.

But he didn't. And she blurted out, 'Don't be ridiculous, of course you don't love me.'

His head jerked. As though she had slapped him. 'Why would I say it if I didn't mean it?'

Panic had her ask, 'Have you been drinking?'

He sat back in his chair, his expression turning to granite. 'No.'

Alice jumped off the bed. She paced the room, trying not to give in to the temptation of opening the bedroom door and bolting. 'You don't love me, Luis…' She waved vaguely between them, attempted a smile. 'What we have is lust and chemistry.'

She waited for him to smile back and agree. She waited for him to make this simple and uncomplicated. Why couldn't they just sleep together like other people? Why couldn't they just revel in the physical, the passion of deep attraction?

But instead, his expression proud, he asked quietly, 'Why don't you believe me?'

She threw her hands into the air. 'Why don't I believe you? Because you don't really mean it. You can't. You're telling me that you love me and want to be in a relationship despite having previously told me that you wanted to remain single.' She paused, and looked at him for long seconds, wondering if she knew him at all. 'Or am I giving too much significance to that word love? Perhaps you use it easily. Perhaps you have said it to every woman you have slept with.'

He walked to her bedroom window. She hadn't pulled the curtains and had opened the window, wanting to sleep to the sound of the nearby sea. He stared out into the darkness for a moment before turning and regarding her, his expression still as hard as stone. And she was reminded that he was descended from proud warrior kings. 'You are the first woman I have ever said those words to.'

She closed her eyes, trying to take a hold of the hot panic running through her. Love was fickle and manipulative. She had had a childhood of witnessing how it could be turned on you, how your love could be used as a weapon to destroy you. She opened her eyes. 'You don't love me. You're looking for something to take the place of the career and life you're leaving. You're looking for something that will take the sting of returning to Monrosa away. You're looking for a new distraction. And that distraction just happens to be me.'

White noise crowded Luis's head.

She doesn't believe me. She doesn't believe me.

'Do you trust in anything that I say?'

She folded her arms, her expression shut off. 'Now... I'm not sure.'

His throat tightened. He should walk away. While he still had some dignity. But questions burned inside of him. 'What has the past week been to you...has it meant anything?'

She backed away. 'This is too much. I thought we were friends; I don't know how to cope with this.'

'Is that all you thought we had—friendship?' He stalked the room, adrenaline pounding through him.

She rounded on him. 'What do you want me to say?' She gestured vaguely between them. 'Why are you rushing this…why are you rushing me? Why are you backing me into a corner?'

He had to get out. Now. Before he said anything else. Shame was creeping along his veins, shutting down his capacity to think. 'Forget that I said anything.'

She dropped her hands. 'Oh, Luis, why did you have—?'

He cut across her. 'You're leaving tomorrow?'

He didn't know himself if that was a question or a statement.

She looked at him with a helpless expression. 'That's what was planned.'

He nodded. 'It's for the best.' It felt as though he was watching himself from a distance. The pain inside of him shutting down everything but a forceful need to protect himself.

Alice watched Luis walk to the door, place his hand on the door handle.

Go. Give me some space.

She wanted to crawl into bed and hide under the bedclothes the way she had used to as a child to drown out her parents' arguments. She longed for a dark, warm space where she wasn't under attack. She wanted to curl herself into a tight ball and hum. Calm the panic that was crowding her head.

His hand twisted the handle.

No! Don't go. I'm sorry. I believe you. But am I crazy to even think that? I want to believe that you do love me. I want to trust you. I want to trust myself... I think I've fallen in love with you too. But is all this misguided, so full of misjudgement and crossed purposes, all so rushed and forced that we'll only hurt one another?

He opened the door. Looked back in her direction. As though waiting for her to say something. But no words would come to her. She was frozen by indecision and the fear that she was being used and manipulated.

He closed the door, his expression rigid. Tears burned the backs of her eyes. What had she done?

CHAPTER TEN

THE WINE BAR door opened, letting in a blast of icy air. Alice craned to see if it was Toni but let out a disappointed breath when she saw that it was a group of office workers. She checked her phone. Nothing. She settled back into her seat, still pretending to be checking for messages and not unintentionally listening in to the conversations of the couples seated either side of her. She sipped her coffee. And tried to process the fact that she had done it. She had submitted her thesis that very afternoon. She still had the last hurdle of the PhD defence presentation to face in a few months' time, but for now she was going to celebrate.

Her phone pinged.

A message from Toni appeared on the screen. She was still in London. She had missed her flight to Dublin. Concerned, Alice typed back a message, asking if everything was okay. Toni messaged back saying that she was stuck in work and couldn't talk but that she was so sorry to let her down.

Leaving the bar, Alice shivered at the biting wind. She had managed to lose her new red hat somewhere in the university and her coat was no defence against the arctic cold sweeping through the streets of Dublin.

A celebration party in honour of Luis's championship win was taking place right now. Alice ducked her head down, fighting to walk into the unrelenting wind. Had it been sunny in Monrosa today? Would they still have daylight? Kara had sent her an invite. She had been taken aback by just how happy she had been that Luis's win was being celebrated in Monrosa...and how desperately sad she was that she wouldn't be there. For a few hours she had contemplated accepting the invite but in the end she had messaged her apologies to Kara, not wanting to take away from the day for Luis...and not sure she could handle seeing him again.

She missed him. Despite having buried herself in her PhD for every waking moment, she missed him with every fibre of her being. She missed his smiles, the way he stirred her tea. She missed catching him regarding her with what seemed like open affection and fondness. She missed the feel of his hand cradling the back of her head when he hugged her. Was that what being in love meant? Missing the other person so deeply you felt as though you had lost yourself? Waking in the middle of the night thinking you heard their voice whispering something to you? She didn't know what love was. Her dad had said he loved her mum. And she had so desperately wanted to believe him. She had wanted to believe that things would get better, that they could be a family. But her dad had used their love and turned it on them, crushing their hopes and dreams. What if Luis really did love her, for now, but what if that changed? What if he stopped loving her? What if he left her with all the scars of panic and zero self-esteem that her mum was still battling?

The entrance door to her apartment block was sticking again and it took her ages to force it open. Inside she gathered up a scattering of mail, which one of her fellow apartment-block dwellers had clearly stepped on, given the boot-shaped imprint that was across some of the envelopes.

She spotted his envelope immediately. It wasn't hard. The heavy cream paper was in stark contrast to the cheap white envelopes from various banks and telecom companies.

She studied the handwriting, the same large, looping letters that she had first seen on the gift card attached to his Christmas present to her. Would she ever find peace? Would her life ever stop feeling so empty? One day, would she learn to face the future with enthusiasm again? Would colour replace the now constant greyness?

Her studio apartment was like an icebox. She checked her boiler and as she suspected the water pressure had dropped again and it was out of action. She topped it up, knowing she should contact her landlord to complain but she didn't have the energy.

Coat still on, she opened the fridge and shut it. From upstairs came footsteps and muffled music and laughter. The girls who shared the apartment were getting ready for a night out. There went her night's sleep.

She contemplated ringing her mum for a chat but instead switched on a side lamp, flicked off all the other lights in the room and collapsed onto her bed.

When would the feeling of numbness leave her? It was six weeks since she had last seen Luis and it felt as though she was living life in a daze. She had somehow miraculously managed to finish her thesis and not get fired from her job, but it felt as though she was sleepwalking through life.

She missed him. It felt as if a part of her was missing. She missed his touches, his laughter, his teasing, his energy, his kindness. But had all those things been real? Had they all been an act, a way of distracting him from his own life? She rolled onto her side, curling her legs up. Had he been using her...perhaps not even consciously? Maybe he had somehow misguidedly convinced himself that he loved her...but that wouldn't have stopped him from breaking her heart at some point.

Her eyes settled on the pile of cream envelopes peeking out from the top of her kitchen cupboards. She should put the newest one up there...but that meant dragging out a chair to reach the top. The reason why she had stashed them there in the first place was that if they were easy to get to then in a moment of weakness she would succumb to reading them.

What was she going to do with them? She had said she would decide once she had submitted her thesis. Including today's letter there were seven letters in total. If she binned them, she could move on with her life. She closed her eyes. But would she always be haunted by not knowing what was in them?

Seven letters. It had to mean something that he had taken the time to write them all to her.

She dragged out the kitchen chair, climbed up and took the letters down. Sitting on the sofa, she placed his newest letter to the back of the pile. They were all now in date order. She pulled the first letter open.

She read it. Checked the envelope to see if she had missed a page. And then read his brief one-page letter again. Dated just under a month ago, it described a trek he had taken with Edwin and Kara into the mountains of Monrosa. And that was all. She opened the next letter. This letter described his agreement with Edwin and his father as to what his new role would be. She nodded as she read the letter, seeing what a good fit his appointment as Chair of Monrosian Sports and Tourism was. The third and fourth letters described his travels throughout Europe as he promoted Monrosa and spoke at mental-health conferences about the benefits of sport and exercise to well-being. She was happy for him. She really was. But not once did he talk about them…about their week together. Sure, he asked how she was, asked if she would write to him, but apart from that, these letters were distant. Why had he even written them in the first place?

She ripped the fifth letter open. Irritated. Disappointed.

What did you want, Alice? Did you really expect them to be love letters? Letters begging to see you again?

She took the letter out of the envelope, a photograph falling onto her lap. And her heart melted. It was a photo of Luis with the cutest ever dachshund. His letter said that he had adopted him from a local shelter and that his name was Elfo. She stared at the photograph. Stared at him, the man who had insisted on staying in London to keep her company. The man who had made her laugh, sigh, feel more alive than she had ever done in her entire life. She stared at the photo and wondered if somebody was capable of pretending care, kindness and generosity to the level he had, without the mask of pretence slipping? She stared at his photo, tears blurring her vision. She was in love with him. She was in love with him for everything that was magnificent about him. But she still didn't know if his love for her was real.

She opened the next letter. Tears blurred her eyes

again when she read about the meeting he'd attended in the Young Adults Together London office to officially launch Stay Strong, their exercise-for-health programme, and his devastation as he fully grasped the pain some of their clients were battling on a daily basis. The feelings of otherness, of not fitting in or belonging to the world, the loneliness. And she cried even more to read of his determination to try to reach as many people as possible, to let people know that they were loved and valued and cherished for their uniqueness.

The seventh letter was short. She read it time and time again, trying to take every word in.

Dear Alice,
Our last time together was not how things should have ended. There are so many things I still need to say to you. Will you consider meeting me in Paris? In the hope that you will, I've enclosed flight and hotel details for you.

I dearly hope you will come, but if you don't I will not write again.

I hope you find the happiness you deserve.

Thank you for a Christmas I will always cherish.
Luis

She stared at the dates on the tickets. He wanted to meet her next week, on February the fourteenth. Valentine's Day.

She held all seven letters in her hands, weighing them, weighing their significance. He had taken the time to write to her. He had made no demands. Instead his letters had been considered glimpses into his life. They had been generous and kind.

And what had she done in return? Shame crept along her limbs. She had accused him of looking for a distraction. When the same could be levelled at her. Weren't his appearance and the days they had spent together a distraction from her PhD? She had embraced his company and the chemistry between them as eagerly as he had. She had initiated and participated in all those emotionally and physically intimate moments as equally as he had. And when he had opened his heart to her, she had shut down like a coward. She hadn't trusted him enough to tell him of the fears that held her hostage to a life so carefully led it was devoid of all colour and hope.

She looked again at the flight ticket. Would she go? She stood and paced the room, a burning anger towards her dad and her own inability to leave the past behind growing in intensity.

'Are you enjoying yourself?'

Luis turned to Kara's quietly spoken question, excusing himself from the group of sports agents and travel-company CEOs he had been speaking to.

Kara waited for his answer expectantly, this party having been her idea. At the beginning, the garden party had had a dual purpose—to celebrate his World Championship win and to formally announce his appointment both as Chair of the Monrosian Sports and Tourism Department and Global Sports Ambassador for Young Adults Together. But then, realising that the party could serve a wider purpose, he had expanded its scope to act as a showcase for everything that Monrosa could offer as a sports and wellness destination.

But the party was also Kara and Edwin's way to privately acknowledge his return to Monrosa...and the family. And Kara's attempt to cheer him up. Even though he continually insisted that he was perfectly happy, they both knew that that was a lie.

He hugged Kara into him and said, 'Immensely.' He gestured about him; the palace's gardens had been transformed into a celebration of everything that was wonderful about the island. 'How couldn't I when you have given me the best party since time began?'

He might have suggested that the party celebrate Monrosa, but it had been Kara who pulled it together in his absence, as he had been travelling abroad for much of the past month, promoting the island as the perfect destination both for professional athletes and amateurs, thanks to its climate and already excellent sports facilities that would be expanded in the next five years in line with the new sustainable-tourism strategy he was devising with his senior department strategists.

In the food area, all the island's leading chefs had come together to produce a five-course tasting menu, using ingredients only sourced on the island. The food producers and their families were helping serve the food to the guests, using the opportunity to promote and educate on their produce. Local choirs and musicians were providing the entertainment. Staff and volunteers from the Monrosian Environmental Protection Agency were giving walking tours of the palace's waterfront, explaining the importance of Monrosa's unique biodiversity and Edwin's strategy for protecting it. And down by the marina, in the late evening sunshine, the various sports bodies were giving demonstrations of the facilities available in Monrosa.

Kara smiled at him, but he could tell that she didn't quite believe his insistence that he was having a good time. 'I sent Alice an invite...she messaged to say that she was tied up with her thesis.'

He shifted away from Kara, closing his eyes for a moment, letting the winter sun heat his face. Trying to shift the knot of disappointment out of his throat. He could have told Kara that Alice wouldn't respond. He had sent her numerous letters over the past month and had heard nothing in return. Not even a message telling him to stop writing to her.

It was close to six weeks since he had last seen her. On the morning of New Year's Day he had escorted her to the car that was waiting to bring her from the palace to the airport, both of them pretending that the night before hadn't happened, and that they were simply friends...or perhaps acquaintances, saying goodbye to one another after spending a few uneventful days in one another's company. They had shaken hands, kissed each other on the cheek and said goodbye, only sharing a fleeting glance before the car had pulled away.

And he had gone back into the palace and, instead of attending his scheduled meeting with his father and Edwin to discuss his future, he had packed a bag, commandeered the royal jet and flown to Courchevel, where he had spent a week with friends. During the day he had skied every black run in the resort and by night he had partied hard. But it hadn't worked. He hadn't been able to outrun his hurt, the humiliation of having declared his one-sided love. And then there had been the guilt—the guilt of knowing that he was letting Edwin and his father down. But also the guilt that he was letting himself down. After a week he had returned to Monrosa, knowing he needed to find a new path for himself in life.

One that would give him a purpose and meaning. One that might fill the vacuum inside of him.

Now he gently asked Kara, 'How are you doing?'

Kara blinked hard. 'Okay.'

He placed a hand on her shoulder and drew her into his side. Affection and concern clogged his throat.

'It's easier now that you are here,' Kara added.

A few days after he had returned to Monrosa, whilst he had still been thrashing out exactly what his role would be, his father still advocating hard for him to take a position in the treasury despite his objections, he had walked into Edwin's office and an argument between Edwin and Kara. Taken aback by how distressed they had both seemed, his first instinct had been to back out of the room, but something had told him to stay. At first they had both tried to deny that they were having an argument in the first place, and then they each claimed that the other person was overly committed to their work… and eventually, asking Kara for her permission to do so, Edwin had told him of their struggle to conceive a baby.

It had been a huge turning point in his life. Edwin and Kara confiding something so personal, trusting him with it, had deeply affected him. He saw the power and connection of family. The power of being there for one another. And, coming from that conversation, he knew he wanted to take over some of their responsibilities—in his role as Head of Sports and Tourism he would use his past experience and contacts to forge a different type of tourism, away from the mass tourism of the past to a sustainable model.

Studying him for a moment, Kara asked gently, 'And how about you, Luis—are you okay?'

A few months ago he would have made a quip,

shrugged off her question with defensive humour. But Edwin's and Kara's honesty, his own rawness since falling in love with Alice, the honesty, the truthfulness he had shared with her in the days they spent together, had him answer, 'Everything went wrong with Alice… I don't know what to do.'

'Listen to your own instinct,' Kara said, then, blinking hard, almost but not quite pushing away a gleam of tears, she added, 'There's always hope.'

He swallowed hard as he watched Kara walk away, knowing that she was thinking of her and Edwin's much longed-for baby. And then he thought about his final letter to Alice that he had sent yesterday. It was his last throw of the dice. At times he wondered why he was putting himself through all of this—what if his instinct that he had told Alice way too soon that he loved her was wrong and in fact she simply didn't love him?

He looked around the party. To the friends and colleagues and old rivals who had travelled from all over the world to celebrate with him. To the locals who had known him as a teenage rebel and had finally forgiven him for the all-night parties he had used to throw in the boat house, the noise travelling across the harbour and keeping half the city awake, causing a flurry of complaints to the palace. He saw his father and Edwin, involved in some grave discussion, his father still reluctantly letting go of power. Relationships were messy and complex…but the essence of life when you got them right.

CHAPTER ELEVEN

THE EXIT DOORS at the airport arrivals hall glided open and Alice stepped out onto the concourse on a wave of uncertainty. Should she turn around? Take the return flight back to Dublin? She studied the overhead signs, one directing her to the taxi rank, another towards Departures and the safe life she knew back in Dublin.

'Miss O'Connor, welcome to Paris. I'm here to take you to your hotel.'

She whipped around at the softly spoken words to find a tall, dark-haired man, entirely dressed in black.

'His Highness Prince Luis sent me.' He took hold of her suitcase and gestured for her to follow him.

For a moment she considered wrangling the suitcase from him, but the man was built like a tank. She was so confused, her ability to think straight a thing of the past, fear taking over instead. She wasn't even certain why she was here. She still had no faith in her judgement. But she knew she had to have some form of closure with Luis. She so desperately wanted to believe that he loved her but a voice in her head was mocking her gullibility. This wasn't how love was portrayed in the movies. This was messy and emotional and so damn scary that she was barely holding everything together.

Their car was parked directly outside the arrivals hall in a no-parking zone. Two airport security men were standing by it. For a moment she thought they were about to ticket them but instead they shook her escort's hand and wandered off. And then she realised it was a diplomatic car.

Inside the car, the driver had the engine idling. Her escort opened the rear door for her and once she was settled he sat in the front beside the driver. She studied the back of both men's heads, it slowly dawning on her that she had seen both of them in Monrosa. Of course—they were Luis's protection team.

She sank into her seat, hoping that neither of them had witnessed her ambush and kiss him that first time at Kara's wedding, or worse still had watched her drag him into the woods on New Year's Eve. They drove in silence into the centre of Paris. At her hotel, The Montclar, she was met by the general manager, who took her directly to her suite, where he informed her that His Highness Prince Luis had arranged for them to dine in an hour's time in the privacy of his penthouse suite.

She nodded and smiled, taking the access key to the private lift that serviced the penthouse, assuring him that she would make her own way there, her smile only fading as her door clunked shut.

She counted to ten. Threw off her jacket. And opened the door again and rushed to the stairwell. She bolted down the five floors and into the reception area. Two protection officers were standing at the penthouse lift. They eyed her dubiously. No doubt his dates in the past would have worn something more glamorous than just jeans and a sweatshirt. She waved the access key at them and stated her name. They exchanged a look, but then one of the men pressed the call button. The private lift arrived within seconds. And its ascent to the twentieth floor passed in the blink of an eye. She pulled back her shoulders as the doors opened, expecting to encounter yet more security personnel standing in a corridor, but instead the doors opened onto a vast sitting room. And to Luis, who was sitting at a desk, working through a pile of paperwork.

He was wearing a white open-necked shirt, the grey suit jacket lying on the arm of a sofa matching his grey trousers. Her heart fluttered and danced to see him. She closed her eyes for a moment, exasperated with herself. Her heart knew nothing. It was a soft, squidgy thing that gave way too easily to lust and easy compliments and promises.

She stepped into the room. 'I'm not in the mood for dinner.'

He stared at her.

She moved towards the desk. Folded her arms. 'So what did you want to talk about?'

'You're angry.'

'No, I'm not.'

She waited for him to say something but he just continued watching her. She clapped her mouth shut against the words bubbling inside of her desperate for an escape. She hated this new side to her, this irrational passion. Life had been so much easier before when silence had come so easily to her. But Luis had unleashed something inside of her and it scared her just how out of control it made her feel.

Why wasn't he saying anything? This meeting was his idea. He was the chatty one. The one who always knew what to say. Panicking, she turned away, afraid of the emotions she was feeling. But at the lift she spun around and admitted, 'Do you know what? Yes, I'm angry. And I hate it.' She moved across the room, stopped in front of the desk, all sense of pride abandoning her. 'I'm angry because I'm here and I don't really know why I came.'

Luis's heart was pounding. For the past week he had been dreading the prospect of Alice not turning up. He had tried preparing himself for the disappointment. And in the hope she would come he had also run through endless scenarios for how he would handle her silence and upset and wariness. But what he had not anticipated was this anger. She was practically sizzling with it. And he was at a loss as to how to deal with it.

Standing in front of him, wearing her trademark black jeans and a black sweatshirt, her silver eyes shining bright with emotion, her cheeks hot, she was throwing down a gauntlet that he didn't understand. How was he supposed to react? What was she looking for from him? He scrambled for a foothold in understanding how to react. And then the words came to him. They were on the tip of his tongue, ready to be uttered, but he held back, knowing he was possibly going to make the worst mistake of his life. He opened his mouth, his heart, his pride, and said quietly, 'You're here because you love me.'

She snorted. 'Do you reckon?' She knew she was being nasty and irrational, something deep inside of her screaming for protection.

'Being in love is scary.'

'Scary? I'll tell you what is scary.' Inside, she shouted

at herself to stop. Why was she doing this? Why was she fighting him? 'Scary is not knowing if you are being duped, if you are reading a situation all wrong. Scary is never being able to trust your own judgement. Scary is being pushed to say things you're not ready to say.' She paused for a breath, the fire inside of her dimming.

'And do you know what's scary for me?' he asked. 'Not being believed in. I've spent the past twenty years fighting my father's distrust. With you, I had thought it was different.'

She swallowed at the softness of his tone, the hurt in his voice. Her heart felt swollen with fear and love and confusion. 'How can I believe you?'

He looked down at his hands clasped before him on the desk. For a moment she had a vision of him walking towards the lift and opening its doors, telling her that their meeting was over. Panic turned her stomach over.

He lifted his head, his expression intense. 'Why can you believe me? How about the fact that you're the first person I have ever declared my love to? And not because I was scared of love in the past…but because I have never fallen for someone like I have for you.'

'We both know that your life is uncertain right now—what if you're confusing the need for certainty and security with love?'

His gaze narrowed, his expression confounded. 'I'll admit to struggling as to what my future direction would be when we met.' He flipped closed his laptop, his expression hard. 'But do you seriously think that I'm so lacking in character and self-understanding that I would open my heart to you just to have a distraction, a new purpose in life? Really? Do you think so little of me?'

His voice carried a barely contained fury. She braced

herself for the fear, for the panic that always hit her when faced with another person's anger. 'Why me, Luis? There are so many other women you could have chosen.'

His mouth tightened. 'Why you? Because you're the bravest, funniest, most intelligent, most contrary woman I have ever met.'

She stood. 'I'm a physical mess around you and I *hate* being so out of control. We could have…maybe we should have…maybe it would have doused the fire between us.'

He stood and moved around the desk with the slow, easy grace of a panther. His eyes bored into hers. 'You can say it, Alice. We should have slept together. Do you think that would have doused what's between us? It would have only made it worse. Do you think it was easy for me not to have slept with you? Do you think I didn't want to strip you naked and make love to you time and time again? Do you know how many times I fantasised about knocking on your bedroom door, or arriving on your doorstep in Dublin, and having sex with you?'

'What stopped you? Why did you push me away? Do you know how that made me feel?'

'I was trying to protect you.'

Her heart felt too big for her chest. She stepped back. Placed her hands on her hips. Testing him. Hating herself for being so needy. 'I didn't want your protection. I wanted your rawness, your desire. I yearned for you to want me without reason…the way I wanted you.'

He dipped his head, and then with a grunt he was moving towards her. He whipped her up in his arms and pushed her against the terrace door behind him, the uninterrupted view of the Eiffel Tower in the distance of no interest to either of them.

His mouth locked onto hers. His breath was hot, his tongue fierce. He wrapped her legs around his waist. She dug her fingers into his hair. Wanting to hurt him. Wanting this so badly.

He pushed up her sweatshirt, muttering a low curse on seeing her black lace bra beneath.

His mouth met hers again, his hand cupping her breast.

It was a duel of a kiss, sending her head and body spinning into a web of lust. Feeling every edge of resistance melt away, and terrified of that fact, she knew she had to test him even further. Breaking away she said, 'Admit it, this is just about lust to you. It was just a cat-and-mouse game to you, to really hook me and get me under your control.'

His hand cupped her breast even harder, and she bit his neck.

He growled. 'No! And you know that… I've never tried to control you. It's your past that's controlling you. Stop pushing me away. Believe in me. Believe in us.' He twisted his head and whispered, 'I love you…'

For a moment she considered giving in to him, giving in to what was in her heart, but the sceptic, the fighter in her, made her whisper, 'How long before you start regretting saying it, though…how long before the novelty of thinking you're in love with me wears off?' She bit down softly on his earlobe. If she pushed him away, if she forced him to see the truth of their relationship, she could save herself from the heartache of being rejected. Her dad never loved her despite all of his declarations and promises. What if Luis was the same?

He groaned. She bit down a little harder.

His thumb flicked across her nipple. Her head fell

backwards as a ripple of pleasure ran through her body. 'I'm a one-woman type of guy; I'm never going to stop loving you.'

She kissed him, her mouth demanding, needing the connection her heart was too afraid to allow. What they had, the emotional connection, couldn't be real. It was too fantastical. Real life wasn't like this. Ending the kiss, she whispered, 'It's lust. Nothing more.'

His eyes met hers, passion and honour shining brightly. 'You're wrong.'

How could he be so certain? 'Aren't you scared?'

She cringed at her badly thought-out question, at the tremble in her voice. Hating the vulnerability she had failed to mask.

His forehead came to rest against hers, his unblinking autumnal eyes searching hers. 'I've never been more scared in my entire life. But for the last six weeks I have been miserable and I cannot contemplate life without you. I've missed you. I've missed your laughter, your smile, your body, the way you roll your eyes…' he paused and kissed her on the mouth, with a rough desperation she understood only too well, but when he pulled back the fire in his eyes was fading '…I've missed the sense of peace you bring to me. The calmness. The acceptance. I've been running away from myself for as long as I can remember, but with you, I've stopped running.' He paused, his voice breaking with emotion. 'Without you I'm not the person I want to be. I'm not the person I'm capable of being.'

He eased her away from the window, stepped back, but she followed and gathered him into her, her heart aching. Against his chest she whispered, 'I didn't want to believe that you loved me, because I couldn't understand why you would.' She drew back and shook her head. 'I'm an introverted control-freak virgin…could two people be more different? I'm broken, Luis. I'm not good for you. You deserve better. You deserve a woman who can love you blindly, who never doubts you.'

His hand touched her cheek. 'You are the calm to my chaos. You get me. I have never met someone who wants to know me like you do, who wants to get beneath the person I choose to show to the world.' Tension lines pulled at the corners of his eyes. 'I love you, Alice…but I need to know that you believe me when I say that. I cannot be in a relationship where I'm not believed.' He paused and planted a slow, tender kiss on her lips, his hands cupping her cheeks. 'Or in a relationship where my feelings are not reciprocated.' His voice dipped into a bare whisper. 'I understand why you are scared of love. Your dad left you so scarred by his actions I understand why you would find it difficult to love…' he stopped and let out a heavy breath, shrugging '…or perhaps I'm over-complicating this and your feelings for me just aren't the same. Maybe I'm not enough…'

Luis waited for her to speak, his heart breaking apart. He had done it again. He had rushed in with both feet, desperate to have her know how much he loved her… but even more desperate to hear that she loved him back. He closed his eyes, cursing himself. He had sworn to himself that this meeting would be calm and unrushed. But instead it was all passion and desperation. Was he, in truth, subconsciously handing her an excuse to back out of what was between them? He turned and looked out of the window. It was starting to rain, fat raindrops running down the glass and blurring the Eiffel Tower.

He walked over to the fireplace, suddenly feeling cold to the bone. He waited for her to speak, the fire behind the glass screen of the modern inset stove doing little to touch the chill in his body.

'You are enough…you are so much it scares me.' She spoke in a bare whisper, her wide eyes reflecting the fear in her voice. She came and stood in front of him, her arms wrapping about her waist. 'My dad hurt my mum so terribly, I'm terrified of ever being hurt like that.'

'I'd never—'

She interrupted him. 'I know you wouldn't. I know in my heart you wouldn't, but I have spent so many years protecting myself, hardening myself to a life where I would be alone, what happened between us was too intense for me to process.' She bit her lip, tears glistening in her eyes. He went to hold her but, shaking her head, she took a step backwards. 'No. I need to explain all of this to you.' She gave a shaky laugh. 'I had my life planned out. A life with little risk of having my heart broken. And then I meet you. And I was so incredibly cross at how attracted I was to you. I watched you in Monrosa's cathedral as you stood at Edwin's side the day he married, and you whispered something to him that had him smile and relax for a few moments and I was hooked. Even from that distance I was hooked by your kindness, your empathy, your energy. And later on you tried to help me when my sandal got stuck, but I was so overwhelmed I snapped at you.' She buried her face in her hands and groaned. 'And then I ambushed you and kissed you. You must have thought that I was crazy.'

He shook his head. 'It was the most wonderful kiss of my life.'

She smiled at that. 'I love you, Luis. I love your spontaneity, your optimism. I know I might grumble about it sometimes but that's only because you are pushing me to go outside my comfort zone, something I need to do.'

He wanted to grin. He wanted to whoop. But he needed, wanted to hear more from her. 'What future do you want for us, Alice?'

She frowned. Shrugged.

He waited.

She cleared her throat. 'I'm not sure…what do you think?'

He shook his head. 'You tell me.'

She frowned even more. 'Why?'

'You said that your dad played mind games with you, manipulated things to control you. Well, I want you to be in control of how this relationship evolves.'

'But that doesn't seem right…it should be equal…it…'

He shrugged. 'I will go at your pace.'

She let out a long, deep breath. 'I love you.'

He grinned. 'So you said. Now, what about our future?'

She bit her lip again. Blushed. She tilted her chin. 'I want to make love with you. I want to move to Monrosa and be with you. I want us to marry and grow old together. I want your babies.' She stopped and looked appalled. In a rush she said, 'Oh, that's not the type of future you meant…you look so shocked!'

He shook his head, fighting for words. And then he realised that the time for speaking was over. Lifting her up into the air, he twirled her around and then, lowering her, he whispered, 'I have never heard anything so perfect in all of my life.'

He kissed her long and slow, only breaking to lift her sweatshirt off. She undid the buttons of his shirt and dropped it to the floor, her hands moving over his bare skin with a slow reverence that kicked his desire up a dangerous notch.

He undid her bra, and stood back, wanting to etch this moment on his brain for ever. When he kissed the perfect pert shape of her breast she gasped, and gasped again when he undid the button of her jeans.

She kicked off her boots as he pulled her jeans down, his hands lingering over the soft curves of her hips and bottom. He laid her down on the rug before the fire, his mouth and fingers caressing every inch of her body, her gasps, the arching of her body, the feel of her hands raking through his hair, over his shoulders, driving him on.

But then, her eyes dazed, she pushed him onto his back and fumbled for the button of his trousers, her mouth planting a hot kiss on his before she mumbled, 'I can't handle this for much longer.'

He immediately flipped her back over, caressed her cheek, his heart ready to explode as he stared into the eyes of the woman who had seen his true self, who had seen his potential, who made him a better man, and in a low growl he said, 'You can decide on what future we have, but I'm in control of this.'

Alice arched her back, warmth and need and desire leaving her barely able to think. Luis ran kisses along her collarbone, his fingers torturing her nipple. She arched even more as his mouth shifted to her nipple, the warmth, the abrasion of his tongue, sending waves of frustrated pleasure through her body. His hands moved over her stomach until he reached her panties. His fingers curled around the fabric and as her back arched in response he pulled them off, his expression fierce. She inhaled deeply, suddenly feeling really exposed. No man had seen her like this. His gaze moved up her naked body, and she blinked at the desire and love in his eyes. 'You are so beautiful.'

Her heart skipped. Her skin glowed and tingled. And she held her breath when he lowered his trousers, her body temperature soaring when he stood over her naked.

He lay down at her side, his hand running over her body in soft sweeps, and then his mouth met hers. His kiss was tender and kind, his fingers caressing. And then he gazed down at her, his expression concerned. 'I don't want to hurt you.'

She smiled at his worry, loving him even more, and whispered, 'I know, and you never will.'

She clung to him when he entered her, gasped at the wonder of their becoming one. Her body arched up to meet every inch of him. Not once did their gazes part. Her gasps were met by his whispers of love and adoration, and she came apart in his arms time and time again, but it was only when he eventually came with her, after what felt like hours of torture, that the most powerful, life-affirming surge of love split her body in two.

And afterwards they lay on the floor, covered by a throw from the sofa, and stared into each other's eyes, no words spoken, their smiles saying everything.

EPILOGUE

'DON'T CRY. THAT'S supposed to be my job today.'

Breaking away from waving at the crowds lining the streets of Monrosa's old town, Alice reached over to touch Toni's hand. Toni looked sensational in her gold bridesmaid's gown, selected to match her own backless ivory lace gown threaded with gold.

Toni flapped her hand before her eyes, laughing and crying all at once. 'I know I'm going to ruin my make-up. It's just that you look so amazing and I'm so happy for you and Luis is going to die when he sees you and everything about this day is so magical.'

Beside Alice, holding Alice's winter wedding bouquet of ruby-red, lilac and midnight-blue roses and peonies, her mum continued to wave and smile at the crowds while whispering under her breath, 'Girls, concentrate.'

Alice and Toni giggled.

Alice waved to the people of Monrosa, who had so warmly embraced her since she had moved to the island, her heart exploding as flashing images of the past year ran through her mind—a book sailing through the air this precise day a year ago. The Christmas week in London and Verbier when she had fallen in love. The day she had moved to Monrosa last April and Luis's excitement as he had shown her around their new home, a modern villa within the palace grounds overlooking the sea. Her work in establishing a palace museum. The book she was writing in conjunction with his father on the history of Monrosa. The hot summer's day when they had been out sailing on the Mediterranean and Luis had proposed to her. How her heart ached when Luis was away promoting Monrosa and Young Adults Together, her pride in how much he was already accomplishing. The thrill, the exultation, the wonder of their reunions. The long nights where they barely slept. Wanting to chat, to connect, to make slow and tender love.

A loud roar went up from the waiting crowd when their open carriage entered Plaza Santa Ana. Climbing down from the carriage, she walked towards the crowd and waved, their applause and calls of goodwill quickening her heart. Once she was certain that the crowd had had a good look at her gown she returned to the steps of the cathedral and to the Cardinal of Monrosa, who was waiting for them, accepting his welcome.

The Cardinal went inside, and they lined up. Toni, who was trembling just about as much as she was, led the way, and, clutching her mum's arm, Alice followed, unable to breathe, her legs shaking so fiercely she was worried they might buckle at any moment. She knew she should smile, should look at their waiting guests. But, totally overwhelmed, she could only focus on the never-ending length of the aisle before them.

And then he stepped out into view. And she sighed

and smiled shyly. His magnificence in his navy-blue officer's dress uniform, the love singing from his eyes and his gentle smile filled her heart with joy and happiness.

Christmas miracles did happen after all.

* * * * *

HOME FOR THE BABY'S SAKE

CHRISTINE RIMMER

For MSR, always.

Chapter One

On a balmy afternoon in early September, Roman Marek stood on the sidewalk at the corner of Carmel Street and Pacific Lane in Valentine Bay, Oregon. His hands in his pockets, he scowled at the excess of arches and scrollwork adorning the facade of the building directly in front of him.

The Valentine Bay Theatre was nothing short of a nightmare—at least, to Roman it was. He'd made his fortune in Las Vegas real estate and he had a definite preference for efficient, light-filled, modern spaces. The last thing he would ever invest in was a run-down, century-old theater in the Venetian Gothic style.

But invest in it he had—in fact, he'd bought the damn thing outright. His mother had insisted. And Roman Marek would do just about anything for his mother. He loved her and he owed her.

As for her ridiculous fondness for the old theater, when Roman was a kid, his mom used to bring him here to watch second-run movies and attend community events. She looked back on those days through rose-colored glasses. And that was why, a few weeks ago, when Sasha learned that the elderly owner had died and the heirs wanted to get rid of it, she had demanded that Roman buy the place.

Buy it, he had. And now he needed to decide what the hell to do with it.

To him, a wrecking ball seemed the most effective solution to the problem—just knock it down and build something better. But demolition wasn't going to fly with his mother. To keep Sasha happy, the building would need to remain standing and to retain at least a semblance of its original design.

As Roman glared at his recent acquisition and continued to consider his limited options, a skinny guy in khakis and a plaid shirt strode past the ticket booth and went inside.

With a shrug, Roman followed. Might as well

have a good look around, get a better idea of what he was up against.

He entered a lobby that was pretty much as expected, with an aged maroon-and-black carpet in a dizzying pattern of interconnected medallions. There were lots of arches, fussy plaster moldings and several Tuscan pillars marching relentlessly toward the back wall. Curving stairs topped with fussy ironwork led up to the balcony.

The good news? Though the air smelled kind of stale, he detected no odor of mold or mildew. He might get lucky and not have to call in a mold abatement crew.

Roman found his way into the backstage area and saw that there was some kind of planning meeting happening out on the stage itself. There were a couple of hot blondes and a few long-winded middle-aged people, all of them sitting in a circle in folding chairs. He eavesdropped without shame as they droned on about a Festival of Fall Revue, a haunted house and a Christmas show—community events, complete money wasters, as far as Roman was concerned. Unfortunately, the former owner had signed on for them and it was part of the deal that Roman would honor those commitments.

Thus, the upcoming events were money wasters Roman could do nothing about. It would be the first of the year before he could get going on his plans to make something useful of this musty pile of concrete and stone.

He stood in the shadows behind a narrow black velour drape, watching the meeting, unnoticed, for several minutes—and not because he was interested in community events.

One of the hot blondes had caught his eye. She wore green shorts and a white shirt and had a pretty face—a gentle oval with wide-set eyes, a small chin and a delicately shaped, shell-pink mouth. The other hot blonde was pretty, too, her face more angular, her pale hair even longer. He would guess that the two of them were sisters, possibly fraternal twins. But he liked the one in the green shorts the best.

As if it mattered in the least.

Shaking off the weird spell the pretty blonde had cast on him, Roman turned away and continued his self-guided tour of the property. Come the new year, when he could finally boot the theater people and community boosters out, he wanted to know where he was going with the building, to have everything in order to start ripping out walls.

The more he looked around, the better he felt

about the situation. It could have been so much worse. The place needed a boatload of work, but it wasn't a bad space. And it was big. He explored the warren of rooms backstage and the large storage and docking area at the rear of the building.

The property could be a killer boutique hotel. Valentine Bay had a burgeoning tourist trade. When the transformation was complete, Roman would have the out-of-towners lining up for a chance to stay here. Already, he was envisioning the extensive remodel that would keep a sense of the old theater and yet be streamlined, modern and welcoming to hotel guests.

By the time he returned to the backstage area, only one hot blonde remained—the one he liked, in the green shorts. Everyone else had cleared out. She was busy on a tablet. Her thick, straight platinum hair fell forward to mask her face as she bent over the tablet on her lap, typing out notes or maybe an email.

He hesitated offstage again, watching her, smiling a little at the tender curve of her back, the way she had her knees braced together supporting the tablet, her lower legs apart, ankles wrapped around the chair legs. She wore battered Converse All Stars and she was so damn cute, even with her sweet face obscured by her hair.

He should move the hell on. But some random impulse held him in place, had him hoping that maybe she would glance over her shoulder and spot him, give him an opening to find out her name.

Just as he was about to give it up and turn away, a tall, gangly dude appeared from the wings on the opposite side of the stage. Roman remembered him, the guy in the plaid shirt, the one he'd followed inside.

"Hailey," said the lanky guy. He had a distinctive voice, low and commanding for a man his size. "At last, I have you alone." He sounded like the villain in some tacky old-time melodrama. All he needed was a tall black hat and a greasy mustache to twirl.

The blonde was not impressed. She didn't even bother to look up as she waved a dismissing hand. "Doug. Don't you have levels to check in the light booth or something?"

"When are you going to let me take you to dinner?"

Her focus still on her tablet, the blonde muttered, "Don't even go there."

"I can't seem to help myself." Doug moved clear of the wings and onto the stage.

"I mean it, Doug. Don't."

But Doug was nothing if not persistent. He took another step. "There's always been such powerful energy between us. Remember senior year? *The Crucible*? I was John Proctor and you were the feisty, wild, troublesome, angry and headstrong young Abigail…"

The blonde did look up then. Roman watched her spine draw straight. Shaking her head, she stood and set her tablet on the chair. "You need to just give it up. You get that, right?"

Doug put a bony hand to his heart. "Don't pretend you don't feel it—bam! Like a bolt of lightning every time our eyes meet. I promise you, no one else ever has to know." He moved in close to the blonde named Hailey.

And then he reached for her.

Roman didn't even realize that he'd let out a low growl until he'd already started to her rescue—only to halt when she grabbed Doug's arm and kicked his legs out from under him.

Doug let out a shout of surprise as he landed on his ass at her feet, center stage. "Ouch," he whined. His wounded expression was pretty damn comical. Groaning a little, he dragged himself upright again, one hand at his back. "That was just mean."

Hailey scoffed. "You'll live—and you should know better."

"There are names I could call you," Doug grumbled.

"Just don't try that again. You'll end up back on your butt."

With a low, derisive sound, Doug turned and limped off the way he'd come.

"It's called harassment, Doug, and you need to quit it," Hailey called to his retreating back. "You come on to me again, I'm giving Mariette a call."

"Leave my wife out of this," Doug grumbled as he disappeared into the wings on the other side of the stage.

Thoroughly entertained, Roman let out a chuckle.

The blonde whirled to face him. He was close enough to her now to see that her wide eyes were a gorgeous lavender blue.

He put up both hands. "Sorry. I saw what was happening and I hung around in case you needed backup."

She regarded him warily. "Who are you?"

"Roman Marek." He tipped his head toward the spot where Doug went down. "That was impressive. You have to do that often?"

She studied him for a slow count of five, apparently trying to assess if he was any kind of threat. He knew he was in the clear when she scoffed and flipped her hair back over her shoulders with both hands. "Please. Men never come on to me. I tend to give off an antirelationship vibe."

He dared to move out onto the stage. "Oh, I don't think Doug was looking for a relationship."

She laughed then. It was a husky, inviting sound. "I'm Hailey Bravo."

The Bravo family was well-known in Valentine Bay. "I went to school here in town. Same grade as a guy named Connor Bravo."

"Connor's my brother—he's third-born, after Daniel and Matthias."

"I remember Matthias, too." Surly and usually high on weed or something stronger, that was how Roman remembered Matt Bravo.

Hailey seemed to sense the direction of his thoughts. "Matt was not a happy guy in high school." A smile bloomed on those pretty pink lips. "But about two years ago, he got married. He moved up near Astoria to live with his wife on her family farm. He *is* happy now—you know, the wonder of true love and all that."

"I'm sure," Roman said with a shrug, though he wasn't. He'd been married twice. Both times, it had ended badly.

A frown wrinkled Hailey's smooth forehead. "You don't look all that sure."

He frowned back at her. "Of what?"

"Love, Roman Marek. Love."

On the contrary, he *was* sure about love—sure that he wanted nothing to do with it. And he should get going. But he liked Hailey Bravo. She seemed so self-possessed and confident. She'd put that Doug character on the floor without breaking a sweat. Plus, she was very easy on the eyes.

"So where are *you* in the Bravo family birth order?" he asked.

"I was born seventh."

"That makes you how old?"

"You ask a lot of questions, Roman."

He gave her a lazy shrug. "I'm a curious guy."

"I'm twenty-five."

He was thirty-two. And he found himself thinking that seven years was an acceptable age difference between him and a woman he might possibly get involved with. Not that it mattered. He had no plans to get involved with any woman anytime soon. "As I recall, there are a lot of you Bravos, aren't there?"

"Ten total, nine by blood."

He wasn't following. "You mean one of you is adopted?"

"No. One of us was switched at birth, so there's the switched sibling and the sibling we grew up with. The one we grew up with is a sibling, too. So that makes ten."

He eyed her sideways. "You're blowing smoke."

"Nope. It's true. One of us was switched at birth."

"Which one?"

"I can't tell you which one." She put a finger to her lips and whispered, "It's a family secret."

"Why?"

"Reasons, Roman. Reasons I'm not at liberty to disclose."

"You're very mysterious." And charming. And so damn cute.

"Not mysterious at all. Not really." As he watched, her sweet mouth turned down at the corners and those fine eyes seemed sad. "We lost Finn years and years ago—he's sixth-born, two years older than me. He vanished on a family trip to Russia."

Roman vaguely remembered the story of Finn Bravo's disappearance. It had happened when Roman was twelve or maybe thirteen, four or five years after he and his mother had fled the only other home he'd ever known, stopping for the night in Valentine Bay. And somehow, never moving on.

Come to think of it, the Bravo parents had died on another trip a couple of years after they lost Finn, hadn't they? Both stories had made the local newspaper.

"We're still searching for Finn." Hailey tipped her pretty chin high.

Roman gave her a long, slow perusal, from the top of her blonde head to the toes of her All Stars—because it gave him pleasure to do so. "I hope you find him someday."

"We will. We Bravos never give up."

The mood had darkened considerably. Now, Hailey seemed both determined and sad. A change of subject was in order. "So what's up with that Doug character, anyway?"

She scoffed. "We were in drama club together back in high school, Doug and me. He helps out here at the theater. And he also pretty much considers it a point of pride to make a pass at every woman who wanders by." She tipped her head to the side, studying him. "Got kids?"

He thought of his little boy and almost smiled. "Why?"

"Right now, we're staging the Festival of Fall Revue. Almost every kid in town will be in it. We can always make room for one more."

He considered telling her he had an eleven-month-old son. She seemed to like kids. But if he mentioned Theo, he would probably end up having to explain what had happened to Theo's mother and that wouldn't be fun.

Uh-uh. It was the wrong moment to go there. "I'm just having a look around the building—and what do *you* do here at the theater?"

Her smile got wider. She looked so happy to be here, onstage in her hometown's shabby old theater. "I work with the local arts council, putting on seasonal-themed shows and programs. It's a community endeavor and we try to get everyone involved." He listened, absurdly enchanted, as she chattered on about how her title at the theater was artistic director. "Also, my sister Harper and I have our own little production company, H&H Productions. In the past year, we've coproduced all the events here at the theater. Frankly, our budget makes a shoestring look fat. But Harper—she's our tech director—can do amazing things. She's a genius when it comes to making something from practically nothing. She's building five major interlocking sets for the Festival of Fall Revue. Wait till you see them, Roman. They'll blow you away."

"Sounds impressive," he said, and found he almost meant it. He could not have cared less about theater sets—interlocking or otherwise. But Hailey Bravo's enthusiasm was contagious.

She gazed up at the catwalk overhead and then out past the lip of the stage, over row upon row of worn, maroon-velvet seats. "The place could use updating," she said. "But overall, it's a great space." Her expression turned wistful. "Unfortunately, it's been sold. We're not sure what the new owner plans to do with it."

Roman made a noncommittal sound and gave no indication that *he* was the new owner she was so worried about. Yeah, he should tell her.

But he just couldn't quite make his mouth say the words. She would only want to know what would happen when the contract with the arts council ran out at the end of the year, and she wouldn't like his answer. That could mean the end of this conversation.

He didn't want that—didn't want her walking away. He was enjoying himself. She was a breath of fresh air, full of energy and enthusiasm.

"So, Roman," she said with a teasing little grin, "if you're here to contribute to the worthy cause of community theater for all the kids in town, I would be only too happy to accept your check made out to H&H Productions—or if you're uncomfortable writing a check to our family business, you can make it out to the Valentine Bay Arts Council. Most of the theater's budget comes through them."

"I might just do that."

"You're a generous man."

"No, I'm not. But I do want to get in good with the artistic director."

Hailey Bravo grinned up at the tall, broad-shouldered guy with the compelling jade-green eyes. He was gorgeous, really, with that jawline cut from granite and that mouth she couldn't stop staring at, that full lower lip and a distinct, beautifully shaped bow on top. His big, hard arms were shown off to perfection by his short-sleeved knit shirt.

And better than mere gorgeousness, those fine eyes gleamed with intelligence and wry humor. She felt downright giddy just looking at him, which made zero sense. Never, ever had she been the giddy type.

But she was giddy over Roman—like, right from first sight. He just rang all her bells in a big way. It had taken her by complete surprise, to feel so strongly attracted.

She hadn't been out with a guy in three years. Not since Nathan, who had been her everything. Other guys just didn't interest her.

Until now…

"Hey." Roman's wonderful, rough voice called her back to the moment. She blinked and watched as he strolled out onto the lip of the stage. He sat down with his legs dangling over the side and patted the space next to him.

She didn't even hesitate, just trotted right over there and dropped down beside him.

"So tell me." He spoke in a rough whisper, for her ears alone, and leaned close enough that she could smell him. Delicious. Like a clean shirt, freshly ironed—and something else, too. Something like the ocean on a cool, breezy day. "How did you get that antirelationship vibe?"

And just like that, without any more encouragement than his simply asking the question, she willingly told him stuff only Harper, who was not only her sister but also her best friend, had ever known.

"There was this guy, Nathan Christoff. I met him my freshman year at UO. Nathan was tall and lean, a great actor, very intense. I was wildly attracted to him, but he was…elusive."

Roman was watching her closely. She couldn't read his expression. Then he said, "So you chased him."

She laughed—at the memory *and* because the stranger beside her had known instantly what she would do. "I did chase him. Shamelessly. Until he finally got honest and admitted that he was completely gone on me, too."

"But…?"

She shifted her gaze downward. Staring at her Chucks, gripping the edge of the stage harder than she needed to, she filled in the blanks for him. "Nathan had stage four leukemia. It was in remission, but he warned me that the odds weren't good. It was likely to come back."

Roman's thick, black brows drew together, and his eyes knew too much. "This isn't a happy story, is it?"

She bit her upper lip and shook her head. "I finally managed to make him see that I just wanted to be with him. He stopped resisting and we were a couple. But he never would come home with me to meet the family, so no one here in town except Harper knew that I had a special guy. We were happy, Nathan and me, for several months. Then he got sick again. He died three years ago." She stared out over all the empty seats, her gaze ranging up to the balcony and then on overhead to the spectacular chandelier. It was eight feet tall, that chandelier. It weighed twelve hundred pounds, an iron-framed paper-and-silk creation in the style of a Chinese lantern.

Roman said nothing, not for the longest time.

They sat there in the empty theater, just the two of them, like they were the only two people in the world. It probably should have felt weird, sharing all that silence with a man she'd just met.

But it didn't feel weird. It felt easy between them. Easy and exciting, simultaneously.

Finally, she admitted, "I haven't been with anyone since he died, haven't wanted to be. After a year or so, I wasn't even sad anymore. Just happy on my own, graduating from college, getting going on the rest of my life here in my hometown." She closed her eyes and shook her head, another laugh escaping. "I can't believe I laid all that on you."

"I wanted to know." He took her hand.

And she let him. His touch was warm. Firm. Heat and something very close to longing skated up her arm and straight to her heart—for all the things she'd honestly believed she would never want again.

Was she getting a little carried away here?

No doubt about it.

She pulled her hand away.

He let go reluctantly—or did she only want to think that he didn't want to let go?

Roman glanced at his watch. It was an Omega, a gorgeous thing, the kind that cost as much as a car and did everything but your taxes for you. She was sure he was going to say he had to get going.

She was wrong.

He asked, "Are you hungry? It's lunchtime. And I remember this fish place from when I was growing up. It's not far from here—if it's still there..."

She knew what restaurant he meant because she knew every restaurant in town. "You mean Fisherman's Korner. It's still open, still serving the best fish and chips on the Oregon coast."

"Have lunch with me there."

"Yes," she said, far too eagerly—and then reminded herself that she really didn't know him. He'd said he'd gone to school with Connor, and he probably had. But she didn't remember any of her older brothers ever mentioning him back then. Not that she *should* remember—but still, she definitely needed to take her own car. "I have to see who's still here and either lock up or get them to do it if they leave before I come back. You go ahead. I'll meet you there. Fifteen minutes, tops."

When she arrived at the fish place on Ocean Road, Roman was waiting outside for her, leaning against a sleek black sports car—the famous one made in Italy, with doors that opened upward, like wings.

"This car," she said, shaking her head, trailing a finger along the gleaming hood. "You'd better write the arts council a check, Roman Marek."

He put his hand to his broad, hard chest, right over his heart. "You have my solemn word on that."

They went inside. The food was excellent, as always, and being with Roman was easy and fun. Even the silences were comfortable. He said he'd moved back to town from Las Vegas and bought a house on Treasure Cove Circle. Hailey knew the house. It was a mansion nestled in its own private oceanfront reserve, surrounded by beautiful old-growth forest, overlooking a secluded stretch of beach.

"I want to see you again," he said as he walked her back out to her car. She gave him her number and when he gathered her close, she didn't resist.

The kiss was just right, a tender, sweet getting-to-know-you kind of kiss. His lips felt so good brushing against her own, and excitement sizzled through her. They both pulled back slowly and just stood there at the driver's door of her Kia Sportage, grinning at each other for a long string of lovely seconds.

"See you soon," he said as he pulled open the driver's door for her.

She climbed in and he shut the door. Then he stood there, the afternoon sun gleaming on his dark brown hair, as she backed from the parking space and drove away.

For the rest of the day, Hailey felt like the living, breathing representation of some old romantic song. She walked on air and danced on clouds. She'd met a guy she wanted to see again. That hadn't happened since Nathan.

She couldn't stop smiling as she sat at the kitchen table in the family cottage she shared with Harper and worked on her plans for the Christmas show—which desperately needed an actual name. Later in the afternoon, she was back at the theater, greeting the parents as they dropped off their children for Fall Revue rehearsals.

It was the usual circus, corralling all the kids, giving them instructions that they immediately forgot. There was some pushing and one of the little girls cried. Hailey consoled and coaxed and loved every minute of it—she always did. But somehow, more so today.

Because she kind of had butterflies over Roman Marek, and for three long years she'd honestly believed that all her butterflies had shriveled up and died.

After the moms and dads returned and took

their kids home, Hailey and Harper spent an hour talking props and costumes—what to make and what to try to scavenge at cut-rate prices or, better yet, for free. Eventually they called it a night and headed to Beach Street Brews for burgers and beers.

The waitress took their orders, filled their mugs and left the rest of the pitcher on the table.

Harper raised her mug. "Here's to us. We did what needed doing for another whole day."

Hailey clicked her mug against her sister's. "We need a name for the Christmas show."

Harper licked the foam mustache from her upper lip, her gaze locked with Hailey's. "Pageant?"

"Bor-ing." Hailey pretended to flick a bit of lint off her shoulder.

"Hometown Holiday?" Harper was watching her much too closely. Hailey was ten months older, and yet in so many ways they were like twins. They read each other's minds, finished each other's sentences, knew when something had changed for the other. "Christmas on Carmel Street?"

"Hmm. Yummy alliteration and the theater *is* on Carmel Street. It has possibilities."

Harper leaned close. "You can't stop grinning. What happened today?"

"I have no idea what you're talking about."

"Liar. Tell me."

Hailey considered holding out a little longer, just for the fun of it. Instead, she surrendered to the inevitable. "Ever heard of Roman Marek?"

Harper's eyes widened. "You met a guy."

Hailey tried not to look wildly gleeful. "Same age as Connor, grew up here, moved to Nevada. Now he's back in town. He's bought the house on Treasure Cove Circle."

"The house with the private forest all around it and the primo beach down below?"

"I'm pretty sure it's the only house on Treasure Cove Circle."

"Tell me everything."

Hailey gave a purposely casual shrug. "He dropped by the theater. We started talking, then later I met him at Fisherman's Korner for lunch."

"So...sexy single dad with kids in the show?"

"No, he said he'd only come in to have a look around."

Harper was still staring at her, laser-focused. "Marek. The name's not familiar." Harper's eyebrows scrunched up. "But if he was in Connor's grade in school, that makes him—"

"Eight years ahead of us." Their mother had held Hailey back a year so that she and Harper could start kindergarten together. "Seven years older than me. Is that *too* old for me?"

"Please. When you were seventeen and he was twenty-four, *that* was a problem. Twenty-five and thirty-two, uh-uh. And there's no reason we would necessarily remember this guy just because he and Connor were in the same grade."

"I told him about Nathan."

Harper's beer sloshed on her hand as she set it down hard. "Wow. You *really* like this guy."

Why pretend otherwise? Harper would know the truth, anyway. "I gave him my number."

Could her sister's eyes get any wider? "Ginormous step forward. I'm so proud of you."

"God. I hope he calls."

Harper poked her in the shoulder affectionately. "Of course he's gonna call." She glanced toward the entrance. "Look. It's Gracie and Dante." Their youngest sister had just begun her first year of teaching history at VB High. She and Dante Santangelo were a couple. They'd started out as friends, then, this past summer, Gracie had rented a cabin on Dante's property. The two had grown closer. Just recently, she'd moved in with him. Dante was a sergeant detective with VBPD. He was also their brother Connor's lifelong BFF. "Dante might remember this guy of yours."

"He's hardly my guy," Hailey corrected. "Let's not get carried away with this thing, huh?"

Harper grinned. "Oh, come on. Let's." She waved Grace and Dante over, then moved to the chair next to Hailey, so the happy couple could sit side by side.

The waitress brought two more mugs and the burgers Hailey and Harper had ordered. There were hugs and congratulations when Gracie announced that she and Dante were engaged. She didn't have the ring yet. They would be shopping for one soon, though.

"Together," Gracie said.

Dante nuzzled her cheek. "She wants to choose for herself."

Harper nudged Hailey in the ribs. Hailey nudged back to let her sister know that she got the message: Dante Santangelo was long-gone on Gracie. Dante, who'd been married before and shared custody of twin daughters with his ex-wife, had always been kind of grim, a determined man, never a happy one.

Dante wasn't grim now. Now, he was openly in love with their baby sister and he didn't seem to care who knew it. He was also nine years older than Gracie, a fact that made Hailey feel even better about the possibility of something good happening with the gorgeous "older" man she'd met that afternoon.

"You two are adorable," Harper declared.

Dante gave her a patient look. "One of us is." Gracie beamed at him and they shared a quick kiss.

Harper nibbled a fry. "We have a question, Dante. Hailey met a guy at the theater today. He said he went to school here in Valentine Bay and he was in the same grade as you and Connor."

"His name is Roman Marek," added Hailey, trying to sound cool and collected despite her silly, fluttery stomach and the blush she just knew was creeping up over her cheeks.

Dante signaled the waitress. "I remember Roman, yeah. Showed up in town like third or fourth grade. Kind of a loner. Smart. Tough, too. He left town for college—Berkeley, I think—and just moved back recently. I heard he bought that big place on Treasure Cove Circle."

"That would be the guy." Harper just kept on grinning.

And Dante was looking at Hailey, waiting for her to explain why she needed to know about some guy he went to school with. "Thanks. I'm, uh, hoping he'll kick in a nice donation to the arts council."

"From what I've heard, he can afford it," said Dante. "He made it big in Nevada real estate."

The waitress appeared. Dante asked for another pitcher and he and Grace ordered food. Hailey asked Grace how her first week of teaching had gone. Grace said every day was a challenge and she loved every minute of it.

Harper wanted an update on Dante's eight-year-old daughters, who were back with their mom and stepdad in Portland right now. An hour went by. More than once, Hailey checked her phone, just in case Roman might have sent her a text or something. He hadn't.

Not that she expected to hear from him so soon.

But there *had* been a real connection between them. She knew he *would* call.

Maybe tomorrow.

Definitely by the day after…

Chapter Two

Roman didn't get in touch with Hailey.

Not the next day, Tuesday. Not Wednesday, either.

He'd decided not to call. It seemed the wisest course now that he'd had a little time to consider the ramifications of getting involved with someone.

He needed to focus on raising his son and getting some new projects off the ground. And he needed *not* to get involved with a woman.

By Wednesday night, he was way too aware that at this point, she had to be annoyed with him for taking her number and then giving her nothing but radio silence.

He found himself thinking of her constantly,

and that somehow made him even more reluctant to call. The last thing he needed was a woman he couldn't stop thinking about. Right now, a casual hookup was about the level of commitment he was ready for. He ought to be trolling Tinder or Casualx, not trying to get to know a former classmate's kid sister.

It was just that he liked her way too much already. That had him feeling at a disadvantage. After all, he'd been completely gone on his first wife, Charlene. He fell for her so hard and deep. He'd declared his love for her early. And often.

She'd sworn she loved him, too.

For a little while. But then she'd shown her true colors.

A year into their marriage, she laughed in his face for being such a fool. She said straight out that she thought love was a crock and what she liked the most about him was his money.

She'd gotten what she loved, taking a big chunk of change off him when they split up. At least it was early in his success. She didn't get as much as she might have if she'd married him a little later or stayed with him longer.

And then there was Nina, his second wife. With Nina, love hadn't entered into it. He'd married her because she was pregnant with Theo. She'd died in a car wreck—just Nina, her new sports car and the date palm she veered off the road and hit head-on. Theo was a month old at the time. At least she'd left his son at home with the nanny when she decided to get behind the wheel drunk.

Bottom line, he had personal baggage to spare and it just wasn't a good idea to go out with a woman he liked too much. The next time he saw Hailey—*if* he saw Hailey—he would have to confess that he was a two-time loser as a husband, a two-time loser with an eleven-month-old son.

She also deserved to know that he was the new owner of her precious theater—and that his plans for the historic building did not in any way dovetail with hers.

He should have told her all that up front. But he hadn't.

So now, he was putting off calling her because he was way too attracted to her *and* he felt guilty for keeping her in the dark about the theater and his sucky track record with relationships.

Thursday morning when he came down to breakfast, his mother was standing at the stove and Theo was in his high chair eating Cheerios and mandarin orange slices off the tray.

"Da-da-da-da!" Theo cried at the sight of him. Roman grinned. For at least a few seconds, he forgot about the woman he shouldn't like so much. He focused on Theo and his big, happy smile.

At this point in his life, Theo had no real concept of the mother he'd lost. He had a grandmother and a father who doted on him. For now, that seemed to be enough.

Roman bent to drop a kiss on his fat, sticky cheek. "Hey, big guy. How's it hanging?"

"Gwat." Theo grabbed a mandarin slice in his gooey little fist and offered it to Roman.

He took it and popped it into his mouth. "Yum. Thanks, Theo."

"Ma-wa-da," Theo replied.

"Eggs and bacon?" asked Roman's mother from over at the stove she loved. It was a chef's dream, stainless steel with giant dials and more than one oven. The one in the Summerlin house he'd bought for her had been even bigger, with even more features. She claimed this one was better, and he knew why—because this one resided in Valentine Bay.

Sasha Marek had not only raised him all on her own right here in Valentine Bay, working as a maid and housekeeper, she'd also recently agreed to move in with him and help him take care of Theo—on one condition: that they leave Las Vegas behind and return to Valentine Bay. Sasha had never liked living in Vegas. To her, Valentine Bay was the only place to be and she wanted her grandchild to grow up here.

He said yes to the eggs and bacon, brewed himself a cup of coffee and sat at the table next to Theo's chair. The little guy kept holding out soggy Cheerios. Roman ate them automatically, straight from Theo's chubby little hand, sipping coffee between bites, staring through the giant windows that looked out on the deck and the wind-twisted trees, with the cloudy morning sky and the blue Pacific beyond.

Sasha slid the plate of fluffy eggs and crispy bacon in front of him. "What's going on with you?"

"Not a thing." He smoothed a napkin in his lap and picked up his fork.

She scoffed. "You think a mother doesn't know when her son is lying to her?"

He ate a bite of eggs and refused to answer. The question was rhetorical anyway. His mother was a wonderful woman, but at times, she displayed definite boundary issues.

A couple of hours later, he was in his home office working on the numbers for a new project he was putting together with a group of investors in Portland and some guys he knew from Vegas and

Phoenix, when he got a call from a woman named Tandy Carson. She introduced herself as the director of the Valentine Bay Arts Council.

"We've all been wondering who the new owner of the Valentine Bay Theatre might be," Tandy said. She must have received the letter his lawyer had sent. She sounded cheerful, though, which probably meant she hoped there was still a chance she could convince him to keep the theater available for arts council use.

There was no chance at all. "You've heard from my lawyer, I take it?"

"I have, yes. And I wonder if we could meet and discuss the situation face-to-face."

"It's all there in the letter. You'll need to find another venue at the first of the year. I have plans for the building."

"I understand. If you would just come by the office, though. The community, the arts council board and I would really appreciate your willingness to talk this over."

It was a total waste of time to meet with her. But it would be downright rude not to. He lived here now. His son would grow up here. He would do what he wanted to do with the theater, but it was only fair to give Tandy Carson her chance to convince him otherwise.

Reluctantly, Roman agreed to stop in at the arts council offices that afternoon.

Hailey woke Friday morning feeling glum.

It was a yucky feeling, the kind of feeling she usually refused to allow herself. Because it was self-indulgent to be glum—especially if you were glum because some guy hadn't called.

Beyond the glumness, she was pissed off. Why ask for her number if he was never going to call?

And okay, yeah. Objectively speaking, she knew that it hadn't been *that* long since Monday. Also, guys failed to call all the time. So what?

Forget him. Move on. It wasn't as though she even knew the man, really.

However…

Well, she really *wanted* him to call.

And that pissed her off even more. Hailey had never been one to wait around for some guy to get in touch. She acted. When she wanted something, she had no problem stepping up and making the first move.

But she didn't have his number and she wasn't willing to track him down at the giant house he'd bought on Treasure Cove Circle. Being proactive with a guy was one thing. Stalking him at his house, well, that was a bridge too far.

Harper had left the cottage early to run errands. Hailey planned to meet her at eleven at a favorite thrift mall, where they would scavenge for treasures to use in the Festival of Fall Revue and the haunted house, too.

This year, the haunted house would be open for three nights—Halloween and the two nights before it. A major hit with kids of all ages, last year the haunted house had earned out and then some. This year, they needed it to be even bigger and better.

Hailey left the cottage at ten, which gave her time to drop by the arts council office on her way to meet Harper. Tandy was there at her desk wearing a determined look and a vintage T-shirt with Surely Not Everyone Was Kung Fu Fighting printed on the front. Her hair stuck straight up in its usual Mohawk, and her flawless dark brown skin made her look much younger than she was.

Hailey helped herself to a cup of bad coffee and took a chair. "Any news yet on the new owner's plans at the theater?"

Tandy flopped back in her swivel chair. "Yeah, it's not good. We need to be cleared out of there on January 1."

Cleared out? Hailey blinked, as if the action could make Tandy's words go away. "You're saying you heard from the new owner?"

"I did. I got the letter from his lawyer Wednesday and gave him a call yesterday. He's firm that he has other plans for the building."

"You actually talked to him, then?"

Tandy nodded. "He even came in yesterday afternoon to listen to me beg. I pulled out all the stops, played on his community spirit, reminded him how much kids need structured afternoon activities, a safe place to gather where they can work together on something bigger than themselves and find a positive outlet for creative expression."

"And?"

"He wouldn't budge."

"Oh, no..." Since she'd learned of the sale, Hailey had been telling herself she would need to be prepared for the worst. But she wasn't prepared. In her deepest heart she'd refused to let herself believe they would lose the irreplaceable space.

"I've been calling around." Tandy pulled a pen from behind her ear and rolled it between her fingers. "We'll find *something*, Hailey. I know we will. And the good news is the new owner made a nice donation to the arts council."

"Great," Hailey said flatly, wishing the new owner had skipped writing a check and given the community thc use of the theater for at least another year. The theater was perfect. There was nothing else in town that even came close. They would end up begging for space on a per-event basis in somebody's barn or a church or the local Grange Hall. It was no way to build the program of her dreams. "Who is this guy?"

Tandy shook her head. "He's not changing his mind."

"Still, it can't hurt for me to give it a try with him, can it?"

"He was very clear that he was not extending our contract beyond what the former owner agreed to."

"I just want to talk to him. A polite conversation. Please."

Tandy stared at her, narrow-eyed. Her pen fisted in one hand now, Tandy held it like a dagger as she clicked the ball point in and out with her thumb.

Hailey kept the pressure on. "It can't hurt to give it just one more try…"

Tandy clicked her pen a couple more times—and then shoved it behind her ear again. "Why not?" She grabbed a document from the stack of papers at her elbow and copied a name and number onto a sticky note. Whipping the sticky off the cube, she handed it over. "Give it a go."

Hailey stared at the name Tandy had written

and couldn't decide whether she felt murderous or sick to her stomach.

At last, very slowly, she smiled. "Thanks, Tandy. I'll see what I can do."

What she *wanted* to do was to wring Roman Marek's muscular neck. As she climbed behind the wheel of her Kia, she slapped the sticky note on the dash. Really, she was way too worked up at the moment to be rational and constructive in a face-to-face with the man.

She probably ought to go home, lock herself in her room and try some deep breathing, maybe a little yoga and a series of calming affirmations to settle herself down. But she was seeing red, and why call when he'd made the mistake of telling her where he lived?

She headed straight for his big, beautiful house on Treasure Cove Circle. Slamming to a stop in the wide driveway lined with giant sword ferns and rhododendron bushes, she flung herself from the driver's seat and soundly slammed the door.

Marching up the gorgeous fieldstone steps between a pair of cedar posts stuck in pillars of concrete and rock, she halted at a front door of iron and glass. Ignoring the bell, she raised a fist and pounded on the iron part of the door. She did it repeatedly, with great enthusiasm.

Soon enough, through the glass lights in the door, Hailey spotted a statuesque form approaching. The door swung inward to reveal a stunning fiftyish woman in a calf-length A-line shirtdress. She had beautiful, wavy hair in every color of gray from silver to soot, hair that fell down her shoulders and over her full breasts in a smoky cascade. Her eyes were the same silvery green as the man who was about to get a full dose of Hailey Bravo in a very bad mood. The woman carried a cute, wide-eyed toddler in her arms. "Yes?"

"Where's Roman?"

Did a smile flit across the woman's amazing face? It was there and gone so fast, Hailey couldn't be sure. They stared at each other. And then, without another word, the woman stepped back, clearing the doorway. She shifted the toddler, so he sat firmly on one arm. The other arm, she swept out toward the impressive stone staircase leading up to the second floor.

Hailey didn't hesitate. She crossed the threshold and marched to the stairs. Mounting them swiftly, she stuck her head into three different bedrooms before reaching the master suite, where the door stood open and Roman just happened to be exiting the luxurious bathroom, naked except for a towel around his lean hips.

Hailey froze in the doorway. It was just possible her mouth was hanging open.

Roman didn't even have the grace to flinch—and really, why would he? Every inch of him was perfect. His chest was downright climbable, laddered with hard muscle. His feet were long and tanned, his legs big, cut, powerful. He looked like the men on the covers of sexy romance novels, juicy books with titles like *Hot Contact* and *Midnight Diversions*. Casually, completely unperturbed, he used a second towel to scrub at his thick, inky wet hair.

"Hailey," he said coolly. "This is a surprise."

Was she starting to feel just a little bit foolish?

So what? She'd come this far, and she refused to turn back now. Not until she'd given Mr. Studly McBastard a giant piece of her mind.

"Let me put something on," he said and went for the towel wrapped around his hips.

Did he think that dropping that towel was going to send her running?

Not a chance. She slapped a hand over her eyes in order not to see him naked when she didn't even like him anymore and she let him have it.

"Three hours, Roman," she accused in a low, angry growl. "You spent three hours with me on Monday. Three hours during which I made it painfully clear to you how concerned I was that the theater's new owner would boot out the arts council at the first of the year. Three hours. That's one hundred and eighty minutes and a whole boatload of seconds during which you might have mentioned that *you* were the new owner in question."

She heard a drawer shut somewhere nearby. Was he getting dressed?

Who cared? She didn't. Butt naked or fully clothed, he was getting an earful and he was getting it now.

She pressed her hand closer to her eyes so she wouldn't be in any way tempted to peek and kept after him. "It's inexcusable, that's what it is. *You're* inexcusable. And aside from how you shamelessly lied to me by omission, Valentine Bay needs that theater and whatever you think you're going to do with it can't possibly be as important as what will be lost when you turn it into...whatever it is you're thinking of turning it into."

"A hotel," he provided mildly. "And you can open your eyes now."

She probably shouldn't trust him, not even about something so minor as whether or not he'd put on some pants. But as each second ticked past, she felt increasingly more ridiculous, her blood at a boil, standing there with her hand clapped over her eyes, wondering what he might be up to while she couldn't see.

She dropped her hand. He was right there in front of her, still barefoot, but now dressed in jeans and a Henley. "You can't do this," she cried, a pleading note creeping in. Because she would do anything—beg, plead, steal—if only she could convince this man to keep the theater going into next year.

"Oh, yes, I can." He said it kindly, an almost tender look in those ice-green eyes. "And, Hailey, I will."

His tenderness did it. All the fight went out of her. She shouldn't have come. She was making a fool of herself. And for nothing, too.

Spinning on her heel, she marched back the way she'd come.

"Hailey! Slow down," Roman called after her.

She didn't hesitate or turn. There was no point in talking to him. He'd made up his mind.

As she took off down the stairs, she saw the beautiful gray-haired woman waiting at the bottom, gazing up at her, the big-eyed child still in her arms. The look of sympathy on the woman's face said it all. She'd heard every word.

"Sorry to, um, burst in like that," Hailey said miserably as she reached the lower floor. The woman gently patted her on the shoulder as she rushed by and out the door.

Fleeing down the fieldstone steps and across the wide driveway, Hailey leaped into her Sportage, gunned the engine, backed fast, turned around and got out of there.

Roman stopped at the top of the stairs.

Clearly, Hailey Bravo wasn't going to slow down long enough to hear anything he might have to say to her. He watched her race past his mother and son and on toward the front door. As he started his descent at a more leisurely pace, he heard her car door slam, the engine rev and tires squeal on pavement as she sped away.

Sasha watched him, her mouth turned down, eyes narrowed in disapproval as he came toward her. He returned her glare.

"Ma," he said when he reached the ground floor and confronted her over the wrought iron newel post. "You can't just send random women up to my room."

His mother gave him one of her elaborate shrugs, the kind that managed to be equal parts dismissive and superior. She'd raised him cleaning other people's houses, often on her knees as she frequently and proudly declared. But no queen could be as disdainful as Ma when she chose to be. "You like her. It's obvious."

Yes, he did. A lot. But he didn't need his mother knowing that. "How can you possibly know if I like her or not? You let her in, eavesdropped on her telling me off and then watched her as she walked out. At no point did you see us together."

"I saw all I needed to see because I saw your face just now as you stood there at the top of the stairs watching her leave. I know your face. I've had thirty-two years to get perfectly familiar with it. You like her and don't you even try to convince me that's not so."

"Ma—"

"We had an agreement and I am only keeping my part of it."

"Wait. What? Agreement? What agreement?"

Sasha gave him zero indication she'd noticed the three question marks in what he'd just said. "What I'm trying to get through to you is that it's not a problem."

"Not a—huh?"

"I'm telling you, *I* like her, too. She's got spunk and it's obvious from what I just heard that she has values, as well. She cares about what really matters in life. And that is why I'm giving you permission to get to know her better."

He stuck his hands in his pockets and shook his head. "Do you *hear* yourself?"

"Don't even try to pretend you have no idea what I'm talking about. We discussed this. You've been married twice. Both times were your choice and both times were disasters. Both times, I warned you—*begged* you—please, not to do it. Charlene was a gold digger and Nina…" She caught herself before she said something bad about Nina with Theo right there in her arms. Nina had been Theo's mother, after all. "May she rest in peace, Nina was not the right woman for you. I understand why you went there, with Nina anyway. You're a good man at heart and you wanted to do right with a little one on the way."

"Ma—"

"I'm still talking. You got married twice, though I tried to warn you against both bad decisions. Catastrophes ensued. And that's why we agreed that you wouldn't get anything started with a woman until I got a look at her and gave you my approval."

He'd made no such agreement. But arguing the point with her would get him nowhere.

She kept right on talking. "And, Roman, what were you thinking, deciding to close down the theater? That is not why I insisted you buy it for me.

I forbid you to turn my theater into some chichi hotel."

Theo, who up till then had sat silent on his grandmother's arm, his head swiveling back and forth between Roman and Sasha like a mesmerized spectator at a tennis match, chose that moment to crow, "Da-Da!" Little arms outstretched, he fell toward Roman.

Roman caught him, turned his ball cap around, dropped a quick kiss on his forehead and leveled narrowed eyes on his mother. "What do you mean, you forbid me? I'm in property development. It's what I *do*. And if ever a property called out for development, that theater is it. I have to do something with it, Ma."

"Yes, you do. You have to make it the best theater it can be for the sake of every man, woman and child in Valentine Bay."

"No, I do not."

"Oh, but you most certainly do. You're a rich man, Roman. And we both know you got your start in very lucky ways. Yes, you worked hard. But you had that nest egg Patrick sent to fund your education."

Patrick. Roman could live his whole life without ever hearing that name again. He'd always wondered if there was something going on between his mother and Patrick Holland all those years ago—but no. That was impossible. Sometimes Ma drove him stark raving out of his mind, but she was a good woman, loyal and true-hearted to the core. Patrick was a married man. Sasha Marek would never put moves on another woman's husband—especially not the husband of Irene Holland, who had treated her like a sister and Roman like her own son.

Roman felt a sharp pinch in the vicinity of his heart, the one he got every time he thought of Irene, no matter how many years went by. *Reenie*, he used to call her. He'd adored her completely—until that awful day when everything blew wide open.

Sasha kept talking, driving her point home. "And then there was that winning Megabucks ticket I gave you on your twenty-first birthday." The year he turned eighteen, she'd begun buying him good-luck lottery tickets for his birthday and at Christmas. On his twenty-first birthday, the Megabucks ticket had hit big. She rubbed it in. "That ticket set you on the road to success. The universe has smiled on you, Roman Marek, and now you need to give back. You can make that girl's dream come true and do something really good for this town."

Theo had started chanting, "Da-Da, Da-Da, Da-Da," as he tried to stick his fingers up Roman's nose. Roman caught his busy little hand, kissed it and reminded his mother, "That girl's dream is not my responsibility and I never cared all that much for this town, Ma. You know that. I'm only here because you love it here *and* because you insisted that coming back here to live would be better for Theo."

She pinned him with a burning look. "Don't be hard and unfeeling. You don't need another hotel. Roman, you need to give that girl her dream."

Really, why was he still standing here? There was no point in engaging with her when she got like this. Without another word, he turned and carried his son to the kitchen to give him a snack.

Behind him, he heard Sasha huff in complete disgust. But at least she let it go.

For now, anyway.

Harper was already at Pacific Bargain Mall when Hailey arrived. They wandered the little shops together, buying old clothing that could be made into costumes and a couple of giant, battered potbellied planters. Spray-painted black, the planters would serve as cauldrons for the haunted house. The kids loved the cauldrons filled with dry ice that produced a lot of spooky smoke, so the more cauldrons the better. They found old chairs, a rickety table and a bunch of fallish silk floral that would help dress the Fall Revue sets.

As they shopped, Hailey tried to decide when to break the bad news about the theater to her sister. It was going to be extra painful to go into it, given that the man who was not renewing their contract in January just happened to be the same guy Hailey had made such a big deal about meeting only a few days before.

Uh-uh. The pain was too fresh. She couldn't talk about Roman with her sister right now. She might start shrieking in fury—or break down in frustrated tears.

Later. Maybe this evening over beers at Beach Street Brews or tomorrow morning during breakfast. She needed a little distance from the humiliation of what had happened just an hour before.

Unfortunately, her sister knew her too well. No sooner had Hailey made the decision to put off discussing Studly McBastard and his plans to turn the theater into a hotel, than her sister said, "Whatever it is, you should just go ahead and tell me."

Hailey scrunched up her nose. "Have we got time for a coffee?"

"That bad, huh?" Harper took Hailey's hand. "Come on."

In the Steamy Bean around the corner, they treated themselves to pumpkin spice lattes.

"Well, that's just crappy on every level," said Harper once Hailey had told all.

"Yeah." Hailey took a slow sip of pumpkin-y goodness and licked the sweet foam from her upper lip. "The jerk never called *and* he's a heartless money-grubber with no social conscience whatsoever."

"Oh, honey. You are seriously ticked off."

Hailey drew herself up tall in the bentwood chair. "Maybe. Just a little."

"You should seduce him. Wait till he falls asleep and then take embarrassing pictures of him and threaten to put them on Instagram if he doesn't change his mind about closing the theater."

"To seduce him, I would have to have sex with him."

"Yep. It's a great sacrifice, I know. But you need to do it anyway, for the sake of community theaters everywhere."

Hailey gave a snort-laugh. She did love her sister. Harper never failed to make a dark moment brighter. "Oh, so you mean it's like my civic duty to crawl in bed with the jerk?"

"Yes! That is exactly what it is. A selfless act of pure love."

"Okay, now you're getting a little carried away."

Harper reached across the café table and squeezed Hailey's arm. "Honestly, though. You all right?"

Hailey drew in a slow breath and exhaled on a determined nod. "I've been better. But I will survive."

Rehearsal was at three that afternoon.

At two, Hailey sat alone at her folding table in the first row of the auditorium. She was working through pre-blocking for the second act of the Fall Revue, which was going to be a circus, especially the finale, when just about every kid in town would crowd onstage and ultimately take a bow. Unfortunately, her mind kept getting hijacked by grim thoughts of next fall, when they would probably be trying to put the show on in a barn, which looked like such fun in those old Judy Garland movies.

In real life, however? Not so much.

"Hailey?" said a husky woman's voice from up on the stage.

Hailey glanced up from her tablet and into the gray-green eyes of the woman who'd opened the door for her at Roman's house. The woman stood downstage, center. She had that sweet little one with her in a stroller.

"Ah-ta!" said the child, waving his chubby hands gleefully. The toy in the baby's left hand had a rattle in it. It made clicking sounds as the little sweetie shook it.

"I'm Sasha Marek," said the woman. "Roman's mother. I wonder, can we talk for a moment?"

Roman's mom. Somehow, it made him seem more human to think of him having an actual mom—and the last thing Hailey wanted was to think of him as human. She was really angry with him, after all, and preferred to picture him springing forth fully formed from the head of a demon or some other purely evil mythological creature.

"Is this a bad time?" Roman's gorgeous mom looked concerned.

And she'd seemed nice enough this morning. People always blamed the mother for what their children grew up to be. But Roman didn't seem at all like the type to be guided by a mother's wisdom.

So yeah. Not this woman's fault that Roman Marek was a jackass.

"Not a bad time at all," said Hailey, and forced a smile. There were a few folding chairs and music stands scattered around up there on the stage.

Stairs led down to audience level on either side. "Have a seat. I'll come up." She ran up the steps and took a chair beside the one Sasha had chosen. "What can I do for you?"

"Well, for starters, I just want to apologize for the way Roman behaved this morning."

"It's not your fault, so there's nothing for you to apologize for."

"Still, I feel guilty." In the stroller, the child let out another string of nonsense syllables and dropped the toy. Sasha picked it up and gave it back.

Was the baby hers? Or Roman's?

"What's your baby's name?" Hailey asked.

Sasha let out a husky laugh. "My grandson's name is Theo."

"Roman's his dad?"

"Yes."

"He's a cutie." The little boy was also yet another major bit of information Roman had failed to share last Monday.

"Roman has a lot of faults," his mother said ruefully. "But he's a wonderful, loving father."

"Good to know." Hailey tried not to sound overly sarcastic.

Sasha sighed—and then changed the subject. "I made Roman buy this theater."

That was a surprise. "You did?"

"Yes. I used to bring him here all the time when he was a boy, during those first couple of years after we moved to town. They offered second-run movies then, two-dollar admission. And there were other community activities for free or for practically nothing. We didn't have much back then, Roman and me. His father, my husband, Roman Sr., had died suddenly when Roman was only two."

"I'm so sorry…"

Sasha gave her a benevolent smile. "We moved to Valentine Bay when Roman was eight. And it meant so much, to have somewhere fun to go for the right price. That's why, when I heard the old owner had died, I asked my son to step up and buy this place."

"You thought it might make a great hotel?"

Sasha rescued the little boy's rattle again, patiently handed it to him and then explained, "Unfortunately, though my son is a loving father and loyal son, he is also thickheaded, with a one-track mind. To him, property should equal profit and profit means money. He doesn't immediately consider how much profit there can be in community activities, in lending a hand, in creating safe spaces for children to grow and learn in. I should have made it very clear right from the start that I meant he should buy this theater in order to make sure it continued to be used for the good of everyone in town, no matter their financial circumstances."

"Are you saying you actually told him to buy it so that it would remain a community resource?"

"I did—or I thought I did. But I didn't make myself clear enough, evidently. I will keep after him to do the right thing, you can be sure of that."

"That's kind of you, thanks." Roman might be impossible, but Hailey really did like his mom. And she was starting to feel more than a little bit sheepish about her actions that morning. "I shouldn't have come barging in on you like that earlier. It's a long story, but I was angry at your son and I did kind of cross a line."

Sasha frowned. "No. Wait. I completely disagree."

"Um, you do?"

"Yes. Absolutely. I love the way you stood up to my son. Roman needs more of that in his life—of people who stand up to him. You may not believe this, but he really is a good man. He's so pigheaded, though. He needs a woman of courage, strength and heart, a woman who will always challenge him to do what's right and always be there for him. Roman thinks he knows everything, but he's wrong, as so many men are."

Where was this going? Hailey wasn't sure she wanted to know.

Sasha leaned closer to Hailey and pitched her voice to a more confidential level. "You should have met his ex-wives. Selfish women, spoiled, with way too much interest in the things that money can buy. He married them anyway—one because she managed to make him believe she loved him when what she really loved were the things he could buy for her. And the other because..." She glanced over at the little boy, who had fallen fast asleep, his chin tipped down, his lower lip adorably pooched out. Sasha went on in a whisper, "...she got pregnant with his son. I have a feeling about you, though, a really *good* feeling." Roman's mom put a hand to her heart. "With you, it will be different."

Hailey blinked. Was this woman *matchmaking* her and Roman? Talk about a stretch. She needed to nip that idea right in the bud. "Sasha, I have a question for you, and I would appreciate an honest answer."

"Of course."

"Are you playing matchmaker?"

Sasha laughed then. "Relax. I know what I'm doing."

"I don't think you understand. There's really and truly nothing to matchmake."

"I think you're wrong."

"No, I'm not. I met your son Monday, right here in the theater. I liked him then, a lot. We even went to lunch together. I thought we had…I don't know, a connection, I guess you could say. I told him things I don't tell other people. He in no way returned the favor. Looking back on the time I spent with him, I realize now that he gave me nothing about himself. He didn't say that he'd been married twice. He didn't even mention that sweet little boy asleep in the stroller. I talked a lot about this theater and said how worried I was because someone had bought it and I had no idea what the new owner's plans might be. Roman didn't reveal that he was the new owner in question. He *did* ask for my number, though."

"But you wouldn't give it to him?"

"No, I gave it to him. And he didn't call."

Sasha waved a hand. "He likes you *too* much. That scares him. But you don't have to worry. He'll get over that."

Hailey folded her arms across her middle. "I really think it's too late now."

"No, it's not. You'll see."

No, she wouldn't. She'd been silly to assume

that Roman was someone special. He wasn't. And she had pre-blocking to get back to. "It's nice that you stopped by, Sasha. And I hate to cut this conversation short, but I've got a million things that need doing..."

"Hmm. I see I've said too much. I do that sometimes."

"Actually, I appreciate your honesty. It's refreshing."

Sasha stood. "I know I'll be seeing more of you."

"You really shouldn't count on that."

Roman's mom gave an easy shrug. "Before I go, I do want to offer to pitch in around here, to help out any way I can."

Hailey grinned then. "First rule of community theater. Never turn down a volunteer." She took a business card from the pocket of her shirt. "That's my sister Harper's number, right under mine. From props to costumes to set painting, Harper runs all the crews. Give her a call. She'll put you to work."

Sasha took the card. "Thanks. I'll be seeing you, Hailey."

"I look forward to it."

For a moment, Sasha just stood there, her gaze locked with Hailey's. Then, a tiny smile on her arresting face, she turned and wheeled the stroller off into the wings stage right, on her way to the door that led to the lobby and the front exit.

Hailey watched her go. She liked Roman's mother.

But as for the man himself, Sasha had it all wrong. Hailey was so completely over Roman Marek. She never should have given him her phone number in the first place, and from this moment forward, she wouldn't be giving him another thought.

Chapter Three

After Hailey told him exactly what she thought of him and then stormed out as fast as she'd blown in, Roman decided he wasn't going to think about her anymore.

He spent the next few hours in his home office, alternately trying to concentrate on the new Portland project and staring off into space, thinking of the woman he was supposed to be forgetting about.

There was no point in thinking of her.

He'd missed his chance with her on more than one level, first by not admitting up front that he'd bought the theater—and then later by failing to call her and rectify his mistake before she found out from somebody else.

Clearly—and understandably—she wanted nothing to do with him now.

And how many times had he reminded himself that he shouldn't be starting anything with a woman at this point in his life, anyway? Yeah, he'd always wanted a family—a wife and several children. However, his two bad marriages had shown him that he just plain sucked at relationships. He was a two-time loser who had no business trying again with a woman. He should be grateful he had Theo and leave it at that.

On the other hand…

Sasha had liked Hailey—really liked her. So much so that she'd given him outright encouragement to pursue her. That was a first. Always before, if Roman wanted a woman, his mother automatically disapproved of her.

Until now.

He would never admit it to anyone—especially not his mother—but he did remember Sasha suggesting that the next time he got married, he'd better seriously consider her opinion of his chosen bride. That had happened after Nina died. Sasha had added that Theo deserved better than to be subjected to his father's terrible taste in wives.

Now Sasha seemed to believe they'd come to some sort of agreement on the issue.

They hadn't.

How could he come to an agreement when he'd been absolutely certain that he would never get married again? Twice burned, after all, was more than enough. Or should have been.

Except he did want a wife. He really did. He wanted a family that included the right woman. He'd always wanted a good woman in his life—and that was where his limitations messed him over.

He was an excellent judge of character when it came to men. And women, too—as long as the woman in question was someone he had no desire to see naked. Unfortunately, his judgment went out the window when it came to a woman he wanted in his bed.

He'd wanted Charlene, wanted her a lot. He'd married her, treated her like a queen, given her all his love.

And look where that had gone. She'd taken him to the cleaner's and walked away without a backward glance.

As for Nina, may she rest in peace, he'd been on to her cold heart right from the first. But that hadn't stopped him from getting involved with her. She'd been gorgeous and tempting. He'd put up very little resistance to her charms. She'd sworn she was on the Pill and he'd used a condom every time.

But there were a *lot* of times.

And so along came Theo. Roman had proposed when Nina was three months pregnant—as soon as he got the results of the paternity test.

Nina had said yes right away, adding, "And no prenup, Roman. I'm not signing one of those. If it doesn't work out, you're going to pay."

He hadn't argued. He'd wanted to be there through every step of the pregnancy, and being married to his baby's mother was the best way to make that happen.

Because Theo was everything. And when Roman felt low about his rotten taste in wives, he reminded himself that without Nina there would be no Theo. So Nina had been a better choice than Charlene, and that meant he'd made real progress in selecting a mate.

So what if his logic was maybe a little bit flawed? A man had to look on the bright side, didn't he?

And that was the thing about Hailey. She *was* the bright side, with that shining platinum hair, big lavender-blue eyes, that sharp brain, smart mouth, sweet body and beautiful smile.

Hailey Bravo was so perfect in so many ways, she'd scared the crap out of him. He'd hesitated to get back to her.

And everybody knew the old proverb. He who hesitated was screwed—or something like that.

Screwed, and constantly thinking about her.

He couldn't help grinning every time he thought of her this morning, showing up on his doorstep, marching right up the stairs. So cute, the way she'd covered her eyes to spare his nonexistent modesty while she gave him a very large piece of her mind.

She was hot when she was furious—okay, yeah. She was hot in the first place. Her fury just kicked the hotness factor up a notch or two.

Hailey was forceful and determined and she cared about the kids she worked with.

What she was *not* was after his money, like Charlene and Nina had been.

And while he was examining his own failings and bad choices, he might as well go ahead and admit to himself that his mother had recognized the goodness in Hailey the moment Hailey stormed in the front door.

He might as well face the truth. Sasha possessed an ingrained ability to see straight to the heart of people, *all* people.

He had no doubt that his mother was right about Hailey.

Hailey Bravo had it all going on and any guy would be grateful for a chance with her. And she'd been on his mind constantly from the first moment he saw her, sitting on the stage with her sister and the others, planning all those kid-centered community events that Ma thought were so important.

Hard fact: he wanted to see Hailey again.

He *would* see her again.

He should have called her sooner, yeah.

But better late than never.

Not five minutes after Roman's mother vanished into the wings stage right, Hailey got a text.

From Roman, of all people. If I call, will you pick up?

Her foolish heart, which was not to be trusted, had the nerve to skip a beat. Your mother just left.

He didn't answer for several seconds. She was about to get back to pre-blocking the second act when his next text appeared. Believe nothing she tells you. And have dinner with me.

She shouldn't. You have a son you failed to mention. Also, TWO ex-wives?

The phone rang in her hand.

She swiped up. "I can't believe I just accepted your call."

"Thank you." He really did have the greatest voice, all deep and manly, with both humor and a shiver-inducing note of authority. A girl could get in big trouble letting herself be seduced by a voice like his.

She taunted him. "You're going to have to do better than 'thank you.'"

"Hailey. I'm sorry." He actually sounded as though he meant it.

Her midsection kind of melted, but she held strong. "Sorry for what, specifically?"

"For not putting it right out there that I bought the theater and I had plans to make money off it—and you're right. I should have told you about my exes up front, *and* about my son. I hate to admit it, but…"

"What? Say it."

"I was afraid all my baggage would turn you off."

Her melty midsection had turned to pure goo. "What am I going to do with you, Roman?"

"We need to discuss that. Over dinner."

She wanted to say yes so bad, she could taste the words in her mouth.

"Hailey, you still there?"

"Yeah."

"It's just dinner…"

"Listen to me, Roman. Are you listening?"

"To every word. Yes."

"I want honesty from you. Don't hold stuff back because you think I won't like it."

"Agreed."

"I'm not happy about your plans for the theater."

"Got that."

"Money isn't everything, you know."

"It's not?"

This guy... "No, it is not. And I'm not going to stop trying to convince you to change your mind about converting an amazing performance space into something you can turn a profit on."

"Of course you're not." He sounded almost pleased she hadn't just accepted that he would do what he wanted with the building he'd bought.

"I love kids," she added.

"I believe that." He said it in a silky tone that caused a tug of awareness low in her belly.

"What I mean is, Theo is in no way a problem for me. And as for your exes, well, as long as they really are exes…"

"Not married. No girlfriends, no one I'm seeing."

She realized she was smiling. Clearly, she was

a total pushover when it came to this man. "All right," she said softly.

"Excellent. Dinner. Tonight."

"Yes."

"I'll pick you up at six."

Should she insist on driving her own car?

As she stewed over that, he said, "You've been to my house. You've met my mother. Chances are, I'm not a serial killer."

"Is that supposed to reassure me? Serial killers have houses and mothers, too, you know."

"Six o'clock."

It really had been so long since a guy picked her up and took her someplace nice to eat. "I'll be ready."

Roman took her to one of her favorite places. It was right on the river in Astoria, with floor-to-ceiling windows looking out on the Columbia, so every table had a gorgeous view, a view that included the four-mile-long Astoria-Megler Bridge that connected Oregon to Washington State.

They ordered drinks and appetizers and watched the darkening sky turn purple and orange, the colors reflected on the water.

"When my sister Aislinn got married at the county building here, we all came to this restaurant to celebrate. I always feel that coming here is special, somehow."

He sipped his Ketel One on the rocks. "So I've done something right finally, is that what you're saying?"

She raised her glass of white wine to him. "To you, Roman. You're pretty infuriating on more than one level, but your choice of this restaurant is stellar."

"Still mad at me, huh?"

"Not really. I'm one of those people who will let you know exactly how I feel about something—but then I'm willing to move on."

"You seem cautious."

"Can you blame me?"

For that, she got a lazy shrug. "Guess not." He seemed to be studying her as he asked, "Doug give you any more trouble?"

"I think, just possibly, that Doug Dickerson might be avoiding me."

"Dickerson? His last name is Dickerson?"

"That's right."

"Why am I not surprised?"

She grinned at him. "And you're not alone in that."

His mouth curled with humor. "I really like that *Dick*erson is avoiding you."

"He's harmless, really."

Roman's mouth flattened as he sat back in his chair. "A cheater is not harmless."

"True. But Doug, well, I doubt he's ever actually cheated. I mean, Mariette, his wife, seems to adore him. And he's kind of a joke to the rest of us."

"You told him to leave you alone and he didn't listen."

"Roman. Doug is honestly not any kind of a concern for me. Let it go, huh?"

He frowned. "Sorry. I thought it was funny, when he wouldn't back off and you took him down. But on further consideration, I started wondering if maybe he's been harassing you."

"He hasn't. Honestly." And a change of subject was in order. "I've been thinking about this morning. I shouldn't have barged in on you. I apologize for that."

"You can barge in on me anytime you want to."

"I was upset, and not just about the theater..."

He leaned in. "I should've called. I wanted to call. A lot. Too much."

"So you *didn't* call? Roman, you have to know that makes no sense."

"Both of my marriages ended badly. As a rule, I have crap taste in women."

She sat back, laughing. "If you're trying to make me feel better, it's a major fail."

"I didn't trust my own judgment about you, that's all. So I blew it and didn't call."

"And then, as you were exiting the shower, I burst into your bedroom, yelled at you and ran back out—and that somehow convinced you that I wasn't just another of your bad romantic choices?"

He sipped his vodka. "Believe it or not, yeah. Plus, my mother really likes you." He was grinning again. "And you should probably never trust a man who's too attached to his mother."

"*Are* you too attached to your mother?"

"She's a pain in my ass. But she's solid as a rock, loyal until death and most of the time, she's right—and please, don't tell her I said that."

They were both leaning in again. Hailey was thinking she liked everything about him. Even the annoying qualities were strangely attractive. He was pushy, but in a charming way. And he was so yummy to look at. He wore a gray button-up rolled to the elbows, showcasing his hard, tanned forearms, which he'd rested on the edge of the table. There was the seriously spendy watch on one wrist and a plain bracelet made of black beads on the other. His hair was so thick, just long enough to kiss the top of his collar, the kind of hair that made a woman long to reach out and touch it—smooth her hand over it to test the texture and then rough it up a little.

She kind of couldn't get over how powerfully she was drawn to him—and more so every time she saw him. It was thrilling. And sort of dangerous. She hadn't felt this way since…

Well, really, not even Nathan had made her feel quite like this.

"I like everything about you," Roman said, as though he'd picked up her thoughts and echoed them back to her. A lovely little shiver went through her. "The way you bite your upper lip when you're trying to decide how much to say. Your laugh. Those lavender eyes and all that determination to make a go of putting on shows in the Valentine Bay Theatre starring every kid in town."

Wasn't that kind of him to give her the perfect opening? "You could help me with that, you know. Change your mind about the hotel makeover, be a hometown hero and give back to your community."

His green gaze tracked from her eyes to her mouth and then to her eyes again. The way he looked at her, so intent, so focused, she could almost feel it as a caress. "I'm not the hero type."

"Roman. You underestimate yourself."

"No, I don't. I know exactly what I am, what I want and what I'm willing to do to get it."

"You mean you're a calculating man?"

"That's right." He tapped the side of his head with his finger. "Everything starts from here with me."

"Everything?"

He grinned then. "Okay, yeah. Except sex. That has its origins a little lower down."

Their waiter appeared. He took away the empty appetizer plates.

When he left, Hailey debated pressing Roman further on the issue of the theater. But Rome wasn't built in a dinner date. She figured she'd said enough on the subject for tonight. "Another thing about your mother. I think she might be matchmaking us."

His response surprised her. "Yeah, she is."

"You know this, how?"

"She pretty much told me so. She said she likes you and she gave me permission to pursue you."

"You're not serious. I just don't see you as the kind of man who does what his mother wants—and today, your mom told me in person that you're pigheaded and no one stands up to you."

He chuckled. "You stand up to me."

She picked up her wine and took a fortifying gulp as the waiter arrived with their entrées.

* * *

Roman kept thinking that the woman across from him was just about perfect. She was not only beautiful and intelligent and funny, but she also had a big heart. He'd discovered he admired that, a big heart.

Who knew he would ever care about the size of a woman's heart?

But he realized now that a big heart mattered.

And she loved kids. Odds were high she would be good with Theo, and she would probably want more children, which worked for him.

He was becoming more accepting of how attracted he was to her, less wary of the emotional danger she represented. She was the kind of woman a man could fall for and never stop. Just fall and fall.

Falling put a man at something of a disadvantage.

But he was willing to let it happen, ready to learn to live with a certain amount of vulnerability to her.

At the end of the meal, they had coffee and shared a slice of chocolate Kahlua silk pie.

He waited for her to set down her coffee cup before asking, "So how would you feel about marrying some guy with a toddler and an overbearing, live-in mother?" He watched her eyes get really big before he smiled. "What? Too soon?"

She ate a bite of the silk pie. "So good…" And then she set down her fork and gamely countered, "I do find you way too attractive."

He liked the sound of that. "So that's a yes?"

"Roman, you need to slow down. It's much too early to start talking marriage."

"For you, maybe. But I'm thirty-two—thirty-two with a little boy who could use a mother. I've always wanted a wife. I like the idea of making a good life with the right woman. I was starting to accept that it just wasn't in the cards for me. I see now I was wrong."

She sipped her coffee. "Your forthrightness is disorienting."

"That's okay. I like you on edge."

"I'll bet. And you know what? *I'm* forthright, too."

"Good. Tell me something I don't know."

That sweet mouth of hers softened and her eyes glittered like twin sapphires. "I'm so attracted to you and…"

This conversation was definitely headed in the right direction. But why had she stalled out? "Say it."

"Well, it's been a long time for me…"

"Yeah?"

She leaned closer and lowered her voice to just above a whisper. "I would be open to a fling with you."

He was half-hard in an instant, and damn glad for the napkin on his lap and the table between them. He quelled the need to reach for her right then and there. Slowly, he shook his head. "Nope. I'll wait."

She sat back. "Um, for what?"

"For the wedding."

She let out a trill of sweet laughter. "Did you propose? Did I say yes? I don't remember either of those things happening, which means that this conversation has gotten way ahead of me."

"I think I should sweeten the deal."

She raised both hands and turned them palm-up in a be-my-guest gesture.

He laid it on her. "When you marry me, I'll give you that damn theater as a wedding present."

She faked a gasp, put a hand to her heart and exclaimed in a cornpone accent, "Why, Roman Marek, I really don't know what to say!"

"That's not all. I'll even remodel it for you—remodel it exactly to your specifications."

"I find I am equally flattered and appalled. You just tried to bribe me to marry you."

"Hailey. I know exactly what I did." Her hand rested on the white tablecloth. He reached across and covered it with his. That she didn't pull away made him want to surge up out of his chair, scoop her high in his arms and carry her out of there.

She said, "You should turn over the theater to the arts council and renovate it for community use as a performance space."

He looked amused. "Yeah. Well, that's not going to happen."

"And I know you're just joking, anyway." Her eyes gleamed even brighter than before and the words came out sounding husky.

He said nothing. He'd already made his intentions clear. He *was* going to marry her. And when he did, she could have the theater—if she didn't make him wait so long that he'd already converted it into a tourist trap by then.

She turned her hand over and gave his fingers a squeeze. "Say you're joking, Roman." It was almost a plea.

He shook his head. Slowly. For a sweet, endless moment, they just stared at each other.

Until the waiter returned to offer more coffee.

Hailey said, "No, thank you," to the waiter.

As for the gorgeous man across the table from her, she hardly knew what to make of him. He was so certain about things, so self-directed.

In her life, in almost every situation, she was accustomed to taking the lead, to making her wishes known and setting about accomplishing whatever goals she'd set for herself. Never before had she met someone who was more dominant than she was, who wrested the lead from her and ran with it.

It had been so different with Nathan. She'd done the pursuing until he surrendered. She'd said what she wanted—him—and he'd eventually given himself to her, though not all the way. He would never come home and meet her family with her. He said his life was one day at a time and meeting the parents just didn't fit with that. She'd argued how wrong he was, but he wouldn't budge on that point.

And oh, he had loved her. She would always have that. Nathan had loved deeply and well, as she had loved him—and their love was made possible because she'd kept after him until he gave her a chance.

Roman was nothing like Nathan. Nathan was a cozy fire on a cold night. Roman, well, he was fireworks and grand gestures, a man who took on the world and wrestled it into submission.

She found being around Roman exhilarating. He wasn't predictable. She didn't really know what he might do or say next. He made her feel off-balance, swept away by some elemental force. She didn't trust how strongly she already wanted him.

But dear God, whatever this was she had going on with him, it was exciting and fresh, uncharted territory. It was also scary.

And good. Really good.

When they left the restaurant, he drove straight to the house on Treasure Cove Circle. Stopping the sleek black car in the driveway, he silenced the purring engine.

Turning toward her in his seat, he caught a lock of her hair and rubbed it between his long fingers. "Silky." He seemed very intense suddenly.

She touched the side of his face. "What? Tell me."

Gently, he guided the strands back over her shoulder. "I want to kiss you, but if I kiss you, I'm not going to want to stop. We'll end up having sex. You'll think I'm weak because I said no and then went ahead and took you to bed anyway."

She stared in those light green eyes and realized she wouldn't mind drowning in them. "Not kissing me then, huh?"

"I'm going to hold off as long as I can stand to." It came out rough. Low.

"So you enjoy torturing yourself?" *And me, too,* she thought but didn't say.

He was staring at her mouth. "Every time you

speak, I want to bite your lips. They're so soft and pink..."

She considered taking the lead herself, just leaning in and claiming his mouth.

But they were moving too fast, anyway. Already, he'd sort of proposed and she'd suggested they jump right into bed.

Really, they could both stand to show a little restraint.

"Is your mom home?" she asked.

"Yes."

"I like your mom. Let's go in."

"No."

"Why not?"

"She likes you, too. She'll monopolize you and say things that embarrass me. I'd rather keep you all to myself, at least for tonight."

"If we're not going in, why are we here?"

"I thought we could go for a walk down on the beach..."

They took the red cedar stairs built into the hillside to get down to the sand. The sun had just set, and the tide was in. At the horizon, a ribbon of orange met the edge of the darkened ocean.

Hailey slipped off her sandals and left them at the base of the steps.

"It's beautiful," she said. "We have a beach out behind the cottage where I live. But it's not in its own little cove, all sheltered and private, like this. Local kids hang out there and so do a couple of families who live nearby, and tourists, too."

He took her hand, his fingers sliding between hers. She felt so good, like her heart was just flying—high up there in the darkening sky, free.

Full of life, bursting with joy.

Hailey loved her work, though she made barely enough money to get by on and now and then people hinted that she ought to find a real job. But H&H Productions was a real job as far as she was concerned. She felt happy and fulfilled, planning the next project, directing any- and everybody in town, pulling a show together on a wing and a prayer.

As a woman, though, something in her had died along with Nathan. She was happy in her life and didn't really expect to ever feel that something stir again.

But then, last Monday, she'd knocked Doug Dickerson on his ass and turned to find Roman standing there, stage right. Something had happened for her at that moment, at her first sight of the big man with the chiseled profile.

A recognition of possibility, maybe. A light going on in the darkness, a match bursting into flame.

She needed to slow down, she kept reminding herself. But how does a woman slow down when she's soaring free and high on whatever that thing is that can happen between her and the right guy?

"Okay, this is about as much as I can take," he said, stopping in the damp, cold sand at the edge of the shore, pulling on their clasped hands, bringing her in close to his heat and solid strength.

Her heart pounded faster, and her breath came swift and shallow. Out over the water, seagulls cried. The waves made that whooshing sound, hollow and soft. The wind, smelling cool and fresh and salty, stirred her hair. Roman trailed his fingers lightly up her arms. Even through the cardigan she'd put on over her sleeveless dress, his touch roused shivers in its wake. He cradled her face in his big, warm palms.

She stared up into those eyes she'd been seeing in her dreams. Conscious thought had pretty much fled. She was all beating heart and trembling sensation.

And then, at last, his mouth was there, meeting hers. So soft, his lips, so pliant. So hungry.

With a desperate little moan, she surged up on tiptoe, lifting her arms to wrap them around his neck.

Chapter Four

Roman breathed her name against her parted lips.

She drank in the sound as his tongue found hers, twining. He was so big, engulfing her in his arms, his hard chest hot against her soft breasts, his erection pressing into her belly, reminding her afresh that this was territory she'd left uncharted for three long years.

He tasted so good and he held her so close. Everything felt magnified—the lovely, cold sifting of damp sand between her toes, the gentle force of the wind against her back. His hands, holding her, stroking her back, were so big and warm. They soothed and aroused her at once.

When he took her by the shoulders and gently set her away, she opened her eyes and stared up at him, stunned, like a dreamer awakened suddenly in the middle of the night.

"Don't stop," she whispered. Surging up, she pressed her mouth to his again. He froze and she braced for him to push her away.

But then, with a low growl, he wrapped her in those hot arms once more and gave in to the dangerous beauty of this wild thing between them.

He kissed her desperately, hungrily, like he would never let her go. Like a storm, he kissed her. She melted into him, her heart crying *yes*.

It was disorienting, glorious, perfect.

And really, he was right. They needed to stop.

That time, they both pulled back at once. He stared at her, his eyes heavy-lidded, more silver than green. His mouth was swollen from making love to hers. She had no doubt she looked as aroused as he did.

Neither of them spoke.

He took her hand again and they continued walking toward the outcropping of rough rocks trailing out into the water that marked off the southern end of his private cove. Still holding his hand, she perched on one of the rocks. He sat beside her on the next rock over.

They stared out across the water. The few clouds had drifted away, leaving a clear sky—a rarity on this section of coast. Slowly, the stars filled the darkness.

It was chilly. Her toes were growing numb. When she shivered a little, he tugged her up off her rock and over onto his. Cradling her between his thighs, he wrapped both arms around her and she let herself lean back into the warmth of his broad chest.

"It's beautiful tonight," she said, her toes still cold but the rest of her warmed by his body heat.

His breath stirred her hair. "*This* is beautiful—having you, right here in my arms—and you're shivering."

"My feet are freezing."

"We should get back."

Reluctantly, she agreed.

It was around ten when they reached the cottage where she lived with Harper. He walked her to the front step. Without hesitation, she turned and lifted her face for his kiss.

He was careful not to let the contact go too deep, pulling back before she was ready to let him go.

"Come in," she invited. "Let's see where this takes us."

"You're way too tempting."

"Why does that sound like a no?"

He rubbed his big palms down her arms and back up in a slow, continuous caress that made her feel heavy and hot down below. "I always considered your brother Daniel to be a real hero."

"Oh, great. You want to talk about my big brother?"

His eyes gleamed down at her and a ghost of a smile played at the edges of that mouth she wanted to kiss some more. "I really admire Daniel, for the way he took custody of all of you when your parents died so suddenly. He was only, what—eighteen?"

"Yeah." Where was he going with this?

Wherever it was, he seemed in no hurry to get there. "I remember he married Lillie, his high school sweetheart, the next year. Lillie… Ostergard, right?"

Hailey nodded. "Lillie was wonderful, a real second mom to all of us. I don't know if you'd heard, but she died."

He stuck his hands in his pockets and frowned down at her. "No. I didn't know."

"Yeah. That was four years ago, right after their twins were born. Lillie had lupus. There were complications. It was a hard time—for Daniel, of course. And the rest of us, too. Lillie loved us so much and we adored her. I was nine when she married Daniel and moved into the family house with us. She loved kids and she showered us with attention. She was like a second mom, the best kind of mom. So interested in everything we did and said, staying up all night to make our Halloween costumes and whole wardrobes for our dolls."

He was watching her so closely. "You loved her."

"We all did. Lillie was the one who taught Harper and me to sew. I never had the patience for it. But Harper, she can whip up something ready for the runway with a few scraps of fabric, a spool of thread and a little rickrack."

His eyes were mournful. "I really hadn't heard that Lillie died. So sorry, that you lost her…"

"Thank you. The good news is that the twins, Jake and Frannie, are healthy and thriving. Daniel remarried a couple of years ago—his wife is Lillie's cousin, Keely, as a matter of fact."

"Keely Ostergard—cute, with strawberry hair and freckles across her nose?"

"That's Keely. She's as terrific as Lillie was, a good person with a generous heart. They have another daughter together, Marie."

"So you're saying that Daniel is happy now?"

"Very."

"Good." A faraway smile tugged on the corners of his mouth. "He and your brother Matt used to get into it, right?"

"How did you know that?"

"I remember at homecoming my junior year, hanging out under the bleachers with the stoners and the other loners like me. Matt was there..."

She knew where that story went. "Let me guess. He was smoking a giant blunt."

Roman's white teeth flashed. "Yeah. We passed it back and forth and Matt complained that Daniel was always riding his ass to shape up, get better grades, start planning for the future. He said Daniel was like some fussy old man, constantly after all you Bravo kids to stay focused and work hard. He griped about how Daniel and Lillie expected you all to be there for dinner together every night and that Sunday-afternoon dinner was a major deal that nobody was ever allowed to miss. I was so damn jealous, wanting what Matt didn't even seem to care about. A big family around the dinner table. Brothers and sisters. As far back as I can remember, it was always just Ma and me."

She stared up at him, still wondering where all this reminiscing about her family was going—and also still longing to kiss him again. "You really should see Matt now. He's so in love with his wife, Sabra. They have a three-legged husky named Zoya and a baby on the way."

"When's the baby due?"

"Next April. Sabra's three months along. Matt's over the moon about it. They made the announcement last Sunday."

"Last Sunday at the family dinner up on Rhinehart Hill?"

"That's right."

"So you still have a Bravo family dinner every Sunday?"

"Yeah—not that we all make it every week, but we try."

He eased his hand under her hair and cupped the back of her neck, his fingers so warm, possessive in the best kind of way. "Invite me for dinner this Sunday."

She pulled back a little to give herself some distance from the seductive heat of him. "Wait. Is this where the trip down memory lane was heading? You wanted an invite to Sunday dinner?"

"I want to meet the family."

She scoffed. "But you *know* my family. You were in school with Connor. You remember Daniel and Lillie. You just told me all about how you and Matt smoked weed together under the bleachers at homecoming."

"Hailey." He drew her close again. She let him do it, tucking her head under his chin, breathing in his clean scent, feeling beautiful and *wanted*, just because his arms were around her—even if she still didn't get exactly what he was after here. "When I say, 'meet the family,' I mean I want to meet them all over again, as your fiancé."

She snapped her head back to look him square in the eye and scolded, "You are so completely over the top."

"It's part of my charm."

"We are not engaged and that means you are not my fiancé. And *that* means it's a little early for *that* kind of 'meeting the family.'"

His gaze held her captive. Not that she minded. She could stare into those eyes of his all night long. He was larger than life, a showman at heart if not by profession. She felt that they were kindred spirits, ringmasters in a world full of clock punchers. "I don't think it's too early," he said. "Not too early at all..." He lowered his head to her slowly.

She couldn't wait for their lips to meet.

And when they did—wow! The kiss was so good. Better than the last one, which had been spectacular.

"I have a huge crush on you," she whispered when he let her go.

He gave her his sexiest smile. "So take me to Sunday dinner because you have a crush on me." He leaned near and whispered in her ear, "Please."

Oh, really. Why not? "All right."

"Excellent."

Two minutes later, she was standing on the step alone, watching him drive away. Her fingers strayed to her lips. They still tingled from kissing him.

In the cottage, she found Harper on the sofa in the living room altering a skirt they'd picked up at the thrift mall. She was watching *Stumptown* on the forty-two-inch flat-screen Daniel had given them last Christmas. When Hailey walked in, Harper pointed the remote and the screen went dark.

"Hey," Hailey objected. "You don't have to turn it off."

"I'll catch it later." She tapped the remote on the cushion beside her. "Sit. Tell all."

Hailey dropped to the sofa, kicked off her sandals and flopped back against the cushions. She stared up at the white beadboard ceiling. "I've just had the strangest, most wonderful evening."

Harper made a low, thoughtful sound. "That's good, right?"

"I'm not sure. Roman Marek says he's going to marry me."

"That Roman. He doesn't fool around."

"I told him I would be open to a fling—and I absolutely meant it." Hailey rolled her head on the cushion to look at her sister.

Harper's gaze was waiting. "You like him."

"I do. But as for the fling, he says I have to wait for the wedding."

"So then, his plan is to drive you mad with desire until you give in and agree to be his wife just so he'll have sex with you?"

She laughed. "He's kind of outrageous, but I like him. I do. He's domineering and yet somehow vulnerable, you know? And funny and smart and definitely up-front about his intentions."

Harper lowered her sewing into her lap and leaned her head back, too. The sisters stared at each other. Finally, Harper said, "You look good, Lee-Lee. Happy in that special way, the loved-up way. It's been a long time."

"Yeah, well. We'll see how it goes."

A tiny frown crinkled Harper's smooth forehead. "Maybe take it slow, huh?"

"Good advice, thanks—however, I did agree

he could come with me to Daniel's for Sunday dinner."

"Pushover." Shaking her head, Harper sat up and bent to her sewing again.

Hailey was never a pushover. She ran the show—at the theater and in her life in general. She had it all under control.

At least, she had until Roman Marek came back to town.

Sunday right on time, Hailey answered the door to find Roman looking amazing and meet-the-family-ready in a cream-colored waffle-stitch sweater and tan pants. He'd brought Theo with him.

"Ba!" cried the little boy gleefully, grinning at her and drooling.

Roman explained, "Ma wanted to go to lunch with one of the women she used to clean house for back in the day. Somehow, she always ended up becoming best friends with every woman she ever worked for. I hope you don't mind if Theo comes with us."

Theo held out the plastic pretzel he'd been chewing on. "Oo-ba?" he asked, still beaming.

Hailey took the pretzel, not even caring that it

was covered in drool. "So glad you could make it, Theo."

"Ah-ga." Theo grabbed for his pretzel back. Apparently, sharing was one thing, but she shouldn't be greedy.

"Here you go." She handed it over. Theo promptly stuck it in his mouth.

Roman was watching her, wearing a look that reminded her of the kisses they'd shared the other night. "Is Harper riding with us?" he asked, scoring thoughtfulness points in Hailey's book.

"She had to drop by the theater, so she took her own car."

For a moment, they just stood there, grinning at each other, until Theo crowed, "Da-Da!" and tried to get Roman to take a bite of his plastic pretzel.

Roman gently pushed his little hand away and they turned for a high-end silver SUV. "Where's the sports car?"

He pulled open the back door and lowered Theo into his car seat. "I call this my Dad Car. I use it when I take Theo somewhere."

"How many cars do you have?"

"I cut back when we left Vegas. Only three now." He buckled Theo in. "This one, the Lambo and a six-wheeled Hennessey Raptor F-150 Super Crew pickup."

"*Only* three, huh? You really need to give the theater to the community."

He shut the back seat door and shepherded her around to the passenger door in front. Pulling it wide, he said, "Marry me and *you* can give the theater to the community."

She sent him a patient look as she settled into the seat. Did she enjoy all this marriage talk way too much? She was so attracted to him, but really, she hardly knew him. To get married, you should be in love, and being in love took time.

Roman shut her door, crossed around in front of the vehicle and climbed in behind the wheel. She almost said something about marriage and love and how it wasn't something to joke about—but then she let it go. She'd made her point and he'd come back with his. Enough said for now.

Too bad Roman just couldn't leave it alone. "What?" he demanded. "No snarky comeback?"

She answered super sweetly. "I never get snarky about something as important as marriage." From the back seat, Theo let out a string of nonsense syllables. "And see? Theo backs me up, a hundred percent."

If anyone was surprised that Hailey had finally brought a guy to Sunday dinner, they didn't let on. When she arrived with Roman and Theo, Connor and Matt and their wives were already there—Connor and his wife, Aly, had brought their four-month-old, Emelia. Liam, fourth-born of the siblings, arrived a few minutes later with his family.

After the meal, Roman handed Theo to Hailey. "I'll be back."

She shared a smile with Theo and asked Roman, "Where, exactly, are you going?"

"Daniel's breaking out the good Scotch in his study. I'm invited—me, and your other brothers."

When Daniel took people to his study and brought out the Scotch, that usually meant a serious talk was in the offing. About someone's life choices, about life changes one of them planned to make. "You don't have to go, you know."

He looked at her so tenderly. "Relax. I can handle your brothers."

She watched him walk away with the others and couldn't stop herself from wondering if her brothers would gang up on him and quiz him about what might be happening between the two of them.

That would be kind of ridiculous. She was twenty-five years old, past the age where a girl's brothers got overprotective when she showed up with a guy.

Wasn't she?

Hailey sat on the family room sofa and settled Theo on her lap. "There. Isn't this comfy?"

Theo gazed up at her, hazel eyes wide and a beautiful smile on his face as he waved a small plastic giraffe at her. He let out a string of happy, meaningless babble, seeming not the least concerned that his dad wasn't in the room. Already, he seemed to have accepted her as someone he didn't mind hanging with.

Really, for a little boy who'd lost his mother at the age of one month, he was so outgoing, so happy and trusting. Evidently, he got what he needed from Sasha—and Roman, too.

"Hi, Hailey."

Hailey turned to find her brother Liam's eight-year-old stepdaughter, Coco Killigan, standing at the other end of the leather sofa. The little girl had Riley, her half brother and Liam's son, in her arms. Riley, like Theo, was big for his age. The little girl seemed to be barely holding on to him. Hailey waved her closer. "Coco, come on and have a seat."

Coco dropped to the cushion next to Hailey and plunked Riley in her lap. She was the cutest kid, with wildly curling dark hair and big blue eyes—and Coco was talented, too. She had parts in several sketches in the Fall Revue, including a brief solo in the finale.

"You know, Hailey," Coco said in a voice so enthusiastic, it made Hailey want to hug her. "I think Riley and Theo are about the same age."

"You're right. Eleven months."

The two little boys were already making conversation in a language all their own. Theo grunted. Riley let out a crowing sound and bounced on his sister's lap.

Coco winced. "Sometimes he squishes me. He doesn't mean it, though. He's just a baby." She bent close and kissed his plump cheek.

Across the big family room, Daniel's three kids were building a Duplo structure under the supervision of Coco's ten-year-old brother, Ben. Hailey suggested, "How 'bout we take these two over there?"

Coco considered the idea and then announced very seriously, "Riley and Theo are still kind of little for Duplos."

"Yeah, but we'll be there to supervise."

Coco brightened. "And then Riley could be on the floor and stop smashing my legs when he bounces."

"Exactly."

So they carried the little ones over there. They

sat cross-legged on the floor and chatted with Ben while keeping Riley and Theo from crawling off or snacking on Duplo blocks.

Eventually, Roman reappeared. He crouched next to Hailey. "How're you holding up?"

She tried her best to ignore the thrill that skittered through her just at the sound of his voice and the sight of him, so large and manly, up close and personal. "We're having a great time. Your son is a dream." She leaned into him, getting even closer. He smelled wonderful, as usual. Like the ocean and fresh sheets—and good Scotch, too. "What went down in Daniel's study?"

Roman gave her a one-shouldered shrug. "I had a drink with your brothers, and we caught up on the last decade and a half. Why?"

"Because I know Daniel. When he breaks out the Scotch, something serious and personal is always discussed."

He guided a lock of hair back behind her ear. The fond gesture stirred something inside her—something a little painful. Something tender and real. "Picture it—four men, gathered in the study that once belonged to your father..."

"What are you getting at?"

"What are *you* getting at? There was Scotch.

We caught up. Last time I got together with any one of them, we were in high school."

"Hmm." She narrowed her eyes at him. "But is catching up serious enough for the good Scotch? I don't think so. I think there's something you're not telling me."

"Good Scotch can be served when there's reminiscing, too."

"You're not going to tell me, are you?"

"Let it go." His voice was rough velvet. And he was watching her so closely, his gaze tracking from her eyes to her mouth and back to her eyes again. She imagined him leaning a fraction closer and claiming her lips in a scorching-hot kiss. Even surrounded by all these impressionable kids, she couldn't help wishing he would make that move.

"Da-Da!" Theo broke the spell as he glanced up from crashing a plastic dump truck into an abandoned Duplo hut and spotted his dad. He plopped back to his butt and held out his arms.

Roman rose, scooped him up and sat down on the floor next to Hailey. "So, what are we building?"

She debated the pluses and minuses of keeping after him about what had gone down in the study.

But hey. If he didn't want to tell her, he wouldn't. She let it go and answered his question instead. "Jake, Frannie and Marie are building a

Duplo castle," Hailey explained, tipping her head at Daniel's three children. "Ben is supervising." She nodded at Coco's brother on the other side of the in-progress plastic structure. "Coco and I are observing the construction and keeping an eye on Theo and Riley."

Riley, who had pulled himself to his feet using an armchair for support, took a few wobbly steps and then crumpled to the floor again. Undeterred, he got right back up on his hands and knees, crawled toward Roman and Theo—and wriggled into Roman's lap. Theo thought that was funny and chortled out a goofy laugh. Roman simply readjusted his position to make room for both boys.

Hailey found the moment way too adorable. And sexy.

The man was just too sexy. And she was so ready for the fling she'd offered him.

Three years without a guy in her bed. And until recently, she'd had zero urge to get intimate with anyone.

And now there was Roman, who was all man in the best *and* most exasperating ways. He'd teased her that she would have to marry him first.

But that was just teasing.

Wasn't it?

* * *

It was after seven when they left the house on Rhinehart Hill. Theo conked out the moment Roman buckled him into his car seat.

When Roman slid behind the wheel, he turned those silvery eyes on her. "Come to my place, just for an hour or two. Ma will take Theo. We'll have a little time alone."

"I'm in," she replied with zero hesitation.

She'd known him for a week—seven days during which she'd been either annoyed or flat-out furious with him most of the time. Didn't matter. She wanted to be alone with him and she wanted it tonight. They needed to get started on the passionate love affair they were going to be having.

Okay, yeah. He'd just said Sasha would be home—home and, like the shameless matchmaker she was, grinning in satisfaction at the sight of them together.

Hailey didn't even care. It was a big house with lots of rooms for her to get Roman alone in.

At Roman's, they found Sasha on the sofa in the family room off the kitchen, watching a Hallmark movie on the big-screen TV mounted above the fireplace.

Roman's mom glanced over as they came in. She smiled with a definite gleam in her eyes. "Hailey." Sasha turned off the TV and stood. "How *are* you?"

"Really good, thanks—and you didn't have to turn off your movie."

"I'll watch the rest up in my room after I put this angel to bed." Sasha took the yawning Theo from her son's arms. "I called your sister and I'm signed up to scout props and paint sets."

"Thank you."

"Happy to help." Sasha pressed a kiss to Theo's plump cheek. "Roman, give Hailey a nice glass of wine, why don't you?"

Roman granted her a glance that spoke of great forbearance. "Night, Ma." He waited until she'd had time to get upstairs before muttering, "Grown men probably shouldn't let their mothers move in with them."

"I disagree—in your case, anyway. You need someone around to remind you that you don't run the world." She paused to give him a chance to argue the point. He surprised her and let it go. She went on, "Plus, Theo sure seems like a happy guy. That has to be at least partly due to Sasha."

"It is—and more than partly," he easily admitted, gesturing her on into the kitchen area.

She stopped near the giant central island and cast an admiring glance around the open room, taking in the dark wood cabinetry, the gorgeous granite-and-wood countertops and the sliding wood-framed doors leading out to a big deck. "This kitchen is as fabulous as the rest of the house."

He gave her a slow once-over, his gaze skating warmly over her turquoise sweater and white skinny jeans. "Wine?"

"Thank you, yes." She lingered by the island as he opened a bottle of red and poured them each a glass.

"The weather's mild. Not much wind. Let's go out on the deck." He flipped a switch that turned on decorative lights strung along the deck railings.

The warm glow pushed back the gathering shadows. Beyond the glass doors, she saw teak chairs and sofas, each with bright-colored cushions and throw pillows. Not a bad setting for the seduction she had planned. They could move it inside and up to his bedroom when things became too intimate.

Outside, he led her to the railing. They stared out at the ocean beyond the wind-twisted trees.

"It's beautiful here." Down below, she saw a cozy backyard area of large rock pavers and grass. "That's pretty down there."

"This way..." He took her hand and led her

down a set of side stairs to the level below, where more glass doors lead into the house.

He noticed the direction of her gaze. "It's a whole, smaller living space on this floor. There's a great room with its own kitchen, two bedrooms, two baths and another big room I've set up as a gym. Other than the workout room, I haven't made much use of the bottom floor. But I figure a separate guest suite never hurts. And maybe when Theo's older, Ma will want a more private space."

"Options. I love those."

Lifting her hand, he pressed his warm lips to her knuckles, causing a flare of heat to burn through her. "Thanks for taking me to the Bravo Sunday dinner." He really seemed to mean it.

"I guess it must not have been too terrible, whatever was said in Daniel's study."

"Not terrible at all. Stop worrying about it." Lightly, he nipped at her skin, a slow, gentle scrape of his white teeth.

She had to suppress a little moan. And she wanted to get closer, so she took a step toward him, until her breasts brushed his hard chest. He must have read her desire in her eyes, because he gave her what she craved and lowered that hot mouth of his to cover hers.

They kissed, there under cover of the upper

deck, wrapped in shadows as the night was falling. It was a long, deep, delicious kiss, one that heated her midsection and had her right on the verge of pulling him back up the stairs, into the house and up to his room.

But then he stepped back. "I'll light the fire."

She blinked up at him and wished he would gather her close once more. "What fire?"

He touched her, skating a finger down the ridge of her nose, tracing the wings of her eyebrows, a bemused expression on his wonderful face. "This way." He led her out under the sky again, where the cloud cover obscured the brightening stars, to a giant stone bowl filled with lava rock. At the flick of a switch, flames licked up through the rock.

"So pretty," she said.

Setting his wine on a low table, he stretched out on the padded lounger beside it. "Come here." She put her wine beside his and started to sit on the next lounger over. But he stopped her by catching her hand. "Here. With me."

It was a tight fit for the two of them, but she had no problem with that. She cuddled in close with a happy sigh. He wrapped his arms around her and slipped a knee between hers.

"This is nice," she whispered.

And then they were kissing again. Long, slow, lazy kisses—or at least, they started out lazy.

But they didn't stay that way. The kisses grew deeper, his caresses more intimate.

She pulled back enough to offer, "Let's go upstairs."

He smoothed a broad palm down her hair and then cradled her chin in the crook of his finger. His eyes were less silver now, more green—deepest green, like in a secret lagoon somewhere in the heart of a thick tropical jungle. "I'm not going to rush you."

"You're not." She grabbed two fistfuls of his sweater, yanked him close again and made herself perfectly clear. "It's been years for me, Roman. I mean, I loved Nathan and I really didn't want anyone else. Not for the longest time."

Something flared in those deep-lagoon eyes, something possessive and raw. "You still love him?"

She went for complete honesty. "Some part of me always will. But I'm no longer wrecked by the loss of him. Meeting you, being with you has made it clear to me that I'm ready to move on. With you. I want to be with you, tonight. You and me. In your bed. Tell me you want the same thing."

"What I want is to marry you."

She sat up so fast she almost fell off the lounger.

"Whoa." He grabbed her and steadied her.

Yanking free of his grip, she stood. "Will you listen to yourself? You won't have sex with me, but let's get married?" She threw up both hands and sat on the other lounger, facing him. "You're making no sense."

He regarded her steadily. Such a good-looking man, all broad shoulders and big arms, a deep chest that tapered to a narrow, hard waist—and a definite bulge at his fly. So hot. And so completely confusing.

"I've messed up at marriage twice," he said. "Both women, I took to bed the night that I met them. I'm not doing that again."

"Roman, this isn't that."

"No, it's not. And I'm going to handle things differently this time. We're taking it slow."

"We've known each other—"

"A week, Hailey—a week, as of tomorrow. A week isn't long enough."

"Oh. Right. Because you're so *restrained*. Did you or did you not ask me to marry you night before last?"

He didn't even have the grace to look embarrassed at the utter inconsistency of his reasoning. "I did. And I meant it, too."

"So you won't sleep with me, but you *will* marry me?"

"I won't sleep with you *now*—and yes, I still want to marry you."

"Who thinks like that? Nobody thinks like that."

"*I* think like that, Hailey."

"Which is my point, exactly." She grabbed her wine and sucked down the rest of it, plunking the glass back on the little table hard enough she was lucky she didn't break the stem.

Rising, he caught her hand. His warm fingers felt just right wrapped around hers. She wanted to shriek at him not to be so tempting when he had no intention of following through. "Come up here," he commanded gruffly. "Kiss me."

"You're just a big tease, that's what you are, Roman Marek."

He was trying not to grin. She could tell by the slight twitch at the corner of his wonderful mouth. "Come on."

She ought to refuse him. But she didn't really want to refuse him. And if he insisted on taking it a little slower, well, as much as she hated to admit that he could be right, and she might wrong, maybe there was a tiny bit of sense in that.

"Come on. Let me feel you close, Hailey. Let

me suffer a little wanting what I'm not going to get right now..."

She let him pull her to her feet. Slowly. Her heart beat deep and hard in the cage of her ribs and her skin felt supersensitized. "I shouldn't kiss you. I should just walk away..."

He gathered her in and bent to nuzzle her cheek. "Please don't."

She tipped her head down.

And he put his finger under her chin and guided her to look at him again. "You're like no woman I've ever known. Everything about you is just right. I could look at you for the rest of my life and never get tired of the sight of you. We don't have to rush into bed together. We really don't."

"It wasn't about *having* to. I *wanted* to."

"And now?"

She gave him a shrug and answered lightly. "Too late. I'm over it. Completely and totally. You missed your chance."

He kissed her then, a long, slow kiss.

She almost pulled away, just to prove her point.

But Roman was an excellent kisser and the past few years had been completely devoid of kisses. So she gave herself up to his strong arms and his warm mouth and the thrilling slide of his tongue against hers. When she did pull back, it was with a soft, happy sigh.

A half an hour later, he drove her to the cottage and walked her to the front step. He kissed her again, sweet and deep and slow, and left her gazing dreamily after him, waving goodbye as he drove away.

Inside, Harper was waiting on the sofa in the living room. "Sit down, kick your shoes off and dish me the deets."

Hailey told her sister everything and they laughed together over the total failure of her big attempt at seduction.

"At least he has honest intentions," said Harper.

"Really? That's what you get from him turning me down?"

"I don't think he'll be turning you down indefinitely."

"Gee, I'm so relieved."

"The way he looks at you." Harper made a show of fanning herself. "Like he's a hungry tiger and you're a plump, oblivious gazelle."

"Now, there's a romantic image for you."

"You should get on the Pill or take the shot. Be prepared."

She couldn't believe she hadn't thought of that already. "You're right. I'll take care of it—and sheesh, it's been so long I almost forgot I need birth control."

The cottage had old-fashioned, wood-framed, single-paned windows, the kind with lots of tiny panes that let in cold drafts in the winter. Harper stared out the windows across from the sofa, her own face reflected at her. She seemed lost in thought.

"You okay?" Hailey asked.

"Mmm-hmm. Just thinking how lucky you are. It's doubtful lightning will be striking twice, you know?"

"Okay, I'll bite. Lucky, how—and what do you mean about lightning?"

"It's a small town, that's all." Harper's voice was wistful. "I probably won't be meeting the love of my life here."

"Okay, hold up." For so long, Hailey had been absolutely sure that Nathan was the love of her life. It seemed somehow disloyal to his memory to even think that Roman might hold that spot now. "One, did I say Roman was the love of my life?" Harper just looked at her and snickered. Hailey continued, "Two—think about it. Lightning has already struck several times in our family and there's no reason it won't strike for you—right here in our hometown. Three..." Hailey softened her tone and gave her sister's arm a pat. "It's not only the romance thing that's bothering you, is it?"

Harper jumped directly to denial. "I love working with you. We're a team, we always have been."

Hailey wrapped an arm around her sister and they leaned their heads together. "Harp. We both know what's going on here. You can just say it. The whole community theater thing doesn't fill your soul the way it does mine." Harper had minored in architecture. She'd spoken more than once about her longing to design the spaces where people lived and worked. And though Hailey would miss everything about having her almost-twin nearby, Harper needed to get out there and live the kind of life that challenged and excited her. "You've got to start looking, sending out résumés, checking out what's available on LinkedIn."

"There's nothing in town."

"Seattle's not that far."

Harper pulled away and met Hailey's eyes. "I do love working with you—and if I go, who's gonna do my job? You'll get stuck with Doug for your tech director."

Hailey snort-laughed. "Okay, now that's really terrifying." But then she grew serious. "You need to do what's going to satisfy you—and yes, Doug's an ass who lacks your genius. But he's capable enough. He could do the job if it came down to it."

"I don't know..." Harper was staring out the dark window again.

Hailey insisted, "Start looking. I mean it."

Harper slid her another glance. "I'll think about it."

In the morning, after Harper had already left for the theater, Hailey answered a knock on the door and found her eldest brother on the step.

"I was just on my way to work," Daniel said. He ran Valentine Logging. It was the family company and the offices were nearby on the Warrenton docks. "Thought I would check in with you, see how you're doing." His square jaw was set. He looked at her with equal parts worry and determination.

It was a look he used to aim at Matthias constantly, but that was years ago when Matt was always getting wasted. In recent years, their youngest sister, Gracie, had taken the brunt of Daniel's big-brotherly concern. Things were better between them now, but Gracie used to complain that Daniel was constantly in her face about every little thing.

As for Hailey, though, she hadn't been the focus

of Daniel's concern in a long while—not since middle school when she'd gotten a C-minus in algebra. And then later, in high school, when she'd dated Jimmy Karnes, of whom Daniel did not approve.

And why did Hailey suddenly feel so defensive? "You saw me yesterday, Daniel. Did I give you some indication that I had a problem we needed to 'check in' about?"

He drew his broad shoulders back and said much too gently, "How 'bout some coffee, Hailey? What do you say?"

Like she had a choice. She ushered him in.

Chapter Five

Daniel didn't take long getting to the point. He sat at the kitchen table, had a sip of the coffee she'd poured for him and said, "So, is this serious between you and Roman Marek?"

"Serious? I've known him for exactly a week as of today, if that's what you're asking."

"You brought him to Sunday dinner. You never bring men to Sunday dinner."

She knew she should just be frank with him—well, up to a point. He was only doing this because he cared, and she needed to remember that. "I like Roman a lot. But no, I don't know where it's going with him and me. It's early days."

"He seems very taken with you, Hailey. The word *smitten* comes to mind. He's also been married twice, and he has a child. And he's older."

"Seven years. It's not that much older. And as for him having a little boy, you'd been married and you had two kids when you and Keely got together." Not to mention, Keely was already pregnant with Marie on the day they got married—not that there was anything wrong with that. But her big brother ought to understand that every relationship was different. There wasn't some boilerplate every couple had to live by. "And I have a question to ask *you*. What, exactly, went down yesterday in your study?"

"What do you mean?"

"Did Roman, er, say something that alarmed you?" If Roman had announced to her brothers that he was going to marry her, she would have to give him a giant piece of her mind. Because, seriously, how could he not know that it was bad form to start planning the wedding when they'd only met a week before—and the bride in question had not said yes?

Daniel shook his head. "Roman didn't say anything that bothered me. I just wanted to talk to you, to be sure that everything's okay with you."

"Why wouldn't it be?"

Daniel rubbed the back of his neck, as though maybe tension had gathered there. "Roman did say he's bought the Valentine Bay Theatre and that he's considering turning the building into a hotel—but then he said he's not locked into that plan yet."

She suppressed a snort of derision. *Not locked in.* Right. All she needed to do was marry him and the community-theater venue of her dreams would be hers.

Daniel was still talking. "I know how much that theater means to you. You've been so happy and excited since you hooked up with the arts council and started developing a year-round program there. So that had me thinking, is this about the theater?"

"This? What?"

"You and Roman, together. Are you dating him because you hope to influence him, get him to forget the hotel idea?" She blinked in surprise at how perceptive her big brother could be.

And he really did look concerned for her well-being.

All her defensiveness just kind of melted away. "You know this really isn't anything you have to get tied in knots over, Daniel. I like Roman a lot." *Enough to spend the night naked with him. Too bad he's saving himself for marriage.* "I also hope to change his mind about the theater. That's all there is to it."

He scanned her face as if looking for clues to what was really going on inside her head. "Roman seems to have done well for himself. And his little boy *is* a cutie..."

"I admit I'm already more than half in love with Theo. He's a great kid, curious about everything—and so cuddly. And that smile of his could light up the world." Already, she'd allowed herself to fantasize about what it might be like to help him grow up.

Daniel said, "I guess it's just..." His fist rested on the table.

She bumped it with hers. "Go ahead. Whatever it is, say it."

"It occurred to me that you haven't ever been all that serious about any guy that I can remember. When you were in high school, you dated, and sometimes you dated guys I didn't approve of, but they really weren't the main thing for you. Your focus has always been on the next show you're involved in or whatever performance project you're putting together. You've been that way since you were little, when you used to stage those skits in the family room involving just about all the other kids in town.

"And I guess all that had me thinking that this thing with Roman had to be really special for you. But then I wondered if you were only encouraging his interest in you in order to try to convince him not to take away the theater. I couldn't decide *what* I thought about that. And then I thought, if it *wasn't* about the theater and you really are falling for the guy, then maybe it was happening too fast, given that you brought him to dinner yesterday and he just moved back to town a few weeks ago." He paused, a frown crinkling his brow as he sipped his coffee. "And so here I am, busting in your door first thing in the morning, unable to stop myself from checking on how you're doing."

Emotion clogged her throat. "You're the best, Daniel."

He almost smiled. "Well, I'm here. And I always will be. You can count on that."

"I do. *We* do. All of us. Thanks for that, sincerely."

He gave a little nod of acknowledgment and she got up and refilled their mugs, mostly just for something to do in a moment when her heart ached.

She felt like a liar. Only Harper knew about Nathan. Harper. And Roman. And that she'd shared the story of her lost love with Roman the first day she met him, well, maybe that made her more serious about him than she was willing to admit to herself yet.

But Daniel didn't know about Nathan. Nathan had been so fierce about her family—that he didn't want to meet them or for her to have to explain to them the situation with him. She knew Nathan had reasoned that he could minimize her future pain by not becoming part of her life back home.

Nathan had been wrong. Keeping him a secret from her family only made her feel cut off from them, which hadn't helped at all. And right now, given Daniel's place in her life as not only her big brother but also a sort of surrogate dad, well, maybe he *should* know.

"Daniel…"

"Yeah, Lee-Lee?"

Her throat clutched with love over his use of the family's baby name for her. "You know how you said that I've never been serious over a guy?" At his nod, she went for it. "Well, back at UO, there *was* someone. Someone special. His name was Nathan Christoff. And I loved him so much…"

And from there, the whole story just came pouring out. When she finished, Daniel got up and hugged her.

She brushed away her tears and hugged him

back, breathing in the woodsy scent of his cologne that always made her think of home. "I haven't been interested in any guy since Nathan," she said.

Daniel took her by the shoulders and captured her gaze. "Until now?"

"Yeah. But I'm not running off to Vegas with Roman, I promise you. So don't get worried all over again, please?"

He dropped a kiss on her forehead. "I'll do my best."

She looked at him, straight-on. "I'm okay, really. Please believe me."

"I do. Just know that you can come to me, anytime for any reason. I might not have the right answers, but I'm always here to listen."

It was one of those days at the theater.

Doug blew out a circuit fiddling around with various holiday lighting effects to use in the upcoming Christmas show. The blown circuit threw the stage, auditorium and backstage area into pitch-blackness, which meant the tech people, including Harper and Sasha Marek, who had come in to help, left for the day. Hailey called the arts council office and Tandy promised to send over an electrician, ASAP.

ASAP turned out to be several hours.

In the meantime, Hailey and Rashonda Kyle, her intrepid assistant director, moved to the lobby, where the lights were still on, and conducted the first half of the afternoon's rehearsals as best they could in the not-ideal space. Rashonda, mother of five, Valentine Bay Elementary PTA president and Tandy Carson's eldest daughter, was as much a town treasure as her mom. Kids somehow always listened when Rashonda gave instructions, so things went more smoothly than might have been expected. Plus, the revue was just what its name implied—a series of skits, songs and dances—so Hailey's rehearsal schedule had the cast broken up into manageable groups.

Not ideal, rehearsing in the lobby, but doable. The electrician finally appeared at a little after three, and by four thirty he'd fixed the problem at a cost of five hundred bucks and change, which he expected to be paid right now or sooner.

Hailey had Rashonda take over running six little ballerinas through their interpretive dance to "Autumn Leaves," and was about to call Tandy and ask who was writing the check when Roman strolled in through the glass doors that led out to the street.

There ought to be a law against a guy looking that good. The man was pure eye candy in a rust-colored sweater and charcoal-gray pants, his sculpted jaw dusted with just the right amount of sexy scruff, big body loose and relaxed, not a care in the world.

"Never mind," said the electrician. "I think this is the guy." He plucked the invoice from between Hailey's fingers.

Roman had his checkbook with him. He signed the invoice and handed over the check. Whistling a happy tune, the electrician exited, leaving Hailey and Roman standing there staring at each other while six girls in black leotards leaped and twirled in the background to the jazz stylings of Cannonball Adderley.

"Roman to the rescue?" she dryly inquired.

He gave her an easy one-shouldered shrug. "It's my building. I like to be sure things are done right—though the truth is, all the wiring in this pile of rubble will have to be replaced during the conversion." He leaned closer and she got a way-too-seductive whiff of his cologne. "*Unless* you give in to your burning desire to be mine forever and become my wife?"

She made herself scowl at him in general disapproval of his hasty wedding plans—not to mention, his heartless scheme to make a hotel out of an important community resource. Scowling, however, was challenging at the moment. He was so deliciously manly, and she couldn't help remembering how good it felt when she had his arms around her. "You need to stop getting married for all the wrong reasons."

He didn't even have the grace to look humbled by his past matrimonial mistakes. "This time, all the reasons are right."

"Sure they are—and I can't stand around arguing with you all day. I've got a show to put together." She started to turn.

He caught her arm and the usual thrill shot through her. "When I quizzed Tandy Carson about the blown circuit, she said the lighting director did it. Who would that be, may I ask?"

"Doug was just doing his job, trying out some lighting effects."

"Dickerson." He was scowling. "That guy's a menace. I should have a talk with him, man-to-man."

"Would you back off on poor Doug? You just said yourself that the wiring needs to be replaced."

He glared at her as though the force of his stare might allow him to see inside her head. "You really don't think it's his fault?"

"I don't. Honestly."

His grip on her arm eased a little. And he said, almost gently, "What time are you finished here?"

"Why?"

"I'll come back. We'll get some dinner."

She should say no. He was controlling and overbearing and he needed someone to hold the line on him.

"Come on, Hailey. Dinner. You and me."

She glanced down at her tatty green UO hoodie, ripped skinny jeans and oldest pair of Chucks. "Casual. I'm talking burgers and fries and a tall Dr Pepper."

"Wherever you want to go, whatever you want to eat."

"Five thirty—six at the outside." She shouldn't be so easy. However, not to be easy was hard to remember when she would prefer to be a whole lot easier, if only he would reach out and take what she'd tried so hard to give him last night.

He still had hold of her arm. With a gentle tug, he pulled her close enough to brush a sweet little kiss to her temple and growl, "I'll be here," in her ear.

Her midsection melted and she felt the foolish, dreamy smile as it formed on her lips. "Get lost. I have work to do."

"Five thirty," he said and released her.

She found herself rooted where he'd left her, gazing longingly after him as he went out the glass doors.

"There goes trouble," said Rashonda out of the corner of her mouth. She'd moved in close as Hailey was busy watching Roman's fine backside walking away.

"Ain't that the truth," Hailey agreed and then clapped her hands to get everyone's attention. "Okay, the lights are on in the theater. Let's take this show onstage."

At Hailey's request, Roman took her to Raeleen's Roadside Grill for the best burgers in town. After the meal, they strolled the historic district to work off the carb-and-meat overload. Roman held her hand. It was a windy, gray evening.

But to Hailey, it seemed the most beautiful Monday ever.

When they returned to his impossibly futuristic sports car, sandwiched themselves inside and tugged down the scissor doors, he turned to her. "Come back to the house with me."

She had a strong premonition that she was asking for a repeat of the night before—a lot of scorching-hot kisses leading to her going home to her favorite battery-powered pleasure enhancer. She should be more upset about that.

She wasn't, though. Not really. Yeah, she wanted a sex life with an actual man again.

But she also had a lot of fun just being with him. She liked trading barbs with him. She felt like he *got* her in a way only Harper and Nathan ever had.

"Take me to the theater," she commanded. "I'll get my car and follow you."

He kissed her. That went on for a while, the two of them craning over the console that reminded her of the bridge of the Starship Enterprise, going at each other like a couple of out-of-control teenagers.

She was the one who finally pulled away. "We'd better stop. It's way too tight in here to keep this up."

He drew her close again, but only to rest his forehead against hers and stroke a big hand down her hair. It felt so good—his caress, the warmth of his breath on her skin.

Finally, he sat back. "You're right. Let's go."

At Roman's house, Theo was already in bed and Sasha had gone upstairs. They went out the back and down to the firepit. He turned on the flames and they sat together on one of the loungers. He wanted to hear about her day, and she shared the details of Daniel's visit.

Roman cradled her closer. She felt his lips brush her hair. "Is he going to be a problem?"

She tipped her head back to see his eyes. "Daniel a problem? Why?"

"You just said he tried to warn you off me."

"No. I said he was checking in with me."

"Because of me. Because I showed up with you at the family dinner Sunday."

"Right..." She let the word trail off, not sure what he was getting at.

"He thinks I'm wrong for you. I'm too old for you and I have a son and I've been married twice."

She wriggled around to face him. "Yeah. He said those things."

"So then, he did warn you off me."

She kissed him, hard and quick. "You need to put on your listening ears."

"Don't patronize me, Hailey."

"Don't be overly sensitive."

"I am not, nor have I ever been, overly sensitive." Those silvery eyes smoldered at her.

Yeah. Overly sensitive. No doubt about it.

Maybe this conversation required a bit of physical distance. She kind of had trouble concentrating on what she was saying when he was too close.

Her brain got all tangled up with the feel of him and the yearning inside her and the scent of him that made her picture his giant bed upstairs with the two of them in it, naked, sheets all tangled, the blankets fallen to the floor.

She pushed at his chest. "Let me go."

He held on and grumbled, "Stay here."

She kissed his stubborn jaw. "I'm only retreating to the next lounger over."

"You never retreat." Those big, hard arms banded closer. "And I like you right here, with my arms around you." He nuzzled her neck, and then nipped at the sensitive skin—his teeth digging in just enough to send bolts of pleasure zipping straight to her core. His hand had strayed up under the hem of her hoodie and he stroked his fingers up and down the bumps of her spine. It all felt amazing—that big, stroking hand of his, the scrape of his teeth down the side of her throat. She longed to start ripping his clothes off, getting down to some serious business right here in his backyard.

But he was unlikely to go there with her tonight—at least, not unless she promised to marry him. That, she was not going to do. They needed a lot more time, the two of them, together, before wedding bells started ringing.

And even if by some miracle he announced that he'd changed his mind and would take her to bed after all, it was wiser and safer for her to get on the Pill first. She pushed at his chest again. "We need to talk, and you are distracting me."

He muttered something disagreeable, but he did release his hold. She got up, tugged her hoodie back down over her hips, smoothed her hair with both hands and switched to the other lounger.

"Daniel does *not* disapprove of you and me getting together," she said firmly.

He levered his lounger down flat, stretched out on his side and braced his head on his fist. "Listen to you. He 'does *not* disapprove.' Double negative. You're hiding something."

"I am not—look. Okay, yeah, he was concerned at first. But he got over it. You have to understand, Daniel's the dad in our family. He takes his role seriously. If he's uneasy about one of us, he follows up and makes us talk it through. I can't say I love it when he knocks on my door and won't go away until he's convinced I'm okay. But I appreciate how much he cares, that he's on the case as our substitute dad."

Roman sat up. He held out his hand. She took it. He tugged her over to his side and hooked an arm around her. "I like it better when I'm touching you."

With a happy sigh, she leaned her head on his shoulder. "I'm telling you the truth, Roman. Daniel and I had a good talk. He understands that I really like you and he's fine now with me going out with you."

"Maybe I should have a talk with him..."

She pulled away enough to give him her sternest frown. "There's no reason to fix what isn't broken. Let it go."

He smirked at her. "You're really bossy. I don't like bossy women, as a rule."

"If you're planning on turning that uncalled-for remark into a backhanded compliment, don't even try."

He chuckled. "Bossy. Yeah. Just like I said."

Roman showed up at the theater on Wednesday afternoon. Hailey was in the middle of rehearsals. She gave him a quick wave and went back to work. His mother was already there with Theo. The little boy liked to nap in his stroller while Sasha painted scenery backstage.

It was the first day of rehearsals for the finale, which included the entire cast. As Hailey had pretty much expected, everything went wrong. Not to worry, though. They still had plenty of rehearsals to whip things into shape before the first performance in mid-October.

Roman hung around for over an hour. Hailey spotted him now and then, lurking in the wings stage left with his son in his arms, looking like every woman's idea of the perfect man, big and fit and handsome—and he loved his little boy. An ovulation-inducing sight if there ever was one.

He was still there when rehearsal ended, though by then, Sasha and Theo had left.

"Dinner," he said, coming down the stairs stage left to join Hailey and Rashonda at the big folding table in the front row. "Finish up and let's go."

She didn't argue. Why would she? She enjoyed his company. Overbearing as he could be at times, his kisses set her on fire, and he was a lot of fun to argue with. Plus, her stomach was growling. If he wanted to feed her, she wasn't about to say no. She and Rashonda gathered up their things and they all three walked out together.

Roman took Hailey to this great little Italian place a few blocks from the theater. After dinner, they window-shopped and then he took her back to his house, where they ended up in the backyard, sharing a lounger by the firepit as the fog rolled in.

She didn't get back to the cottage until almost midnight. Harper was already in bed.

The next morning, early, she went to her doctor and got a contraceptive shot. Roman couldn't hold out against her forever. Eventually, she would get lucky and she needed to be fully prepared.

Friday, they went to dinner and a show in Astoria. When he dropped her off at her place that night, he wrangled another invite to Sunday dinner at Daniel's.

She had a condition. "Bring Theo *and* your mom."

He joked that his mom cramped his style, but he agreed to invite her. Sasha said yes. They all rode together in Roman's SUV—a.k.a. the Dad Car.

The afternoon went well, Hailey thought. Sasha got along great with everyone and Theo was universally adored. Gracie and Dante Santangelo came. They had Dante's eight-year-old twin daughters with them for the weekend. The twins, Nicole and Natalie, had struck up a friendship with Coco Killigan. The three girls hauled Theo and Riley around with them for most of the afternoon as Daniel's three little ones followed in their wake. All the kids seemed to love hanging out together, even smart and serious ten-year-old Ben Killigan, on whom Nicole Santangelo just possibly had a crush.

From then on, for Hailey and Roman, a pattern was established. As September became October, they were together constantly—two or three evenings a week and always on Sunday at Daniel's. Hailey really was gone on him. He was such a great guy, even with the occasional dickish and domineering behavior.

He asked her and Harper to plan a party for Theo's first birthday and she happily agreed. She would have done it for free, but he insisted on paying H&H Productions the going rate. When she explained to him her plans for Theo's special day, he called her a genius and asked her to marry him yet again.

She smiled and sweetly said no.

He still wouldn't sleep with her. He was very hands-on, though, in the best sort of way. Whenever they were alone together, they shared endless, steamy kisses and some pretty intimate caresses. But he always called a halt before the main event, after which he would suggest that they should get married.

Was she tempted to say yes?

Maybe. A little—or even a lot.

But it was much too soon. Neither of them had mentioned love and love should come first before two people started talking about saying "I do."

And they weren't in love, were they?

Her mind shied away from the question every time she started to consider it. In her life, she'd been in love with only one man, and since she lost

Nathan, she'd honestly believed that he had been the one, *her* one. She'd been so sure that true, forever love would never be hers again.

However, this thing with Roman felt...special. Powerful. Her love for Nathan seemed so long ago now, a beautiful, bittersweet interlude, not the grand passion she'd once believed it to be. That made her sad.

And then she would remind herself not to get too serious—about the past *or* about Roman Marek. She was having a great time with him. For now, that was more than enough.

On October 7, Theo was a year old. The following Saturday, they threw the birthday boy a party at the house on Treasure Cove Circle. H&H Productions filled the place with balloons and streamers and passed out party hats and whistles. Roman had invited every child in Hailey's family—meaning all the kids who attended Sunday dinner at Daniel's. Even Nicole and Natalie Santangelo came up from Portland for the event.

Sasha had ordered a giant cake shaped like a truck. They had wagon rides, bubble catching and a parade through the house. The bigger kids built a castle out of oversize colored blocks. It was Theo's job to knock it down, with Riley's help—to cheers and applause from everyone. And then they had story time, which consisted of Ben Killigan reading *Mr. Brown Can Moo! Can You?* as Coco led the others in making animal sounds at the end of each rhyme.

Later, after Theo had blown out his candle, Sasha served cake and ice cream and Roman took a bunch of pictures of Theo with bits of cake and green icing all over his face.

Harper leaned close to Hailey and declared, “No doubt about it. Our best party, ever.”

They high-fived each other on that one.

Hailey was still grinning after everyone left. Harper hung around to clean up, heading out the door when everything was pretty much done. Roman took a worn-out Theo upstairs for a much-needed nap.

That left Sasha putting a second load in the dishwasher as Hailey wiped down Theo’s high chair tray. When Hailey turned for the sink, Sasha had just shut the dishwasher door. The cycle started with a whooshing sound. Hailey just happened to glance directly at Sasha and saw that there were tears running down her face.

“Sasha, what…?”

“Nothing,” Sasha said, sniffing. “It’s nothing at all…”

Hailey tossed her sponge into the sink and

scooted close to Roman's mom. "Come here…" She pulled the older woman into her arms.

At first, Sasha stiffened, but then she gave in and let Hailey hug her. They stood there at the counter, holding on to each other as the dishwasher whirred softly beside them.

Sasha sobbed. "Sorry, so sorry…"

Hailey rubbed her back and reassured her. "Don't be. It's okay."

"You're right, I know you are. It's going to be okay," whispered Sasha. "They *promised* it would…" She lifted her head and they stared at each other. Sasha sniffled and brushed at Hailey's shoulder. "I'm soaking your shirt."

"Don't worry about that." Hailey turned enough to grab the cube of Kleenex a few feet down the counter. She whipped a couple of tissues out and passed them to Roman's mom, who dabbed at her eyes and blotted her wet cheeks. Hailey set down the box and took Sasha gently by arms. "Now, what's going on?"

Sasha cast a worried glance toward the arch that led to the front of the house and the stairs leading up to the bedrooms. "I don't want Roman to see me like this. I've been planning how to tell him for the last several days. I don't want it to be with tears running down my face. He can't stand it when I cry—which I never do, really. He likes to think he can make anything right, and seeing me or any woman cry makes him feel powerless. Powerlessness is not a good fit on my son."

Tell him what? Hailey wanted to demand. But instead, she said gently, "Theo will want a story before he'll go to sleep. That leaves a few minutes, at least, before Roman comes back downstairs. And whatever it is, you've got nothing to worry about. You know Roman. He'll be right there for you."

"I do know, yes. It's just that I haven't figured out *how* to tell him…"

Hailey didn't know whether to push for information or just provide reassurance and let it be. She settled for offering encouragement. "You're amazing, Sasha. Whatever's happened, you're going to be fine."

Sasha chuckled through her tears. "I do love your can-do spirit."

Hailey gave a rueful smile. "That's me. Keeping it on the sunny side—and I need to know. What can I do? How can I help?"

They stared at each other. And then Roman's mom dabbed at her eyes one more time and whispered, "I have breast cancer."

Chapter Six

When Roman entered the kitchen, he found Hailey and his mother huddled together by the dishwasher.

They both startled and whirled to face him. Hailey pasted on a smile. Sasha had red eyes and a nose to match. She'd been crying.

And Ma never cried.

He went right to her. "Ma, what's the matter?" Hailey stepped back and he took his mother by the shoulders. She looked down at first, but then her gaze rose reluctantly to meet his. "You've been crying." He didn't mean it as an accusation, but somehow, it kind of sounded that way.

Ma looked wrecked. It tore something inside him to see her so gutted. She hadn't had an easy life, and after he made it big, he'd sworn to himself that she was never going to suffer over a damn thing ever again.

"Oh, Roman…" A sob escaped her and the tears started falling again. She swayed toward him and he wrapped his arms around her. "I'm sorry. It was…such a great day. I think I'm feeling extra emotional, seeing our little boy so happy. I really wasn't going to cry over this. I most definitely was *not* going to cry…" She most definitely *was* crying. He felt completely useless as sobs shook her slim shoulders.

Hailey, behind him, pushed a box of Kleenex into his line of sight. He pulled some out and gave them to Ma to replace the soggy ball she had clutched in her hand. "Here, Ma. Fresh ones…"

She took what he offered and dropped the used ones on the counter. Nobody said anything as she blew her nose and wiped at her eyes.

Finally she drew herself up straight. "We should sit down. I will tell you everything."

Behind him, Hailey hesitantly suggested, "Maybe I should—"

She didn't get to finish, because he and Ma commanded, "Stay," in unison. Ma continued, "I want some coffee and then I'm going to explain the situation to both of you."

A few minutes later, they sat at the table, the three of them, each with a hot mug of coffee to hold on to. By then, Ma had pulled herself together. She wrapped her hands around her mug and launched into her story.

"A week and a half ago, I went in for my routine yearly mammogram..."

Okay, he might be somewhat oblivious to the possible health hazards that befell women, but even he knew what was coming as soon as she said the word *mammogram*.

How bad is it? Are you going to be okay? What do you need? What can I do? A thousand questions bounced around inside his head, each one warring for the first chance to come out of his mouth.

But he said nothing. He waited for her to say all she had to say before demanding to know how he could make everything better.

"They called me back for an ultrasound. The lump appeared malignant, so I went in for a biopsy, a procedure where they extract some of the tissue from the lump to test."

"Wait. How do they do that?"

His mother looked bewildered. "Do what?"

"You said they extract some tissue. Using what?"

"A needle, Roman."

"You went to that by yourself?" She should have told him. He should have been there.

"No, Roman. Matilda went with me." Matilda Graves was one of the women she used to work for, one of the women she'd become good friends with over the years. He hated that she hadn't told him sooner. But before he could start in about that, she dabbed at her eyes again. "It's definitely cancer."

"Cancer." His brain didn't seem able to process the word.

"Yes, Roman. I have breast cancer."

Suddenly, that Matilda Graves had replaced him at the scary procedure involving a needle didn't seem all that important.

Several obscene words scrolled through his brain. He kept them in. "Ma..." He laid his hand on hers and she put her other hand on top of his. They both squeezed at the same time.

"It's not *all* bad." She stared at him through eyes identical to the ones he saw when he looked in the mirror. Right now, they were pleading, hopeful eyes. "The lump is malignant, but the biopsy results showed it's not particularly fast-growing. They're going to do surgery, remove the lump, a margin of surrounding tissue and a few of what they call sentinel lymph nodes to test—those are the ones closest to the tumor, which are the first places the cancer would go if it spread. The doctor seemed confident that I will have a full recovery. I don't have the gene for breast cancer and the lump is very small. If the lymph nodes are clear, there's a high likelihood I won't have a recurrence."

"But what about radiation? And chemo?"

She was nodding. "I will have radiation therapy starting a few weeks after the surgery."

"And then?"

"That will be it. Unless the sentinel lymph nodes are affected. If they are, there will probably be more surgery and either chemo or some other systemic cancer drug, in addition to the radiation."

The lymph nodes *would* be clear, damn it. He wouldn't have it any other way.

Hailey said, "So we're rooting for clear lymph nodes and radiation only."

"Yes." Ma was nodding.

Roman had to say it. "You should have come to me as soon as you got the results from your mammogram."

Eyes defiant now, Sasha stared him straight in the eye. "Pardon me if I wanted to enjoy my grandson's first birthday without you and everyone else worrying about my health."

Now he felt like a jerk. "Sorry, Ma," he muttered.

She squeezed his hand again. “You’re a good son, but a very bossy one.”

Over her shoulder, he saw Hailey’s lips twitch and knew she was suppressing a smug little grin because he often called *her* bossy.

“Don’t,” he said flatly to the gorgeous and exasperating woman sitting on the other side of his mother.

Hailey widened those lavender-blue eyes at him, playing innocent. Which she was not. “I have no idea what you’re talking about.”

“Roman,” his mother chided. “Be nice to Hailey. She’s a woman of fine character, with a big heart. It’s your duty and privilege to treat her right.”

“Thank you, Sasha,” Hailey said with a brilliant smile.

“It’s only the truth,” Ma replied.

Just what he needed. The two of them ganging up on him. He wanted to order them to back the hell off. But Ma had cancer and was going to need surgery. It wasn’t a good time to get on her case.

As for Hailey, he liked having her around, and if he gave her too much grief, she might just leave.

He took the high road and asked mildly, “When’s the surgery?”

“I was waiting to schedule it until I talked to you.”

“The sooner the better,” he said.

Sasha drew in a slow, steadying breath. "I agree."

"And I need to get with your doctor, get all the details."

"Of course you do," his mother said dryly. "You can come to the surgery consult."

"I'll make a list of questions we need to remember to ask."

Sasha nodded. "I do feel so much better now that you know."

Which is why you should have told me right away, he didn't let himself say. "Good."

Ma gave him a brave little smile. "First thing Monday morning, I'll call the doctor and say I'm ready for the next step."

Hailey kept thinking she ought to go, that she ought to leave mother and son alone to speak privately.

But when she said as much for the second time, Sasha made her position clear. "Don't go. I want you here and Roman needs you here."

Hailey slid a glance at the man in question.

He met her gaze. "Stay."

An hour later, Theo woke from his nap. Hailey and Roman took him for a walk around Treasure Cove Circle. Back at the house, they sat on the floor with him as he played with his toys. Theo yawned a lot. The big day had tired him out. As for Roman, he seemed quiet. Thoughtful. Hailey helped with dinner and then with the cleanup afterward.

At a little after seven, Sasha took Theo upstairs. “You two have a nice evening,” she said. “I’ve got friends I need to call and a good book to read.”

Hailey and Roman sat in the family room. Kicking off their shoes, they got comfy on the sofa and pretended to watch a thriller on the big-screen TV.

About halfway through, Roman pulled her in tight and bit her ear lightly, causing a sweet string of sparks to flare across her skin. “How much do you care about seeing the rest of this?”

She turned her head enough to kiss him. “Not even a little bit,” she whispered against his parted lips.

“Well, all right.” He aimed the remote at the screen and it went dark, dropped the device on the coffee table and then guided her down to the pillows until they were stretched out on their sides, face-to-face. With a look of great concentration and a slow glide of his index finger, he traced the curves of her eyebrows and the shape of her chin. “Your skin is like something from an old, sappy poem.”

"Is that somehow a compliment?"

He nodded. "Smooth as satin and velvet, cool and pale and perfect."

"Perfection is way overrated."

"Look at you. Not only perfect, but modest about it."

"Roman. I am far from perfect and we both know that."

"You should stay the night." His voice was tender. "I don't want you to go."

"You're being so sweet and direct." She threaded her fingers through this thick hair. "You are not okay, are you?"

He shifted even closer and caught her mouth in a lingering kiss, a kiss that wasn't really about sex, but more about communication, a conversation without words.

When he let her mouth go, she said, "Your mom's going to have a smooth surgery and a quick recovery. I'm sure of it."

He pressed his forehead to hers. "It wasn't easy for her when I was a kid. They didn't have a lot, my dad and Ma. Just each other and, eventually, me…"

She stroked the hair at his temples some more, soothing him. "Tell me about your dad."

"I really don't remember him. Ma says he was kind and gentle. He was a groundskeeper for a rich couple, up in Seattle. Ma was the housekeeper and cook."

"How did he die?"

"Fixing a tire. The jack didn't hold and the whole car came down on top of him."

"Oh, my God." She rested her hand on his broad chest, right over his heart. "That's awful."

"It must've been, for Ma. Like I said, I was too young to really get what had happened. Ma kept her job, though, cooking and cleaning in the same house, for the next six years." Something in the tone of his voice alerted her. She lifted her head enough to watch his eyes. He glanced away and then back. "What?"

She had a sense that there was more he could have said, about those six years after his father died. But she didn't want to push him. She wanted him to open up to her in his own way and his own time. "Nothing. So, after your dad died, you stayed in Seattle..."

"Until I was eight."

"And then?"

"Then we left Seattle, Ma and me, in an old car piled with everything we owned in the world. It wasn't a whole lot. Ma stopped for the night at the Ocean View Motel."

"On the Coast Highway, just as you're coming into town…"

"That's the one. Cheap wood paneling, squeaky box-spring beds in the rooms. The ice maker in the alcove by the office didn't work." His eyes were far away, recalling that time. "Ma managed to talk the owner into giving her a job as a maid. We lived there at the motel for a few months, until she'd scraped enough together to get us an apartment—a dump, that apartment, not much better than our ugly room at the Ocean View. Ma was relentless, though, a hard worker with a will of iron. Within a year, she had jobs all over town, taking care of people's houses. She rented us a little place of our own and here in Valentine Bay we stayed."

"Until you left for college…"

"*She* stayed, even then. When I made money in Vegas, I convinced her to move there. I always swore that when I grew up, I would take care of her in style. I bought her a nice house, made sure she had plenty of money of her own, everything she could ever need. But all she really wanted was to come back and live in this town. She loves this place."

Hailey kissed him. "So what you're saying is, you've given her what she wanted most. You came back here, where she wants to live, and she gets to be with her son and her grandson, too."

He stroked a hand down her arm, slowly, and then trailed his fingers back up again. It felt so good—the way he touched her, the absolute focus in those silver-green eyes when he looked at her. "What I want is for her to be happy, to have the best of everything. She deserves that. I guess I just never let myself think that something like cancer would get her. I hate that there's nothing I can do to make sure she's going to be all right."

"There's a lot you can do, and you're doing it. She'll get the surgery and the recovery will be quick. And you'll be right there with her all the way."

He moved in even closer. She felt his breath warm across her cheek. And then he nipped her earlobe, a tender little bite that sent a surge of desire arrowing down into the center of her. "You sound so sure…"

She pushed him back enough to capture his gaze again. "Why wouldn't I be? She's caught it early, it's not an aggressive form of cancer and her doctor seems confident that she's going to beat it without a lot of debilitating treatment."

"But you just never know."

She laid her hand on his cheek, loving the feel of

him, the rough texture of his beard scruff against her palm, the press of his hard body so close and warm. "Sorry, Roman. You don't get absolute assurance. But in your mom's case, you do get about as close as you can to knowing that everything will turn out right."

"Not like that guy you were with in college." He watched her intently.

Sadness had weight. It pressed on her heart. "No. Your mother's cancer is not like Nathan's. His illness was in remission when I met him, but it was stage four leukemia. He was afraid it would come back. And it did."

Roman caught a hank of her hair and wrapped it around his fist, tugging it tight. It hurt, a little, in a pleasurable way. His eyes burned into hers. "Stay."

Her heart melted—along with her midsection. She kissed him and gave him her answer against those lips of his that were so soft compared with the rest of him. "Yes."

For a while, they didn't stir from the sofa. He held her close. Their kisses started out restrained, tender and exploratory.

But there was fire between them, and each kiss made it burn just that much hotter. His erection rubbed against the cove of her sex. Even through the barrier of his clothes and hers, she felt him so acutely, wanted him so very much.

"I can't wait anymore," he said on a low groan.

She laughed, a husky, hungry sound. Because she *was* hungry. For him. For all the magic she would finally get to share with him. "I'm so glad. Because I'm definitely having sex tonight, one way or another. It would be downright cruel of you to make me have it without you."

He sank his teeth into the vulnerable curve of her neck—just enough to make her gasp in delight at the sharp sensation. Then he kissed the spot he'd bitten. "I'm not sure what this is, what we have together, you and me—but I do know I like it very much."

She stretched her head back, giving him better access. "You *like* it?"

"I do, yes."

"And that's why you keep demanding that I marry you?"

He made a low sound, like a growl, against her throat. "Exactly. Quit putting me off. Say yes and let's get married."

"What is this, a business deal? We'll shake hands and you'll whip out the contract? I'll sign on the dotted line, after which we'll seal the deal with a hot night of great sex?"

"Nothing wrong with an honest transaction, between equals."

"Roman, you're such a romantic." *Not.*

"I know we'd be good together and I think you know it, too. You're everything I want in a wife. Smart and gorgeous. With a big heart—and see? I get that now. The heart. It matters. You're all that, and you keep me honest. I don't really like that you take zero crap from me, but I respect you for it."

"Stop. The sheer beauty of this proposal is killing me."

He held her gaze, so determined. And hot. Really hot. She felt a little breathless just from the intensity of that look in his eyes. "Think about it."

She would—she *did* think about it. All the time. But no way was she saying yes to him. Not yet, anyway. Not until he understood that there had to be love, that love was the first thing, the real starting point. Not until he could say that he loved her with all his heart—say it and mean it. Not until she could do the same.

She tried, gently, to make him understand. "There has to be love, Roman. Love takes time and care."

His eyes darkened. "So then, that's a no?"

She kissed him again, a soft, brushing, tender kiss. "You're not real comfortable with the subject of love, are you?"

* * *

Roman had no idea how to answer her.

He loved Theo and he loved Ma. But his one foray into loving a woman he wanted had not ended well. He'd been so sure Charlene was the one for him. He'd planned to love her to distraction for the rest of their lives.

It had all been a lie—from the first, on her part. On his, well, by the end he knew he was a fool, all bleeding heart and yearning soul, while she was just there for the cold, hard cash.

He didn't really know if he could go there again and he preferred not to give the subject all that much thought.

Hailey brushed another soft kiss across his mouth. "Let's table the love talk *and* the marriage proposals for now, huh?"

He felt relief—and disappointment, too. He didn't want to go to the love place. But he really wanted to marry her for all the reasons he'd already laid out for her. Why couldn't she just accept that they should be together and do things his way?

It was a ridiculous question to be asking himself. He knew that. They were the same, the two of them, each accustomed to taking charge. And he actually liked that about her, too, even though it meant she had strong opinions on what needed doing and how to do it.

"Deal," he said, and nuzzled her cheek, breathing in the scent of her skin, a heady combination of vanilla and roses and that indefinable something that was Hailey and Hailey alone. The smell of her was as tempting and addictive as the rest of her.

He took her mouth. Invading the slick wetness beyond her parted lips with his tongue, he tasted her deeply, aware that he was breaking his own promise to himself. He'd fully intended not to give in, not to take her to bed until he had her agreement to marry him. But he needed her tonight like he needed to draw his next breath.

"Stay..." The single word escaped him of its own volition.

She drew back enough to look directly at him. Her cheeks were flushed. Her eyes gleamed with heat and hunger. "I already said yes. I said it that first night when you took me to dinner at that great place on the river in Astoria, where I proposed a fling. I've kept saying it. I haven't changed my mind."

"Good answer." He yanked her close and claimed her mouth again, reaching down to take the round globes of her pretty bottom in his two hands, feeling the sweet resilience of her flesh beneath the fabric of her jeans. Shifting her on top of him, he guided her to straddle his hips and swung his legs over the side of the sofa, bringing them both to a sitting position.

He went on kissing her, loving the way she sighed his name into his mouth as he stood.

"Hold on," he advised, licking the two words onto her plump lips.

"Wait a minute."

He groaned at any delay in his upcoming gratification. But all of her concerns did need addressing. Pressing his forehead to hers, he asked, "Yeah?"

"Well, I was just thinking—you know, about your mother. I mean, what if we're noisy? That would be awkward."

Noisy sounded pretty damn good to him. As for her concern? Easily dispelled. "I promise you, I like my privacy as much as the next guy. I would not have taken this house if the soundproofing wasn't state-of-the-art."

Her smile bloomed slow and extra sweet. "All righty, then. Let's go." She twined her arms and legs around him and he carried her up the stairs.

Inside the master suite, Roman paused at the door, his mouth locked on hers. With a flick of one foot, he swung the door shut behind him, backed up to it and kissed her some more.

She tasted so good, like all the things he'd thought for too long he would never have. And it was not only the taste of her that drove him wild. It was also the way she kissed him back—so eager and shameless, sexy little moans escaping her.

Unwrapping her legs from around him, she slid down the front of him, rubbing his hardness as she went, making him hurt for her in the best sort of way.

When her feet touched the floor, she pulled back enough to gaze up at him through starry eyes. He engaged the lock.

And then he yanked her close again and took that perfect mouth of hers once more.

She was going to need something to lean on before he took her to the bed, so he turned them as he kissed her, until her back was pressed against the door.

He got the hem of her knit shirt in his two hands and lifted it. Her mouth still fused with his, she raised her arms for him. The kiss broke as he whipped that shirt up and tossed it away.

Glancing down, he saw she wore a lacy pink bra that held up her small, round breasts like an offering. A growl escaped him. "So beautiful." Cradling the pretty little mounds in his two hands, he swept his thumbs over the silky skin, so smooth and plump above the lacy cups.

She reached behind her and undid the clasp.

He glanced up from his big paws cupping her delicate flesh and into her luminous eyes as the bra came away in his hands. He said something guttural. It wasn't really a word. Just need and appreciation—and the good kind of pain a man feels when he's strictly denied himself but can't bear the deprivation for one moment longer and is finally about to get what he needs.

With twin flicks of her fingers, she let the straps drop down her arms. The bra fell away.

Irresistible, those pretty swells tipped in dusky pink. He took them, bare now, in his hands. She moaned as he bent his head to get his mouth on her. Heaven, the taste of her, the feel of her nipple, turning tight and hard, elongating against his tongue, vanilla and roses filling his head.

He molded the gorgeous shape of her, his hands cradling her ribs, palms sliding lower. Her skin was like velvet. Her body moved eagerly, swaying toward him, offering him everything—now.

At last. Tonight.

His clothes confined him. He wanted them off. She stared at him, her mouth a soft O as he whipped his shirt over his head and tossed it away, then ripped his zipper wide and shoved his pants down along with his boxer briefs. Kicking the tangled mess away, he raised one foot and then the other, bending to pull off his socks.

"Roman..." Her tone was reverent, those eyes of hers neon blue. She reached out and pressed her soft hand flat against his chest. He caught that hand, cradled it, raised it to his mouth to kiss the heart of her palm. They stared at each other, a long look full of heat and need.

Still holding her gaze, he dropped to his knees. She sucked in a sweet, sharp breath as he brushed his fingers over her belly, undid the button at the top of her jeans and pulled the zipper down. Her lacy white panties came into view. He pushed the jeans a little lower and smiled at what he'd revealed.

"So beautiful," he whispered, leaning in, pressing a kiss to the shadow of her cleft behind the flimsy barrier of satin and lace.

Pretty as they were, those panties had to go.

He hooked his fingers under the elastic waistband and slid them down until they met the jeans. And then he took everything—the jeans and the panties—sweeping them away down those fine legs of hers.

Her silvery hair swung forward, brushing his shoulder, warm silk against his skin, as she braced her right arm on his other shoulder and got her feet free. With her toe, she nudged the twisted wad of fabric out of the way, reaching down to remove her bright purple socks.

He caught her by the waist and then gently pushed her upright, until her back was against the door. Gazing down at him, her hair sliding over those fine bare breasts, she took a shuddering breath. There was so much of her he couldn't wait to get his hands and his mouth on. He was so hard right now, it hurt.

A good hurt, the best. To see her naked, before him. To have her at last. She destroyed his control. The scent and sight of her, the sound of her breathing, the random moan that escaped those lips he couldn't wait to kiss again… All of it took him away to a place where there was only the next touch of her hand against his skin and the sweet way she whispered his name.

For now, for tonight, she made him forget that life was too damn fragile, and a man could plan and work and scheme and prepare—and still, he couldn't always protect the ones who mattered. Some things were beyond even his iron control.

He was lost in her and he needed that—at least for tonight.

She watched his face as he lifted a hand and laid it on her upper chest, his middle finger touching the tender groove where her delicate collarbones came together. Just the feel of her skin was so much to him—everything. So smooth. So alive.

He trailed his hand down between those pretty breasts, over the sweet curve of her belly, to the neat landing strip of pale hair between her silky thighs.

She said his name again, sweet and low. All breath and yearning.

He dipped a finger in. Wet. Warm.

She moaned and rocked toward him. He used his other hand to hold her in place as he rubbed with his thumb on the sensitive nub at the top of her cleft and slid another finger into her perfect, wet heat.

Her body rocked against him, eager, needful. He glanced up as he put his mouth on her. With a long, desperate groan, she let her head fall back against the door.

He went on kissing her, using his tongue and his fingers to drive her higher. She tasted so good, of roses and woman and the sweetest surrender, so beautiful and so completely *his*.

He whispered encouragements, driving her higher, until she reached down and grabbed his head between her hands. She fisted his hair as he felt her go over, her body milking his fingers, pulsing on his tongue.

And then she was pulling at him, urging him upward. He rose and she met him, claiming his lips in a long, searing kiss.

"Bed," he said, "now," when they came up for air.

She bit her upper lip and confessed, "I'm, um, not sure I can walk yet."

"No problem." He scooped her into his arms and carried her over there, setting her down on the turned-back sheets and then sliding in next to her, taking her mouth in another lengthy kiss. That time, when they paused for breath, he remembered the awkward stuff that needed to be said. "I have condoms."

She leaned up on an elbow and gave him a dewy little grin. "I got the contraceptive shot right after I started trying to seduce you."

He caught a lock of her hair and rubbed it between his fingers. Silky and fine, just like her. "Excellent."

"You mean my trying to seduce you or that I got the shot?"

"Both." He smoothed the lock of hair and guided it behind her ear.

"Well, okay, then." She went on, "There hasn't been anyone since Nathan. He'd only ever been with me and before him, I got tested, so I'm clean."

He nodded. "I got tested a few months ago. There's been no one since then."

She leaned close. Her soft breast brushed his chest and her sweet scent excited him. "Okay, then. I think we can skip the condoms if you're comfortable with that."

His answer was to haul her tightly against him, cradle the back of her head and guide her mouth down to his.

That kiss of his? It set Hailey's world on fire.

She lost herself in him, in the way his big, hot hands claimed her body, commanding and so very thorough, as though he needed to memorize her skin, learn every dip, swell and curve. She'd been frustrated, she would openly admit, at how long he'd made her wait for him.

But this—now. Tonight…

She might never admit it to him out loud, but tonight was worth the wait.

He kissed his way down her body and spread her open for his mouth and hands again. It was heaven—so quickly, he sent her soaring into the stratosphere once more.

When her heart and mind stopped spinning, she tugged on his shoulders and begged him, “Please, Roman. Come up here. I need you with me, *in* me. I need you now…”

He didn’t argue or hold back—not this time. Not tonight.

She reached for him, opening her legs to make room for him. He settled between her thighs, leaning up on his elbows, framing her face between those wonderful hands that knew just how to touch her, just how to make her body burn.

His quicksilver eyes held her, *owned* her.

She met them happily and whispered, “Please. Now,” as she reached down between them and wrapped her hand around his thick, ready hardness, guiding him to where she needed him.

He came into her slowly, his gaze holding hers, his jaw set and determined. It had been such a long time for her. He was big and she was tight.

But she was ready, so ready. And the way he filled her, stretching her, felt so good.

With a last strong flexing of his hips, he was in her to the hilt. They stared at each other, both breathing fast.

"You okay?" he whispered, lowering his head to her, brushing a kiss against her parted lips.

"Good." She stroked a hand down his hard flank, glided a finger up the bumps of his spine. He groaned at her touch. They were both sweating. "*So* good..."

He warned, "Hold on..."

"Oh, yes."

He took her mouth and started moving—slowly at first but picking up speed. She slid her hands down and grabbed on tight.

And after that, well, everything got hazy in the best kind of way. They rolled on the bed, tangling the sheets beneath them as he moved inside her, so deep. So perfectly right. She came up on top and rode him, grinding against him, feeling him so deep within her, all the way to her hungry heart.

And then they were on their sides, facing each other. She flung a leg over him to bring him even closer. He moved within her, deeper than ever, it seemed.

Until she felt her climax barreling down her spine, lighting up the core of her, moving outward from there, filling her body with heat and light.

She felt him throb inside her, spilling into her as she pulsed around him, nothing left of her but sensation, glorious and free.

Chapter Seven

It was still dark when Hailey woke.

She had no idea how long she'd slept. Roman was wrapped around her, spoon-fashion. He must have turned out the lights after she dropped off to sleep. She smiled to herself at the memory of what had happened between them in this big bed just a little while ago.

But how long ago, exactly? Was it morning already? She had no clue. Her phone was in her purse downstairs on one of the kitchen counters, if she remembered right—and the alarm clock was on Roman's side of the bed. Carefully, she shifted, trying to turn over and check the time without waking him.

She managed to turn over, but then his eyes opened.

"I could get used to this." He smiled sleepily and she felt a light brush of a touch under the covers as he skated a hand up over her hip and down into the cove of her waist.

She got up on an elbow so that she could see the clock. "It's after four."

His hand kept moving, sliding out from under her arm, brushing the curve of her breast, caressing her shoulder and finally easing around the nape of her neck. "Don't even think about leaving." He rubbed, massaging, down her nape and back up. It felt good.

She let out a pleasured sigh. "I should text Harper, just to let her know where I am."

"I might allow that."

"Oh, thank you so much because I wouldn't do *anything* without your permission."

"If only you could say that with just a hint of sincerity."

She gave a low laugh. "Too bad I left my phone downstairs."

He traced the line of her jaw and brushed the

back of his hand over the curve of her cheek. "I'll go down and get it for you. In a minute."

"So...if I stay—"

He silenced her with a finger to her lips. "There is no *if* about it."

She caught that finger and kissed the tip. "Won't that be weird—I mean, for your mom?"

"Can't say for certain. I haven't been with anyone since we moved in here and she had her own place in Vegas—but my guess is no."

"No, not weird for her?"

He shook his head slowly. "You said it yourself that first night at that restaurant you like in Astoria. Ma's matchmaking us. Plus, she wants me to be happy and you make me happy."

Well, now. Wasn't that nice to hear? "Yeah?"

He leaned in. "Yeah." His lips met hers.

That did it.

They spent another hour reacquainting themselves with the fabulousness of having a sex life together.

It was after five when he went downstairs and returned with her purse and his fancy watch, which he'd left on the end table by the sofa. She sent Harper a text. Then she and Roman snuggled in together and went back to sleep.

* * *

In the morning, Hailey was happy to find that Roman had guessed right about Sasha.

When they came downstairs at seven, his mom and Theo were already up. Sasha stood at the stove and Theo sat in his high chair happily banging his sippy cup against the tray with one hand, eating dry cereal with the other.

"Da-da, hi!" the little boy crowed and drank from his cup. Roman went over and ate a raisin from his hand.

"Good morning." Sasha gave Hailey a warm smile. Any apprehension she might have had about getting judged on the morning after faded like mist in sunlight. "How about some French toast?"

"I would love some." Hailey went to the pod coffee maker and brewed herself a cup.

"Hi!" Theo greeted her with a big smile. He had milk on his chin.

"Mornin', Theo." She bent to wipe it off with her thumb and then offered to help with the meal, but Sasha shooed her to the table.

It was nice, the four of them in the big, light-filled kitchen. Comfortable. Like they were all family.

Was she getting ahead of herself here?

Maybe. A little. But so what? Last night had been beautiful.

And wonder of wonders, the morning after was, too.

Hailey headed for the cottage at a little after nine. She found her sister sipping coffee and hemming a costume for one of the Fall Revue skits. A pile of them sat on the chair next to her.

"Nice night?" Harper asked with a sly little grin.

"The best." Hailey poured herself yet another cup of coffee, took the chair on the other side of the stack of costumes and pitched in turning hems.

Later, Roman, in the Dad Car with Sasha and Theo, picked up Hailey and Harper for Sunday dinner. At Daniel's, Sasha spoke openly about her diagnosis and her upcoming surgery. She got a lot of hugs and encouragement from everyone. After dinner, Roman dropped Hailey and Harper off at the cottage, where Hailey packed a bag and drove her Kia to the house on Treasure Cove Circle.

That night was every bit as amazing as the one before. The next morning, after breakfast, Roman walked her out to her car. "What time are you done at the theater today?"

"Six, possibly seven, depending on what comes up…" She tossed her overnight bag across the seat to the passenger side.

He caught her arm and pulled her close. "Come straight here." The scent and strength of him surrounded her. She felt kind of weak in the knees, remembering last night and the night before—looking forward to future nights. He seemed to be thinking along the same lines. "Spend the night."

She pressed her lips to the hot column of his neck. "I can't stay over every night."

"Yeah, you can."

"Roman…"

He smoothed his big hand down her hair. "Start with tonight. Stay with me tonight…"

Somehow, she'd forgotten how to tell him no. "All right. I'll stop by the cottage first, though. I need to pick up a few things."

He eased his fingers around her nape, pulling her close to drop a sweet little kiss on her forehead. "Ma'll have dinner ready at six, but there will be leftovers. You can eat whenever you get here."

"I'll grab something at the cottage."

A muscle twitched in his jaw and she knew he wanted to insist that there was plenty to eat right here at his house. But he let it go with a nod and brushed a kiss across her lips.

She jumped in behind the wheel and headed for the theater.

* * *

Hailey was surprised when Sasha showed up at the theater to help that day.

"I like to keep busy," Roman's mom said. "Theo's with Roman at home, and there's a lot to do here. We need trees in autumn splendor painted on one of the sets. I can do that. I'm quite a talented scene painter, as it turns out. Just ask Harper."

Hailey took her arm and pulled her into a corner backstage where they could have a little privacy. "How are you feeling?"

Sasha reached out a hand and pressed it fondly to Hailey's cheek. "It's a small tumor. I feel fine. We're well before the stage where I would start getting sick from it."

"Do you have a date for your surgery?"

"Yes. Tuesday, a week from tomorrow. My doctor says I should be pretty much recovered within a week after that—two at the outside. And before the surgery, I'll be able to help the kids get in and out of their costumes for both performances of the Festival of Fall Revue." The first performance was this coming Saturday night and then there was a matinee on Sunday.

Hailey wanted to grab her and hug her. "You're a trouper."

Sasha cast a glance upward, at the catwalks and

lights overhead. "I love this old theater." She grinned at Hailey and leaned close to whisper. "And I'm not letting Roman turn it into some pretentious hotel."

"Yeah. I wish I knew what to do to stop him." *Well, other than marry him, but that would just be wrong on so many levels.*

"I'll come up with something." Sasha looked determined. "Maybe I should threaten to move out and leave him to make his own beds and cook his own meals—except, we have a housekeeper who comes in a few times a week, so the cleaning and bed making would get done anyway. He's even offered to hire a cook if I ever get tired of preparing the meals." She sighed. "So my threats tend to ring a little bit hollow."

Hailey said, "I keep hoping he'll see the light when it comes to the theater, that he'll do the right thing out of the goodness of his heart."

Sasha declared, "He *is* a good man."

"Just occasionally misguided," Hailey added.

"And did I mention pigheaded?" Sasha asked.

"I believe you did—the first time we met, as a matter of fact."

That evening, Hailey grabbed a quick dinner with Harper. It was almost eight when she arrived at Roman's house.

He greeted her with a long kiss at the front door. Then he took her bag from her and pulled her inside. "Let's go upstairs." He picked up the baby monitor from the table by the stairs and led the way.

On the upper floor, the door to Sasha's room stood open. Hailey glanced in. No sign of Roman's mom. "Is your mom still downstairs?"

He didn't break stride. "She left at five, said she needed to meet a friend."

The door across from Sasha's was shut. "I take it Theo's in bed?"

Roman ushered her into the master suite, set down the monitor and shut and locked the door. "He's asleep. And I'm hoping he stays that way." He headed for the walk-in closet. "This way…"

She followed him in there. "Are you okay?"

"Of course." He set her bag on a dresser. "I emptied this dresser for you." With a sweep of his arm, he indicated the double row of empty hangers along one wall and the shoe racks beneath them. "And I cleared that area, too. I can make more room if you need it."

Real affection rose in her. She wanted to throw herself in his arms and tell him she adored him—however, she was also onto his game here. It was called *Keep pushing Hailey until she agrees to move in*. "Thank you, Roman. But it's just an overnight bag."

He scowled in the sexiest way possible. "Bring more clothes. Bring *all* your clothes. There's plenty of room."

She took his hand, a sweet, warm shiver sweeping up her arm at the simple contact. "We should talk."

He slanted her a dark glance. "So that's a yes? You'll move in?"

"Come on. Let's sit down." She led him to the sofa in the sitting area of the suite. They sat side by side. She kept hold of his hand and wove her fingers between his. "We don't have to rush this."

His brow was all crumpled. "I want you with me."

"I *am* with you." *I love you.*

The three little words took form in her mind and the breath fled her body. Carefully, she drew in more air and reminded herself that it was still so soon, early days for their relationship. Love was a very big word and she shouldn't rush into it.

She *wouldn't* rush into it. She cared a lot for him, but she was not making that leap to calling it love.

Roman was the ultimate domineering male. If she didn't slow this down, he would roll right over her to get his way. She needed to set boundaries so that he didn't overwhelm her.

"But I'm not moving in," she said. "Not now. Not yet."

"When?"

"I can't answer that question at this point. We need time, Roman."

"*I* don't. I know what I want and it's you."

"And I want you." She held his gaze, unwavering. "I want to be with you and I'm not going anywhere, but you have to stop pushing me to move in. Please."

They shared a sort of mini stare-down. And then, slowly, he seemed to relax. At least marginally. He lifted their joined hands and kissed her knuckles, one by one. "When I decide what I want, I go after it."

"I'm here, Roman. With you. Here is where I want to be. But I'm not ready to move in yet, or to stay here every night."

He almost smiled. "You're stubborn."

"Isn't it wonderful that you're not?"

That brought a dark chuckle. "Okay. You got me there."

"I'm staying tonight." She scooted even closer and leaned her head on his broad shoulder. "Can we just start with that?"

He didn't answer. Not in words. But he did tip up her chin and cover her mouth with his.

Hailey woke to a faint sound downstairs. Through the darkness, she saw that Roman's eyes were open, too. She whispered, "Did you hear something?"

He tucked her head under his chin. He was so warm and big, and it felt so good, to have him all wrapped around her. "It's just Ma coming home. Go back to sleep."

"What time is it?"

"After two."

Was that odd? For Sasha to be out so late?

It seemed unlike Roman's mom, somehow—but why shouldn't a grown woman stay out as late as she wanted to?

Not my business, Hailey scolded herself. Roman gathered her closer. She felt his lips brush the crown of her head, the warmth of his breath ruffling her hair. Deeply content, she let her eyes drift shut.

In the morning when Hailey and Roman came downstairs, Sasha was up, making breakfast, humming to herself, looking rested and happy, clear-eyed and more beautiful than ever. Theo sat in his high chair, babbling away, sippy cup in hand.

"Lee-lee!" He held up his chubby arms to Hailey and her heart melted.

Roman said, "Be warned. He's got sticky fingers."

She was already sliding the tray out of the way and scooping him up against her heart. He offered his sippy cup and she pretended to drink from it. "Delicious. Thank you."

Holding Theo on one arm, Hailey put out the place mats, napkins and flatware. Roman made coffee—for Hailey first and then himself. Hailey put Theo back in his chair as Sasha plated Western omelets for the adults and then gave bits of scrambled egg to the little boy.

They sat down to eat.

Roman couldn't keep his mouth shut. "You came in late, Ma. Everything okay?"

Sasha's lips curved in a radiant smile. "Yes."

He held his mother's gaze for a little longer than necessary, waiting for her to say more. She didn't.

Hailey suppressed a grin of her own. Roman reminded her of Daniel, back in the day, when she or Harper or Gracie stayed out past the curfew he'd set for them.

But Roman wasn't Daniel.

And Sasha was no curfew-breaking teenaged girl. "Eat," she instructed her son.

Shaking his head, Roman picked up his fork and did what his mother told him to do.

Harper chuckled. The knowing sound sent a tingle of annoyance down Hailey's spine.

It was past seven that night and they sat at the kitchen table in the cottage, cutting out construction-paper leaves in three colors—brown, red and gold. The six ballerinas in the "Autumn Leaves" number would strew them about the stage as they danced.

Her sister advised, "You should just get in your car and go on over there."

Hailey cut out another leaf. "If I go over there every night, he'll have me living with him before you know it."

"So?"

"Roman and I have known each other for a month. And the first week doesn't even count because he failed to call when I gave him my number."

"Your point being?"

"We're moving too fast. We need to slow it down a little."

"No, you don't. Life's too short. You need to be with the man you love."

Was her face beet red? It had better not be. Hailey set to work cutting out another leaf. "I never once said that I was in love with him."

"You're so cute when you're blushing—look at me."

Hailey huffed out a hard breath, lifted her head and glared at her sister.

"Just go," Harper said.

"I can't go barging in on him when I insisted that I was staying home tonight."

"Sure, you can. Go."

"What if he's busy?"

"My guess? Whatever he's up to, he wants you there while he's doing it. The worst that can happen is he's not there and you come back here." Carefully, Harper took the scissors from Hailey's hand. "He wants to be with you, and you want to be with him. It's just nonsensical that you're here and he's there."

Roman opened the door as she ran up the front steps.

"I missed you," she said softly.

He pulled her close, kissed her deeply and led her up the stairs. She noticed he had the baby monitor with him again, and Sasha's door was open when they passed it in the upper hall.

But the question of where his mother might be

never came up. He pulled her into the master suite, shut the door, turned the lock and began getting Hailey out of her clothes.

When he took her in his arms again, she found she was very glad she'd taken her sister's advice.

And in the morning, Sasha was right there in the kitchen with Theo when Hailey and Roman came downstairs. Roman's mom hummed a little tune as she dished up oatmeal and buttered the sourdough toast.

Hailey had no idea what had made Sasha so happy. Whatever it was, more power to her. With surgery and radiation treatments in her near future, Roman's mom deserved all the joy she could get.

The week kind of flew by. Hailey hung out with her sister for a bit every evening, but she slept with Roman every night. Roman gave her the alarm code and a key to the front door so that she could come on in whenever she arrived. She did consider saying no to the key. It seemed another big step in their relationship and she still felt they were moving too fast.

But she wanted to be with him, and he wanted the same thing—and as Harper had advised her, life was too short to waste it pushing happiness away.

Friday night when Harper returned to Roman's

straight from the theater, she saw he was in charge of the baby monitor again. "Sasha went out?"

"That's right," he reported, "with her mystery friend. She called me a few hours ago, said she wouldn't be home until late."

"She was at the theater this afternoon for the final run-through."

Twin lines had drawn down between his eyebrows. "I have no idea what she's up to."

"Roman." Hailey got him by the collar of his white shirt, went on tiptoe and kissed him. "Whoever this friend is, your mom seems really happy."

"You're right."

She kissed him again. "I'm right, *but*...?"

"It's just, well, she hasn't been with anyone that I know of, not for years and years. She went on a few dates when I was in middle school, but that was it. I don't think she went out with any guy more than twice back then."

"So you think it's a guy, too?"

He smirked. "Meaning *you* think it's a guy?"

"Kind of seems like it to me."

"Maybe she's got a hot thing going with one of the women she used to work for—and don't give me that look like you suspect I might be a gay-bashing dinosaur. Whatever makes her happy, I'm good with that."

"I was not giving you a look," she chided, and kissed him again. "You're a good son."

He bent close, pressed his lips to the side of her throat and growled, "Come on upstairs. I'll show you just how good I am."

Hailey spent all day Saturday at the theater. It was the usual pre-opening-night pandemonium. Sasha was there, too, helping to pull it all together. Roman dropped by with Theo around three, just to check in. Hailey kissed him hello and Theo reached for her.

She took him. "Next year," she promised the little cutie, "when you're two, you can be in the Fall Revue and the Christmas show right here on this stage, just like all these other kids." Or at least, he could if she managed to get Roman to see the light and give up on making a community treasure into an upscale hotel.

Theo watched her mouth move, transfixed, and then let out a bunch of cheerful nonsense syllables.

"Oh, yeah," she agreed as if he'd spoken in English. "You are so right about that."

He giggled. "Lee-Lee..." With a sweet little sigh, he laid his head on her shoulder.

For the next half hour, she carried Theo on her hip as she ran a chorus of six-year-olds through a last-minute rehearsal of a song about a scarecrow and a gray squirrel. When Theo started to fuss, Roman took him, gave her another kiss and said he'd see her when she got home that night.

She stood stage left, bemused, staring after him, thinking that his house really kind of had begun to feel like home to her.

And then Doug called for her and Rashonda to help run a last check of sound and light levels. Hailey went back to work.

By seven, all the seats were filled, and the curtain rose. There were fluffed lines galore and too many missed cues, but that was part of the charm of putting just about every kid in town onstage. And with an audience of parents and community boosters, the Festival of Fall Revue was bound to be a big hit.

They got a standing ovation when the curtain came down. And when the show was over, the Valentine Bay Community Club served coffee and cookies in the lobby for everyone to share.

Sasha didn't make the meet and greet in the lobby. Rashonda said she'd left shortly after the curtain call. When Hailey got to Roman's, he was manning the baby monitor.

"I better be meeting this guy of Ma's soon," he groused.

She wrapped her arms around his neck. "Your mom deserves a private life, Roman."

"And I deserve to know what the hell's going on with her."

"She seems really happy, whatever it is."

He grumbled something under his breath. She kissed him. That ended the grumbling—at least for a while.

The matinee the next day went more smoothly than the opening performance. A few of the seats were empty, but the audience was every bit as rapt and enthusiastic as the one the night before. Too soon, it was over and everybody took a bow.

Next up—the haunted house and then on to the Christmas show. And after that, who knew? Roman hadn't changed his mind—yet—about kicking them out of the theater as of January 1.

Monday, Hailey helped strike the Fall Revue sets.

And Tuesday, Sasha was scheduled for her surgery. Harper and Daniel's wife, Keely, volunteered to watch Theo for the day up at the Bravo house so that Hailey could be there for Roman and his mom.

Roman drove Ma and Hailey in the Dad Car to Valentine Bay Memorial.

He tried to look calm and unruffled. But he wasn't. He hated crap that he couldn't control. Ma had better come out of this in good shape or there would be hell to pay.

Hailey, in the passenger seat, kept sending him smiles and reassuring glances. She always read him way too damn well. He shouldn't like that he was practically an open book to her, but he did. She knew him. Never before had he felt that a woman he wanted had a clue what went on inside him.

Ma, in the back seat, seemed calm enough. He kept shooting her glances in the rearview mirror, on the lookout for signs she might be freaking out.

She caught him doing it twice. The first time, she gave him a reassuring smile. The second time, she said, "I'm fine, Roman. Stop worrying."

He wanted to argue that he wasn't worrying, but why lie? She'd diapered his ass when he was the same age as Theo, and she'd raised him mostly on her own. She had radar for pretty much everything that was going on with him. "I'm trying, Ma," he said.

Her doctor had explained that the pathologist would be available today and would be checking the lymph nodes immediately after they removed them. If the sentinel nodes were clear, Ma could go home by the end of the day. If not, the surgery would be longer because they would need to take and test more lymph nodes. Should that be the case, she would have to stay overnight, at least.

The lymph nodes had damn well better be clear.

At Memorial, they had valet parking. But he decided to park the Dad Car himself. He let Ma and Hailey out at the entrance and headed for the parking garage, getting lucky and finding a space right away. In less than five minutes from dropping them off, he was striding between the wide glass doors, headed straight for the sign-in desks.

And at that point, he was holding it together—on edge, but dealing. But then he saw something that made him want to start throwing chairs at windows and putting his fist through walls.

Ma stood not far from Reception—with the one man in the world Roman had never wanted to set eyes on again. Hailey sat on a nearby chair, looking like she didn't quite understand what was happening. As Roman kept walking, Hailey glanced over and saw him coming. She started to get up, but he shifted his gaze away from her.

All he could see right then was Ma in the arms of Patrick Holland, the man who'd destroyed their lives and left them destitute when Roman was eight years old.

Chapter Eight

"Reenie! Reenie, please," the eight-year-old Roman had begged.

He didn't understand what was happening, didn't know why Reenie was so angry at Ma.

Everything was very, very wrong. But Roman knew he could make it right. Because Reenie loved him. Reenie would never send him away.

"Don't be mad..." He was crying like some little baby, tears and snot running down his face as he tugged on Reenie's shirt, trying to get her to look down at him.

But Irene Holland wasn't looking at him. She shoved him away. He staggered, almost falling, as

Reenie kept shouting at Ma. "You cheating little whore! I was your friend. I treated your kid like my own. And this is how you pay me back? By stealing my husband?"

Ma was standing really straight. "I did no such thing," she said, her voice low, but shaking a little. "I didn't. I wouldn't. Irene, you know me better than that."

But Reenie wouldn't listen. "Liar!" She screamed the word. "I want you out of here. I never want to see your face again. I can't stand the sight of you."

"Reenie, no!" Roman tried to grab her again.

But Ma caught his hand. "Roman," she said in that voice of steel, the one he knew meant he had to obey. "Stay by me."

"But—"

"Shush," she commanded.

He shut up, but he couldn't stop crying. He stood there, whimpering and sobbing, rubbing his wet face with the hand Ma wasn't holding.

Patrick, Reenie's husband, came running out of the house. "My God, Irene! What are you saying? Sasha didn't do anything."

A horrible, screaming noise came from Reenie. She turned on Patrick. "Oh, didn't she? All of a sudden, you want a divorce and she did nothing?

I see how you look at her. I see how she smiles at you. You think I can't guess what dirty business you've been up to, the two of you, sneaking around behind my back?"

Patrick started to say something else.

But Ma spoke first. "Stop. We'll go." And she turned, pulling Roman with her, toward the four-car garage and the cozy apartment above it where they'd lived for all his life.

Reenie shouted terrible things after them, while Patrick said she was crazy, that she didn't know what she was talking about. Patrick called to Ma to wait. But Ma didn't stop or look back.

Roman did look back. He saw Patrick wrap both arms around Reenie. She struggled as he pulled her into the house. The door slammed behind them.

"Roman," said his mother, her voice gentle, but firm, "keep moving. Come on."

He turned his face to the garage again and shuffled along after Ma. He wished he could get smaller, so small that he wasn't here, in this bad place where Reenie had pushed him and didn't love him anymore and Patrick had to drag her back into her house.

In the apartment, Ma got his suitcase and put it on his bed. "Pack everything that belongs to you." He just stood there and cried. Ma's eyes got softer. "Oh, baby..." She knelt in front of him and took his wet face between her hands. "It's okay, Roman. We will be okay."

"Ma, I'm s-s-scared."

She grabbed him close and hugged him tight. "Sometimes people say bad things when they're hurting. Sometimes they get all mixed up in their minds and they say things that aren't true. But you have me and I have you and we will be all right. I love you so much and I need for you to be my strong, big boy right now." She pulled a tissue from her pocket. "Here you go. Blow your nose and let's get packing."

Two hours later, with everything they owned piled in the car that was older than Roman, they were ready to go.

Roman was a big kid. Big enough to sit in the front seat. He got in and buckled up like the big boy Ma needed him to be. Ma got in behind the wheel.

But before she could drive them away from that place, Patrick came out of the house.

He leaned in Ma's window, his eyes full of sadness. "Sasha. Please. Don't go."

"Step back from the car, Patrick," Ma said, her voice so tight, like a wound-up spring.

"Just listen for a minute. Just let me fix this problem."

Ma stared straight ahead. "Your wife needs you."

"I will talk to her, work it out with her. We'll get a divorce and you and I will be together."

Ma sucked in a hard breath, like Patrick's words had knocked all the air out of her. "What are you talking about? I'm no home-wrecker. I have never in any way encouraged you."

"I know. But I think you do care for me—and Sasha, I love you."

"Don't say things like that." Ma hissed the words.

"Not even if they're true?"

"Go back to your wife," Ma commanded as she started up the car. The engine lagged, then caught.

"Sasha, please. At least let me give you some money before you—"

"Go back to Irene. I don't need your money. Roman and I will be just fine. I never want to see you again."

The car started moving. Patrick fell back. Ma clutched the steering wheel hard and drove them away from there.

As the glass doors closed behind him, Roman shut down the voices and too-vivid images of the past. He kept walking, headed straight for his mother and the man she'd once insisted she never wanted to see again.

Ma must have seen movement in her peripheral vision. She looked over and met his eyes.

That was when she pulled out of that bastard's hold and stepped in front of the guy, like she was protecting him—protecting Patrick Holland, who didn't deserve to touch her hand, let alone have her using her body as a shield for him. "Roman, calm down."

He froze in midstride and somehow managed to keep his voice low. "Really, Ma? *Him?*" About then, he realized he was almost as furious with her as he was with the man who had messed his wife over so bad, she'd blamed Ma and kicked her out on the street.

"Roman," Ma said. "We'll discuss this later."

Okay, she was right. This was neither the time nor the place for him to beat the shit out of Patrick Holland. "Just get him out of here. Now."

The waste of space behind her chose that moment to speak up. "Roman, be reasonable." He stepped around Ma and kind of eased her behind *him*. Like he was a big hero and she needed protection from her own damn son.

"Go back to your wife," Roman said.

"Roman..." It was Hailey. She stepped in close,

took hold of his arm and said, soft and gentle, the way you would to someone who was out of control, "Maybe we ought to—"

He spoke right over her, his gaze glued on Holland. "Get. Out."

And Ma stepped from behind Holland again and got right in Roman's face. "This is not about you," she whispered.

Behind her, Holland shook his head. "I shouldn't have come."

"Figured that out, did you?" Roman sneered, as Ma glared at him like *he* was the problem.

Holland said, "I just couldn't *not* be here." He muttered the words at the industrial carpet beneath their feet. And then he looked directly at Roman. "Your mother asked me not to come. She didn't want to upset you. She was right," he said. "I'll go."

"No," said Ma in the voice nobody argued with. "*I* want you here." She stuck her hand behind her, and that bastard took it as she said to Roman, "I should have done this better. But I didn't, and here we are."

"Roman, please." Hailey tried again. "What matters right now is what Sasha wants. Just consider the situation, just—"

He patted her hand and cut her off a second

time, accusing Ma, "*He's* the one, isn't he? The one you've been staying out half the night to be with?"

"Yes, he is," Sasha replied, chin high, eyes full of fire. "And if you don't mind, Roman, I would like to stop making a scene at Reception. I need to let them know I'm here and ready to prep for my surgery."

Surgery. For a moment, the sight of Holland had wiped everything but rage from his mind.

"Roman…" Hailey squeezed his arm again and he finally got what she was trying to tell him.

Right now, all that mattered was what Ma wanted. Whatever it was, even Patrick Waste-of-Space Holland, she would have it.

"Okay, Ma." He took a step back. "Whatever you say."

The tension in the air thick enough to cut with a knife, they all trooped upstairs to the surgical unit, where Ma announced that she wanted Holland with her during the prep. She asked that Roman and Hailey remain in the waiting room.

Roman had wants, too. Right now, first and foremost, he wanted to punch Holland's lights out. If he couldn't do that, he longed to march back down the curving stairs and walk right out those sliding doors, not once looking back.

But punching Holland really wouldn't solve anything. And Ma was still Ma, no matter how infuriated he was with her. No way he could walk out on her at a time like this.

He and Hailey sat side by side, between a potted palm and a table set out with water and coffee, not far from the hallway that led back to where the action was. Ten minutes passed. He knew because he couldn't stop glancing at his watch. Hailey read something on her phone and didn't say a word.

Not that she had to say anything. Like Ma, she had that talent for seeming calm and unconcerned, minding her business at the same time as he just *knew* she was reproaching him without speaking, without so much as a single meaningful glance.

In the end, he couldn't take it. Exerting effort to keep his voice low and without heat, so no one nearby would be disturbed or likely to eavesdrop, he said coolly, "You have no idea about any of this."

She shut down whatever app she was using and met his eyes. "And whose fault is that, Roman?" Her voice was just as quiet and neutral as his had been.

He felt like the bad guy here. Hell. Maybe he *was* the bad guy.

Yeah. Probably he was.

She raised her phone again. He realized she was about to return to whatever she'd been reading.

Gently, he laid his hand over the screen. "I'll tell you. Everything."

Her face got softer. "Okay." She dropped her phone into the tote bag she'd brought with her. "I'm listening."

So he just went ahead and told her outright what she'd no doubt already figured out—that Patrick and Irene Holland were the wealthy Seattle couple his parents were working for when his dad died.

He went on to explain that the Hollands had no children of their own and that, while Ma continued to keep the huge house and cook the meals, Irene was only too happy to play substitute mom to Roman. "I called her 'Reenie,' and I loved her almost as much as I loved Ma."

But there was trouble in the Hollands' marriage.

"As the years went by, Patrick Holland fell out of love with his wife—and *in* love with Ma." Looking back now, Roman realized that Ma must have had feelings for Holland, too. But Holland was a married man and completely off-limits to someone like Ma. For Ma, marriage was a sacred trust. Not to mention, Ma had great fondness for Irene, who had treated her like a sister and Roman like her own.

"I was eight when my safe, happy life with the Hollands was blown all to hell." He quickly explained the ugly scene that had gone down the day Patrick Holland asked Irene for a divorce. "So Ma and I came to Valentine Bay."

Roman wanted to leave it at that. But Hailey was watching him. Those eyes of hers saw too much, and he wanted to marry her, which meant he was supposed to communicate with her.

He said, "I didn't know it at the time, but somehow Patrick found out where we'd gone and started sending money to Ma."

As Roman learned later, Holland had sent a check every month. Sasha sent the first check right back. "But then the next month, he included a note explaining that if she didn't take the money, he would show up on her doorstep to speak with her about it. From then on, she put the money in the bank but refused to spend any of it—until I was ready for college. I wanted to go to Berkeley. I knew we couldn't afford that. Then Ma told me she had it covered. That was when I learned about the checks Patrick had sent."

"She'd saved it up for you."

"Yeah. At first, I refused to take his money. But Ma kept after me." She'd argued that he could pay it all back eventually, but he should make use of it for something important, and education mattered. "So I took Patrick's money and got my degree in business and finance." He'd worked fast and hard, graduating in three years, debt-free. "Four years after that, I'd made my first million."

"That was quick. From straight out of Berkeley to a millionaire in four years." She gave him one of those looks, a look that said she wasn't going to just sit there and let him tell her only what he was willing to admit to.

Oh, no. Hailey Bravo had to have the whole damn story.

He explained about the lottery tickets Ma used to give him and the one that had paid off big. "So I got a little windfall the year I graduated."

Blue eyes got bigger. "*Another* windfall? You're a lucky man."

"So I've been told," he said flatly.

She bit her upper lip, like maybe she was trying to keep from grinning at him—or saying something he wasn't going to like. "Go on with the story."

"So I made my first million and as soon as I made it, I paid Holland back, with interest. Sent that bastard a check with a note that said he'd better take it and cash it and stay out of our lives. That I was doing just fine now, and we didn't need his help. That was it, I thought. Patrick Holland was out of the picture for good." He let out a laugh, a quiet one with zero humor in it.

Hailey leaned closer. She took his hand. He twined their fingers together. It felt good—just to be touching her. He was glad, really glad, that she was here.

She asked, "So then, what happened with Irene?"

Reenie...

Even after all the years since she shoved him away as she yelled all those evil accusations at Ma, just the thought of Irene Holland still made a hollow ache inside him. "I've got no clue. Like I said, I thought we were over and done when it came to the Hollands."

Hailey just looked at him, for the longest damn time. Finally, she advised, "Stop giving orders and start listening, Roman."

"Smart-ass," he muttered, and brought her hand to his mouth. Her skin was so soft and cool against his lips.

"You said it yourself."

"Huh? Said what?"

"Roman, your mother wouldn't let him near her if Irene were still in the picture."

"Maybe he divorced her. That *was* his plan."

Hailey said nothing. She did give his hand a squeeze. But he also got one of her looks—infinitely patient, but with a side of irony.

He saw movement in his peripheral vision. It was Patrick Holland emerging from the hall that led to the prep and surgery area. A nurse was with him.

Holland had spotted them. He kept coming. Roman stood. Hailey rose with him.

"Your mom wants a word with you," the older man said.

Roman glanced at Hailey. She gave him a quick nod and a little smile that somehow communicated she would be right there, waiting for him—with Patrick Holland, evidently.

Hailey sat down again and Roman went to meet the nurse who had waited to lead him back.

"This way." The nurse took him to a small room with accordion doors making up one wall. Just about every piece of medical equipment known to man was in that room. The equipment was mounted to the rolling bed in there and to the wall behind it. Way too many wires and tubes seemed to be hooked up to Ma, who lay on the bed under a blanket pulled up to her waist. She wore a mint green hospital gown that made her look old. An elastic bonnet hid her thick hair. She gestured at the chair on the right side of the bed. He sat in it.

"I'm all ready to go," she said, "and they've put something in the IV that's making me feel nice and drowsy. But I'm hoping they won't come for me until I've said what I want to say to you."

He had about a thousand questions and he longed to bark them at her, rapid-fire. But he did remember Hailey's advice. "I'm listening, Ma."

She reached out and clasped his shoulder briefly. Warmth spread through him. Despite his current resentment toward her for springing Patrick Holland on him out of the blue, he remained mindful of what a good mother she'd always been, through all the years of his childhood—and recently, too.

Some people considered him a hard ass and those people were right. But he loved his mother unconditionally, no matter what she pulled on him.

"Contrary to what you may think, Patrick did love Irene," she said.

Roman couldn't stop himself from scoffing. "He broke her heart. I was only eight, but I was there, remember? I saw what he did."

"The heart is a wild thing, Roman Marek. You can't tame a heart. You can only do what's right and that is what Patrick did. He stayed with his wife. He took care of her. He remained Irene's husband until her death." The words came at him like knives.

"When was that, her death?" He spoke around the sudden tightness in his throat.

"Eight years ago. Irene had early-onset Alzheimer's. It was diagnosed a year after she kicked us out of her house. She died from complications of the disease. Seven years ago, one year after her death, Patrick contacted me. He asked to see me. I *wanted* to say yes. But I told him no. Because I knew how my seeing him would upset you."

Guilt took a hard poke at Roman. Even if he had no use for Patrick Holland, he didn't like being the reason Ma had told the man no. "But now you've changed your mind." Did that sound like an accusation? Well, maybe it was.

Ma simply agreed with him. "I have, yes. I called Patrick the night of Theo's birthday party, after I told you and Hailey that I have cancer. Patrick never remarried. He's here now because I need him. This..." She gestured at the tiny room, the machines and equipment pressing in close. "It all has a way of putting things in perspective."

More than one unkind comment rose to his lips. Roman bit them back.

Ma said, "Roman, Irene was right all those

years ago—not about any betrayal. There was no betrayal. Well, except in my heart."

He didn't want to hear this, but then he found himself demanding, "What are you saying?"

Her gaze didn't waver. "I'm telling you the truth, and the truth is that, after your father died, I fell in love with Patrick Holland. It happened slowly, over time. I never told Patrick how I felt all those years ago. I never told anyone, and I never gave him any indication that I would be open to him on an intimate level. I kept my wild, willful heart locked down. I did what was right and kept my distance from him—and in the end, the day came when it all broke apart, anyway. We had to start over, you and me. And we came through it. It wasn't easy, but here we are. If I survive this cancer—"

"Ma. Don't say that. Of course you'll survive."

She gave him a real smile then, but her eyes were weary, full of the knowledge of how fickle fate can be. "If I survive—for as long as I survive—it's *my* time, Roman. Mine and Patrick's. Irene is gone and Patrick is retired now. Time goes by too fast and both Patrick and I refuse to waste another day of it. We've done the right things. We've kept our promises. It's enough. Patrick and I are through denying what we have together. I love him. He is the man for me. What we have has lasted through a lot of lonely years and it will weather any storm."

He had no idea what to say to the things she was telling him. So he kept his mouth shut.

She reached out and clasped his shoulder again, her grip firm. "I hate to see you suffer over this, Roman. I truly do. But for me and for Patrick, the time has finally come for our hearts to lead the way."

Chapter Nine

"I understand Roman has a year-old son," said Patrick Holland, making a bold stab at conversation now the nurse had led Roman off to see Sasha.

Hailey gave him a smile. He seemed like a perfectly nice man to her, tall and lean, handsome in a low-key way, with graying hair that had thinned a little at the hairline. "That's right," she said. "Theo's the sweetest little guy around, curious and smart and loving. He's also into everything, like most kids his age. He's staying with my sister and sister-in-law for the day."

Patrick was nodding. "I always wanted kids."

His brown eyes were sad. "Wasn't in the cards, however."

"Sorry," she said, for lack of anything better.

He gave a one-shouldered shrug. "The years go by and all of a sudden, you realize it's too late and you're just going to have to learn to accept that."

She made a low sound of understanding. "We never did get introduced. I'm Hailey Bravo."

He gave her a wry little smile. "Patrick Holland—just in case you didn't catch it in all the excitement so far."

Was that somehow a dig at Roman? She drew her shoulders back. "Yeah, well. You can't blame Roman for being surprised to see you here this morning."

"I'm not blaming him." Patrick met her gaze squarely, adding softly, "I promise you."

Her protective annoyance at him wilted. "Sorry," she said, for the second time.

"Don't be." Patrick seemed completely sincere—and she realized she believed that he *was* sincere. After all, she knew Sasha. Roman's mom would never waste her time on a man who wasn't worthy of her. "Roman is not my biggest fan," he said mildly. "But that doesn't mean I don't think the world of him."

"You do?" The surprises just kept coming.

"I do. He's taken excellent care of Sasha and I understand he's a great father to his little son."

"He is."

"Plus, I always had a soft spot for him."

Would it be totally disloyal to Roman if she asked why? She decided to risk it. "Why?"

"He was a sweet little boy, friendly. Curious and open. And so smart…" Patrick seemed to catch himself. "Am I saying too much?" Before she could decide how to answer that, he added, "If I'm overstepping, you only need to say so."

"It's okay, really." Was it? She wasn't sure. "Roman told me what happened when he was little—the major events, anyway."

Patrick said nothing for a minute or two. He sat very still. When he spoke, it was somberly. "It was a difficult time—especially for an eight-year-old boy caught in the middle of an ugly scene he couldn't understand."

She wanted to pat his shoulder, to offer him comfort for all the troubles of the past. But she really didn't know him all that well. She settled for a slow nod and a quietly spoken, "Yes," in agreement.

After that, they were both silent, waiting.

Eventually, Roman reappeared. He sat down on her other side. She took his hand.

The real waiting began.

* * *

An hour and a half later, the surgeon came out to talk to them.

The surgery had taken a little over an hour. They'd removed the tumor and a margin of healthy tissue around it, as well as the sentinel lymph nodes. The margin was clear and so were the lymph nodes, meaning there was no sign at all that the cancer had spread beyond the tumor itself.

Sasha would have radiation starting in four weeks. And that should be it. The doctor was confident that she was one of the fortunate ones. She would heal quickly, and her chances of a recurrence were equal with those of a woman who had never had breast cancer at all.

There was a lot to be happy and grateful for.

Roman and Patrick went in to see her in Recovery.

Eventually, she was moved to a regular room. Hailey got to see her then and to offer a careful hug and heartfelt congratulations on Sasha's excellent prognosis.

Sasha looked worn out, but peaceful, too.

After a few minutes, Roman came in. Hailey left him with his mother and went on out to join Patrick in the waiting room.

She sat down next to him. "I'm thinking they should be releasing her soon."

Patrick glanced at his watch. "It's after six. It shouldn't be too long now."

Hailey excused herself for a quick trip outside, where she called Harper, shared the good news and promised she would be there to get Theo as soon as they made Sasha comfortable at home. She'd been back in the waiting room for ten minutes or so when Roman emerged from the long hallway.

Patrick got up and went back to be with Sasha.

Roman came and stood over her. "Let's get the car."

"She's ready to go?"

"Yeah, just about." He seemed withdrawn. Maybe angry. Or maybe just exhausted from all the stress of a long, difficult day.

She rose and took his arm. Tugging him close, she brushed a quick kiss to his cheek. "You're the best," she whispered, feeling a need to reassure him.

He gave her a crooked smile. "Don't know about that, but you've been great today. Thank you."

"Anytime." She would have kissed his cheek again, but he turned his head and their lips met. The light kiss reassured her that, though he might not be happy about Patrick showing up, he did seem to be coming to grips with the situation.

She followed him out to the parking garage. They climbed in the Dad Car and buckled up.

"We'll go now and pick up Theo," he said, as he turned on the engine and put the car in Reverse.

She sent him a puzzled frown and suggested, "Maybe we should just take your mom home first."

"Patrick will take her."

"Wait." She put her hand on his arm. "I'm confused. We're not driving her home?"

He shifted back into Park and dropped his hands from the wheel. "No. Patrick is driving her home."

"I had no idea."

"Sorry. When I went in to see her that last time, she said she would ride with Patrick. I should have said something before I hustled you out here to the car."

"It's okay, it's just… Well, Roman, I can't tell if you're hurt or angry or what's going on with you."

He stared blankly at the concrete pillar in front of the car. "They want to be together. He's staying over."

She stifled a gasp. "At the house?"

"Yeah."

Her arms ached to grab him and hug him really hard, but he didn't exactly look in the mood for hugs. Carefully, she asked, "You're okay with that?"

"It's what she wants. I'm going to have to learn to be okay with it because Patrick Holland isn't going anywhere."

That night, they had the baby monitor with them in Roman's room.

"I think I might need to hire a nanny," Roman said, after they turned off the lights and it was just the two of them, naked under the covers in the dark, whispering together before falling asleep. "Ma's not going to be in any condition to corral Theo for at least the next week. And who knows what, exactly, is going to happen after that? She's made it very clear she's going to be with Patrick, so there's that."

"I'll help." Hailey slipped her arm under his and rubbed soothing circles over the warm skin at the base of his spine.

"That feels good." He tipped up her chin with a finger and brushed a kiss across her lips. "And yeah, we might be able to manage in the next week, the two of us. But you've got your haunted house and your Christmas show to deal with and I've got a project in Portland I'm working on. It's going to require more of my time as things move along."

"You're saying you won't be able to depend on Sasha to take care of Theo?"

"She's in love with Patrick. She's planning a future with him. I don't see her living here in this house for very long."

Hailey pulled back and sought his gaze through the shadows. "You mean she'll be moving to Seattle to be with Patrick?"

"I don't think so. She told me that Patrick's retired now. That means he could live anywhere. And you know how she is about Valentine Bay. She's never really wanted to be anywhere but here. I'm guessing they'll get a place together, here in town."

"She told you she wanted a life with Patrick?"

"Yeah. Laid it right out there. Schooled me but good."

"It seems so sudden, you know?"

Under the warm cocoon of blankets, he stroked a hand over the curve of her hip. "She said she's been in love with him for years, that now is their time. I can't argue with that, even though I want to."

She framed his wonderful face between her palms. "You're angry at her."

"Yeah. I know my anger is irrational. I know I'm still reacting to Patrick as though I'm eight years old and I've decided it's all his fault because I can't let it be Ma's or Reenie's."

"Because you loved your mother and Irene unconditionally."

"Yeah. When I was little, Patrick was the disposable one, as far as I was concerned. Ma and Reenie were my world."

She stroked the hair back from his temples. Really, he never ceased to surprise her. Sometimes he could be so thickheaded and controlling. Times like now, though? She just wanted to hug him close and never let him go. "So then, you get that Patrick Holland really isn't the bad guy?"

"Didn't I just say that? I know I need to get over what happened all those years ago. But I'm not over it."

"Okay..."

He gave a rough chuckle. "You're way too damn patient with me."

"You're right. I'm amazing."

"Marry me." Those silvery eyes gleamed at her, determined as ever.

If he could just say the *L* word, she might be ready to consider it. But he hadn't. And it really was too soon, anyway.

Wasn't it?

She met his gaze and tried to figure out a gentle way to turn him down. Again.

He got the message before she found the words. "Can't blame me for trying." He kissed her lightly. "What else you got for me?"

She gave him a slow smile. "Hmm. How 'bout a distraction from all the emotional turmoil you're feeling that you actually understand pretty well, but still find hard to deal with?"

"Was that a criticism?"

"No, it was a compliment—to your ability to see through your own issues to the truth."

He scoffed. "Right."

"Roman. Focus. Do you want a distraction, or don't you?"

His big hand skated down her thigh and back up again, raising sweet shivers as it went. "Why don't you show me exactly what you have in mind?"

She eased her arm down between their bodies and wrapped her fingers around him. "Like this?" She gave a firm stroke. He thickened in her grip.

"Yeah," he said gruffly. "That'll do just fine."

The next day, Hailey left for the theater at eight in the morning. The Fall Revue was over, but the haunted house would be opening in less than two weeks.

Roman kissed her goodbye at the door and missed her the moment she was out of his sight. She did that to him, made him want to be with her all the time. He didn't let himself think about that too much—about how attached he was becoming.

Sometimes the way he felt about her reminded him a little too much of how far gone he'd been over Charlene back in the day—only now, it was even worse. He not only wanted Hailey, he *liked* her. A lot. It bothered him how much.

But then he reminded himself that Hailey was nothing like Charlene. Hailey was good—a good woman. She wasn't trying to get closer to his wallet. All she wanted was him.

Still, sometimes he was certain he wanted *her* more. And that seemed dangerous in ways he preferred not to think on too deeply. If she'd just marry him, he knew his apprehensions would fade. He could stop worrying about losing her.

When a woman like Hailey said yes, she meant it. If she would only say yes, she would be his for the rest of their lives. Yeah, his previous marriages had ended in disaster. But it wouldn't be like that with Hailey. Everything was different with her.

He was in his office at eight thirty, trying to simultaneously entertain Theo and check email and messages, when his cell lit up with Hailey's name.

He answered with, "Missed me, huh?"

"It's only been half an hour."

"I know how you are. You get sad when I'm not there."

"Yeah, well. Aside from my devastation at being away from you for a whole thirty minutes, I talked to Rashonda." How was it that just the sound of her voice soothed him?

He was a goner for her, no doubt about it. "That's the woman who helps you in rehearsals, right?"

"Rashonda does a lot more than help in rehearsals."

"Noted."

"Da-da, hi!" Theo had grabbed onto his pants leg and was pulling himself upright. Roman gave him a wave as Theo made it to his feet.

"That my favorite little guy?" Hailey asked.

"How'd you guess?"

"Put him on."

Roman put the phone to Theo's ear and watched his eyes widen as he listened. "Lee-Lee!" he announced and then crowed with happy laughter. Theo loved Lee-Lee.

Which was even more reason she should marry

Roman immediately. He pulled the phone back and said to her, "So you talked to Rashonda…"

"She knows someone who might be interested in the job as Theo's nanny. Someone really good with kids, Rashonda said, and with great references. She won't be available long. I'll text you the number."

As soon as he hung up with Hailey, Roman called the prospective nanny. Lois Chetfield answered on the first ring and said she could come by in an hour for an interview.

Roman knew Lois was the one as soon as he opened the door and saw her standing on the porch in tan pants, a dark-green shirt and practical-looking shoes. She was in her forties with a warm smile and sharp eyes.

"You're hired," he said.

Lois smiled patiently. "First, we should talk and then I want to meet your son."

So he went through the motions of interviewing her and watching her with Theo, who took to her right away, grinning and babbling at her in his mixture of short words and nonsense syllables.

Lois stayed for over an hour, during which two of Ma's friends came by to see how she was doing. Lois knew both women. They stopped and chatted with her as Theo sat in her lap, drooling contentedly, chewing on a rubber banana.

Then Patrick came downstairs. It struck Roman anew how bizarre his life had become. Patrick Holland was staying in his house, sleeping in Ma's room…

Roman really needed not to think too hard about that.

Ma's two friends reminded him of chirping birds, all bright and chipper and fluttery as Patrick introduced himself. He led them upstairs for a visit and then walked them to the door when they left.

A few minutes later, Lois left, too. Roman started contacting the references she'd given him. He got nothing but glowing reports of her nanny skills.

It was probably the fastest nanny hunt in the history of child care. By noon, he'd called her back and hired her at the hefty hourly rate she required. Lois would start working tomorrow. She would take care of Theo from nine to five, weekdays. She was also willing to make herself available periodically on weekends and even to travel on occasion so that Roman could take Theo with him when he had meetings out of town.

Two more of Sasha's friends came by. Like the first two, they brought casserole dishes. It was the same routine as earlier. Patrick appeared and introduced himself, then led them upstairs.

That evening, dinner consisted of the food brought by Ma's friends during the day. Ma said she felt better and insisted on coming to the table to eat. Hailey was still at the theater, so it was Roman, Ma, Patrick—and Theo in his high chair.

Except for Theo, who chattered happily away at no one in particular as he stuffed bits of cooked vegetables and meat in his mouth, nobody said much for several minutes.

But then Ma turned to Roman. "Matilda and Rose mentioned that you were interviewing for a nanny today." Matilda Graves and Rose Sampson were the ones who'd shown up while Lois was getting to know Theo.

"Her name's Lois Chetfield," he said. "I hired her. She starts tomorrow."

"According to Rose and Matilda, Lois is an excellent caregiver."

"I think she'll work out fine, yeah. Theo warmed right up to her."

"I'm glad." Ma hesitated before adding, "I'm not deserting you, Roman—or Theo, either. I will be stopping by often to spend time with you and my grandson. And whenever you need me, I'll be right here in town. You only have to call."

"I appreciate that, Ma. Thanks," he said, and meant it. Mostly.

He slid a quick glance at Patrick and then back to Sasha. "So you two will be getting a place together?" he asked, as though he hadn't already assessed the situation and realistically determined what was bound to happen.

Ma and Patrick shared a long glance. They looked apprehensive, like they were afraid of his reaction to their plans. He supposed he couldn't blame them. So far, his response to Patrick's appearance in Valentine Bay had been less than reassuring. He knew he needed to do better, to accept that they were together and also that they actually seemed happy that way.

"Yes, we are going to look for a place," she said at last, "and we're getting married next week, at the county clerk's office. I want you to be there."

So, then. Just like that, they were getting married. Why couldn't it be that simple between him and Hailey?

"Roman?" Ma wore a worried frown. "Will you be there?"

He realized she'd read his silence as resistance. "Of course I'll be there—and, uh, congratulations."

His mother gave him a careful smile and a regal nod. "I'll invite Hailey, too, for our second witness."

"She would like that." Roman spoke gently—he thought.

But then Ma said, almost plaintively, "We just want to finally get started on our life together."

Across the table, Patrick doggedly speared a fork into his broccoli salad. He looked as uncomfortable as Roman felt, which had Roman thinking that for seven years after Irene died, when Patrick and Ma had every right to be together, she'd refused him. She'd told Patrick no because she knew that the mere mention of Patrick Holland made Roman's adrenaline spike.

Seven years was a long time and Roman needed *not* to be the guy who kept his mother from being happy. He was getting the picture that his animosity toward Patrick was unfounded, anyway. It was just the remnants of the terrified little boy he'd once been, a boy who felt his world crumbling and needed someone to blame.

He set down his fork. "Okay, let me just say this. Ma, I want you to have what *you* want. That's all I've ever wanted for you." He turned to Patrick. "Until yesterday, I had no idea that what Ma wanted was you. That's been a stunner for me, but I'm dealing. Make her happy. You do that, you'll make *me* happy and we'll get along just fine."

The knot of tension in Patrick's jaw seemed to

ease a little. "That's more than fair," he said. "I love your mother very much, Roman. Seeing her happy means the world to me."

Later that night, in bed, Roman brought Hailey up to speed on the situation with his mom and Patrick Holland.

"So you were right," she said, marveling at how well he'd assessed the situation.

"They're getting married and getting a place together." He pulled her a little closer and kissed her neck—using his teeth.

"Ouch!"

"That's for sounding so surprised at how perceptive and intuitive I am."

She laughed. "Why do I have the feeling that anything I say right now is only going to get me into hot water with you?"

He made a growling sound and nuzzled the spot he'd just nipped with his teeth. "Say I'm sensitive and deeply insightful."

She dutifully parroted the words.

And he kissed her. The kisses got longer and deeper. By the time Roman turned out the light, Hailey was thoroughly satisfied and completely content.

The next day, Patrick found a three-bedroom

beachfront house that was available month-to-month. He and Sasha would move in on November 1 and start the hunt for a house they wanted to buy.

Sasha healed quickly. A week and a day after her surgery, she and Patrick were married at the county offices in Astoria. Roman and Hailey served as their witnesses. Following the brief ceremony, the four of them shared a wedding lunch.

Out in the restaurant parking lot a little later, there were hugs all around. Even Roman and Patrick managed a sort of half hug and a handshake. Finally, the bride and groom climbed into Patrick's Jaguar XJ and took off for Seattle and a five-day honeymoon at the Four Seasons.

Over the next few days, Hailey spent long hours at the theater. Every night, she came home to Roman and Theo—and yes. Roman's house had very much begun to feel like her house, too.

On October 29, the Valentine Bay Arts Council, in association with H&H Productions, opened the second annual haunted house at the Valentine Bay Theatre. The event ran for three nights, culminating on Halloween.

Last year, the haunted house had been a big success. This year was even bigger. They had triple the number of visitors, resulting in three times more revenue than the year before.

When Hailey got back to Roman's after locking up the theater, it was after ten and Theo was in bed. Roman had ordered dinner from that great Italian place in the historic district. He'd gone all out, with tall, white candles, fancy plates and flatware and a beautiful bottle of wine from Tuscany.

She was tired but feeling pretty great about a job well done. And Roman was wonderful, listening attentively while she talked about how cute the kids were in their Halloween costumes, how they all loved to scream their heads off when a vampire rose from a coffin or a skeleton dressed in rags popped out of a hidden alcove. She bragged shamelessly about how much money they'd made.

He raised his wineglass in a toast and suggested, "Marry me. You can have the theater."

Her heart kind of twisted. He was an amazing man in so many ways—thoughtful and generous and gorgeous and so very good in bed.

But, come on. How many proposals was she going to get without the three most important words in them?

Should she go ahead and say it first, hope he would finally take a hint if she just put it right there? *I love you, Roman. Do you feel the same about me?*

She set down her own glass of wine in order

to resist the temptation to upend it over his thick head—and it was right then, as she considered dumping her wine on him, that the scary truth of what she'd just admitted bloomed within her.

I love him.

She truly did. There was no more slowing it down, waiting till later to examine her true feelings. She loved him.

He was her guy, her *person.* She loved him in the deepest way, and she wanted to be with him. She might even be willing to say yes to him, take the leap and marry him, though they hadn't been together for all that long and a step as serious as marriage shouldn't be entered into hastily. A decision to get married could not be rushed.

Still. She wanted to be with him and, even in the short time they'd been a couple, she'd come to count on his presence in her life, to look forward to coming home to him after a long, challenging day at the theater. Already she couldn't imagine her world without him in the center of it.

He mattered to her. So much. She loved him, she did.

But she didn't want to say yes to him now, not like this, when she was kind of pissed off and a little bit sad that he couldn't just relax and let things happen naturally now and then. He had to wrestle every situation into complete submission.

Well, she'd never been all that good at submitting and she wasn't starting now. It was too soon for marriage. Really, what was the big rush?

Just in case he hadn't heard her the other times she'd said it, she reminded him, "I would never get married for a theater, Roman—not even the Valentine Bay Theatre. I really wouldn't."

"I want us to be together."

"We *are* together." Sometimes she felt a little guilty about how "together" they were. She didn't spend enough time with Harper anymore. Lately, she only saw her sister at the theater. She felt neglectful, leaving her best friend and virtual twin living all alone at the family cottage.

Yeah, it had been bound to happen eventually. They each needed to have their own lives, to follow their own paths, or whatever.

Still.

She'd fallen for Roman so hard and so fast. She needed to slow him down a little, catch her breath. Give them both time, let this amazing connection they shared ripen.

Like fine wine from Tuscany.

He was watching her closely. "I'm blowing it,

huh? Next time there needs to be a big rock and me on my knees."

She picked up her wine again. Alcohol solved nothing, but sometimes a girl needed her wine. She resisted the urge to take a giant gulp and sipped slowly as she chose her words with care. "It's not about the ring or you getting down on one knee. It's really not, Roman. We need more time before we make that kind of decision."

"*I* don't. I've already made my decision. I want a life with you. I want to get going on that."

She gestured with her glass—at the dinner he'd laid out with such care, at his house where she pretty much lived now, at him and her and Theo sleeping upstairs in his crib. "We do have a life. I love what we have. There's nothing to 'get going' on. We are already 'going.' We're together and I want us to stay that way, keep working together, supporting each other, building a life, you and me."

"And how long is that going to take—until we've supported each other enough, worked together enough, built enough of a life that you're willing to walk down the aisle to me?"

"Um, a while. It's not a race, Roman. It's a process."

"A process. That's one of those words people say when they're planning to drag something out."

"I'm not dragging anything out."

"Great. Because I want to firm this thing up."

"Firm it up?" Now she was gritting her teeth so hard, she wondered if her back molars would crack. "Roman, love isn't a business deal."

"Maybe it ought to be. A business deal makes sense. It's an honest transaction."

"And love isn't? What is going on with you, really? I don't understand you sometimes. You're the most terrific guy in so many ways and then you…"

Wait a minute.

Why was she lecturing him?

More important, why was she holding out on him?

No, she wasn't going to marry him. Yet. But someday, yes. Someday—and not all that far in the future—she really did see it coming. The two of them.

Together.

As wife and husband.

So what could she do right now to ease his mind a little? What could she do to encourage him to have a little patience with the process?

Even if he couldn't make himself say the important words, *she* could give them to *him*. She could open her heart, let him in, let him see how important he was to her.

She drew in a slow breath and made herself say it. "I love you, Roman. You're the guy for me. I love you very much."

The look on his face right then? Priceless.

For a moment she saw all the sides of him. The sexy, powerful, often overbearing man; the scared little boy exiled from the only home he'd ever known; the loving son and father—and the Roman who held her close in bed, the Roman who ordered Italian for ten o'clock at night and put out the white tablecloth and candles and poured the good wine, because no matter when she got home from work, he wanted her to have a great meal and a chance to tell him all about her day.

She was about to grab him and hug him and promise him that it would all work out right in the end, if he would only have a little bit of patience.

But then he said, "So if you love me, why don't you just say yes, and we can get married?"

It was yet another molar-cracking moment. She forced a level, reasonable tone. "I just think it's too early for us to get married."

"Too early? No, it's not. If you love me, then what's the problem? You just need to say yes."

"Roman. Do *you* love *me*?"

He blinked—not as though he didn't love her.

More as though it went without saying. "Of course, yeah. I do."

She didn't know what she felt. Relief. Frustration. Confusion. Sadness. All twisted up together into something that hurt. He'd just managed to say he loved her without using the actual word. "Why is it so hard for you to say the words *I love you*, then?"

"They're just words, Hailey. Words don't make it real."

"Maybe they don't. But words matter. Words are our most effective way to communicate. And if you can't tell me you love me without my having to drag it out of you, then I don't understand why you're so surprised that I keep saying no to us getting married."

"What does that mean? That you're never saying yes to me?"

"No, it doesn't mean that I'm never saying yes. I fully intend to say yes to you."

"When, then?"

Her patience with him was fraying. "Why does that sound like an ultimatum?"

"Why are you answering my question with another question?"

She exerted considerable effort to keep her voice low and calm. "You're being unreasonable, impatient and completely unfair." And she couldn't just sit there. Frustration with him made her restless. She pushed back her chair and rose. "Is it that you don't trust me? You think if you don't 'firm this thing up—'" she air-quoted "—like a business deal, I'm going to cheat on you or betray you in some other way or just—I don't know—walk out the door someday?"

He pushed his half-full plate away. "I didn't say that."

"Good. And I really hope you're not thinking it. Because getting married too soon is no way to guarantee anything. Rushing to the altar is not a solution to whatever doubts you're having. We need time to work out—"

"Slow down. What did you just say? Whatever doubts *I'm* having?" He stood. "I'm not the one with the doubts. You're the one who won't say yes."

They were facing off across the table—the beautiful table with the pretty candles he'd set out just for her. She really didn't want a showdown.

Slowly, she sank back to her seat and tried, again, to speak quietly and without heat. "Roman, it's not about doubts. I don't have doubts about you."

He looked down at her bleakly and muttered, "Yeah, you do."

Did she? At a moment like this, maybe. A little. But she did love him, and she knew they could work it out if he would just stop seeing a ring and a wedding vow as an all-around solution to every single problem. "No, I don't have doubts. I love you and I have no doubts about you and me as a couple. I think we're a great match. I only want us to—"

He showed her the hand. "Leave it, okay? Just leave it alone." He grabbed his plate and carried it over to the compost bin. A stomp of his foot on the pedal and the lid swung up. He dumped in his half-finished meal, stepped to the sink, rinsed the plate and stuck it in the dishwasher. "I'll be in my office."

Scooping up the baby monitor from the end of the counter, he disappeared under the arch that led back to his study, leaving her sitting there alone wondering what the hell had just happened.

Chapter Ten

In his office with the door shut, Roman sat at his desk and stared at an Andy Burgess painting on the far wall.

Really, he wondered, what the hell was the matter with him?

He had a real problem here.

The problem was called love, and who did he think he was fooling?

Not Hailey. Uh-uh. Not fooling her. She had his number. He was behaving irrationally, unreasonably and also unfairly. She deserved better.

Too bad he didn't seem to be able to make himself do better.

How hard could it be to open his damn mouth and just say it.

I love you, Hailey.

He winced at the mere thought of those words coming out of his mouth. Those words didn't *feel* like a good thing. They felt like a dangerous thing. A thing he could never step back from.

That wasn't normal. Was it? For a man to duck away from the very thought of telling his woman how he felt about her, what he wanted from her?

Which was forever, and with love.

But then, really, as for the love, well…

He just wanted to skip to forever and leave all the messy feelings behind. He didn't do feelings well. She needed to accept that, deal with it.

Move on to the two of them making a life—and that meant it had to be more than just living together.

He was a traditional kind of guy. If people wanted to be together, they should damn well suck it up and make a real commitment. There should be a ring and vows and a contract.

Why couldn't she see that? He wanted her and she loved him, and they needed to just get the hell on with it.

Which circled him right back to the basic problem.

He was completely in love with her. He would do anything for her.

All the messy, hungry feelings he had for her put him at a complete disadvantage. And that was unacceptable.

What he'd gone through in his two bad marriages was nothing next to this.

What if he lost her?

What if she woke up one day and realized that she didn't really love him, that she was still in love with her precious Nathan and would be forever? That the dead guy was the one she really wanted, and she was only settling for Roman?

What if she considered him, Roman, a bad bet for forever?

And, come to think of it—*was* he a bad bet for forever?

The indications were certainly there. He loved her, but somehow he couldn't get the actual words to come out of his mouth.

And what about patience? Another check in the negative column. He was not a patient man. He'd just walked away from Hailey, left her sitting at the table all alone because she wouldn't just give in and do things his way.

He knew he ought to get back out there, apologize for being an ass, make it up with her…

Right then, his phone pinged with an IM from one of his partners in the Portland project. He read it and responded. There was a reply to his reply. They started working through a few kinks in the project.

Two hours later, he was still in his office. An hour after that, he stretched out on the leather sofa under the window.

When he woke up, he could hear Theo on the baby monitor, babbling away to himself. Out the window, he saw the gray light of morning.

As he crossed the kitchen on the way to get Theo, he saw the note Hailey had propped against the fruit bowl on the island.

Left early. Having breakfast with Harper. I'll be back around five.
Love,
Hailey.

His first thought was that it couldn't be that bad between them. She'd signed it "Love, Hailey," hadn't she?

His second thought?

He was acting like a douche and he needed to make it up to her.

What he didn't really want to do was talk about

it. He had a feeling they would just end up in another argument if they tried that.

So where did that leave them?

Hell if he knew.

Lois showed up right at nine and took over with Theo. That freed Roman to deal with some loose ends on the Portland project until around eleven, when Ma and Patrick arrived back from Seattle.

He knocked off working to welcome them home. They were way too affectionate with each other for a couple well into their fifties if you asked him. And so damn happy. In fact, Ma looked ten years younger than she had when they left, which was quite the feat considering she'd had breast surgery less than two weeks before. Roman decided he could get along with any man who could make Ma that happy. Even Patrick Holland.

They all—Lois and Theo included—had lunch together. The newlyweds were excited to be moving into the house on the beach. "Our first house together," Ma announced with stars in her eyes.

Patrick had it all set up. Movers would arrive from Seattle with his stuff tomorrow. He'd hired a couple of local guys to pack up Ma's things and deliver them to the new place.

Ma's girlfriends Matilda and Rose dropped by at a little after three that afternoon. They all four sat around the living room drinking gin and tonics. Roman visited for a few minutes when they first got there, just to be polite, but then he retreated to his study, emerging at five to take Theo from Lois.

By then, Ma's girlfriends were gone. Ma and Patrick were in the kitchen, cooking together. The air smelled of Ma's famous teriyaki chicken with pineapple rice. They were laughing about something, the two of them. Patrick leaned in close for a quick kiss.

Married and happy.

The way he and Hailey ought to be.

Roman kept on walking. He found Lois and Theo in the family room. She left and he took Theo back to the kitchen, putting him in the high chair, giving him some apple slices to gnaw on.

"Roman," said his mother. "Set the table, please."

He was putting the plates around, including one for Hailey, when he heard the front door open.

A minute later, Theo banged a fisted apple slice on his tray and crowed, "Lee-Lee!"

Hailey swept into the kitchen in paint-spattered jeans and a black T-shirt with Keep the Drama on the Stage printed across the front. "Theo!" She went straight to him, ate an apple slice from his hand and kissed his fat cheek with a loud smacking sound.

And then Ma was turning, holding out her arms for a hug.

Hailey went to her. "So good to see you. How was Seattle?"

"Wonderful. But it's so nice to be home."

Roman's gaze collided with Hailey's as Ma enfolded her in a hug. Hailey gave him a questioning smile. He tried to look adoring and apologetic but wasn't sure if he succeeded.

The evening progressed well enough, he thought. They ate. Ma wanted to spend some time with Theo, since she was moving out tomorrow. She and Patrick took over with him, to play with his toys and blocks for a while and then to get him ready for bed and read him his stories.

That left Roman and Hailey alone in the kitchen. Together, they cleaned up after the meal. As they cleared the table and loaded the dishwasher, he kept dreading the moment she would bring up their disagreement the night before—and the way he'd walked out on her and never come upstairs to bed.

She didn't mention it, though. She was quiet. He wondered what she might be thinking and then was instantly afraid she might tell him.

By the time she started the dishwasher and hung

up the dish towel, he knew the moment of truth had come. "Let's go upstairs." She offered her hand.

He just...couldn't do it. Not right then. "Listen, I need to deal with a few things. I'll be up soon."

She gave him a long look, those astonishing lavender eyes full of all the things he wasn't letting her say. So beautiful, everything he wanted but probably should reconsider the wisdom of having.

Because he really wasn't up for it. Never had been. It was good she wouldn't marry him. He wasn't fooling anybody. He didn't know what the hell he was doing when it came to relationships. And he would make a terrible husband.

"Okay, then," she said gently. "See you soon."

He watched her walk away and wondered what the hell was wrong with him.

In his office, he did zip. He stared at that painting of a midcentury modern house across from his desk and thought about the damn theater, about how he'd kind of lost his desire to make it into something it wasn't, how next year or the year after, Theo would be old enough to take part in the Fall Revue, visit the haunted house, sing a song in the Christmas show. Having Theo was like getting a continuing education in what really mattered in life.

An hour meandered by. Now and then, his

phone beeped. He ignored it. For a while, he played a video game on his laptop, just throwing away the time until he finally had to climb the stairs and figure out what to say to the woman in his bedroom.

He thought about Charlene and Nina, about how he hadn't really known his ass from up with either of them. He'd tried to do better with Hailey, to have a real relationship with her, one with give-and-take and all that stuff he didn't really get.

But he was just plain bad with give-and-take, at least when it came to a relationship. He liked to give the orders and have them obeyed.

And yet, he had learned from the debacles of Charlene and Nina. Both of them had asked how high when he'd said jump—Charlene, until she was ready to dump him. And Nina, until she'd delivered the healthy son he'd demanded of her. Looking back, he realized that the thing with Charlene had been only infatuation. As for Nina, she'd been the means to an end: Theo.

He got it. He needed a woman who could and would stand up to him. Hailey was that woman.

And he was in love with her—in love for the first time in his life.

All he really needed to do right now was to tell her so.

Except she wouldn't marry him and every time

she said no to him, he grew increasingly certain she would never say yes. Because she was a smart woman and she knew he wasn't up for the real thing.

It was after nine when he finally climbed the stairs. He tapped on his bedroom door before he opened it and found Hailey sitting up in bed with her tablet.

She set the tablet on the nightstand and held out her hand. He went to her, his heart pounding deep and hard in the cage of his chest, dreading whatever would happen next, not sure what he would say and feeling pretty damn certain that whatever came out of his mouth, it wouldn't be the right thing.

But then she pulled him down to her and lifted her mouth to him like an offering. He took it, starving for her—and for a while, it was all right.

More than all right. Just the two of them, Roman and Hailey, holding each other, loving each other with their bodies when the words weren't working. Inside her, moving together with her, slow and so sweet and then faster, harder, deeper—it felt like anything was possible, that they would get it right.

Afterward, as they lay naked side by side, he waited for her to say something. The silence stretched out and he tried to figure out how to start. But nothing came to him. And she remained quiet, the way she had been down in the kitchen after Ma and Patrick took Theo upstairs.

Like she didn't know what to say to him. He probably shouldn't be surprised. He had no idea what to say to her, either.

Was this how it died between them? In silence, because what else was there to say?

He pulled the covers up and gathered her to him, wrapping himself around her, breathing in her scent of roses and sex, memorizing the silk of her skin.

The next morning, Roman was already in the shower when Hailey woke up.

She felt a stab of sadness, for the distance between them that seemed to yawn wider with every moment that passed.

And then she pushed the sadness away and joined him in the shower. They made love again, the way they had last night, with few words and a whole lot of feeling. When she came, she almost cried out her love for him.

But she held it back. Love seemed somehow an issue between them. She didn't want to rub it in, that he had such trouble saying the words. Would it be rubbing it in to scream it out in the middle of an orgasm?

Somehow, it seemed so. She kept the words in.

Yeah, she wanted to try again to talk it out. But she had the feeling that that wouldn't go well. She really didn't want to push him. Maybe just giving him space, waiting for him to start the conversation, was the wisest course.

So she waited.

When she got home from the theater that evening, it was just her and Roman and Theo. Sasha and Patrick had moved to their new place. The house seemed too quiet, especially after Theo went to bed and it ended up being a repeat of the night before.

Roman retreated to his office and she went upstairs. When he joined her, around ten, they made passionate love and then turned out the lights.

She didn't sleep well. They needed to talk. But she had this feeling that it really would be better if he started the conversation. At least that way, she would know for certain that he was ready to deal with what had gone wrong between them—or, wait. Not "what had gone wrong," but "how to make things right."

Willingness wasn't everything. But it was a start.

"You seem off, Lee-Lee," Harper said that afternoon. They were at the kitchen table in the cottage, going over Harper's set design for the Christmas show, which was now officially titled *Christmas on Carmel Street*. "You okay?"

Hailey glanced at her sister, who sat hunched over her laptop, her acres of blond hair piled up in a bun that had slipped precariously to the side. Really, she could tell Harper anything. But right now, she kind of didn't know what to say about her problems with Roman. "Yeah. I'm okay."

Bun bouncing, Harper bumped her with a shoulder. "Liar."

"You're losing your bun, Harp."

Harper dropped her stylus and shoved at the bun, which only made it droop a little farther to the left. "You're evading. Is it Roman?"

"Yeah." Hailey got up, took the elastic from Harper's hair and redid the bun to her satisfaction. "There." She dropped back to her seat. "But I'm not ready to talk about it."

Harper picked up the stylus again and made a few quick changes to her rendering. "That man is completely in love with you—or he was the last time we were all at Sunday dinner together."

That had been a few weeks ago. What with the fall festival, Sasha's surgery, followed swiftly by her sudden marriage to Patrick and, after that, all the scrambling to set up the haunted house, Hailey and Roman had ended up passing on dinner at Daniel's.

A whole lot could change in a matter of weeks. Communications could shut down. Love could turn into something else, something dark and unhappy, filled with resentment and dissatisfaction. And an awful, empty silence.

The kind of silence that could mean it wasn't going to work.

And she really didn't want to talk about Roman right now. "How's the job hunt going?"

"I've sent out some résumés and I have a couple of interviews coming up, one in Seattle and one in Portland."

"Great."

"Lee-Lee, are we changing the subject?"

"How did you guess?"

"He gives you too much grief, he'll answer to me."

Her sad heart lifted a little. "I'm counting on it—now, can we fit in a charming shop with a door that opens?"

"Yes, we can."

"And how 'bout a snowman and a couple more

festive-looking Victorian lampposts with wreaths hanging on them?"

"You're the director."

"And don't you forget it."

When Hailey got home to Roman's that night, she found him and Theo in the kitchen. In the past, she would have gone straight to Roman for a hello kiss. But one look at his face and, well, kisses just didn't seem like a very good idea.

He stood at the fancy chef-quality stove and rattled off the dinner menu. "Roast chicken, oven potatoes and salad."

"Sounds good." She went to the sink and washed her hands. "Can I help?"

"I've got it all under control."

Of course he did. Theo chose that moment to wave his hands and call her name. At least someone seemed happy to see her. She sat down on the floor with him and they played with his blocks as Roman put the dinner together.

They ate. She cleaned up the kitchen while Roman took Theo upstairs.

He was still up there when she finished loading the dishwasher, so she grabbed her tablet and sat on the sofa in the family room to go over her calendar for the next couple of weeks. Very soon, her schedule would get tight again as they ramped up the Christmas show.

She checked email and made an appointment with Tandy Carson at the arts council. They needed to start discussing possible venues for next year. She wanted a meeting with the council and the volunteer staff at the theater.

They needed to get everyone on board, have them all reaching out to neighbors and friends, anyone with a barn they rented for events or a church that might be open to letting them use their fellowship hall. It hurt, to lose the theater. But that wasn't going to stop her. There would be other performance spaces. She refused to let this setback get her down.

She heard footsteps on the stairs and her heartbeat accelerated as Roman entered from the front room. She met his eyes as he came toward her.

His face gave her nothing.

Something was going on here and it wasn't good.

"Busy?" he asked, coming to stand in front of her with the glass coffee table between them. He was so handsome, in gray pants and a dark shirt that clung to the strong shape of his chest. His beautiful eyes watched her too closely—but distantly, too. He had a large manila envelope in one hand and the baby monitor in the other.

Her throat felt tight. So did the back of her neck and the muscles of her belly. Like her body was drawing into itself in preparation for a blow. She set her tablet on the table. "No, not busy at all. Theo?"

"Asleep." He set the monitor on the table a few inches from her tablet.

She made herself ask him, "What's going on?"

"We need to talk."

For a split second, she forgot how to breathe. But then her lungs started working again and she sucked air in a strange little gasp. "Okay." It came out weak sounding.

Suck it up, Hailey. Whatever's going on here, don't be a wimp. Sit up straight and face it head-on.

He reached up with his free hand and raked his hair back from his forehead. "Hailey, I..."

She caught her upper lip between her teeth, worried it—and made herself let it go. "You what?"

He gazed at her steadily. A muscle ticked in his jaw. "This isn't working, you and me."

Words. She'd always been so good with them. But right now, she had none. Just a pathetic little "Ah," a sound full of hurt and surrender, followed by an incredulous, "You're breaking up with me? Just like that, you're breaking up with me?"

"I can't be what you want." He watched her so tenderly. The jerk. "You need to move on."

Anger. It made her earlobes hot and her chest burn. "That's crap. I can't… I don't…" She gathered her scattered wits and demanded, "You're just giving up? You're not even going to try?"

He held out the envelope. "I want you to have this."

She eyed it, sorely tempted to spit on it—whatever it was. But fine. Sure. She snatched it from his fingers, undid the clasp and pulled out the papers inside.

It took her a minute to understand what she was looking at. Her mouth dropped open. "You're giving me the theater?"

"I already have. You have the deed in your hand, transferred to you, and I've recorded it with the county. It's official. You own the Valentine Bay Theatre."

She wanted to toss the papers in his face. But no. That wouldn't be right. Her town needed the theater and whatever was going on here with him and with her—it had nothing to do with the deed in her hand. It was the right thing, for him to give the theater to her so that she could make sure it served Valentine Bay.

"Thank you," she said quietly. "I'll make certain it's put to good use."

"I know you will."

Silence. Empty and endless.

She should argue, come up with all the reasons he needed to rethink this, to realize how wrong he was. And she needed just the right words, the ones that would make him see all the good that they had, that they *were*, as a couple, together—to make him realize the enormity of what he was throwing away. She needed the words that would change his mind.

But her throat had clutched tight. Hurt and fury pulsed through her.

And a sad little voice in her head whispered, *Come on, Hailey. When are you going to face the truth and admit that he's right?*

It took two people. And he wasn't *there*, not really. He was no longer *with* her, except in bed. And sex was important, yeah. But you couldn't build a relationship on it. Not one that could last.

Right now, in all the ways that mattered, he had checked out on her. He'd left the premises, abandoned the field. Ever since the other night when she'd dared to bring up the subject of love, he'd only been going through the motions of being with her.

And she needed to face hard reality.

If he was willing to dump her because she wouldn't marry him yesterday or sooner, to destroy what they had because any talk of love made him uncomfortable—hey. Who was she to try to argue him out of it? Who was she to call him wrong? Why in the hell should she fight to stand beside him?

She rose to her feet. "What are you saying to me, Roman? Be crystal clear."

Something flashed in those ice-green eyes. Pain? Panic? Whatever it was, it was gone in an instant, a shade drawing down, leaving only cool distance and a will of steel. "It's over, Hailey. We're done, you and me."

Weakness swept through her. She wanted to beg him for just one more chance. The hurt was so deep, her knees almost gave way.

But she didn't let them. He would not see her break.

She would walk out of this house with her shoulders back and her head high.

"All right, then," she said mildly. "I'll pack my stuff and go."

Chapter Eleven

Hailey went home to the cottage, where the porch light was on and the windows dark. Harper was probably out with friends or even at the theater.

Yeah, Hailey knew that all she had to do was call and ask her sister to please come home. Harper would be there in an instant, ready to comfort and console, to take Hailey's side absolutely, to call Roman Marek every bad name in the book.

But no. Right now, she felt held together by frayed thread and spiderwebs. She couldn't break down yet. She needed a little while—to put her things away, to be numb and quiet and completely alone.

She carried in the two suitcases of clothes and

other belongings she'd brought back from Roman's. It wasn't a lot of stuff, really. But putting it all away in her little closet at the cottage—it just felt so final.

They were really, truly over, her and Roman. She wouldn't see him again, not on purpose—not him or Theo, either.

And that was another blow. Theo.

She would miss him so much. His silly, happy laugh. The way he called her name, his chubby arms reaching for a hug, when she entered the kitchen at the end of the day.

She sank to the bed and then fell back across it on a pile of bras and panties she'd been just about to put away.

Sweet Theo.

Would it hurt him as much as it hurt her—to have her disappear from his life? Should she have insisted on saying goodbye to him?

Or was that just her own pain speaking? Maybe it was better not to make a big deal of it, better just to vanish from his world. It wasn't like he would understand what was happening, however she handled it.

And it had been only a couple of months since she'd entered his life. Surely, he couldn't have become too deeply attached in that period of time.

Could he?

She stared blankly at the beadboard ceiling. It was blurring now as the tears welled and got away from her, dribbling down her temples and into her hair.

"Hailey? What's happened?"

Blinking the wetness away, Hailey lifted her head. Her sister hovered in the doorway to the bedroom.

"Harp." She sat up, sniffling like a total wimp, swiping a hand at her eyes and under her nose. "Surprise," she said, and sniffled again. "I'm home."

"Oh, honey. What's happened?"

"Roman broke up with me."

Harper's big eyes got bigger. "No."

"Yeah." She held out her arms. "I think I really need a hug."

"Aw, sweetheart…" Harper stepped to the bed and gathered her close. "Lee-Lee, honey. I might have to kill him. But, babes, it will be all right."

Having her sister's arms around her allowed her to let the pain come. She ugly-cried.

Twenty minutes later, she was blowing her nose and giving Harp the full rundown on How Roman Dumped Hailey.

"What an absolute rat bastard," Harper said,

once the tale had been told. "And not in an illegitimate way. In the *bad* way, the bastard-by-choice way."

Hailey sniffed. "He's just scared."

"Don't you dare defend him."

"I'm not." Hailey crossed her heart. "Don't you worry. He had his chance and he's not getting another one." She sagged against her sister. "Help me put all my stuff away?"

Harper stood. "Uh-uh. Later for all that." She grabbed Hailey's hand and pulled her to her feet. "Right now, we're going to open some cheap wine and say more rude things about Roman."

"He gave you the *theater*?" Harper hit her forehead with the heel of her hand. "You didn't really just say that, did you?"

Hailey stuck her glass under the spigot of the box of sauvignon blanc and filled it to the rim. Again. "Consolation prize, right?" She knocked back a big gulp and shuddered. "Lucky me."

"Lee-Lee. I can't get my head around it. You *own* the theater."

She raised her glass. "Yeah. I'm sure I'll be happy about that. Eventually."

"It is a very good thing—for us. But even more so for this town."

"I know." Hailey heaved a long sigh and said glumly, "I can't wait to tell Tandy that we don't have to go scrambling to find a place for next year—or any year."

"It's huge." Harper seemed unable to find a word big enough.

"Yeah. Aside from the small issue of my broken heart, life is good."

A few days later, after the crying and the bad-wine-drinking was over. After she'd announced to the arts council and all the wonderful volunteers who worked with her at the theater that never again would they go scrounging for venues. After she'd met with a lawyer who would be helping her figure out how to run the theater for the community's good without losing her shirt. After she'd told herself a thousand and one times that she was through with Roman Marek, that he could crawl through ground glass, naked on his knees, for another chance with her and she would tell him to turn around and crawl back where he came from.

After all that, well, she started to wonder if maybe she should have tried a little harder to work it out with him.

Maybe she should have listened and nodded when he said it was over—listened and nodded and then calmly informed him that she was going upstairs to bed and they would talk about it in the morning.

Maybe she should have said—again—that she loved him, adding this time that she knew he loved her and he wasn't going to scare her away.

Being in love was magical and transformative, sure. But it was also hard—especially when a woman and her love didn't see eye-to-eye. Roman didn't have a lot of experience with loving a woman and he didn't exactly excel at compromise.

She should have been more patient.

By Sunday, when she went to dinner at Daniel's, everybody in the family knew that Roman had ended it with her and given her the Valentine Bay Theatre as a parting gift. Unsurprisingly, Daniel coaxed her into his office and brought out the good Scotch.

She went ahead and told him that she was considering tracking Roman down and seeing if maybe he was ready to try again.

Daniel advised against hasty action on her part. "He should come to you. Begging. But first, I need to put my fist through his face."

Hailey forbade her big brother to do any such thing. "Stay out of it. I mean it, Daniel."

Reluctantly, he agreed to let her run her own life. And then he said, "You've got heart and brains, a lot of energy and a hell of a work ethic, Lee-Lee. You also know what you want and you're willing to go out there and get it. One way or another, you're going to be fine."

Monday morning, bright and early, Sasha appeared in the open doorway of the office space backstage, which Hailey had cleaned out and fixed up for herself.

"I had a feeling I might find you here."

Hailey got up from behind the ancient metal desk that had probably been there since the theater opened back in 1925. "It's so good to see you."

Sasha grabbed her in a hug. "I've missed you." She took Hailey by the shoulders and they smiled at each other, wobbly smiles. Both of them were misty-eyed.

Hailey said, "You look great. How's married life treating you?"

"I'm happy. So happy…"

"That's what I wanted to hear. Radiation starts next week?"

Sasha nodded. "First treatment is next Monday."

"I want you to call me—you know, if there's any way I can help."

"I will. But it's pretty straightforward. I just use the special cream they'll give me, eat well and expect to feel tired sometimes."

"Call me anytime. I'm there." Hailey made a mental note to check in with her Tuesday or Wednesday after that first treatment.

Sasha brushed her hands up and down Hailey's arms, a fond gesture and a soothing one, too. "Speaking of calling, I've been wanting to reach out to you. But I've held off. I kept thinking Roman would come to his senses and admit that he can't live without you. I really didn't want to interfere—well, not too much, anyway."

They both laughed at that, soft laughter that didn't last long.

Hailey told Roman's mother the truth. "I love him so much, Sasha. And I miss him. And I miss Theo, too..." Her eyes filled, but she sniffed the tears back.

"And they miss you." Sasha gathered Hailey close again. "My son can be such a fool." When Hailey pulled back a little, Sasha held her gaze and said, "Roman is very good at taking control but not so much at risking his heart."

"No kidding."

"Hailey, he's completely in love with you. And that means when he finally figures out that throwing away what he wants most of all is no solution to anything, he will be showing up on your doorstep and doing whatever he has to do to convince you to give him another chance."

"Great. Have you met me? I'm not the kind of woman who sits around waiting for a man to get past his issues and reach out."

Sasha's sad smile brightened. "It just so happens he's in Portland for meetings on some project he's been planning. He took Theo with him. And Lois."

"Do you know what hotel they're staying at?"

Now Roman's mom was full-on beaming. "As a matter of fact, I do."

Roman's hotel was a boutique Hilton downtown, a block from Pioneer Square. Hailey found a SmartPark nearby and walked the short distance to the hotel entrance.

The lobby had a bar in it, all very luxe—browns and blacks with pops of rich color and accents in rose gold and brass. She went straight to the front desk and asked for Roman's room number—no, she didn't expect the tall, beautifully groomed woman whose name tag read Beatrice Sinclair to give it to her.

But she took a flier on that anyway. "Which room is Roman Marek in?"

It didn't work. "Let me check on that for you," said Beatrice pleasantly. "Your name?"

Hailey gave the woman her name and Beatrice called the room. After a quick exchange with whoever answered the phone, the clerk glanced up at Hailey. "Mr. Marek is in meetings all day and unavailable."

"Is that Lois? Let me speak with her."

Beatrice managed to ignore Hailey's request without seeming rude about it. "Yes," she said to the person in Roman's room. "Hailey Bravo. She's right here." Beatrice glanced at Hailey again. "Your phone number, Hailey?"

She rattled it off and Beatrice repeated it into the phone, thanked whomever it was she'd been talking to and hung up. She gave Hailey a kind smile. "Is there anything else I can do for you?"

"Apparently not. Have a great day, Beatrice."

"Thanks so much. You, too."

Hailey went to the bar, ordered a coffee and debated what to do next. There wasn't a lot to debate. She'd wanted to catch him off guard, but that probably wouldn't be happening.

Resigned, she got out her phone and texted him. I'm in the lobby of your hotel and I want to speak with you in person. Now, if possible.

An endless thirty seconds later, he replied, Go home, Hailey.

Well, that wasn't very promising. But she'd come this far. She wasn't leaving without seeing him. She sent him a middle-finger emoji and settled in to enjoy her coffee.

Roman, who had excused himself from his meeting and stepped out into the hallway when he saw it was Hailey who'd texted him, muttered a filthy word at her middle-finger reply and returned to his meeting.

It was winding down, that meeting. They would break for lunch and reconvene at two. Still, he tried to keep his mind on track.

Until that damn text, it had all seemed important, nailing down the details, getting everyone's agreement to move on to the next step—but now, all of a sudden, he just didn't give a damn about the next step. It could all go to hell and he wouldn't really care.

Who did he think he was kidding, anyway? He'd been miserable since he dumped her.

And now she was at the hotel.

And okay, it couldn't work out between them. He'd already decided that, acted on it, ended it.

But he should probably go talk to her, explain that she needed to give it up, forget about him.

It was over and she had to learn to accept that—they both did, because he was having some trouble getting the memo himself.

Not that he would tell her that.

No. He would be firm and gentle—well, as gentle as he was capable of being. He would remind her that it could never work, and she needed to go home.

"Don't you agree, Roman?" asked Darrin O'Kelsey, a good man from Phoenix who'd put in almost as much capital on this deal as Roman had.

Roman had no idea what he was supposed to be agreeing with. And right this minute, he didn't care, anyway. "I'm sorry, Darrin. Everyone, I've got an emergency I really need to deal with." *A four-alarm fire by the name of Hailey Bravo, to be specific.* "I'll catch up with you in the afternoon."

They all made understanding noises and agreed they would see him later, that whatever the issue was, they hoped it would work out all right.

"Thanks, yeah. So do I." And then he was out of there, striding along the hallway between the meeting rooms, racing down the wide stairs that led to the lobby floor.

He spotted her immediately, in a brown coat and

jeans and short harness boots, her thick, pale hair tumbling down her back. She sat at the bar, laughing at something the bartender had said.

For a second or two, he was frozen in place, just listening to the sweet, husky sound of her laughter, glaring at the bartender, who didn't need to lean that damn close.

Right then, it all came blindingly clear to him.

It was no good. Sending her away from him had accomplished exactly nothing, except to make him miserable.

And what about her? Had she been miserable, too? He knew she had. He shouldn't have done that—hurt them both that way.

Okay, yeah. It scared the hell out of him, how much she meant to him, how empty it all felt without her hand in his.

But breaking it off with her was no kind of solution. He was half-dead without her, just going through the motions. Whatever she wanted, she would damn well have it.

She wouldn't marry him? Fine. He would learn to live with that, somehow. For as long as she would put up with him, he needed to be there, together, with her.

Whatever she wanted, however she wanted it—that's how it would be.

If only she would just give him one more chance.

The bartender caught him glaring. Hailey followed the other man's gaze, turning on the barstool, spotting him standing there. They stared at each other.

God, she was so beautiful. That skin like cream, cheeks strawberry-pink from emotion, or maybe the cold outside. Those eyes that saw into his soul.

No, he didn't know right then—what she wanted, why she was here…

But he couldn't bear one more second with all this distance between them. He went for her. She slid off the stool and met him halfway, in the central seating area.

They stopped with no more than two feet of space between them, beside a pumpkin-colored barrel chair.

His arms ached to reach for her.

And yet he didn't dare. "Hailey." His voice was a low, desperate rumble.

"You came." Her eyes were so hopeful—and that was a good sign. Right?

He fisted his hands at his sides. They wouldn't stop wanting to grab her. "I was planning to tell you…" The words got all turned around in his throat.

"What?" she asked and then seemed to answer the question he hadn't asked—or had he? "Yes," she said firmly with a quick nod of her head.

"Hailey," he said again.

"Yes." She stared up at him, lavender eyes pleading, yearning...

And he was yearning, too...

And then, all at once, the words were there. "I love you, Hailey. I love you so damn much. I didn't know. I never guessed..."

And she cried, "Oh, Roman. Yes!"

And then she was in his arms. He lifted her, until he was holding her up off the floor, her body soft and perfect and willing, her mouth under his, opening. Inviting.

Someone shouted, "Get a room! The place has twenty floors of 'em."

Someone else whistled.

And someone slow clapped.

He didn't care. Neither did she. They kissed for the longest time, right there in the lobby of his hotel, holding on tight, promising without saying a word that never again were they going to let go.

When the kiss finally broke, he lowered her until her feet touched the floor. Bending a little, he pressed his forehead to hers. "Just one thing..."

"Anything."

"One more chance. That's all I'm asking. Give me one more chance. And however you want it, that's how it will be."

"Yeah?"

"Yeah."

"Say it again. Say the words."

"Hailey Bravo, I love you."

"Oh, Roman. That sounds so good."

"And will you give me a chance?"

"I will. I love you, too. And I was thinking…"

"Yes."

She chuckled and brushed her soft fingers into the close-clipped hair at his temple. "I was thinking a compromise."

He could do that—compromise. For her, he could do just about anything. "Yes."

She blinked up at him. "Did you just say yes to a compromise?"

"As long as you really mean it, that you're really going to give me another chance?"

"I do. I mean it. Yes, I am."

"Then I'll compromise the hell out of whatever works for you."

And she smiled, a slow smile, one that was achingly sweet. "You're serious?"

"I am."

"Roman, I want a little time."

"You got it."

"I want us to live together, the way we *were* doing, you and me and Theo. I want to build a life. I want us to be engaged."

"Engaged?" This compromise of hers was starting to sound pretty damn good. "Are you saying yes to me?"

She nodded, a slow, careful movement. "Yes, I am, Roman. I want you for my husband. I want to be your wife. And it won't take forever until that happens, I promise you. But I'm just not going to rush it. I want a little time. I want six months, with us living together, practicing compromise and patience."

He tried to grin. "You mean the things I'm really bad at?"

"You'll get better."

"Because practice makes perfect?"

"Because I love you and you love me and we're both motivated to create the best life we can, together, for us and for Theo."

"You're right. I'm in."

"Good. And then we'll get married in the spring."

For a half a second or so, he couldn't find words. But he rallied. "Clarify for me."

"Of course. What do you need to know?"

"You're telling me yes?"

"Yes, I am."

"We're engaged and you'll wear my ring?"

"Yes, we are, and I will. Happily. Forever."

He stared into her incomparable upturned face. "God. I missed you."

"And I missed you. So much. Never pull that kind of crap on me again."

He'd figured out a few things during the endless, awful days without her. One was that a guy needed to admit his own damn culpability outright. "I really screwed up."

She laid her soft hand on the side of his face. It was everything—that touch. "You did," she answered tenderly. "You got scared."

"Damn straight, I did. I'm an overbearing ass."

"Yeah, kind of." Her thumb brushed his lower lip and her eyes stayed locked with his. "On occasion."

"I don't deserve a second chance. But you just said yes and I'm holding you to it. Hailey, I swear to you, this time I won't let you down."

"I know you won't. I do believe in you, Roman. I believe in *us*."

He caught her hand, opened her fingers and kissed the heart of her palm. By then, he *knew*.

He was certain. This was real. They were going to work it out. "Let's go upstairs."

"Yes. Please. I need to see Theo. I've missed him so much."

"Lee-Lee!" Theo cried when they walked in the door of Roman's suite. Hailey had never been so glad to see anyone—well, except maybe Roman a few minutes ago, downstairs.

The little boy was already standing, kind of propped up on the arm of a club chair. He took off on his own two feet, staggering toward her with his arms outstretched.

"Theo." She crouched and opened her own arms wide. "I have missed you so much!" She gathered him in, her gaze locking with Roman's over the silky crown of his head. "How long's he been walking?" she asked in wonder.

His voice was rough with excitement—and happiness. "He's been trying, but this is the first time he's made it more than a step or two."

"Amazing."

"Yep. Looks like all he needed was the right motivation."

Theo commanded, "Lee-Lee. Up!"

She scooped him into her arms, kissed his fat cheek and rocked him from side to side. He was so solid and warm, and he smelled like fresh bread and baby wipes. With a tiny sigh, he laid his head on her shoulder. She had Theo in her arms and Roman at her side. All was right with the world.

It really didn't get much better than this.

Roman gave Lois the afternoon off. She had her own room down the hall and said she'd be heading out to explore the shops at Pioneer Place. Roman ordered room service and they had lunch in the suite, the three of them.

He had a meeting that afternoon he couldn't get out of. Hailey hung out with Theo in the suite. The little boy was napping in his travel crib when Roman returned, thus giving him and Hailey an opportunity for a more intimate reunion in the bedroom.

She had duties she couldn't shirk at the theater tomorrow, so she went home by herself that night. As she was leaving, Roman pressed the key to the house into her palm. "I'll be back tomorrow afternoon," he said. "I'm hoping that when you come home from the theater tomorrow night, you'll be coming home to me."

She kissed him. When she dropped back to her heels, she replied, "I'll be there."

And she was.

The following Saturday, they left Theo with Sasha and Patrick and went together to pick out a ring. Hailey chose a single gorgeous round diamond on a platinum band.

Sunday, the three of them went to Daniel's. Sasha and Patrick came, too. There were congratulations from all the Bravos—both for Sasha and Patrick on their recent marriage and for Roman and Hailey on becoming engaged.

Hailey got a little bit worried when Daniel and her brothers disappeared with Roman into the study at the front of the house. But they all emerged smiling an hour later and no one was injured that Hailey could see.

At home that night, Hailey asked Roman what had happened when he went off with her brothers.

He tipped up her chin with a finger. "You know the rules, Lee-Lee. What happens in your brother's study stays in your brother's study." And then he kissed her, and she forgot everything but the feel of his lips on hers.

Six and a half months later, on the last Saturday in May, Hailey and Roman were married on the stage of the beautifully refurbished Valentine Bay Theatre. Half the population of Valentine Bay sat out in the auditorium to witness the occasion.

Harper was the maid of honor and Daniel gave the bride away. Hailey's other sisters—Grace,

Aislinn and their switched sister, recently retired movie star Madison Delaney Larson—were also attendants.

By then, the groom had had plenty of time to fully accept that Patrick Holland was a fine man, a man worthy of Sasha's love. Roman had asked Patrick to be his best man and Patrick had said he would be honored to stand up with him.

Both Hailey and Roman wanted eighteen-month-old Theo for their ring bearer. Theo was walking comfortably on his own by then, but he had a habit of changing direction at the drop of a hat.

Sasha got the job of corralling him. The little boy wandered off course more than once—during both the wedding march and the vows that followed. But his grandma always guided him back to where he belonged.

It was a simple ceremony presided over by Tandy Carson, an ordained minister of the Universal Life Church. When Tandy gave Roman permission to kiss the bride, he peeled back her short veil and whispered, "Finally."

"Totally worth the wait," she replied as his lips met hers.

* * * * *

MILLS & BOON

Coming next month

THEIR ROYAL BABY GIFT
Kandy Shepherd

The woman's wet dress clung to her body making no secret of her curves. She was a scandal in the making.

He grabbed a striped towel from a stack on a nearby lounger and threw it around her shoulders, another one around himself. "Keep your head down and walk as quickly as you can," he said.

She attempted a faster pace but stumbled and he had to put his arm around her to keep her upright. He scarcely broke his stride to pick up the phone she'd dropped when she'd fallen.

"Are you hurt?"

"Only…only my pride."

"Are you staying at this hotel?"

She shook her head and wet strands flew around her face, sending droplets of water on him. "I…I only came here for lunch. My hotel is in the older part of town."

"I'm in the penthouse here. There's a private elevator down to my suite. I'll take you there."

"Please." She was still shivering, and her eyes didn't look quite focused.

He had to get her—and himself—out of here. Edward kept his arm around Ms Mermaid as he ushered her to the discreet private elevator. If people didn't recognise him, a scandal could be averted.

Within minutes they were in the expansive suite where he was living while his Singapore house was being gutted and refurbished. He slammed the door behind them and slumped in relief. No one with a camera could follow him here. He turned back into the room. Then realised he had swapped one problem for another. Standing opposite him, dripping water on the marble floor of his hotel suite was a beautiful stranger—and her presence here could so easily be misconstrued.

"Thank you," she said. "I could have drowned." Her eyes were huge, her lush mouth trembled. Hair wet and dripping, makeup smudged around her eyes she was breathtakingly lovely. A red-blooded male, no matter how chivalrous, could not fail to feel a stirring of attraction. "I…I can't swim, not enough to save myself. But you…you saved me."

Continue reading
THEIR ROYAL BABY GIFT
Kandy Shepherd

Available next month
www.millsandboon.co.uk